THE CRUCIFIX IS DOWN

THE

CRUCIFIX

Contemporary
Short
Fiction

IS DOWN

edited by
Kate Gale
and Mark E. Cull

Red Hen Press

2005

The Crucifix Is Down
Copyright © 2005 by Red Hen Press

Cover art *Bleeding Heart II* (mixed media) by Italo Scanga.

Cover design by Linda Zartaroglu
Book design by Mark E. Cull
Typeset by James Harmon

ISBN 1-888996-34-X

Library of Congress Catalog Card Number 2005901775

Published by Red Hen Press

The City of Los Angeles Cultural Affairs Department, California Arts Council, Los Angeles County Arts Commission and National Endowment for the Arts partially support Red Hen Press.

First Edition

ACKNOWLEDGMENTS

"The Nightingale," by Margaret Atwood. First published in *Nightingale*. Copyright © 2000 by Margaret Atwood.

"Distance of the Moon," by Italo Calvino. First published in *Cosmicomics*. Copyright © 1968 by Harcourt Brace & Company and Jonathan Cape Limited.

"Denver Omelet," by James Harmon. First published in *LA Miscellany* as "Napa Valley." Copyright © 2002 by James Harmon.

"The Ones Who Walk Away From Omelas," by Ursula K. Le Guin. First published in *New Dimensions 3*, 1973. Copyright © 1975 by Ursula K. Le Guin.

"Long Distances," by Jewell Parker Rhodes. First published in *Peregrine VII*, Summer 1989. Copyright © 1989 by Jewell Parker Rhodes.

"Bearded Irises," by Candice Rowe." First published in *Berkeley Fiction Review*, Issue 19. Copyright © 1999 by Candice Rowe.

"Roan," by Diza Sauers. First published in *The Missouri Review*, volume XVII, number 2. Copyright © 1994 by Diza Sauers.

Contents

Preface

The twin pillars of the Judeo-Christian ethic and Hellenism have been toppled with the groundwork of romanticism leaving a mindless swirl of consumerism and human bees trapped in a global and massive hive mentality. There are those who walk away into the darkness, outside the human light, swirling madness and find themselves off the island. The Greeks feared exile, early Christians feared Purgatory. Without a sense of home, there is no exile to fear. The mythic underpinnings have dissolved, leaving chaos. The pillars of civilization have crumbled and the roof that housed our egos, longings, and madness has eroded. What is left is naked desire, and the cruel materialism of Western civilization.

Our strength is in our ability to barricade ourselves from truth, to brainwash ourselves into believing the life of the hive is the only life, to believe that the shell we inhabit is us. We inhabit the netherworlds of the Inferno as a matter of course. Damnation isn't what happens when the furies come to get you. It is every waking moment, every breath we take in the fetid air of the twenty-first century. The life of the imagination lives on, clarifying this space in history when populations can be wiped out with a rain of bombs, left ruined and blighted. In this madness, we live with a sort of soul pox, a malaise in intellectual life in which what passes for life is merely existence. Perhaps, the serfs didn't have it any better.

What has technology brought us? We are not more human or more divine. We rain fire and brimstone as surely as any Old Testament God, we ravage and we kill. The strong countries do not succor the weak—Haiti, Afghanistan, the Sudan. The fundamental question of the twenty-first century may be what constitutes walking away from Omelas. The writers in this collection endeavor to push the envelope of human imagination, to ask ourselves outside of ourselves into the realm of being, walking away from the hive into the beyond where imagination meets the horizon and then dips beyond it. To the other side of truth and into the space of dreams.

THE CRUCIFIX IS DOWN

Keala
Francis

The Clot

THE CLOT ON THE FLOOR grows and oozes. By the time my bridge group comes over to play, it looks like a mud puddle. After two hours—even as I ply them with fake butter scones and non-fat chocolate croissants—the stench becomes too much and my bridge group goes away. They are a catty bunch, so I am not so sad to see them go, but I am a little. I try to remove the clot by blotting it lightly with a white towel, pressing down with the tips of my creaky fingers. The clot stays.

One afternoon, two limbs appear, forking arms held aloft out of the clot on the carpet. They wave at me when I come out of the bedroom in my bathrobe. They are non-threatening, but scare me enough that I walk past at arms' length. They sway toward me as if to embrace me, but perhaps to strangle me. I'm not sure.

These arms continue to wave at me when I come out of the bedroom. Or when I come out of the shower. Or if I just happen to forget for one second that they are there when I watch my shows. Then they wave like hell. Somehow they know I'm not paying attention and they wave to be noticed like a child who bangs the pot when you're on the phone.

The weeks go by and suddenly two legs pop out just a body's length from the arms. They are young legs, still unsure of themselves. Although they do not stand, the legs wobble knock-kneed like a young doe taking her first tentative steps. I am a little shocked at this. The arms, however, seem quite pleased at the new arrival and hug the knees into a yoga position. I have skipped my yoga classes for the last some months. The yogi—or whatever you call these yoga teachers nowadays—called after I'd missed two weeks. She probably thought I'd died. I just was tired of never being able to touch my toes. She stopped calling when I told her that.

Besides, I am still in demand—at least for the arms. When I come out of the bedroom, the arms leave off fawning over the legs and wave invitingly, but the legs cross. The legs—I must admit—are very shapely. I am a bit jealous in fact. In high school, I got whistles at my legs. Those boys thought I was a looker. Even now, some of the older men in the park give me a toothless hoot, but that's usually after they've cheated on their low-sugar diets. After all, my legs have blue-popping veins, deep-purple capillaries, and lumpy folds. My legs are old. The clot has produced limbs that are youthful.

Perhaps I could try them on, I think.

The legs are too unfriendly, though, so I decide to touch the waving arms to teach those legs a lesson in courtesy—it is my house and my carpet and my clot, after all. The arms lightly pat me. They act like a parent drying a four-year-old, carefully patting her down before she sits on the car's new leather seats in her wet, bright-yellow suit. Charlie and I never had enough money for leather seats, and I let my children sit wet if they wanted. Cloth stinks sooner or later. Wet or dry. My daughter has leather seats.

The arms beckon me closer, and I kneel next to them at a distance from the legs. The legs couldn't care less.

I decide to give the waving arm-hand a manicure. For a clot-engendered armsandlegs—when do you call it a body?—the nails are quite nice with full-white half moons at the cuticle. No nail biting possible, I suppose. I used to chew mine raw, but now that my teeth are pearly white and fake as the butter, my nails usually just crack on their own. I paint the arm-nails sunshiny red because I no longer like the color for myself—my daughter told me it was unseemly for an old lady to wear red. Besides, I never paint my nails anymore. The pinkish-brown skin of the arms sets off the red nicely.

The legs are noticeably distraught with this new friendship between the arms and myself. The legs straighten and refuse to move during the manicure. The arms—always friendly—wave energetically when I finish and I tell them to be careful not to smudge the polish. I know, I say, I used to smudge mine all the time for I never had the patience to watch paint dry.

I do make a conciliatory attempt to paint the toes, but the legs thrust the feet into the carpet, bending the toes under so I can't reach them. Why an armsandlegs would have such disparate personality traits is beyond my comprehension.

I take to talking to the armsandlegs. I tell them that my curtains are too old and if Martha Stewart saw them I would be scolded. She would gasp at the faded blue-and-turquoise shag rug. The children used to pretend it was the ocean and fake swim in this sea in the summer. Their children—my grandchildren—keep their shoes on in the house and never swim in the carpet. I have heard their mother—my daughter—tell them not to even sit on the carpet. Better than no ocean at all, I once said. I got yet another—Oh Mother!—and left it at that. It's too dirty, she says.

Perhaps I am a dirty old woman.

The legs seem to relax when I tell these stories, so I keep talking. I tell them about the time Charlie and I took a road trip. I start to cry because I miss Charlie, and the arms beckon to me. Even the legs pull up at the knees in a nice way. No, I say, no I'm okay.

Charlie was always tall, dark, and handsome. Even as he aged, Charlie never stooped. He never went through a mid-life crisis. He always loved me, usually tolerated me, and often ignored me. My daughter doted on him. Perhaps I was always too silly for her? I don't know. But Charlie she loved with abandon, and he'd put her on his knee and read her stories from the Bible, from history books, from famous authors. Jack loved Charlie, but he also enjoyed baking with me. Jack was my son, too. He is in the Peace Corps in the Congo. I told him to wear bug spray and drink bottled water. He laughed and kissed me on the cheek. Take care, Mom.

My bridge group calls to tell me that I am not allowed to play with them until I clean up my dirty room. They might as well tell me to clean up my dirty self. I am too tired to shower these days and because the food delivery guy says he'll deliver all the meals daily now, I figure I can live without the bridge group. As I said, they're catty.

They all came to the seniors park after me, and Margaret, Ann Jean, and Linda all came together. They had needed a fourth, and I was thrilled when they asked me—out of all the women in the park—to join them. Margaret colored her hair; Ann Jean did aerobics; and Linda was a seventy-year-old Goldie Hawn. I felt like I was that oldest lady in The Golden Girls, but maybe I just watch too many t.v. shows.

I ask the meal delivery boy if he has a girlfriend. He smiles and says he's not supposed to talk about his personal life. Well, what can he talk about, I ask. He can't talk about much because he has to deliver more food to other people who are sick like me. I'm not sick, I say. That's true he says, you're not as sick as some.

So I talk to the armsandlegs. I start to sit next to the clot, inching a bit closer each day as it seems they listen more intently. The arms wave more slowly when I move closer—I feel like giving them one of those pink scarves they use in that rhythmic gymnastics event. Even the legs will dance for me now to make me smile. The arms have convinced them that I am not harmful or mean. I have watched this take place. I pretend to watch my shows, and out of the corner of my eye, I watch the arms. They pat the tops of the thighs and point to me. At first, the legs straighten flat out as a sign of disbelief. But as the days go on, and as I spend more time near the clot, the legs begin to listen to the arms.

I like the arms because of this. They are the only ones who have made me feel nice in a long time.

I take to sleeping next to the clot, but still a bit away so as not to fall in. The arms urge me closer each night and when I sleep they lay a hand on my shoulder like my grandmother used to do when I would sit at the foot of the sofa. The arms rub my head and play with my stringy hair as if I were still that young girl.

My granddaughter never lets me hug her for too long. My daughter has said something to her, I'm sure. I once confronted Alice. But she said she refused to talk to me about this right now. Why couldn't I move to a home like a normal old person? Why I couldn't, I said. I still walk on my own two feet and still have a brain in my head. Oh Mother! she said. She started to cry.

The armsandlegs have no face for tears. But they are tender and I now respond to this tenderness with silent tears, curling my old self up on the carpet. The armsandlegs love me next to them. The legs almost seem happy, and start bouncing the feet on the floor whenever I come closer. They are impatient like I am. But for what?

The phone rings one night. My daughter is calling. She rarely does, so I guess my bridge group has told her about the clot. I am coming over to clean you up, she says. Your bridge group (ha! I was right) told me that you are living in filth. I am not, I say. It's just taking me time to clean this clot. What the hell are you talking about mom?

I hang up. The armsandlegs both reach for me. I need them and I am tired. I lie down on my back right next to them and the legs flutter with excitement. They must love me to want me so close. The arms reach across me and hug me closer. I almost fall into the clot. I push myself away. The legs straighten out. The arms wave frenetically.

They don't acknowledge me for two days. The delivery boy stops coming into the house and now leaves my food on the doorstep. My daughter threatens to "clean me up" one of these days. My bridge group knocks at the door. Ha! I pretend that I am not home. We know you're in there, Carol. That's Margaret. She's always the one to gossip, so she always talks. All three of them need to learn a thing or two about silence. I have. So have the armsandlegs. The arms, I realize, have never clapped or snapped their fingers or made any sort of noise.

On the third day, the armsandlegs forgive me. I tell them I love them and ask them if they love me. The legs point their toes and throw themselves straight into the air. I want to hop on and play airplane like I did with Charlie when we were dating. I'm afraid I'll break my back now, though. I feel tired and my head hurts. The arms hug themselves then stretch to the toes, in a bodiless, perfect jackknife.

| Ray Gonzalez | *The Crucifix is Down* |

THE LAST CRUCIFIX is down off the wall, an outline of its cross standing out from the faded paint, the Christ having hung there for twenty-six years. The tenement apartment once contained fourteen such crucifixes, but the old woman has died at ninety-six and her family has taken them all away except for this one overlooked inside the closet. Three days after the apartment is cleared of the woman's belongings, the forgotten crucifix slips off the rusty nail and lands on the closet shelf, no one around to hear it fall, the thud on the wood announcing that it has landed with Christ's figure face up, its plunge off the wall forming a tiny dust cloud. The cross is eight inches long, the figure about six, its ivory-colored plastic cracked. Two more days go by before the apartment manager shows the place to a potential renter, the crucifix lying flat on the shelf and not seen when he opens the closet. He shows the apartment to four other possible tenants, but the place is not rented. Five days after the last inspection, the crucifix moves two inches closer to the edge. Three days later, painters are sent in because the manager thinks he can rent it after a painting of the ugly, turquoise walls. The closet doors are half open, so the two-man crew doesn't notice the bottom three inches of the cross, with Christ's feet and knees, teetering on the edge of the shelf. They paint the two main rooms in two days, saving the closet for last. One painter almost steps on the crucifix that is now lying, Christ down, on the floor. He calls to his partner, but the other painter is touching up in the bathroom. The discoverer picks up the crucifix and sets it on the kitchen counter where they have piled old nails, a twisted fly swatter, and other objects of a previous life. He paints the closet and notices the silhouette the crucifix left in the layers of grime that cover the rest of the wall. Before he paints that area, he stands back and observes the pale form left by the cross. Though he is not Catholic, he goes to the crucifix on the counter and finds it under old newspapers his partner found in the bathroom. He touches the cracked plastic Christ and is trying to recall something about his long dead father and priests, when a chilling cry scares him back. He drops the cross on

5

the counter and runs into the bathroom. "What the hell?' he asks the other painter whose face is pale, the guy shaking in his splattered clothes. "I saw her," he says in a low voice, a brush with fresh paint dripping in his hand. The bathroom is empty, half the wall behind the tub painted yellow, the rest peeling its ugly pink. "I saw her sitting right there in the tub, covered in an Indian blanket. She was saying something like a prayer, then she held a Jesus up to me." Both men step out of the bathroom as this is described. The bathroom painter takes his baseball cap off and wipes the sweat with a painted hand. "She held one of those crosses up to me, then she was gone." He goes into the kitchen, and his partner follows, noticing the bleached outlines of other crosses on the bedroom and living room walls, places they have already painted over. He hears a rustling of newspapers and notices the rising strength of the paint fumes in the apartment. His partner, still shaking, is searching the crumbled newspapers for the crucifix. "I saw a cross right here earlier," he says. The two search the counter, but the crucifix is not there. Silently, they go to the closet and find the crucifix nailed to a spot that has already been painted, one nail at the top of the cross, one nail through the Christ's chest, and one nail through his crossed legs, the nails thicker and longer than the old ones they found the first day when they were preparing the walls—the heavy spikes shattering the plastic, while pinning the Christ deeper into the crucifix. No one remembers who ran out of the apartment first.

Margaret
Atwood | *Nightingale*

PEOPLE DIE, and then they come back at night when you're asleep. By the time you're my age this happens more frequently. In the dream you know they're dead; funny thing is, they know it too. The usual places are a boat or a forest; less often a cabin or an isolated farmhouse, and even more rarely, a room. If a room, there's often a window; if a window, there will be curtains—white— or heavy draperies, also white. Never Venetian blinds: they don't like that kind of lighting, the day or night falling in slantwise through the slats. It makes them flicker even more than they normally do.

Sometimes they're friends, and they want you to know they're all right. That kind might make a remark or two, nothing earth-shattering. It's like the screen when you turn off the television, one of them said—it's just a loss of contact. Another one—the setting was a woodland walk, in fall, orange and yellow leaves, that crisp smell—this one said, Isn't it beautiful?

Some don't say anything. They might smile, they might not; they might turn away once they know you've seen them. They want you to see them: that's the point. They want you to know they're still around and they can't be forgotten or dismissed.

Procne turned up the other night. Got in through the window, I guess. Right away I wished I'd taken a pill: that would have shut her out. But you can't take pills all the time, and she waits. She waits until I'm unconscious.

You shouldn't have let him lock me up in that shack she said.

The location was a room; the window in question had white curtains. We've been through this before, I said. You weren't locked up. You could have opened the door. Anyway, I didn't know.

You knew, she said. You repressed it, but you must have known. You weren't an idiot, though I might be giving you too much credit.

Of course I knew there'd been a first wife, I said. Everyone knew that, it was a matter of public record. But according to him you were dead.

Typical, she said. That's what they want you to think. I might as well have been, but I wasn't. I was working like a slave to keep body and soul together. Meanwhile you were swanning around without a care in the world, getting ready to take my place. Having your dress fitted for the big event. Some dress too, seed pearls all over it and slit to the navel. What of piece of tat. I wouldn't have been caught dead in it.

I had to, I said. I had to get married. He raped me; what else could I have done? You know how people talk. It was that or slut city. Don't tell me you were jealous of the dress.

Jealous? she said. She gave a kind of caw. Not for an instant! I knew his ways, never washed his feet, meat breath, what a pig. Believe me, you were welcome to that part of it. I only wish he hadn't cut out my tongue.

That is a paranoid fantasy, I said. He never did that. You made the decision not to speak, is all. I expect you were sulking. But the tongue part of the story is just a misreading of a temple wall painting, that's what people say now. Those things weren't tongues, they were laurel leaves, the priestess was supposed to chew them and hallucinate, and prophesy, and—

You and you archeology, said Procne. That's a cover-up. He cut out my tongue all right. He knew I knew too much. You don't want to face the facts.

Maybe he had his reasons, I said. Men in power often behave a little strangely in their private lives. It's the stress they're under. They have to make decisions all the time, they need a break. Sometimes they dress up in maid's uniforms, or ankle chains, that sort of thing. Not that I'm excusing his behavior.

I knew you wouldn't excuse it. That's why I decided to send you the message—to let you know I wasn't dead after all. I wove it into the wedding veil we were making, so you could hardly miss it; lucky you were smart enough to decode the embroidery. *Procne is among the slaves*, is all it said. I didn't put *Set me free*, I didn't want to influence you one way or the other, I wanted to let you make your own decision about that, you could even have ignored it. But I wasn't going to keep my trap shut just to spare him the embarrassment. If I could have got out, I would have crashed the wedding. What really burns me is that he completely neglected our son.

You mean that boy of yours, the one you killed and cooked?

I did no such thing. He floated that cheap talk-show story as a way of discrediting me. I never laid a finger on poor Itys, but with me gone and his dad so tunnel-vision about you, the boy was neglected and naturally he got in with a bad set. I think they were sniffing glue, doing sacrifices in vacant lots, that kind of thing. I wasn't my fault he ended up as a hash.

In my opinion, I said, the two of you just pulled him to pieces between you. It happens so often in these custody cases.

Fine for you to talk! If you hadn't been such a piece of jailbait, walking around in your bath towel at the age of twelve, none of this would have happened.

How can you say that? You were my sister! You were envious of me my whole life!

I wanted you to avoid the mistakes I made, that's all.

The window was open at the bottom, there was a breeze, the curtains were blowing. The air smelled of apple blossom. I really wish you'd leave me alone, I said. It's over, it's long ago. You're dead now, and he's dead, and I'm too old for all this garbage.

You're never too old for it, said Procne. Then she started turning into a bird, the way she always does. It's unsettling to watch, especially the beak part, and when the feathers come out around her eyes. When I look down, the same thing is happening to me. I am her sister, after all; these things run in families. She's a different kind of bird every time but I'm always the same. She was the clever one, she had the talent; I was more limited. This is when I know in the dream that I'm dead too, because at the end of the story he killed us both.

Then Procne flies out through the window, and so do I. It's night, a forest, a moon. We land on a branch. It's at this moment, in the dream, that I begin to sing. A long liquid song, a high requiem, the story of the story of the story.

Or is the voice hers? Hard to tell.

A man standing underneath our tree says *Grief.*

Jillian
Umphenour | *Morton's Cow*

BOSSY, ONE OF JOE MORTON'S COWS, ran away yesterday. It was reported she went looking for greener pastures. Joe was said to have been in a quandary since he truly believed that pastures didn't get any greener than his . . .

Betty Lou was Bossy's mother, and reportedly, one of Joe's favorite cows. She set a good example for the others and was never heard to utter even one harsh word. Betty Lou was stupefied when questioned about Bossy's dissatisfaction, "Joe gives us everything we could possibly want: plenty of good food and water, a warm place to sleep. Our entire family is here to love and support her. Why, I've spent my whole life here. It's good enough for me. It ought to be good enough for her! It's not like it's boring here, for Pete's sake! There's plenty of room to stretch our legs. Joe's pasture has always been green enough for the rest of us. I don't know what the heck Bossy was talking about. We can walk all the way to the fence on the east side and see Herbert's cornfield. Or go to the west and look through the fence and see Wiley's Tractor Repair. If we want to. Why in the world would she want to leave such a nice place? Well, I honestly thought she was happy, Lord knows she should have been. I sure do miss her though. I hope she comes home soon. Well, if not, she'll always be my little girl."

Hanna, a friend of Bossy's, was quoted as saying that Bossy was the smart one of the herd. Evidently, Hanna wasn't happy either. She couldn't explain just why, but she did say that she was afraid to leave. "I envy Bossy," she mooed, "she's got guts to go after her dreams. I'd have gone too but I have my calves to think of . . . I can't just up and leave them. They need to be with their mother. And I certainly wouldn't dream of taking them out into such a cruel world where they would end up on someone's dinner plate. My babies won't end up veal cutlets! At least here, they got friends and family. Joe would never do them any harm. But believe me, as soon as they're all grown and have families of their own . . . I'm leaving here, too. Believe me . . . someday I'll leave too."

Billy, the bull of the herd, was disappointed that Bossy was gone, but he took solace among the other heifers. He told reporters, "Yeah Bossy was one fine

10

bovine, oh man she was sweet! Definitely one of my favorites. I will s-u-r-e-l-y miss that babe. But, as they say, 'no sense crying over spilled milk'. . . . As far as I'm concerned, there's way too many heifers and way too little time . . . oh hey, speaking of which, I gotta get going, got a date . . . later dude."

Some people may have said Bossy was an instigator, but she gave darn good milk and lots of it, which made Joe a very happy man. So. He called the police for help getting her back. Mabel Johnstone, a reliable witness (since she's the receptionist at the police department and known as the town gossip as well) reported that she heard Joe Morton's call to Officer Hardy. This is the conversation she claims to have heard:

"Officer Hardy, this is Joe Morton. You gotta help me. My Bossy's gone!"

"Calm down, Joe. What's a Bossy?"

"You mean who! Why she's just one of my best cows! She's gone and you've got to find her. Why . . . I've looked everywhere and she's just nowhere to be found. Oh Lord . . . I hope nothing's happened to her. Oh Lord I love that cow so. Can you please find her for me Hardy?"

Officer Hardy, an extremely patient man, promised to do his best, then asked, "So what does she look like, Joe?"

"Well Hardy, she looks like a darn COW you fool, you know what a COW looks like don't ya?" Joe snapped.

"No need to get snippy there Joe! Of course I know what a darn COW looks like! We only got about two thousand of 'em in town though. You don't suppose she's got any distinguishing marks or tattoos that might help me find her, do ya Joe? You'd hate for me to bring you the wrong cow now, wouldn't ya?" Officer Hardy was a compassionate man who loved his job and got it done right. His wife Mae was very proud of him . . . but the impression Mabel Johnstone got was . . . Joe Morton just wanted his cow back. He didn't care about that now.

"Well her body is mostly black but with a few small white spots, her legs are white with a few small black patches. Left ear's black and her right ear is tagged, it's white. A square black face and big sad brown eyes. She's a good lookin' spry heifer. Is that enough for you to find my girl? Oh, and she was last seen headin' west on the highway, supposedly lookin' for greener pastures, they say. Please Hardy, you just gotta bring my girl back to me. I gotta go now, before I make an even bigger fool of myself. Oh, and thanks Hardy." Joe hung up.

Mabel Johnstone also reported that directly after the phone call, Officer Hardy was hot on the trail. He questioned everyone and anyone who may have seen her before she left or when she took off down the highway that day. He had an artist draw up a sketch from Joe's description. He put out an APB on Bossy. He was known as an officer who always got his man. A cow wasn't any different as far as he could tell. He knew exactly what to do and when. So he did.

Everyone was talking about Bossy. She was reportedly the biggest news to hit town since Grandpa Worley's misadventure a year ago. The rumor on the streets, as I heard it, was that, in his typical drunken stupor, wearing only his stinky, sweat-stained undershirt and boxers, Worley drove his tractor right into Marge Olsen's living room. He stumbled off as he proudly exclaimed, "Dolores, I'm home. Where's dinner? You're not Dolores! This isn't my house."

He promptly threw up on her family heirloom carpet. Marge was evidently fuming mad at that point. Shotgun in hand, she was about to put him in a world of hurt. But instead, she simply flung him out into her front yard on his butt. Word has it, he's still working and paying on repairing the damage he did to her house and yard. Word has it she kept his tractor too. That she loans it to him to do his farming.

Once again, Mabel Johnstone reported that a week later Joe got the news from Officer Hardy, "It seems your Bossy hitched a ride on a hay truck headed for California . . . cleaned out his truck by the time they got there, too, incidentally. The driver dropped her in Hollywood, said she was looking to be a moovie star. It may be hard to find her in a place like that. You know as well as I do, in big cities like that . . . all the cows look the same. I did speak to an officer down there in the Hollywood office. He informed me that she hadn't committed any crimes or been in any accidents. No reports on her at all. I guess that's good news. She's most likely doing ok. If you want me to keep looking for her I will. It'll be like finding a needle in a haystack though. Joe. We could search for her til the cows come home (sorry, no pun intended) and still not find your Bossy. I'm real puzzled here Joe, what do you want me to do next?"

Joe explained to Hardy that this wasn't the news he'd expected, instead he'd expected his Bossy would be home where she belonged by now, out in the pasture with the rest of his cows . . . she had no business going out there to Hollywood to make moovies. "Aw good golly Hardy, I don't know what to do either. This sure is a fine mess. Please keep this under your hat cuz I don't need any of my other cows gettin' any newfangled "BIG" city ideas. One more runaway cow right now might just push me right over the edge. I need to think. These are desperate times indeed." It appeared this cow thing had him in quite a state . . .

One month later, Joe reported that he received a postcard from Bossy. Postmarked Hollywood. She evidently was quite happy there. The STAR of a string of Jersey Maid commercials. Wondered if Joe had seen any of them yet. She had a big-bucks-moovie-contract and no intention of ever coming back, except maybe for a visit. Next year.

As Joe told it, she'd written on the postcard that she was sorry, but she needed more than Joe had to offer her. She felt so trapped there. She couldn't breathe. It was stifling. She needed to express herself. Be creative. Be more than just a piece of meat and a quart of milk. She believed there was more to life than just standing around chewing her cud all day. She wasn't sure Joe would understand this now, but hoped that someday he would. And forgive her. She didn't mean to hurt anybody; she just *had* to be *free*.

An anonymous witness observed Joe in his kitchen . . . talking to himself, "How could she do this to me . . . after all I've done for her. I gave her everything she ever asked for. Everything she ever wanted! I loved her. This is where she belongs. Lord knows I tried to make her happy." Joe pulled out his hankie to wipe something from his eyes. He stared at the postcard in his hand for a long time, then tore it up and threw it in the garbage.

Joe went out to check on his cows. The screen door slammed behind him.

| Dennis | *Portmanteau* |
| Must | |

I'VE A HABIT of dragging people around.

Only matter is, you couldn't tell. My chalk-stripe, navy blue worsted suit, white shirt, foulard tie, and the calfskin-cap-toed shoes disguise my baggage. An hour or two over a drink, you still wouldn't know what I really do.

It varies from month to month just how many. There are some regulars. The jazz pianist, the preacher, the worrier, the teary-eyed sentimentalist, the callow youth, and the woman with alba skin and hair the shade of fire. They only show themselves when I'm alone. At such times they exhale collectively and appear.

My wife, Alma, they've taken to, however. Each has slept with her. I don't object, whereas you might think I would. I'm not a voyeur. Instead I'm enlightened by the delight she enjoys in the diversity. Each causes her to reveal a different side of herself.

For instance, the keyboardist. He seduces her by whistling chord progressions of one of her favorite ballads. First he'll announce the chords in each bar, say, "OK, C minor seventh, F seventh, D minor, C sharp diminished, then back to C minor and F seventh." Then he'll warble the changes.

All the time rubbing the small of her back, always a prelude to coitus.

The woman with the alba skin and fiery orange hair, she I like to think is a Rabbi's daughter. She has very long legs and fingers that you might imagine are a cellist's. Her lips are a deep vermillion and bud-like. When she laughs they open niggardly, suggesting a violet breathing behind them. Alma enjoys the reticence of the Rabbi's daughter. How she approaches her with stealth and a fragrant breath. The tongue caresses Alma's neck and aureoles with deliberateness. Alma giggles and shivers. The Rabbi's daughter moves down the body.

Soon legs are entwined. And Alma is singing the keyboardist's progressions. The Rabbi's daughter's only sound is a sustained A sharp, two octaves above middle C.

The preacher gets her attention only on week nights when Alma returns home from work, literally exhausted. He's insistent in his own guarded way. "I don't see enough of you. Don't you love me anymore? Let me massage your feet. Tell me the problems you encountered at the office today." All his tired lines. One invariably works. Especially the massage or his share-your-troubles ploy.

Invariably Alma and he ride off to a perfunctory release. Neither is too excited about it. The preacher for all his earnestness is unable to touch these parts of Alma that the keyboardist and Rabbi's daughter provoke.

When I watch them an ennui sets in. Often I fall asleep before he moves to the missionary position.

The lachrymose sentimentalist places a photograph of Alma's deceased mother over the headboard. Looks very much like Alma, actually, when I first met her. The mother is sitting in a wing chair, smoking and laughing. Her legs are crossed and a pleated skirt falls just above her knee. The mother's eyes are illumined with a "you're winning me over" smile. There's a very seductive message in the way she has tossed back her head, the long braid flying out to the side of her lovely face with abandon.

A maudlin sadness generates the couple's embrace. Alma's deceased father was a stone, a providential husband and father, but a stone nonetheless. The libidinous nuance suggested in the photograph went unanswered by him. Alma mourns for her mother's loss both while she was alive and now. The sentimentalist sobs and commiserates with her. A prelude to an embrace. A release from this sadness and all the others they can think of.

The callow youth she addresses as the instructor. "Do this. Oh, please, not that. This. Yes, that's better." It's a very small step removed from masturbation. At times she prefers the latter, but he'll get better, she reassures herself.

Only out of some wizened sense of charity does she prevail the worrier to come in off the balcony (he's always threatening to leap) and accompany her in the bed. She knows that this effort of mercy will be fruitless, however; at some time during the night she will hear the slider doors to the balcony open and see the shadow of the worrier shuddering alongside the wrought-iron balustrade and staring ten floors below.

Alma thinks I'm shallow. She doesn't like the way I cock my hat to one side of my head. Forever she is scolding me that the part in my hair is crooked. "Did you look in the mirror, Edward?"

Little does she know about looking in a mirror. She glances in one and sees her gums receding, the strands of gray, the mole under her left eye that she calls a beauty mark. I see those characters smirking at me. I can't afford to look in a mirror, for God's sake.

Alma treats them better than she does me. In fact they are deferential to her. Catering to all her needs. It's me they are indifferent to. "Get a life," they say. And when the worrier ratchets up his anxiety about wanting to leap off the balcony, the others begin to exhibit signs of anxiety. They whisper among themselves, seeking some way to ease him back to stability. "We'll miss him terribly," one will cry. "We're family," another will assert. It's seems if one of their members is threatened, they all are. If one bolts on his own volition, underneath all the fuss is a sense he'll pull the others like catfish on a string along with him.

No, they are never solicitous with me. Yet it is I who carry them about on my back.

It's why I've come up with this scheme.

I'm going to force the worrier to leap. He keeps threatening, obviously gaining some satisfaction from the rest being solicitous of him. Coddling him. I say if he wants to do it, he should be brave and leap. That's the way I will frame the issue. "Worrier, if you keep threatening to leap, I believe you are only doing it for the pity the others heap upon you. They don't want to be left alone. Further, I suspect that if you do in fact leap, one will come down with the desire to do the same. It's infectious, you know? This desire to take one's life. I would never consider it. Oh, no. But you have. Yet, unlike the others, I have no sympathy for you. Further, I think you are pusillanimous. A coward, yes. I would have much more respect for you if indeed you were brave and took the plunge. It would all be over in a matter of seconds. But a word of advice: stay clear of the tree. It might break your fall. The last thing you need is to finally muster the courage to leap, then have the grand event be compromised by your getting hung up in its branches.

"Ignominy. You've suffered enough of that, Worrier.

"So what do you say? I will accompany you early to the balcony, and in the morning's gray mist, you'll fly. How does that sound? Better than taking the leap. Huh? Is it a date?"

My scheme.

If the worrier does indeed climb upon the balcony's railing, and if the other characters in my charge are convinced of his determination to plunge . . . it's at that very point in time they will flee my head like starlings out a barn loft. For where the worrier goes, they follow. His fate will be their fate. And that's when every character looks out for himself. I'm convinced of it.

Alma will have a new man come daybreak.

| Cecile | *Infatuation* |
| Rossant | |

*MA IS HER NAME. She is at the end—standing at the end of the hall or seated be-
sides his bed watching the TV screen until the last of the credits scroll by—and the
beginning.*

*Because Ma is always waiting for the slightest acknowledgement of her presence,
she hears the beginning of every one of his utterances with the utmost clarity. "Ma!
When you go Ed's, buy me a box of cigarettes." She precedes Lem. For Ma, being
there for his beginning was akin to witnessing a miracle.*

I caused a dilemma when I dragged Di to Lem who was lying near enough but
who was just too lethargic etceteras, to get up to meet her on his own accord.
He is the type to stay in bed, even starve in bed so long as he has enough cigarettes to fend off hunger and enough stamina to bring on and hold an erection
if a beautiful woman happens to stroll by. I came too late.

If ever he is forced to earn some money to pay for his fully blossomed
smoking habit he refuses to handle any material except metals. He believes
anything else, and perhaps rightly, will speed up his physical decay or even
more repugnant, coat him in the unbearable film of its own deterioration.

Lem once explained that metallic by-products inlay the skin in an oily
metallic dust that he thinks act as a preservative. He works for weeks at a time
at a die manufacturing plant nearby. On break, he often rubs the machine oil
into his hands, face and forearms, and down the front and sides of his jeans.
I have loved Lem, presumably for his supreme detachment, which I have been
perpetually unable to achieve. He needs few categories for things and even
fewer for states of being.

I have wondered at times that he probably doesn't even recognize that chickens with their heads axed off are hopping around the planet . . . somewhere.

Today Lem showered. To do so he stands in the dark hallway of his apartment.
The shower is a length of rubber surgical hose, hardened and darkened with

age. He attaches the hose to a joint in the water pipe and loosens the outer ring. Water leaks through the joint. He lifts away the floorboards beneath his shower. Standing on two exposed joists, he directs the water dripping off his body to the gap between. The apartment beneath his is abandoned. A couple of months ago, Lem positioned a metal basin below the hole to catch the falling water. Lem smokes as he showers. "I would fucking freeze otherwise." he says. The ashes also fall through the hole in the floor.

Di is not worth talking about. She serves something as crass as other people's interest in her body. I am not unkind to her. If Lem asks me to bring her to his place, I never refuse. But we don't have much to say. We have really nothing in common. For example, I can't share in her understanding of Lem—not at all.

Di is beautiful. She has a kind of beauty that hooks into you. I stare at her when we ride the train together. I'm not even sure what I'm thinking about. She sits across me cross-legged and bobs her floating leg up and down like a dog. That disturbs everyone on the train. I can see that some of them would give a lot just to touch her with the tip of a finger. They can't grasp how little she has to offer. For Di, intensity always wins over complexity. I can't accept that kind of selfishness.

She and Lem don't talk at all. In exclusive concentration they move towards each other with controlled and efficient movement, like dancers . . .

It is not that I hang around to watch. It is something I understand afterwards, when Di has already left. It is the way Lem pins himself to the bed after she leaves, as though he wanted to remember how each part of him was involved in the performance that they just completed. Lying there, Lem draws a mental picture of himself. He likes what he sees.

Thinking about their relation sends shivers down my back. I have to walk somewhere, fast, to a public place. Five blocks away is a diner. I order coffee and read the long menu and the paper if available. When the place gets crowded I ask for a danish, a small salad or a large tomato juice. I never want to eat something that might put me to sleep. In a little while, I'm seeing other couplings. Once it was the cook's hands cracking eggs, tossing fries, managing a pen and his burgers. Last time, Sunday afternoon, I couldn't stop looking at the plastic flowers in the window. How the leaves bounced every time someone left or entered the place.

Today's waitress refills my cup. I stay seated for a sip or two.

Lem is not at home. I have his keys that I only use after ringing his bell at least ten times. Six months ago I accidentally walked in on Di and Lem. They didn't notice me. Both lay on the bed in Christ on the Cross positions—Lem flat on top of Di. It was so quiet I could hear their even heavy breathing. They were barely moving. Unfortunately, I picked up on the caterpillar-segment-like movement of Lem's sweet behind and knew that they were joined. I tiptoed down the hall; the floorboards creaked. I didn't dare look around, one view of them was good enough for a lifetime.

Luckily, today Lem left the window open. A fresh wind blows across the room. This morning I bought artificial flowers and throw them on his bed just to check their effect.

I'm staring at the flowers when Lem walks in. He lies right on top and closes his eyes. His long hair falls across the pink and yellow petals. His smile rises on a face lit by a warm orange glow. Later the face is ashen blue. I want to pull him out of bed but I just sit there until the sun goes down. The room is in almost total darkness when Lem finally sits up, lights a cigarette and says hello.

| E.C. Stanley | *It's About Justice* |

EACH VISIT TO SEE MY DAUGHTER at her various foster parents was a new and delicate torture. But one can, with time, get used to anything. They say. And it had been five years. This particular neighborhood was grim. This particular foster mom, openly hostile. In Andrea's eighteen months there I never saw the foster father. "Lucky for you, Mom," Andrea said. But grinned.

The family had four 'fosters,' they called them, plus two of their 'own' children. Neither parent had an income apart from raising other people's children. They had been at it now for sixteen years. I tried to imagine the mother as she might have been at the beginning. I haven't done so well myself, losing two adopted children. This foster mom, I estimated, must have lost between thirty and forty. Well I couldn't do it. If I could, I would start over with another child this minute. I am still young. And I think too I have forgiven myself. All my craziness earlier. The year we lost Andrea. And maybe they were not so crazy after all—all my foolish, futile attempts to challenge enough about her past to change it. Considering what was about to happen to us next. Which is the story I wish to tell now.

Andrea and I had the usual wonderful weekend. Two movies, her choice in fast food, ice skating at the local mall. Our last official act each visit was a shopping spree at Food Lion. A standard meal at the foster home consisted of canned corn, canned pork and beans, canned applesauce; and on weekend nights, hotdogs. The foster parents did allow Andrea to keep her own fresh veggies and fruit as long as she would store them in her room. We'd buy totally green bananas Andrea kept suspended in her closet and claimed sometimes lasted until my next visit. Hard-as-a-rock green mangoes, slick black avocadoes, when Food Lion had them, lasted even longer. Then there were the dried apricots and nuts.

Andrea and I were usually rather manic the last few hours of these monthly visits. We had our parting rituals worked out, so leave-taking could be as painless as possible. I'd stop the rental car out in front of the dreary tract house, as if I were some visiting school chum. Andrea would swing out of the car with her sack of fresh produce. I'd say, "Have a terrific week at school, Sweet." She'd say, "Talk to you Tuesday."

We were allowed two ten-minute calls a week.

"And talk to you Sunday, Sweetie," I'd cry. "Love you a lot!"

This time was different.

We went through the same routine as always. But while I was wheeling the car around in the narrow roadway, to head out in the opposite direction for the airport, Andrea set the bag of produce in the driveway and came running alongside the car. I thought at first that she was teasing. Or about to show me some new cheerleading stunt.

Until I noticed her eyes.

And that her breath was coming in tight little pants.

Like a dog.

I don't know how I got out of the car. I had to go back a few minutes later, steer it out of the middle of the road, and park.

"I'm sorry. I'm sorry." Andrea was trying to smile, but huge tears pelted the bodice of her pink silk shirt. Where it stuck, it looked like blood soaking through.

"It's all right!" I grabbed her fiercely. "I feel exactly the same each visit."

"Y-y-you do?"

"Usually I cry the first fifty miles. Then I curse the next two hundred. All the stewardesses on Southwest know me."

A sharp rapping at the grimy bay window turned out to be the foster mom, mouthing 'no body contact,' like the cur she was.

I said as much out loud. "That bitch from hell."

This cracked Andrea up. It was the first time she'd ever heard me curse.

We separated. But very little. Just enough to saunter, arm in arm, up and down the badly cracked sidewalk. Careful to keep within sight. But instantaneously forgetting the foster mom the minute our backs were turned. We had learned to do that. Oh I would have fifty miles of awful anxiety returning the rental car, would the bitch report me? If she did, I'd probably have to get another court order for my next visit. Which was costly. And Phil would yell for weeks. "So what gives, Sweetie?" I dredged up a Kleenex from my purse.

Andrea brushed her bangs back, stalled.

"What's got you worried? Honey, please tell Mamma. Is it my leaving? Or what?"

Now everybody, everybody working with an abused child that is, has got to have help. I personally believe that a true friend, one your own age, with children of her own, may be the best help available. In today's world. Of course most people say, therapists. Our family had had—oh let's see, close to a dozen professional counselors at that point. Andrea alone had had seven; both foster kids and employees of the state tend to move around a lot. And I had had three. Two of them helped.

One of mine, the one who taught me how to ask what I just asked, moved away after just six weeks of helping. Her husband was transferred to Missoula, Montana, of all places. I still phone her occasionally. She and Andrea never met. What she taught me is this: "Do not suppose that you can read Andrea's mind. Sometimes you can, of course. And that's good. That's terrific. You have a lot of insight. But what I want you to remember every precious moment you are with your daughter is: Ask. Ask!"

I asked.

"What is it? What's got you worried? Is it my leaving—"

Now that's the mistake, see? I had learned to ask. But I was still supplying easy answers—To protect myself?

Ever since Andrea has begun to outgrow her fear of promised retaliation by her birth parents—or perhaps just learned to live with it—she has become an uncommonly honest young woman. Too honest for most people. Too honest for me, I realize now. What, for example, would I have done if she had spelled it out, what she was planning to do? Report her to the latest in the revolving-door of therapists the state supplied?

Tell Phil, my husband?

Every time I brought Phil another fear, suspicion, intractable problem about Andrea or the system, he began to yell. He could not help this.

Tell my therapist? Two or three sessions into treatment, with each of them, they would calmly inform me that they'd like to help me, but the first step would be to admit that I had to give up on my adopted children.

This is where the good friend came in. The very first thing I did when I returned to my home outside of Denver was phone my friend Susan. Sometimes even, from the airport, jammed into a row of well-heeled salesmen at the phone bank, before I took the bus to my car in the long term lot. Susan always had some good advice. Usually she was so far ahead of anybody's therapist, I was amazed. Perhaps because she knew these children were perceived by me to be my children. Whether or not they'd ever be able to live under our roof again. It was the one thing that made me able to endure the pain.

Meanwhile Andrea had noticed the tear stains and was rippling the new silk blouse out away from her body, edging backward toward the house, avoiding my eyes.

"*Zoooo, jung laydee,*" I called, gathering strength, my best friend Susan's strength—the saving phone bank less than three hours away now. "'*Don't jew trust me vith jur pro-blem?*'" I tried mimicking one of the latest shrinks.

"Oh, on a lot of things," she said.

"'A lot of things?'"

I was back on track here, see? Open-ended questions. And I think Andrea

22

might really have confessed, but at exactly that moment, one of her foster brothers stuck his pimply head out a rusty screen door at the side of the house and yelled, "Andrea! It's your turn to set the dinner table. And you know it."

Andrea blanched. "I hate it here."

I said quickly, "But that's not the problem."

Andrea said, "No, that's not the problem."

I agreed, "No."

"OK," she turned and yelled. "I'm coming."

"We don't have any privacy on the phone, Andrea," I prodded.

"I know," she murmured. "I want," she mumbled, in one airless gulp, "to change my name to Ann."

Ann?

"You know, like you, Mom."

The smile on her face. That blazing sunburst on her face?

"Well?"

That smile was like one of those kindergarten drawings where the sun in all its cadmium glory o're-takes the world.

"What's your, our middle name, anyway?" she looked mercifully down. A grateful mother could get sunburned in that smile. "Mid-dle name, Mom," she lilted after a while.

I wasn't sure I remembered. My rushing blood had spurted too much good news to the head. Eventually, however, "M-m-ma-bel?" I admitted.

"Mabel!" How she hooted. "Oh I love it!"

"You're delirious, daughter of mine." And I burst into tears.

"Ann Mable Lewis," she whistled softly. "'Oh, Mabel are you able?' Ann Two!" She leaped back to salute me even as foster mom began shrilling again, back there in the distance, that someone named Andrea was about to lose her allowance for the week. Seventy-five cents. "So what if boys get to do that 'Junior' stuff! I don't care. I am satisfied with this. And don't you ever forget it." She was looming close, shouting from the effort of trying to put it into exactly the right words. Words I could, mercifully, not understand at the moment. But would remember. Later.

"'Cause from now on out, I'm you. And that enough for me. Can you re-member that? That's important. That will have been enough. OK? Mom? Mother! Are you listening?" Though before I could even begin to respond, she grabbed me, wrenched our heads into line to where we could both see this miraculous sun seeping out from under an inglorious gray cloud and about to disappear into one of the two Dempster Dumpsters at the end of the street.

We had joked about the summer sun dead-ending in the dumpsters before, many times, declaring with mock glum, 'Story of our lives!' We'd named the bright new green one on the left, Ms. Kansas. For breaking up our happy home. And the rusty one on the right, Loser Louisiana. For failing to prosecute Andrea's—that is, Ann Two's birth parents, on the testimony of a minor. But what does she mean, 'will have been enough?'

"Look, Mom." Oh she could read my mind, this daughter. "I've got to get out from under this cloud. You understand that, don't you?"

"Oh but Annie," I cried as the sun dipped delicately toward the garbage. "You have. You have!" The sky a wound.

"And back when everybody was telling you to forget it! Well, you didn't forget it—You knew I was your daughter."

"Of course. And you deserve a new name. And, Annie, please believe me, it will be the greatest honor of my l-ll-l—" I prepared to go on babbling for hours.

"What I'm saying is, you're my role model." She'd begun to nudge me back toward the house. "If you think about it. And you will think about it. You never listened to a soul but Mrs. Drescher." My friend Susan. "And you never, never said die."

"Standing out there thicker than thieves, in the complete dark. Just waiting for a car to knock you side-winding. Missy, I don't have to tell you, you're grounded. And, yessiree, that means cheerleader practice too."

"We are so, so sorry—" I launched in. "Mrs.—uh Felter, to have delayed your dinner. Please, please forgive us. This once. It was something truly special—"

"Well, I have other children here. Andrea knows that. And you, an adult. You're supposed to be responsible. How do you 'spect her to learn when—"

"Bye, Mom." Ann Two slipped gracefully behind the torn screen door, two nut-brown fingers lingering, raised in our familiar 'V for victory' salute.

"I inten' to report you both," foster mom buzzed on.

"Have a terrific week at school, Ann," I yelled hysterically.

"I'm you." This lilting out from the dark, dark house.

"Talk to you, Cutie, on Tuesday!"

"You're as silly as she is." The foster mom.

Ann reappeared briefly, in a distant window, smile blazoned across her mouth, cheeks, throat, blouse, blushing the blue then black of a bruise, in the flickering light of a television tube. "Love you, Mom. Forever. And don't you forget it." Pantomimed.

"I love you, too, Ann Two."

And she had told me everything. Knowing I'd be too overjoyed to notice. But trusting me to remember her words. Just as she had trusted me not to report the almost forgotten missing line in all this she'd demonstrated months before. She'd been planning it that long.

At least two—possibly three—visits earlier we had been sitting in a

McDonald's, idly discussing her future. College was still two years away. When she was eighteen, she could live with us again. She wanted to live at home the first year of college, or so. About this she was adamant. Afterwards she was going, like everyone else, into a dorm. She was going to be normal—

"We'll live together again," she grinned like a vixen, carefully slathering ketchup onto another skinny McDonald's fry, "when you get old. On my imaginary island."

When she was just a little girl, oh, sometime the first year we had her and her brother Huey, she once told me that when she grew up she was going to buy me an island exactly like the one in the painting that hung over mine and Phil's bed.

"'Only sun, and sand, and sea gulls.'" I nodded my head.

"Tell me again," Andrea said, pushing back the empty food cartons but folding and refolding her crumpled paper napkin, "what the university is like." Kansas never let her cross state lines for a visit. "Can you really see the mountains from your apartment? What kind of Volkswagen will I have? Think it'll be too late for Dad to re-teach me violin?"

Twenty minutes of questions, hopes, dreams and descriptions later, Andrea abruptly reached for that same folded and refolded paper napkin, whipping it dramatically aloft, and shaking it out, like Houdini about to disappear.

"You, madame—" she smiled. "*You haf bene zee participahn in an astounding zientifeeq esperimon deefying the imageenacion.*"

Although language play was clearly one of our oldest and truest pleasures, there was something new in her voice, something well beyond the sideshow huckster. It stung like molten steel, so that goose pimples massed at the base off my spine, shot off toward my hair. "*Vat has bene thees espeera-mon?*" I asked from my chill.

Andrea grabbed a flimsy plastic fork from the pile on her tray and lifted it dramatically to her mouth. "Are you ready, *Mesdames, Monsieur?*"

"*Ciertement.*" Certainly not. Still I could not move as, wide eyes narrowed to mine, delicately poised fork shaking not at all, Andrea carefully tongued out a huge chunk of the steak sandwich she'd finished eating twenty minutes before.

"*Voila! Exactement.*" She smiled, pushing the lump, unchewed, practically to my nose.

"Andrea! That's gross," I cried.

She blushed.

"Gross and disgusting! Have you lost your—"

"*Zoe sor-ree, Madame,*" my daughter smiled.

"Well, what on earth? And, please, put that down."

The well-preserved bite of steak sandwich was still balanced aloft while Andrea herself leaned across the clutter, upending a carton. "I've figured it out," she stopped inches from my nose. "Come on!" Suddenly she dumped the steak lump into the mound of clutter. "Let me drive." She stood. "I've got something to tell you," she flung over her shoulder. "It's about justice!" Heads turned in the McDonalds. And she was out the door.

I had trouble finding correct change, ordering a cup of coffee-to-go, fastening my seat belt.

"I've figured out how to do it," she said the minute she accelerated the cherry red rental car onto the Interstate. I had taught her to drive myself, the year before. She was a natural. "I know how to get them, Mom!"

Oh, God, not this again, I thought.

"*I have figured it out.*" She was yelling, triumphant, leading a football cheer.

"Oh, Andrea, no."

"'*Oh, Andrea,*' Yes."

A few years back it had become an obsession. Retaliation. And exposure of the cult her birth parents raised her in. The wrong therapist and the wrong moment. Or the least tiny flaw in this ebullient girl?

"Andrea, sweet, I—" About the only thing I agreed with the current therapist about: Andrea should not even be let discuss it. When she did, she became—well, not herself. "—I've promised." I was hurt. "My visits depend upon it. And you know that."

"But Mom!" She gripped the steering wheel and checked the road before and behind before turning full face. "It's still going on."

I was the one to look away. "Oh God I hope not."

"But you know it is. It's still happening to other kids."

"Andrea, we tried. Your Dad and I—"

Spent our last dollar—lost every successive legal battle. Meanwhile amortizing every cent Phil had vested in state retirement from his twenty years of teaching. This after he lost his tenure over the scandal. And only has a part time job in Colorado. We will, literally, never be able to retire. But you cannot tell a child this. As you cannot tell a child that two district attorney's offices essentially refused to accept the testimony of a child, for a crime against that child.

"Look, Mom. Just be my friend here. The girls at school? They'll never know me. They can never know me. The cult took that from me before I was three."

"Andrea, we are not allowed to speak of a cult."

"*Let me finish.* I have thought it over. There IS a loop-hole—"

Our kids struggle with justice. While we worry about retirement.

"So. Mom. You've promised not to talk of it—" voice molten steel again, "—because no one's ever been able to produce a body, right?"

"Ummmm, Andrea, honey, my visits—"

"Got you now," she grinned and clicked and re-clicked the automatic door locks, to emphasize that we were speeding seventy miles an hour down the

Interstate. "*Jew are my priz-son-ere*! No one has ever been able to produce a sacrificed baby's body, RIGHT?"

What dooms my daughter is not so much what she has had to live through. 'The luck of the draw,' she shrugs forthrightly. It's that she can claim no past, no personal history. If she tells the truth, society has declared that no one sane will ever believe her. She'd have been better off being abducted by flying saucers. So common wisdom is.

"That uh," I hear her voice from far away, "that uhm, bite of meat?"

I duck my head.

"Well, I'm not sure you noticed, Mom, but it wasn't 'macerated.' We learned that word this week in English III. Aren't you impressed?"

No one will ever believe her.

"They put baby's liver under the microscope," Andrea suddenly sucks in a wheeze, "scientists recognize it, right?"

That is, except me.

"Anyway," Andrea stares off down the expressway, "that's what I figured out last year in Biology II. I failed Biology I, because I refused to cut up a cat. That's really funny, isn't it? But I found my *solu-ci-on-nee*, in Bio II."

I am not allowed to believe her.

"Well?" Triumphant again. "Mother! Are you listening?"

That is, if I want to see her again, before she is eighteen.

"Mmmm, Andrea, sweet, you're scaring Mom a little. Will you let me drive now, Sweetie? You're upset."

She allowed me the least little irony of a smile. Then whipped the cheery red rental car to the shoulder of the busy Interstate. "Yo," she remarked smartly, when I pulled out too close in front of a rapidly approaching eighteen-wheeler. And had to swerve dangerously onto the shoulder again.

"Sorry," I said.

"Apology accepted, pard'. But that would prove it, wouldn't it? Baby's liver! Wouldn't that prove it? Couldn't be a finger or a toe now, could it? Wouldn't prove it was dead, right? Just chewed up a bit—Played with just a teensy bit. Toyed with—Sorry. I said, sorry, Mom. Cut it out!"

For, in self defense, I'd begun mowing down a steady stream of rubber markers meant to remind you, you had drifted from your lane.

She put her fingers to her ears, squalling, "*Calm* down, *Mom*."

So how do you talk to a sixteen year old with a dozen-plus cigarette burns on her abdomen tied, in her memory, which seems absolutely A-OK on everything else, to having refused to participate in six ritual murders, two of them of new-borns? Or what would you say to a sixteen-year-old who four years ago was told that she would never have children, and was at an astronomical risk for various cancers because of her extremely early sexual abuse?

I mowed down a couple hundred more thudding markers, for emphasis, before mouthing in perfect Chicago-mob lingo: "*So dat's how you could do it, huh?*"

It struck as intended. Andrea shrieked with laughter and slapped the dashboard. I did too. We screamed and shouted out our outrage. Our isolation. Before I pulled the rental car back into the thunderous quietness of a lane.

Eventually, "Can we have some music?" my daughter asked. "I adore you, Mom," she added when she had located, miraculously for Kansas, a Bach chorale.

"I love you too, daughter of mine."

I also loved her enough to know I had to offer to go for her. "So how long would it take me to uh—to, you know—to learn to—" I asked.

"Oh no." Andrea's response was immediate. "No, thank you. Though I knew you would offer!" She patted a drum roll on the dashboard, in ecstasy. "Took me three months. But you're a klutz."

"Also," she added, more woodenly, some miles later, "they never trust a stranger. And they mmmm, don't cater much to middle-aged women. The old fertility angle, I suppose. Sorry, Mom."

This child was sixteen. Sixteen! But I couldn't afford the luxury of sentimentality. The cult my daughter reported used all its fertile females as breeders. These women were forced to deliver at home, so there would be no records—No record of birth, no possibility of murder. In fact, Andrea's responsibility to breed for them is why they'd hypnotized her. Brainwashing her to return.

A youth spent. Hours every afternoon. In a darkened room, a little girl with a tape recorder. From age four. My little girl—Stop. "Wait!" I yelled.

Andrea jumped.

"Granted." I was yelling now. "Granted, it may still go on. Or, granted you may have even found a way to bring them down. But—" It was dirty, but it was the one advantage I had left to press, "have you ever once considered that your desire to return and 'get' them might be—in some unconscious way only—" I tried to soften it, but it had to be said, "—might be somehow influenced by all that brain-washing they did about how you'd have to return?"

It worked instantaneously.

Or so, anyway, she let me think.

She crumpled like a spent puppet, throwing herself almost to the floorboard of the car. To dangle there, almost listless, suspended by the shoulder strap of her seat belt.

"Look, Sweetie," I cleared my throat after she eventually groped for my hand. "I will never forget what you have taught me today."

She began to cry more seriously.

"And when you are back at home? When your are eighteen. If you still want to. I will discuss it then."

Pure unadulterated worship flushed her face.

"That is," I couldn't stop myself, "if they still haven't been exposed by legal means. Trends turn. This current tendency to deny all reports of—ss-SS—" Satanism. I was still afraid to voice it. "Oh, honey! I know it hurts. But try not to think of it so much as repudiating you, as repudiating the horror of it all. You of all people should understand why people simply refuse to believe it." I was fatally off target.

A thin trickle of saliva escaped her lips, but nothing more. "So at eighteen then? OK? But even then, never, ever, with your going alone. Is that clear? Andrea, look at me. I mean it. I want you to promise me that you'll wait. And that you'll take me with you. I mean, if you have to go?"

She wiped away the dollop of spit, but didn't raise her head. Then, silence, and another five miles of busy Interstate not seen by us.

"So I'm a dope?"

"No." Said to a crown of glossy chestnut hair more beautiful to me than any sunset. "No. You are the sweetest, bravest girl I've ever known. But you still have to promise."

We shook on it, one crooked arm bent backwards—but all ten fingers and toes, showing that they were not crossed. Our standard practice.

"Well all right, then!" I could breathe, I could live. "I didn't want to do it, you know." After our shake, she shot up from her slump, as suddenly as she had crumpled. "But someone has to do it. Ooops. I don't mean you, Mom. I really don't."

She was a teenager, I hoped momentarily, after all.

"I fantasized once that I did it though." Eyes big as pies, hands trundling through every pocket for a tissue. "Everything was going fine til someone suspected me. You know? They come up to me? So even then all I have to do is swallow it, right?"

"Andrea, please. My flight leaves in less than an hour. Can we uh please?" I really don't think she heard me.

"I go straight to an emergency room and all. I slit myself open—"

"Andrea!"

"Oh well, maybe they could just pump my stomach—"

"That's more mutilation fantasies, Andrea. And I am NOT going to listen!"

Five years ago, when she was first hospitalized, after her brother Huey precipitously joined the Coast Guard and and my husband Phil was blamed for her V.D., Andrea scratched known cult symbols into wrists, her ankles, her left breast. Now she blew her nose, long and pompously, "But, mutilation with a cause."

"And you know I'm going to have to report some of this."

"You're beginning to s-ss-sound," she tinkled away like bells in a wind chime, "like my f-f-f-foster m-mom."

Oh, I did report her. I told her no-good therapist. I told the no-good supervising case worker. I told Phil. He busted his Meerschaum pipe into the keyboard of the cherished harpsichord he built himself. And yelled, of course.

I told my therapist, not one of the two good ones. Who concluded I had handled it all wrong.

Finally, I told my best friend Susan, who said, "Look, whatever you do about Andrea, you've got to get yourself another therapist."

Two weeks later I interviewed the second good one. I stayed with her until her husband moved to Missoula as explained above. Three months later, less than a week after the visit where Andrea set the grocery bag in the driveway and renamed herself Ann Two, she disappeared.

Phil and I immediately bypassed the red tape of any foster care bureaucracy, who had left their brief accusatory message, on our answering machine. We hired our own private investigator. We told him he would find Ann in the medium-sized Louisiana town where her birth parents still lived. I told the detective what she was there for. I do not think that he believed me. But we gave him her list of seventeen adult cult members authorities there had failed to investigate or prosecute all these years.

Six weeks later we had to let the investigator go. My father had called and offered to cash in the C.D. that takes him to Florida six weeks every winter, to the time share with his poker buddies. Phil said no. Then he threw the telephone in the kitchen trash can yelling, No, no, no. "There has to be an end somewhere," Phil screamed as he kicked and kicked at the garbage can and the phone, the coffee grounds and egg shells. Then he began to hiccough and shriek, "SHE'S DEAD ANYWAY! Can't you," hic hic "can't you feel it?"

He has never once yelled again. What he had been yelling against, or bracing for—the worst—had happened. Our daughter Ann was in fact two days dead though it would be three more weeks before we learned it. Her once nutbrown body gone heavy sunset colors beneath caked layers of mud. Stuffed into a manhole a good forty-eight hours before Dad gladly offered to give up Florida. Phil was right again.

Police analyzed the contents of her stomach routinely. For alcohol and drugs. Of course there were none.

A quietened Phil flew United Airlines to New Orleans. Took a pathologist acquaintance of his along. First time I realized Phil had listened to my accounts of visits with Ann. But nobody believed Phil either. Least of all his now-ex-friend, the University of Colorado pathologist. So who knows what testing he did? Just that they found nothing. Except my broken, tough and tender seeker of justice. Ann Two.

| Karen J.
Cantrell | *Isn't That Why You Came?* |

Wednesday

ELI'S COUCH WAS BIG and hard and modern, not very comfortable under relaxing circumstances, and Martha was not feeling relaxed. As soon as Eli returned with the cappuccino she was going to tell him that she couldn't do this any longer. A week of unsuccessful wrestling with the vision of Stacy, the young redheaded Viking who had been sleeping in Eli's guestroom—or wherever she had been sleeping—had forced this decision. Even now hearing the gush of steam in the kitchen, she could see Stacy pulling up her shirt after dinner to show Eli her belly, Eli pulling up his shirt in response, his hand tracing the long line of Stacy's hip. It should have been Martha tossing the salad in Eli's kitchen, not Stacy. And it should have been Eli and Martha on the inside waving good night to Stacy, Garth de Guzman and all of Eli's other dinner party guests. "You and Stacy ought to get along fabulously," he had said. But Martha knew exactly how that light brush below the belt felt.

At the same time, Martha really had no claim. She and Eli weren't really supposed to be having a relationship. Whatever they had was tenuous and elusive, fairly new and hardly linear.

She accepted the cup and stared into the foam as Eli sat down in the opposite corner of the couch and made small talk about real estate he had been seeing. They both sipped their coffee and waited. "So," he finally said. "Garth de Guzman called. He wanted your phone number." Eli explained the project that Garth wanted to discuss with Martha. Then he paused. "I told him you were hot in bed."

"Good," she murmured feeling his words against her skin, not sure whether she had been slapped or caressed. Was it possible he was jealous? Her horoscope that morning had said that her partner really wanted a lifelong commitment. Could Eli be her partner?

He set his mug down on the table and leaned toward her. "Shall we?" He nodded toward the bedroom.

"Oh, I don't know."

"Isn't that why you came?"

"Because you hope but do not expect to have free time this week?" She was paraphrasing his last week's email. "But if you do, my company and cunt are both welcome, *querido mio*?" She looked at him. "Cunt. It has an ugly sound."

"How long it took you to bring this up," he whispered then defended the word as the 19th century word of choice among doctors and lay people.

"It has a pejorative connotation."

"It's a perfectly acceptable English word. I could argue that it's prudish to disagree."

She let her head fall against the back of the couch and exhaled loudly.

"Okay," he conceded. "Prude is one thing no woman ever allows herself to be called."

"How did I get here?" she mused.

"There was a cool looking woman at Amanda's party, who seemed interesting though somewhat reserved, and towards whom I experienced that hormonal *je-ne-sais-quoi* with which we are both familiar."

She closed her eyes.

"You'd be more comfortable on the bed." He slid across the couch next to her. "You can use the bathroom first."

Maybe this was why she came she thought lying down on top of his quilt.

Eli entered the room and began stripping off his clothes, hanging them neatly over the back of a chair. "You don't want to go to your meeting with a wrinkled skirt, do you?" he asked climbing under the covers, waiting while she sat up and undressed. And then she was tasting the toothpaste on his breath, feeling his skin against hers, his fingers, his mouth. They were still tentative and hungry. He said he had been pining for her. She said she didn't believe him. He tried to sneak inside. "It might be better for you," he said.

"It would be better for you," she answered.

So he handed her the foil disk from the nightstand, and uncoiling the latex she admitted to having been thinking about him.

"Tell me," he said. "We would probably both enjoy it."

But she wanted her pleasure without having to describe it. Whereas he had no qualms about asking her to roll over, adjusting the pillow under her hips, arranging her legs. He said her back was lovely and he liked propping himself on his elbows, cupping a breast in each hand. Eli's coming she thought hearing his four sharp little cries.

Entwined afterward, she rattled off her list of things to do including finding a musical drama class for her youngest son who had recently been inspired.

"He should talk to Maria," Eli said.

"Who is Maria?"

"Mi amor de Caracas."

It was hard to be middle-aged. She got up and found her clothes, realized she was late for her meeting. He lay in bed watching her.

"Do you think the people at your meeting will be jealous?"

"How will they know?"

He grinned and pulled on a robe. "It's impolite of you to just come over for sex and leave so abruptly."

She fixed her lipstick in his mirror. "Do you think Garth de Guzman is really going to call me?"

"We should see more of each other."

She kissed him on the lips. "We'll talk or email, figure out a time to go out, to see and be seen."

Friday

In the kitchen washing dishes, she felt a sudden twinge in her left breast. The hot water rinsing her favorite mug, the sound of the video game her boys were playing in the next room, the lazy rhythm of a weekend night without plans crystallized in her mind. But of course nothing life changing was happening. Even if sperm could live inside a woman's body for three or four days, the condom had been spermicidally lubricated. It was just part of the ongoing cycle. Ovulation came every month.

Sunday

Her horoscope said that a personal tie was moving center stage. *You should move forward with confidence and high expectations. You might be feeling extreme emotions: elated and overcome. But this is because of the intensity of the relationship.*

Her older son walked into the room. "That guy who was here the other night dropped by while you were gone."

"Oh yeah?" she said as nonchalantly as possible. "Eli? What did he say?"

"He was in the neighborhood."

She and Eli traded messages, and when her son heard Eli's voice on the machine he asked, "Why does that guy want to talk to you so badly?"

Eventually Eli got through. "There's a long weekend coming up," he said. "It would be nice to get out of town. I haven't gone away in ages."

Isn't That Why You Came?

Wednesday

Your new lover identifies closely with your life goals. Together you can reach a higher realm, something impossible to achieve alone.

"My cab driver was a woman," Eli said once they were seated. "She flirted with me all the way here, but I was thinking about you."

"I'm glad we have a waiter then. My ex-husband had a talent for saving waitresses, big-eyed girls with sad stories, the kind you meet in diners out west."

He leaned across the table and raised his eyebrows. "He also had a talent for impregnating you."

His words brought back Friday night's twinge. Her breasts had been feeling heavier. "I didn't think you had any interest in pregnancy."

"Not in the product, but the idea of making a woman pregnant, seeing the effects on her body . . . That's exciting."

Thinking of the tiny purple flowers on her nipples, leftovers from their lovemaking, she asked if he wanted to leave his mark on her. She imagined that he would enjoy lactation.

"You know I am neither shy nor embarrassed about sexual matters," he said. "If more people were open about their fantasies, there might be more light-hearted and guilt-free indulgence in this most universal of recreations." He paused to look at her. "Of course the notion of leaving marks on a lover holds a perverse territorial appeal, but don't worry, I'm just enjoying your company at the moment. I'll find another way to leave my mark on the world."

They had gone out to see and be seen, so she asked whom they had seen, but he said he had forgotten to look.

Thursday

Seeds you plant now should bear robust fruit.

Eli called in the early evening before meeting friends for dinner. "My fabulous bachelor lifestyle," he sighed. But before she could respond the little one started talking to her and wouldn't be quiet. "I'd better go so you can take care of your brat," Eli said.

"Careful," she said and hung up.

The little one stood with his hands on his hips. He said that he didn't like Eli. Eli should never have agreed that his room was messy. His posture, the little line that marked his forehead when he frowned were so much like his father's. She looked for pieces of herself in the lengthening and slimming boy who was still her baby. The one who still let her hug him, for now.

Eli had said that she was the only one he knew who had children and actually lived with them. He called motherhood exotic. At the same time he believed no one should be reproducing.

Friday

Eli's horoscope said that October 15th was the *moon of conception, of ideas as well as life, pregnancy, birth, and babies.* Fortunately, Columbus Day was early this year.

Saturday

"I like her," Eli said as soon as the small dark woman with the French accent had shown them to their room, turned up the heat, and minced away. "She's saucy."

Martha closed the door and lay down on the bed. Eli announced that he was going to the bar. She told him to go on, for despite Eli's protestations of needing very little sleep, Martha had been the one to drive the twisty country roads while he napped. Still it had been a pleasant drive: the sun had shone, even if the leaves had not quite changed. It was good to be out of the city, to see mountains and small towns. The room was warming up and the bed was firm.

He was sitting at the dark wooden bar sipping scotch from a martini glass. He said that Chantal, the French woman, had poured Scotch up to the brim for him. An older couple who had been at the bar when they arrived was still there. Martha ordered a glass of wine, which was not filled to the brim, while the older woman finished her story of why they had left the city for the country. Eli then told a story about driving in the country looking for a rodeo with Maria.

"Were you angry about having to do all that driving?" the woman asked Martha.

"Oh I'm not Maria." Martha put her arm around Eli and smiled across him. "I just met this guy back in the last town."

The woman laughed a little too loudly. Then another couple arrived, her dinner companions, and she repeated this story for them. As her husband conversed with their friends, Eli told the woman stories about his "active bachelor" days, the parade of women who had been through his apartment, the things they hid where only their successors would find them.

"They left things in order to come back," Martha said. "It's superstition."

"No," Eli insisted. "They hid things on purpose. I was constantly being confronted by angry women holding dusty boxes of Tampax or half-used bottles of moisturizer, forgotten panties, hairclips, demanding to know where these things had come from."

The older woman tittered.

"You must have loved it," Martha murmured.

"I had to defend myself. I would point out the dust. Surely the dust must have meant that it was old and forgotten."

Martha couldn't let it rest. "You didn't tell them that you'd bought those Tampax for them, to be a good host?"

"Which is worse, an outright lie or an omission?"

"An outright lie," said the older woman.

"It depends," Chantal said from behind the bar.

Martha saw Eli looking at her.

They ate at the inn because Chantal said the chef was French and the older woman assured them that he was good.

"I'm a charming guy," Eli said after Chantal had seated them and taken their order. "Why are you so guarded with me?"

Martha sipped her wine and glanced around at the Victorian décor. The two couples from the bar were on the opposite side of the dining room.

"I have always been truthful with you."

"What do you want me to say?"

"Talk to me. Tell me about yourself."

But she knew where shared confidences led, to intimacy, to the pleasure of talking about love. And she remembered the rules, the lines he had drawn that first night when he had offered to walk her home, when there on the sidewalk he had told her that she seemed lonely and that while sex would ruin their friendship, he wanted to sleep with her in his arms. Her boys were away at summer camp for another two days, so she agreed. He smiled then and ran his hand along her hip.

He had stripped completely before the window while she came to bed in a thin kimono feeling uncertain and stiff, out of practice. He had pulled her head to his shoulder, then pulled away to run his hands over the silk. First the back, then the front, and then as the sash loosened, inside. He said he missed breasts, that her breasts were pretty and her hips were fuckable. He missed sleeping with someone, but he didn't really miss sex. Then he said that for a moment he had actually wanted to be inside her. She remembered how nice it was to feel skin against skin, the sweetness of exploration in the dark. In the morning he still talked about friendship while taking pains to make sure her coffee was just right.

Now she was alone with him in the country. Alone in a restaurant peopled with strangers. "I'm just playing by the rules," she said.

"What rules?"

"The ones you laid down in the beginning."

"What did I say?"

"You said you didn't want to have a relationship with me."

"And then I forgot," he said under his breath.

An extended family sat close by speaking a foreign language that she couldn't quite hear. "You said you didn't want to have sex with me because it would ruin our friendship."

Chantal brought the appetizers; Eli practiced his French with her before she left.

"Go on," he said. "What were the other rules?"

"I wasn't supposed to tell Amanda, and I still haven't."

"I haven't told her either. I believe in privacy. Anything else?"

Across from them a man talked loudly about his garden. She turned back to look at Eli. "No expectations."

"No expectations," he repeated looking at his plate. "I'm glad I set things out so clearly. We do still have a friendship, don't we?" They each took a few bites. "I would miss you if you weren't in my life, and I don't just mean the sex. But the no expectations rule was right."

"Because of Stacy?"

"She's a head taller than me!"

Martha smiled and sipped her wine.

"Stacy is one of the dearest people in the world to me, but I haven't slept with her. She slept on the floor. You're the only one I'm sleeping with right now. The only one I've spent the night with in the last three years." He took a bite and chewed it slowly. "At least I think you're the only one I've spent the night with."

"You can keep reading," he said from between her breasts.

"Okay," she said and pretended not to be distracted until he looked up at her and said, "Your breasts are very full tonight." He rubbed his face back and forth between them and looked up at her again. "I just thought you should know." Her period was still a week away. Quickly she reached over and turned out the light.

He asked if she preferred her condoms to his. She said she had the extra sensitive kind. "Oh that's for me," he said. "I have ribbed for you." He liked having her put the condom on him. He said it felt motherly. She insisted it was foreplay.

"I want to call you Mommy," he said.

"I like Martha better." She tapped on the white band around his testicles.

"My cock ring," he said. "I wear it because it makes me very aware of my genitals. Most women say they like it too. You should pierce your nipples. Then you would have the same constant awareness." As though she wasn't already far too aware.

He said he liked perversity. Anything would do. She told him she liked things the way they were. "You're so reticent," he said. "But your body isn't reticent at all."

Sunday

They had hiked halfway up the mountain when they stopped to catch their breath. From here the route they had followed was partially visible, but the path overhead was impossible to see. Eli noticed the snow first. Tiny white grains that started and stopped as though the sky was spitting at them. They didn't feel right, these icy grains. They didn't fit with the trees dressed in green summer foliage, patched with rust and yellow swatches.

They drove into town for dinner, to a rustic place with wooden beams in the ceiling and a fire in the hearth, a place for secrets, where sitting side by side on the banquette, Eli asked her about breastfeeding and she admitted to its pleasure.

"Where do you feel it? In your uterus?"

"Babies are very good suckers."

"I'm good at sucking too, aren't I?"

"Yes, you suck very well." She told him about the universality of pregnancy, how secretaries, messengers, corporate vice presidents all had something to say about it. How her body swelling with new life had connected her to nature, biology. A tiny limb stretching inside made her dress ripple whether she was cooking dinner or proposing new business.

If the night before had relaxed the rules, the food, the wine, the firelit dimness further loosened the need to be glib and witty, tough and careful. The stories began to slip out, stories about parents and siblings, Martha's marriage and her boys. And then Eli told her that Maria was coming in three weeks.

"I think you two would get along, but what's going to happen while she's here?"

"I think I will disappear," Martha said at the same time grasping at his word "while." It had a temporary flavor, unlike the finality of "when."

"I want to keep you in my life," he said. "Although we may have to stop sleeping together. At least for a while."

In bed he told her which of the things she had said that day excited him. He told her which tones of voice he preferred. He asked about her fantasies—he would do whatever she told him to do—anything, no matter how perverse or kinky or ordinary. "You're inexperienced, but I like the noises you make. And I could probably sleep with any woman once, but only a good set of breasts will bring me back." He grinned and pulled the covers over his head. "I'm a bad influence."

She wondered if maybe she was his science project, someone to push in order to discover her limits. What would she do with him? What would she do without him? Without his encouraging murmurs of "good girl, good girl."

Monday

He woke up early and returned to bed smelling of Colgate. And after making love, brushing her teeth while he showered crossed another boundary of intimacy.

He waited in the car while she bought the boys a pumpkin at a farm stand, then quoted Pablo Neruda as she drove them back toward the city, the poem about running away from his lover in Calcutta, leaving his old shoes behind. He asked when her children were coming home and she told him she had one more night. He said he hadn't had his fill of her, so they dropped her bag and the pumpkin off at her place and she gathered what she needed for the morning.

It was hard not to hear some of his messages, even though she stayed in the next room. A woman had invited him to her dinner party and he called to accept. He made plans to attend a museum opening with someone else, and then he stepped into the living room to call his business partner. Pacing back and forth before her he talked money into his cordless phone. Then he opened his mail and showed her how much the bank had valued his assets. His talking about money sounded like wooing.

"Do you want to hide something?" he asked while she was taking off her clothes.
"I need all the things I brought."
"Do you need your condoms?"
"No. It's too late."
"Too late for what? Your cycle?"
"Um hmmm."

Isn't That Why You Came?

Saturday

He called in the morning and she arranged sleepovers for the boys. After a movie, sitting on her couch sipping herbal tea, she told him how much the little one had liked the pumpkin; he told her about the dinner party; it all felt familiar and comfortable. Thoughts of him had made her feel happy during the week. She teased herself with wondering if what they had could have turned into something longer, nothing serious, but the possibility of dinner parties with an even number of friends, going to the planetarium with her boys, sharing books, all had their appeal.

He checked his messages while she washed her face. She heard him commenting about "more houseguests," but wasn't sure whether he was talking to her or to himself. In bed he said that she deserved someone more committed than he.

"Oh yes," she said from across the sheets, "I knew in the beginning that you were more of a short story than a novel."

He laughed. "I'm more of a comic book," he said reaching for her.

Sunday

There were dirty dishes in the sink, abandoned by last night's hurry to get everyone out of the house, but now the hurry had dissipated. Time had run out. She let the alarm sound through the clanging of pots and pans, the clattering of utensils, even though she knew that detergent could not wash away what she felt.

Eli appeared in the kitchen doorway. "Why did you leave?" He looked puzzled and sleepy, almost vulnerable. She turned off the water and dried her hands, then went over to embrace him. She was going to miss having a naked man in her house. She was going to miss Eli and his four little cries in the dark. She promised to bring him a cup of coffee if he went back to bed.

"Hi mom! I came home by myself."

Stepping out of her bedroom, she saw her older son standing just inside the living room eyeing Eli warily.

"Good morning," Eli said. "Your mother told me that you had a sleepover last night. Was it fun?"

"Yeah, but now I've got a lot of homework to do." The boy scuttled into his room and shut the door.

"Perhaps this will be good for him," Eli told Martha. "Perhaps it will do him good to realize that his mother is human."

Monday

Eli's email asked about her son's reaction. But *she deserved someone more committed than he.* Another line had been drawn and she had to enforce it.

Tuesday

Querida,

You're just disappointed that a really enjoyable interlude in your life—and mine—is drawing to its inevitable conclusion. You're hurt and probably jealous that I haven't chosen you over Maria to whom I've been committed for a decade, and who at my request has abandoned both her high-paying job and entire life in Caracas to join me here. You're upset by your son's untimely entrance on Sunday, which might have been worse had he arrived twenty minutes earlier.

You'll have to deal with the fact that Maria will be here on Saturday, just as I'll have to deal with your having other lovers and your life going on as if I was never there. You're not the only one who's hurting. Don't demean a meaningful, if fledgling, relationship just because it must come to an end.

It would be healthy to talk. I offer you hugs, kisses, and not one word of insincerity.

E.

Enjoyable interlude, inevitable conclusion, chosen, committed for a decade, a meaningful if fledgling relationship that must end. Each word struck her in a different place. She had ignored her own warnings and allowed that insistent desire to feel special sneak inside. But now, "While Maria's here" could no longer be construed as temporary. Maria was coming to stay. It was a plan, it was his choice.

"Martha," he said. "We need to see each other."

"There's nothing to discuss. We had an affair. It lasted a couple of months, and now it's over."

"I still think it would do us good to look each other in the eye and talk. I know I would feel better. Can't we still be friends?"

"We were lovers. We were always lovers. Only lovers. And there is a difference between not committing and not committing because of commitment elsewhere." He had been asking Maria to move here for years.

"You're getting what you wished for," she said. What difference could it make to know whether she had been a last fling or the final straw that brought Maria from Caracas?

"I'm going to do what I can to make it work."

"I should hope so."

"I still care about you."

But that was the one thing that she could not forgive, his encouraging her to care.

She hung up the phone and rested her head on the desk. She wouldn't cry at work, but she could give into melancholy for a few minutes, to anger and self-flagellation. She had been so silly to wonder if her horoscope was aligned with his! Indignation alternated with despondency as she poked at the void that had been Eli. But riding the waves of resentment, fury, rage, submerging under those of woe, despair, and misery, she felt a stirring of her consciousness. A pattern was forming, becoming familiar, and almost within reach. She knew this cocktail and recognition dawned as she pinned her pensiveness upon the impending arrival of her old friend, biology.

Wednesday

The blood reminded her of the theory of menstruation as a form of cleansing. There was satisfaction in the way it was wiping the slate clean.

Garth de Guzman called to invite her to a museum opening. "I'm a member," he said, "So I can get myself and a guest in for free. Eli and other people that you know will be there. What do you say?"

| James | *Denver Omelet* |
| Harmon | |

"ROOM FOR RENT: single female with a furnished two-bedroom apartment looking for responsible roommate. $500. Utilities included. No pets. Cat lover a plus."

How nice. To rent an already furnished apartment room with a single female. And cost of utilities included. That meant you could let the water faucet run all night long and the next day too, but you would not have to pay a cent. "No pets." We did not have any pets. We used to have a goldfish, but it died. "And cat lover a plus." We were big cat lovers. When we were younger, we had a little cat. He would sit in the kitchen sink and our mother would scoop him out and throw him on the floor. She called him a headache, but his real name was Rex. He did not like too many people, but he liked us. We used to smear mother's lipstick on his lips and pat a little blush on his cheeks, and dance with him all morning long until it was time for our naps. Rex loved this game. At night, he would curl up on our bed. Not mother's bed, mind you, but ours. He really was mother's cat, but he liked us the best.

It was just too bad that we are not female. The ad did not say that the roommate had to be female, but we guessed that the woman who paid for the ad meant that. We remembered how we tried to put an ad in the paper to rent out one of our rooms. We told the man at the ad office that we wanted to rent the room to a nice Christian person, because mother always told us to stick around nice Christian people. But the man at the ad office said, "You cannot make any discretion concerning race, creed, or sexual preference." So maybe the woman who paid for the ad was not allowed to say, "For women only."

We did not mind because we did not need an apartment. We were reading the ads because father told us we should always read something because that was how you get smart. We liked to read the ads because they were short. And, when no one was looking, we would always peek at the "Adult Masseuse for Hire" ads. Father said, "Adult means dirty filthy stuff." When we were driving to the market, we passed an adult bookstore and we asked him what an adult bookstore was and that was what he told us.

Once, we hired an adult masseuse. Her name was Rhonda. She made house calls. When she asked what our name was, we lied and said Gary Simmons. That was our landlord's name. We were worried that he might throw us out of our apartment if an adult masseuse came by, so we went to a motel across the street and rented a room for the night. We told her to meet us there. We ended up paying thirty-five dollars for the room and one hundred fifty dollars for the masseuse. That was too much money. In the ad, it said, "I answer all your needs," and the word "all" was capitalized. But all she did was rub our backs.

We had heard about these masseuses who were really call girls and really answered all your needs. Kenny told us. He also told us that the adult masseuse we hired had ripped us off. He knew because he used to be a sailor in the Merchant Marines. Kenny had lots of interesting stories. We met Kenny at the hospital where we delivered blood plasma. Kenny was our friend. When we drove up to the back of the hospital where the deliveries were dropped off, Kenny would be there. We usually found him smoking a cigarette. Kenny was a physical therapist and he hated his job.

Once Kenny said, "All my patients have one foot already in the grave. No one under eighty, you know? I mean, for once, I'd like to deal with a pretty dancer with a sprained ankle."

He lit another cigarette using his old cigarette. Whenever he was upset, Kenny would smoke a lot. "God I hate old geezers. I hate massaging their brittle muscles and feeling those varicose veins move around under their skin. You know what else I hate about old geezers?"

"What do you hate about old geezers?"

"The smell. They all got the same smell, like decaying flesh."

Kenny said, considering the racket he was in, and the lousy pay he got for it, he deserved a call girl every now and then. He gave us a few phone numbers and the names of some good call girls and we thanked him, but we never called the call girls. When he asked us how the call girls were, we told him that we lost the phone numbers. Then he wrote them down again, and the next week he asked us again. We told him that we lost the paper with the phone numbers when we got the blood plasma car washed. He stopped giving us the phone numbers after that.

He said, "If you didn't want my help, you could have just said so."

We drove a little Hyundai that said, "Caution: This Vehicle Contains Human Blood" on the side windows. Sometimes, we would drive our blood plasma car around the industrial parts of the city where all the prostitutes stood around, thinking that maybe we should stop and see what one of them would do for a twenty dollar bill. We never pulled over, but sometimes we would drive around the same area three or four times. Our boss, Ari Yosarian, used to ask us how we managed to rack up such a huge gas bill and why we were always late with our deliveries. We would tell him that we had to take the detour because the road was under construction. This was true. The roads we traveled on were always under construction.

However, one time we were driving along the industrial section of town, and we thought to ourselves, "If that light up ahead turns red and a prostitute is there, maybe we should let her in and she can give us a quickie." Kenny called that sort of a thing a "quickie." We had never had a quickie before, but Kenny said that they were good sometimes.

"It hits the spot," Kenny said.

Well, what do you know? It was a red light and we had to stop, and believe it or not, there was a prostitute on the corner. But then, all of a sudden, we did not know what to do. The light would not be red forever, so we had to be quick. We had to unroll the window to talk to the prostitute. But what if she was an undercover cop? Kenny said you had to be careful because you never knew if the prostitutes were undercover cops. We had to play it safe. We had an idea. We unrolled the driver side window, pretending that it was hot and we needed air, but it really was hot, so we did not have to pretend. Then we leaned over and unrolled the other window on the passenger side. We unrolled all the windows in the car. It was a long light. Then, as we unrolled the back window, we caught the prostitute's eyes for a split second. We were going to call her, but the light turned green. We did not know what to do. The car behind us honked its horn, so we stepped on the gas pedal and drove away. We felt ashamed of ourselves.

We had a teacher who told us, "Never let an opportunity pass you by." His name was Mr. Green, but he let us call him Ron. We did not want that opportunity to pass us by, so at the next street corner, we made a right turn. Then we turned right again at the next street corner and then right again, going all the way around the block. But when we came to the corner where she had stood, she was gone. We looked around. She was walking into a deli across the street.

We missed our opportunity. But then again, maybe it was not a missed opportunity. Maybe she was not even a prostitute. Maybe she was a woman who liked to show off her body. Whenever mother spotted a woman like that, she said, "Will you look at that skimpy little Jezebel? What a disgrace." We used to laugh when she said that, because how did mother know they were all named Jezebel?

We put our newspaper down and looked out the bus window. There was nothing to look at but the road. There were mountains and trees and houses and offices, but they all blended in with the road. We were on our vacation. We had not been on a vacation since we lived with our parents. They used to take us to the mountains and go fishing to Yosemite every year and stay at a motel. Mother always wanted to go camping, but father said he did not want to sleep where there were bears and rattlesnakes, and have to wake up in the middle of the night to use an outhouse. So we stayed in a motel instead. This was the first vacation in fifteen years. Our boss, Ari, had made us go. When payday came around, he noticed that we had accumulated five weeks of vacation time and sick leave, and scolded us.

"What the hell were you thinking of? You want me to get in trouble with your union?" he asked us. He picked his nose when he talked to us. He always picked his nose. Mother never let us pick our noses because it was a dirty habit.

We told Ari that we did not want him to get in trouble with our union. We had forgotten about our vacation time. So he told us he did not want to see us at work again until we had taken at least one week's worth of vacation time. We asked him what we should do or where we should go.

"How the hell should I know," Ari told us, "go wherever the hell you want. Why should I care?"

We asked Kenny where we should go, and he said that we should go to the Wine Country in Napa Valley. "You'll meet lots of drunken women up there." Then he laughed at us and said, "You lucky devil. I wish I could go with you. Gorgeous scenery too."

We asked him what we should do up in the Wine Country with all the drunken women and gorgeous scenery. He told us that we should go wine tasting, of course.

"There's all these single women who go up there with their girlfriends to soak in the culture and the wine, but they always end up soaking up more wine than culture. But there's nothing wrong with that. It's easier to hit on them that way."

"How do you hit on them?"

"Well, you walk up to one of the women. And then you introduce yourself, make small talk, you know, the usual. Then, when you're both a little more familiar with one another, you say to her that you notice she's a bit intoxicated and, being a Good Samaritan, you would like to drive her back to your place where she can sleep it off," Kenny said, winking his eye twice.

"What if she doesn't want you to drive her back to your place?"

"What? Well forget it then. Bad idea. Instead, what you do is you sweet-talk that girl into going with you on a little balloon ride. Tell her the fresh air is just the thing she needs."

"Balloon ride?"

"Yeah, they got these hot air balloons you can rent. Real classy. They got this catering company that prepares you a picnic basket with wine and cheese and stuff so you can have a picnic in the sky. Great view. Very romantic. And you're in luck because I got a friend who can get you a cut-rate deal on one of those balloon rentals. I tell you, your girl will love it."

"She will love it?"

"If experience has taught me anything, it's this. Women will always go for that mushy stuff. I kid you not."

We thanked him for his advice and decided it would be a good idea to go to Napa Valley and try some mushy stuff with a drunken woman.

It was a good day for a bus trip. That is what the woman who sold us the sixty-three dollar bus ticket said to us. She was right. Her name was Genevieve. We woke up extra early that morning so we could make it to the bus station in time. We had enough time to order some breakfast, so we went to Pete's Diner across the street. We sat in the counter because we like watching the cooks prepare our meals. We asked the waitress if we could see a menu. Her name was Gilda. We looked the menu over well. It was a good menu because it had pictures of the different meals you could order. Everything on it looked good.

We looked at the Kid's Menu. One of the meals was called "Eggsy Weggsy." Next to it was a picture of a smiling egg with a topcoat and a cane made out of bacon. We laughed because we thought Eggsy Weggsy was a funny name for scrambled eggs and bacon.

We looked at the regular menu. The Lumberjack Special looked good. You got two eggs, any style, with your choice of hash browns or country-fried potatoes, four strips of bacon, two sausage links, two flapjacks, and your choice of grapefruit juice, orange juice, or cranberry juice now for a limited time for six dollars and fifty cents. When Gilda came around, we ordered the Denver Omelet and a coffee because that cost four dollars and fifty cents and we did not have a lot of money in our wallet.

A young woman dressed like a cowgirl came in and looked for a seat. She was upset because there were no tables and she had to sit at the counter, and the only seat at the counter was next to us. We said good morning to the woman dressed like a cowgirl and asked her if she had looked at her menu. We told her to look at the Kid's Menu and showed her the picture of the Eggsy Weggsy. We all laughed.

Then we became nervous. We did not want to talk to her anymore, because we were afraid we had run out of things to say. We had already said good morning and we should have left it at that. Now she wanted to talk. She told us her name was Millie and that she drove a truck. We told her we delivered blood plasma to the hospital. That was something to talk about.

"Oh really?" she said and she crossed her legs, "What's that like?"

We said it was good. She said she was glad that it was good. Then we said it was good that she was glad that it was good. She laughed at us for saying that. We wished that our breakfast would come soon so that we would not have to talk to her anymore.

Millie was nice. She had nice legs. Kenny once said some men go for the legs and others go for the chest. He asked us if we went for the legs like him, but we did not say anything, so he slapped our back and laughed. We tried not to look at Millie's legs too much. We looked at her face. Her eyes were nice too. It looked like she had soft hair. Not too many women who drive trucks have soft hair. She made us feel uncomfortable.

"You know," Millie said, "you're very sweet. And polite, too."

"Really?"

"Yes, really. I don't know. I guess I'm marked for life or something. All the men I meet only want to jump my bones."

"You should tell them that they should not jump on your bones because you could get hurt that way. Kenny's a physical therapist," we said, but then we became nervous.

"Who's Kenny?" she asked. She brushed a strand of hair away from her eyes.

"We should not talk about Kenny behind his back," we said.

"I understand," Millie said.

Then the breakfast came. We started eating and looked at our plate but not at Millie. She asked us if something was the matter. We said we were hungry. We put some ketchup on our Denver Omelet. We asked Millie if she wanted some ketchup. She said she had nothing to put it on. Finally, the waitress brought Millie her food and we were glad, because we thought that if she ate she would stop talking. But she kept talking. She said she did not get to talk to too many people when she was driving. She used to have a CB radio but it broke down, and anyway she did not use it much. She just listened. But she liked to talk. She liked to talk to us, she said. We thought she talked to us too much, but we did not say that because she might get upset.

We finished our Denver Omelet and paid the waitress with a ten-dollar bill. The menu said that a Denver Omelet was three dollars and fifty cents and that coffee was a dollar, so that meant that everything together would cost four dollars and fifty cents. But we forgot about the tax and the waitress' tip. When the waitress asked us if we wanted any change, we told her that she should keep it all.

Millie said, "That's awfully generous of you."

We did not know what to say, so we wiped our lips and got up to leave.

Millie said, "You leaving already?"

We said we had to or else we would miss the bus. She said it was nice talking to us, and we said it was nice talking to her and we left and bought a newspaper and got on the bus. We could not wait to read the ads. We would read the ads all the way.

Terry Wolverton	*Temperance*

"I don't drink."

It was an announcement, a declaration made, not in response to a particular question nor to any offer of refreshment, but out of the blue. She spoke the words with all the fervent resolve of a line scarred into the sawdust at our feet.

I had arrived only minutes before. It was one of the first things she told me about herself. Not the first thing, which was something about the neighborhood she lived in, nor the second, which was most likely about her job. Still, very little time had passed before she made it a point to let me know, "Oh, by the way, I don't drink."

"Excuse me?" Maybe the music had gotten louder, or maybe my attention had wandered.

"I don't drink," she repeated. She said it like a warning, or like a test. This was something she definitely wanted me to know if I was going to think about dating her.

It was a test I didn't think I was likely to pass, but I wasn't even sure I was interested in dating her. She was someone Eric knew, Eric from the office, and he kept saying to me he had this friend, I ought to give her a call. So one day I did, explaining about the office and about Eric, and I suggested we might meet at this little dive in my neighborhood.

She could have told me then, I guess, could have suggested some other place, and maybe she regretted that she hadn't. Maybe that's why she blurted it out like a secret she just couldn't keep.

She was cute enough, though not as tall as I usually like. Not really my physical type at all. She had that kind of thin blond hair that can look stringy if it's not washed often enough or not well shaped, but hers looked shiny and styled, cut blunt just below the line of her chin. I'd be lying if I said I knew the color of her eyes.

She seemed like a nice girl, and maybe that was the trouble. Nice girls always seem to get a little more unhappy when they hang around with me.

Her features were pleasant, maybe a little bland, but they grew noticeably sharper as she made her declaration. Her assertion hung in the air between us, like a smoke ring that refused to dissipate, until there seemed nothing for me to do but bite.

"Why not?" I asked like I wanted to know.

She didn't answer, but gave me a look. It was a look full of pre-dawn hangovers and DUI's, of trying to keep quiet while puking in the toilet at work. It was a look full of darkness and all the more bitter for it, and as I studied her gaze I knew suddenly, and with absolute certainty, that I could get her to drink, no problem. That very night, if I chose. It wasn't that I cared whether she drank or not, but I suddenly recognized that her announcement was not a test, but a dare, and I began to feel excitement for the first time since I'd arrived.

I leaned closer to her, extended a hand that grazed the fine hairs of her forearm. "That takes guts," I said to her, with the full-throated sincerity of an actor in his first big part.

She blinked twice; it was not the reaction she'd expected. I had caught her off-guard and it made her nervous. She shrugged one shoulder.

When the bartender approached, she ordered a club soda. Considerate, I asked, "Will it bother you . . ." before ordering a whiskey sour.

This is not what I ordinarily drink; I'm not sure I'd ever had a whiskey sour before that night, but I saw her give it an envious glance when it was set down before me and I knew my instincts were on-target.

She sucked hard on the straw plunged into her Collins glass of soda, and we commenced a desultory conversation, that kind of first-date chit-chat when neither party has decided if the other one's worth their while. She told me about her dog, Hector, a mutt she found on the street, how she had to bathe him everyday or else he smelled bad.

Who knows what I told her? Maybe some story about hitching to California when I was seventeen and never leaving. I was pretty sure I'd never told Eric I grew up here.

She must have decided that she liked me a little bit, because she started in on her last relationship, how it began, how it ended. We were on our second round, and I asked her casually, "Would you like the cherry?" I held out the blue plastic sword impaling the orange and the maraschino, glowing lurid red.

She hesitated, but I could tell she felt stupid, thought that to refuse would make her seem rigid and uptight, so she said, "I guess, thanks."

I'd made sure to give the sword an extra swirl in the top of my glass before handing it over, and her eyes widened as her tongue tasted the whiskey-soaked fruit.

"Thanks," she said again, and fidgeted with her cocktail napkin, tearing one long shred from its edge.

I took a sip from my glass, setting it down with an air of deep satisfaction. "They make a good whiskey sour," I declared, then said, "Oh, I'm sorry."

"It's okay," she assured me, if a little grimly.

Then I must have told her my own tale of lost love, something with plenty of tragedy; maybe it had an ocean as a backdrop. Her forehead creased in sympathy, and she lay a warm hand on top of mine.

At that point I excused myself, took a trip to the restroom. I wanted to leave her alone with my beverage, give her a chance to think. I took a long time, washing my hands under a stream of lukewarm water, passing a flat comb through my hair in front of the mirror.

When I returned, my glass was not on the same side of the napkin as I had placed it before getting up. I pretended to take no notice, re-seated myself on the bar stool, and asked, "Miss me?" with a winsome grin.

She returned a thin smile; I couldn't tell if it held guilt or sarcasm. Still, she seemed happy enough to see me, because the next topic of conversation was about her childhood. As these kinds of stories go, hers was neither the most harrowing nor the most joy-filled I'd been told. No overt brutality, no bucolic holidays. Just a mother who disappeared—mostly quietly—into a prescription drug addiction. She told it simply, with neither theatrical self-pity nor that tough fragility—a kind of calculated brittleness—I've seen some girls adopt. This made me almost like her; she seemed more vulnerable to me now, human, and I almost began to have second thoughts about my scheme to sway her resolve.

But by that time it had all gone beyond me. When the bartender returned to check on us, she piped up, "Make that *two* whiskey sours," as if the impulse had just occurred to her, as if she hadn't been thinking about it for the last half-hour or more, turning it over and over in her brain, a devil whispering into one ear, an angel in the other. I made sure my face conveyed just a hint of surprise, curiosity without judgment, and she offered a small shrug as if to say, "Nobody's perfect."

When the bartender set the drink before her, she embraced it like an old friend, gripping the stem of the glass in a hearty grasp, and tossing back a full third of it in a single gulp. Her eyelids fluttered shut as she savored the taste of the booze and sweet lime; a tension eased out of her shoulders. She turned to me with a smile less tentative than before.

I might have expected to feel something then, a victory of confirmation at least, but the moment was anticlimactic. I understood then that it had been a foregone conclusion all along, having little to do with me, really. Whether it was an elaborate form of self-deception or a calculated strategy didn't really matter; this was a routine she had perfected through repetition. When I told the story to Eric the next day, he looked genuinely shocked, demanding, "How could you do that to someone? How can you live with yourself?" but I said, "Don't you see? I gave her someone to blame."

After her second drink she became quite flirtatious, scooting her bar stool close to mine, running her hand along my thigh, as if hidden mechanism of control had been sprung. Her voice grew louder, her stories more animated. She leaned her head on my shoulder and I felt her hot breath against my neck.

After we closed the bar I walked her home; it was the least I could do. She kept bumping her hip against mine as we walked the deserted blocks to her neighborhood; then she'd giggle and apologize. She'd become little-girlish, talking in a kind of feathery, whispery voice, as if I were someone bigger, older, someone with power over her, someone to beguile.

I could see the scene as it unfolded in her brain: how she'd relinquished her will to me, and now she was mine to do with what I liked. I saw how she'd woven me into her story, caught me up like a fish in a net. Soon I'd begin to stink. I was supposed to be the next stranger she woke up beside, the next item she'd add to her list of personal shortcomings.

But I was tired of her now.

When we reached her doorstep, she pushed her body against mine; her mouth reaching up for a kiss seemed like a bottomless cavern. Lightly, I pressed my lips to her forehead, a quick peck, not unfriendly but disengaged. Then I plucked the keys from her unsteady hand and released the lock to her bungalow apartment. I held the door for her and, once she'd entered, let it close gently behind her.

I was halfway down the courtyard when the door struggled open, and she leaned out into the mist-filled pre-dawn air. "Hey!" she called after me. Her voice was a mess of confusion. "Where're you going?"

"Home," I replied. "You get some sleep."

I didn't wait for her response, but turned and headed along the pavement, refusing to feel the eyes that followed my retreating back as it disappeared into the gray light of not-yet-morning.

| Jewell Parker | *Long Distances* |
| Rhodes | |

J IM COULDN'T REMEMBER the moment when it had happened, let alone why. Was it in the supermarket buying kidney beans or touring through Allegheny Park with its man-made pond when he knew just from looking at her, he would have to go California? Knew from fixed stares, drooping mouth, her restlessness.

Knew he'd have to leave his humid and river-choked valley with its steel mill-sooted hills to drive across plains, Rockies and desert until sand gave way to heaving ocean. And for what? Her dreaming?

3,000 miles. A man could get lost.

Barbara showed him a postcard picture book of California. Flat-topped roofs and pastel stucco. Palm trees bent by breezes. He'd be trapped by distance. Sunshine.

"We'll be pioneers," Barbara said.

He wondered if he'd miss shoveling snow, crushing ice while sprinkling salt? If he'd miss the ugliness of brick homes with rain slicking off slant roofs into mud-packed gutters? He'd never see the three rivers overflow.

Would he miss driving over cobblestones, getting his wheels caught by streetcar tracks the city was too cheap to dig up? Or parking on hills with the car in gear, the tires turned towards the curb?

He'd miss his mother.

For what? Barbara's dreaming? Or his fear she'd go with or without him? No matter.

Jim had traded in his muscle Chevy for a dreamboat Chrysler. A 300 with a red interior that wasn't as bright as the red metal outside and never would be. The skinny ass man who sold him the car said it would get him around the world if that's where he wanted to go. He said he didn't. But Barbara had been sold with that line. And here he was driving on a stretch of highway about ready to cross into INDIANA WELCOME. A truck was coming out of Indiana, flickering its headlights to low. It started to rain. He turned on his windshield wipers, his high beams. Night driving was dangerous. But Barbara couldn't wait another day. Had to leave at midnight to make better time. Now she and the kids were sleeping.

He looked at the trip odometer, 270 miles. At least two more days and nights of driving 800, 1,000 miles a day. No unnecessary stops. No motels. Barbara needed to get to Los Angeles fast, to make it big. Somehow. He'd drive until his mind warped and then maybe he'd forget his guilt. Forget his Momma's unnatural quiet, forget her solemn shuffling about the house. Forget her leaning out of an apartment window, watching them pack up as if she couldn't believe it. Forget her refusing to say or wave goodbye. Jim wished he had a drink. He'd promised to call his Momma from Wheeling. But it'd seemed like too soon. He plain forgot to call at Dayton.

He looked in the side mirror and saw the Ford his father-in-law, Joseph Wright, was driving. Joe was no comfort. For weeks, Joe told folks at the Pier Point Bar, "No way I'd allow my baby girl travel from Pittsburgh to LA alone."

"What you mean alone, Joe? Jim's going. He's her husband, ain't he?"

Then Joseph Wright would puff his chest, suck his gut, and glare until the person nervously admitted, "Ain't right to let a woman travel alone. Not with two kids."

A dozen slicks and low-lifes had told Jim that Joe was drinking bourbon and calling him a faggot. But what was he supposed to do? Beat up on an old man? Have his wife holler? Jim gripped the steering wheel.

Since the first time he called on Barbara, the old man kept one-upping him. Jim remembered being seventeen, squirming on a plastic-covered sofa, his hands itching with sweat. Joseph Wright, an ex-cop, had a bit of money. He had a bit of Irish too. He was freckle-faced Negro and proud of it. Jim was just poor and black.

Joseph Wright slipped in questions like artillery fire:

"Where you been, boy?"

"Home." He remembered how his plain, brown-faced Momma could make a cramped apartment seem like the world. Make you never want to leave. He promised he'd never leave.

"Where you going, boy?"

"Uh, work, sir. I be wanting my own butcher shop." He liked the feel of a cleaver ripping away flesh from bone and the soft whishing sound of bloodied sawdust beneath his feet.

"What do you want with my girl?"

That one he couldn't answer.

Looking at Barbara with her head leaning up against the window and slightly cocked back, breathing through her nose in a slight snore, he still didn't know. Now she didn't look so pretty and when she was angry, she seemed less so. Maybe it was the old man that made him want her. Him with his attitude that his baby girl was so special and Jim was just another no-good hood from the streets.

Jim sighed, pressing the aching small of his back into the vinyl seat. He was twenty-six. Still poor and black with a wife longing for the "opportunities" of California. She used to long for him.

At sixteen, Barbara was eager to do it anywhere. He remembered her hitching up her dress, begging him in the laundromat. Together they moaned; he had a kid. Responsibilities. Barbara was smart: she finished school. He dropped out to cut beef full-time. God, how his Momma screamed. Wasn't a man supposed to support his family? What choice did he have?

Another pretty baby. Barbara was less eager to do it. She started spreading her legs again when she started talking California. He rubbed himself between her thighs until the world and regrets faded.

His Momma never liked Barbara. "She attracts men like bugs to flypaper. Her uppity Dad is a yellow fool. Too bad her Momma died." Then she would grin, smack her hips, before uttering her final condemnation. "Spoiled."

The smell and sound of stale heat passing through vents sickened Jim. He felt like rolling down the window, but the cool wind would cut right back to the children. His two daughters, Tonie and Jackie, almost smothered beneath blankets, were two squirrelly balls in the back. He wondered when his Momma would see her grandkids again. No more dressing them in white and carrying them to church to sing, shout and Praise The Lord. Who would she rock and sing lullabies to? It was his fault they were leaving. Dammit, why couldn't he say No to Barbara? He should've called his Momma from Dayton.

A yellow sign with a vertical ripple told him the road up ahead was curved. Jim took one hand away from the wheel. His right hand adjusting the turn of the wheel was all he really needed. He loved the feel of cars. Even this one. And as the green fluorescent speedometer showed his increase in speed, the better he felt. 70, 75, 80. Without looking in the mirror, he knew the old man would be straining his car up with him. He could just about hear Joseph Wright cursing. Joe needed to be with his daughter more than he needed to breathe. "What do I need?" Jim thought.

As the asphalt turnpike straightened itself out, Jim lowered the speed. He didn't understand his feelings, but it didn't much matter. If he understood everything, he'd still hurt. Understanding didn't ease pain.

He was eight when his Momma told him matter-of-factly his Dad and Sondra were gone. They were at the kitchen table eating collard greens and rice. Even at eight, he'd understood the attraction of the neighbor woman with her flowery dresses and jasmine perfume. Him and his Dad both laughed and smiled at her jokes. He understood his Momma was too fat, awkward and glum around Miss Sondra. Nonetheless he'd kicked the wall and tried to hide his crying. That night he slept on his Daddy's side of the bed. Curled in the crook of his mother's arms, touching her round face, he promised he'd never leave. She didn't ask him to say it. But he was eight and thought words had power. Each night thereafter, before uncoiling the sofa into his bed, he whispered, "I'll be here." And when he married, it was simple enough to live in the same tenement, three floors down and across the hall.

Barbara hadn't threatened to take the kids. He couldn't even use that excuse. The car was pulling him further away from his mother.

At that point where the skyline met the road in his vision, Jim was sure he could see her. Her breasts sagging, her eyes dim. Was there a difference between what the two of them were feeling? His mother, flat in bed, hearing the sound of no one breathing; him, maneuvering through rain, hearing the car and bodies exhaling the same heated air. Who would care for his mother? He wished he could turn on the radio. There were buttons to push rather than knobs to turn. Too much noise though. Besides he'd probably only get country.

Jim wanted to piss and buy some coffee. A red neon sign blinked, *Food, Gas, 5 miles, Terre Haute*. He would call his mother and tell her he loved her. He would get change. A hundred quarters. Call her every stop from a pay phone. First Terre Haute. Then St. Louis, Topeka, Denver. Would she weep?

He wanted to hit something. Wanted to run the car off the road. A twist to the right, and into the embankment. Kill them all. Metal, concrete, blood. The car would pleat like an accordion. He wished he could see Joseph Wright's face then. Yeah. What would Joe say seeing his daughter smashed up? Her toes meeting her elbows; her head twisted off. What would Joe do?

Jim missed the exit. A dairy truck hauling cows rumbled past. The rain was easing. He looked at his watch. 4:28 am. His Momma was probably asleep now. He should wait 'til morning. After he crossed the Mississippi, Columbia, Missouri then. He'd call her there. Veins popped up like worms along his hands. What if she refused to talk to him? He stumbled a bent Kool of out his right pocket. He lit the cigarette, dragged deep, and smoke filled his lungs like a caress. He exhaled. Smoke blanketed the dash. He stubbed the cigarette out.

"Barbara," he whispered plaintively. "Barbara."

Her eyes opened. Disoriented, she registered the night, the bold headlights whizzing by, Route 70 heading across the Wabash River and into Illinois.

She turned her head to the left and looked at Jim. "What is it?"

He grit his teeth and stared straight ahead at the road.

"Would you have gone without me?" His voice was barely a whisper. The heater's fan kicked in again.

"Yes," she said.

He felt like the time a line drive hit him in the gut. Wind went right out of him. Driving was easy. Automatic. He concentrated on feeling the murmurs of the engine.

The sky was clear. He switched off the wipers and rear window defrost. Barbara was sleeping.

Kansas City. Maybe he'd call his mother then. She's be up. 10:00 a.m. Tuesday was laundry day. She'd be gathering clothes, stuffing them into her cart to wheel them to the laundromat. She needn't worry anymore about shaking out sawdust, starching his collars or lifting bloodstains from his shirts. He'd probably miss her if he called. When the phone would ring, she'd already be out the door, racketing her way down the steps.

He'd call her that evening. After dinner. In Wichita.

Maybe Colorado Springs? Yeah. She'd have more time to adjust to him being gone. Another 1000 miles he'd be in Los Angeles. His family needed him. Jim pressed his foot hard on the gas. Los Angeles. He'd call his mother there and tell her he loved her nonetheless.

"Pop?" It was Jackie.

"Sssh. You'll wake your Momma and sister up."

"Tonie keeps kicking me."

"In her sleep, she don't mean it."

Jim watched his daughter scowl in the mirror. She was resting her chin on top of the front seat, next to his shoulder, her fuzzy blue blanket covering her head like a nun's cloth.

"Can I help drive?"

"Come on, but be careful."

Jackie lifted her tennis shoed foot over and onto the front seat. Jim, with his right hand, grabbed her by her collar and pulled her down between him and Barbara. Jackie shifted herself onto his lap. He relaxed, feeling her small hands gripping his two hands on the wheel.

"Wow. I ain't never drove on the turnpike before."

"You just keep your eyes on the road so none of us don't get killed."

Jackie clutched her father's hands tighter.

"Can I turn on the radio?"

"No."

"Aw, Pop."

Jim nudged her head with the side of his jaw.

Together, they watched the road. A clear, straight line to the horizon. Him looking over the arch of the wheel, Jackie right beneath it. It felt good to have company. He needed the distraction.

"Look, there's a dog, Pop. Running across the road."

Jim didn't see anything but he pumped the brakes anyway so Jackie could be satisfied they wouldn't hit the animal.

"And there. It's a raccoon. See it. Scootin' across the road."

"Nothing's there."

"It is."

Jim pumped the brakes. He felt his heart lighten at his daughter's silliness. He reached up and adjusted the rearview mirror so he could see her face while she drove. He slowed for a deer, a wily, old fox. Joseph Wright must be thinking he's driving crazy. Jim didn't care. Jackie was the child most like himself. Tonie took after Barbara, feminine and sweet when she wanted something. Jackie was the one who should've been a boy.

Feeling her shoes bang his knees, her spine curling into his chest, and a stumpy braid tickling his chin, Jim felt more her father than any other time he could remember. They were alone in the car, driving to California. The sun was coming up.

"Angels are digging out the sun to wake up the world," said an awed Jackie. "Digging it right out of the earth."

"The sun doesn't come out of the earth."

"Does so," she said, fiercely whispering, staring at him through the mirror. "Right now it's half in and half out."

"Who told you that?"

"Grandma."

Jim felt shaken. He remembered his Momma telling him such things too. Telling him that stars were God's words in light. The moon, His mirror. Rainbows were the fluttering glow of angel's wings. The horizon was the blue gust of God's breath. All of a sudden his mother's presence was real.

"If Grandma said it, it must be true," Jim whispered.

Jackie tried burying her face in his shoulder.

"I didn't want to leave," said Jackie.

"I didn't want to go." Jim hugged his daughter closer, and hearing, feeling her soft shuddering sigh, he had a clear sense of what a damn fool he'd been. He turned off the headlights and the rear window defrost.

"You think she'll forget me?" asked Jackie.

"Naw," he said. "Grandma loves you."

"How? Not backwards loving? Grandma says backwards loving hurts." Her words flew. "Then, the hurt turns to hate. Grandma was hurting. She didn't want to kiss me goodbye."

Jim stared straight ahead at the gray roadway. He didn't want to look up and see her reflection in the overhead mirror. He didn't want to look up and see her looking at him. "There's a cat," he said, pumping the brakes, trying to stop

59

his headlong drive. In his mind, he lost the image of a road map. He couldn't see a red-marked line named 70 winding its way to California. He saw him and his daughter marooned in a car, whispering secrets.

When the sun was halfway up in the sky, Jackie fell asleep. Her hands slipped off his hands and he could feel her fingers lightly touching the hair on his arms. "Jackie?" All the women in the car were sleeping.

In the side mirror, Jim looked yearningly at Joseph Wright's car. He wished the old Ford would catch up with him. They could drive side by side past cornfields and wheat, at least until the Rockies.

Sunlight was baking him. He couldn't slip off his jacket without disturbing Jackie. He cursed under his breath. In the grease-slicked patches on the road, he saw shreds of rainbows. The sun loomed. He knew the angels were moving it.

If Grandma said it, it must be true.

Anne
Randolph

Burnt Barn

"Why you want to go out to Wyoming?" Mama asked.

I never said.

"Krissy, Krissy Warren. Make something of yourself. Pick one thing and do it well."

I had to do things my way. I should have listened, should have heard. I thought I loved him, he would take me away.

"Krissy . . . make something . . ."

I know, ". . . of yourself." And Mama, I did. I made a mess.

I felt for his children. They had seen so much. I thought they would love me if I was just good to them. But I lost everything. All those things from our family house. When we moved them out here—out west to real winter cold—I would have put them in the big house, but he needed his space. I didn't want to be like you and Dad. I thought if I would accommodate. If I would just let him have his way.

Movers unloaded our stuff, Mama—yours and mine—in the barn, the old barn. He built the new one for the cattle and a corral for the horses and goats. But in the old barn, it was safe, no stinking animals there.

I woke up in the night, worried about the cold, the weather fighting against the hardwood from the South, from moisture to dry. So dry here. I couldn't make myself go out there for a while, for about a year. No place for my things in the house. I knew I had to check, but knowing our stuff was in a barn, safe, was enough.

That April morning when I went out to check, I was horrified. I found my boxes, our boxes, torn and scratched. Corrugated crinkles pushed out. Holes eaten out of the edge of the paper cartons, from the boxes you mailed. Something happened. Mice nibbled on the boxes, all year long. The glue devoured.

One box, marked "Childhood," was scratched the worst. Mice ate my dolls. Not their whole bodies, just the stuffing out of their plastic legs and arms. My dolls looked like monsters, mold covered heads once baby faced porcelain, with doll stuff dangling: their frayed arms, their frayed legs.

My favorite Madame Alexander baby doll wrapped in paper, torn by rat claws, with legs shredded. I pretended it didn't matter. I pretended I didn't care; but I did. What's a grown woman doing with dolls anyway? Even if they had been hers? He had all boys.

The pictures. His cats. You wouldn't think we'd have cats and rats in our barn; but we did. Ranch cats, their stink. I used to like cats, but these wild ones, farm cats—I've got to poison those cats—their stench. Cats picked the box with the pictures for a cat pan. Like they knew, they knew what they'd done—his son's cats. Barn cats are supposed to pee outside, scratch in dry dirt. Not farm cats, not ranch cats; they pissed on the top of the picture box, again and again.

I opened that box: family photos, pictures of my past melted, shiny like daguerreotypes, some metal thing, yet paper melted silver. People I know, their faces now faded silver and pink; and a shiny blue, smearing their image to no faces at all.

That big picture, the one you loved, ruined. That picture of Papa's sister, her four children, gone, only their dresses left behind. What good is a family of dresses, of children with no heads? Dangling dolls, melted relatives found before the disaster.

Elgar worried about his third boy; this son wasn't tracking. Elgar knew something was wrong. His own adult son, so sweet, so good looking—his personality changed, defensive, irritable. Must be the alcohol. We knew about the drinking, but there was something else that made the meanness come out. So hard to wake in the morning. He slept on the floor of his bedroom in the big house. Then he slept in the loft in the barn; his choice, not mine. I was afraid he would fall.

That night Elgar's son called from the bar, the one bar in town, and talked frantic, about how he wanted to make something of himself. "You see what I'm saying," he said about twelve times. No, we did not see. He filled with anger, distrust, disgust. Wounded, unable to feel. His anger roared.

That night we smelled the heat. Elgar woke first. Sensed something, that burnt smell, the barn, a corral away. Elgar sensed the smoke. Worried for the horses, he ran outside. The new barn was fine; the old barn in flames. Took twenty minutes for the volunteer fire department to mobilize, to get up the mesa, get that far out to the house.

I threw on a jacket and shoes. You don't want to wear slippers in an emergency, too unsafe. Elgar's shadow flickered in the flame light. He dashed to the barn. Just stood there.

Burnt Barn

His son's Mercury parked close to the barn, the driver door open. Odd. A gulf of flame, swarmed through the roof of the barn. Heat pulsated like at the steel mill. The barn engulfed, flambeau. I only thought of spoiled pictures and dolls with their scraggly arms.

The door to his car still hung open. I didn't think for a minute that his son was still inside. Elgar knew. He tried to push the barn door open, too much heat, scalded his shoulder. An explosion. The blast threw him against his son's parked car, broke his arm.

"Mama, I watched the barn burn and saw only faded pictures. His son, his middle son, gone."

Idling

THICK, BLOWING SNOW; a stiff wind. Out on the lake, a car, idling. Headlights illuminate mottled white. Inside the car, where the four of them sit, it is warm and bright.

Now they'll never get where they thought they were going. Too anxious. They blame Aaron and no one's surprised. Didn't compensate for the conditions.

"Had your mind on something else," said Nancy, with a smirk and an insinuating but not unsympathetic glance at Sandy. Sandy doesn't say a thing-just stares out the window at the rippling sheet of snow.

"You had your hand on something else," said Jeff. And that much was true: he had his hand on Sandy's thigh.

"Two hands on the wheel," Sandy was saying the instant before it happened, covering his hand with her own. Giving him a chance to feel her equal desire before insisting he act responsibly, take his hand away. But he didn't. His hand rested lightly on the smooth material of her skirt.

But that wasn't what caused the accident. It was the conditions. Two hands on the wheel would not have helped. "It's the snow," he says.

"It's your driving," says Jeff.

Sandy says nothing, keeps staring out the window. A loud crack, like the report of a gun, then silence, Nancy thinks she felt the car move.

"What was that?"

"What was what?" asks Jeff.

"That sound. The ice."

"So what?" says Jeff. "You think we're gonna fall in?"

Nancy doesn't know what to say.

"We couldn't fall through if we wanted to." Jeff started bouncing up and down on the back seat to illustrate the point. Nancy slapped him on the arm. Aaron laughs. Sandy doesn't. She'd been the voice of reason in the phone relay. Aaron tried to talk them into coming; she tried to talk them out. Nancy and Jeff—the mediators—trying to get Sandy together with Aaron. But reckless Aaron really wanted it. Sandy did too. But she was afraid.

"Look," he'd said, "if we don't all go, none of us goes. Tell her that." They did. And she finally gave in.

Sandy, just before they hit the icepatch, tried to lift Aaron's unhelpful but unresisting hand; he let her put his hand back on the wheel. But he wasn't going to cooperate. Just then they'd felt the car lose traction, like losing contact with the earth: the car slid sideways, nearly flipped——Sandy anyway had felt the tilt on the passenger side as the tires left the ground—but Aaron turned the wheel and by some miracle just when Sandy thought the car was headed irreversibly up and over the tires fell back to the ground: all this in a moment as they'd hurtled down the embankment and onto the frozen lake, sliding who knows how far, spinning too, so now they could not know, even if they could get the spinning tires to grab the surface, whether they were facing the road (and the hill they couldn't climb with any car) or the deeper part of the lake.

"Maybe she distracted *him*," said Nancy.

Well, who wouldn't be distracted by those black tights emerging out of that skirt so high above the knee, the stretched material smoothly defining those slender legs, crossed at the knee: the dark black lines of the nylons, the flesh that peeks through. Drawing his eyes from the road. So much like an invitation to touch. You couldn't improve those gradations with an airbrush. And with that short red jacket that doesn't reach below her hips, there is just that mini skirt that she can't with her modest little tugs keep from riding up. The bottom of it isn't three inches from her cunt. How could you resist trying to put a careful hand upon that perfect thigh?

Still, that wasn't why they left the road.

"No one could drive in this. Look at it: you can't see past the hood."

Sandy clenched her fist around the material of her skirt and held her tongue.

"We have to do something," said Jeff.

"Yeah right," says Aaron. And that was that.

The setting of the sun didn't improved things any; they needed the headlights to see it was still snowing. And had it ever snowed like this? The car was enclosed in four shadowed bedsheets rippling in the wind. And the wind whined, whistled, moaned, sometimes even almost shrieked.

"You'll freeze to death," said Nancy.

"Josh'll come by eventually," says Jeff.

Sandy sat still, arms crossed, eyes directed at the wavering darkness. Aaron imagined she felt his eyes upon her, but she didn't look back. He caught, reflected in the window, the defiance or the anger or the sadness in her face. He glanced back at her legs. An elegant door, shut tight.

"I'll go," said Aaron.

"Shut up," says Sandy.

"Anyway, Josh'll get here before you could get help." Jeff wanted to help. He also wanted confirmation. Aaron called Josh as soon as the car stopped spinning.

"Sure," says Aaron. "He'll be here."

They can feel the modulated force of the wind pushing against the side of the car. They feel the heat pouring in, too hot on their knees. They can't hear the engine.

"You should shut the engine off and start it up again every twenty minutes so you don't run out of gas," said Nancy.

"That's if you think you're going to freeze to death," says Aaron. "Josh is on his way. We got plenty of gas."

"How's he gonna get through this?" asked Sandy.

Aaron was talking to Nancy and Jeff, but he was looking at Sandy, hoping she'd see his face in that window, see how serious he was. (Isn't that what bugged Sandy about Aaron: that he was never serious?) "Josh? He can get through anything. He's got. . . ."

Sandy did look at him. But her anger did not waver: "You're nuts. It's a whiteout. Why don't you just conserve the fuel like she says."

"I'm telling you. . . ."

But Aaron isn't even sure he's gotten through. He won't tell them this. But there was a lot of static on the phone, and then the battery went dead. Truth is, he isn't even sure it was Josh on the other end.

". . . and this old boat gets great mileage."

"What made you think we were gonna be able to make it through this anyway?" says Sandy.

"Who wants to stay home on a Friday night? Hang out with the parents? Watch TV?"

"It wasn't supposed to be this bad," Jeff helped.

"Just shut the car off," says Sandy. The tone tells Aaron this comic defiance of common sense isn't winning him any points. But he doesn't reach for the key.

"How do you get mileage when you're standing still?" Nancy asked.

"Standing still? You kidding? We're chasing ourselves around the sun right now at the astonishing rate of 68,000 miles per hour."

Comments like that just made things worse. Sandy closed herself up as though she were cold, despite all this heat pouring in. Aaron took off his coat.

Jeff opened another beer.

"Shut it off," Sandy repeated and she seemed about to reach over and grab for the key.

"I can't," he says, managing an appropriate tone. "If I shut it off, we'll never get it started again." He'd had to jump it to get it going. He pointed to the gauge. It wasn't recharging. Not a good day for batteries. "Don't worry we've got plenty of gas. Josh is coming; one time, he got through more than this . . ."

"You've never seen more than this," says Sandy.

"Doesn't matter," says Jeff, "we got blankets and food and body heat. We could hold out way past this storm."

"We got carbon monoxide. . . ."

They hadn't thought of that. Snow building up all around them; how long until it obstructed the exhaust?

"The heat from the pipe's gonna keep it free," says Jeff.

But they weren't sure.

"Okay," says Jeff. "No going to sleep."

"At least two people have to stay awake at all times," says Nancy. "The moment one of them falls asleep, the other one shuts off the engine, just in case."

Sandy tried cracking the window, but it seemed to be frozen shut.

"How were you planning to get home?" says Sandy.

There's always someone with cables.

How long could they hold out?

The conversation grew old.

"We got condoms. We got games."

"Yeah right," says Sandy.

"At least it's comfortable in here."

The dome light's on, the map light's on. They've got provisions like crazy: food and beer and blankets. No one's worried because there's nothing to worry about. Josh is coming. There's plenty of gas. It keeps them warm.

They talk about what they're doing. They eat, drink. They try the radio, but it's all static.

"We got food; we got beer. We got blankets," repeated Aaron.

"Beer makes me piss."

"So piss in the bottle."

"Easy for you," says Nancy.

On one side the doors are pretty much pasted shut by the wind, and on the side they're frozen shut from an ill-advised car wash. Not that it would be absolutely impossible to get out. But think of it: no one's ever seen snow fall or wind blow more belligerently: heaven's sifters have overturned. None of the four is new to winter: they know. A wind like this shoots it all at you like tiny shards of glass: you gonna take your dick out in conditions like this? You gonna expect a young lady to raise her skirt? And Aaron has to tell them, because this has happened before, if they do manage to force open the door, they won't be able to shut it because the mechanism will then be frozen in the open position.

"It'll smell terrible."

"Put the lid back on."

"Then how we gonna tell the piss from the beer?"

Sandy didn't laugh. She was looking forward now, out the windshield.

There's no doubt she sees Aaron looking at her, trying to draw her eyes toward him, but she doesn't turn to him. Some process is going on in her mind, some story she's part of is getting told over and over.

"Are you mad at me?" he barely whispered. She shakes her head.

It is, it turns out, possible, to rig a kind of funnel out of a plastic bag and an empty beer bottle. You cut a small hole in the corner of a zip lock bag, stuff that into the bottle, then hold the mouth over your cunt as you stand on the seat. Then you have Sandy hold the bottle while the boys turn away—

"I've had sex with you for God's sake."

"Yeah well you've never had to help me pee before and you're not gonna start now."

"And *you're* not gonna watch either," says Sandy.

"Turn the light back on. You want me to piss on the seat." She'd held it as long as she could.

You stick the end with the hole far enough into the beer bottle and keep it still and pee into the bag, which bloats a little and pulls the end up to the bottlemouth, but they're lucky; none of it spills. In these close quarters it smells stronger than you'd expect. "This is gross," says Sandy and she has an urge to let go when the warm amber bulge stretches the bag under her hands so that she fears it's going to just let go. Nancy lets out a little panic scream and the boys turn around and Nancy and Sandy simultaneously tell them to shut their eyes but not before they get an eyeful. They high five and giggle.

Nancy and Jeff, who've had more beer than Aaron, who's still on his first, or Sandy, who hasn't had any, have empty bladders for the moment. Aaron decides if he has to go, he'll just hold it. He has no idea what Sandy will do. Maybe that's why she's not drinking.

Aaron asks, "You sure you don't want a beer?"

"No thanks." Her voice is not cynical, not even unfriendly, maybe with just an edge of something. Aaron wonders whether the beer would dull the edge or sharpen it.

"Sorry about this," he says.

And it looked like she was almost gonna smile. Maybe she wasn't so angry anymore. If so, he couldn't see why, unless anger just doesn't have much of a shelf life, at least not with Sandy. And she looked at him in a kind of tired way that didn't add much to his understanding. He didn't have any idea what it would take to pull her over the line, back to the hopeful, carefree, adventurous way she'd felt when he pulled into her driveway and she popped out of the door of her white house in the newest, sexiest clothes she owned, and glanced around at everyone and laughed and said, "I can't believe we're doing this." Maybe she could be brought back to that; maybe not. If *he* was gonna do it, there was only one way. He said, "Think of this. Here we are, we're hurtling through the universe in a machine that eats gas to no purpose."

"It's keeping us warm," says Nancy.

"Yeah, but what's the point of our warmth? Isn't this a perfect image of the whole shebang? The universe itself, this giant machine, generating and expending energy that keeps us all alive, but that's it; designed for a journey, driving and driving, but not taking us anywhere."

"We're not driving anyway," says Nancy.

"68,000 mph," says Aaron. "The earth is a warm dot with limited gas in the infinite coldness."

"Wow, that's profound," says Jeff. But Nancy thought it was interesting. Sandy smiled for the first time as though she too found something in it. Although she herself held out for God. Still, the reaction was promising; Aaron kept going. "You know I heard there was this French guy; I think his name was Duchamp-I'm pretty sure-who took this toilet and set it on a pedestal or something and called it a work of art. I think they call it 'Duchamp's toilet.' Anyway . . ."

"I'd take Duchamp's toilet right now." Jeff's groaning like he has to take a dump; Nancy hits him.

"I think he should have taken a car and rolled it out onto a lake in a storm and stuffed a bunch of people in it and just started it up and let it go until it ran out of gas."

"You said there's plenty of gas," said Sandy.

"How much gas is there?"

"Less than when we started."

"And Josh is coming, right?" says Nancy.

Not fast enough for Jeff.

"Hold your noses everyone; I apologize." Desperate attempts at every door to jar the windows open. No luck. Frozen solid.

And then, "Thank God for zip lock bags." Nancy'd crawled in the front to give him plenty of room.

Still static on the radio, must be in some kind of ravine that blocks everything out. Bored as hell, eventually Jeff and Nancy go at it. He puts a hand on her tit; she sees Aaron's eyes in the mirror, tells him to kill the light. He quickly does. Everything goes black until Aaron and Sandy adjust to the small beam of the map light. All he can see now is the dashboard, the perfect art of Sandy's thighs, and the outline of her face.

Jeff and Nancy are obviously practiced; once the lights are off, they're alone. She compliments his technique and grunts and groans, says "yes," and "more" and "that's it, right there. Slow. Yes. . . ." and the uninhibited pleasure in the sound of the voice, makes you think that's exactly the effect music exists to counterfeit. Aaron's hardon strains against his pants like a trapped rodent: like if his dick had a thumb it would unzip his fly itself. He can see Sandy's legs uncrossed, thighs about as far apart as they can get in that tight skirt.

Having rapidly debated the move and come up with no prudent course, not even a definitive hypothesis, he places his hand on the closest thigh, right at the edge of her skirt. He can only imagine the expression on her face as she turns toward him, flips off the map light, grabs his hand and pushes it under her skirt between her thighs. He hears the static sound of the skirt hiking up and feels the tingly resistance of nylon fabric over her crotch—and the warm, wet softness underneath, the bulge of her lips, the hard nut of her clit. His hand is her instrument; she rubs it over her in the pattern she wants; he just lets it go limp, or does his best to, to give it to her, but it's hard to do. No matter how he tries, his hand doesn't want to submit to her control. And he's afraid she'll be disappointed, think he's trying to pull away when all he's trying to do is let go of his own hand.

"Maybe they'll give us a turn in the back," he leans over and whispers, and he hopes they'll do it soon as he's not sure he's not going to burst right here and now whether she touches it or leaves it alone. Sandy juts her pelvis forward into his hand and moans; he feels the pulsation of her orgasm as she presses his hand still to ride it out.

"Hey what's going on up there," says Jeff. And that's all that saves Aaron from soiling his pants.

"You're not," says Nancy.

"Why not," asks Jeff.

"She's a virgin."

"So's he."

It's true; they are. They are virgins.

"I'm *not* a virgin."

No one says a thing, expecting, perhaps, the story that will confirm this- although Aaron is already pretty much convinced.

"Excuse me?" says Nancy.

"How can you *be* a virgin?" says Sandy, who has obviously thought this out.

Idling

"Let me explain," says Jeff, but Sandy won't have any of it.

"She's right," says Aaron, who has picked up what he figures is Sandy's logic, although it never occurred to him she would think like this: "you can't *be* something you've never *done*. If you're a painter it's because you paint; if you're a chef it's because you cook. If you're a virgin, it's because you *don't* fuck. Does that make any sense?"

"And if you get laid, you lose your virginity?" Sandy adds. "What is that? So you are something you've never done and you lose something you've never had. It's disgusting."

"Fucking backwards," says Jeff, yawning, opening up another beer.

Nancy thinks this one out. "But 'cold,'" she says, "is a lack of heat."

"And what is 'virginity' a lack of? There's a word for not having had sex, but is there a word for having had sex?"

"It's just economics," says Aaron. "A woman increases her value by pretending this nothing is something and that she has it and that it's valuable. It's easy; just give it a word."

Another loud crack. They hear the noise like an explosion. And the car shakes, just a little, or seems to. Hard to tell with all the movement going on in there.

Nancy screams. "The ice is breaking."

That's what it was, a sudden crack in the ice sheet that covered the lake, a rift that ran, no doubt, from one end to the other.

"It's not breaking," says Aaron.

"This car is heavy."

"It wasn't even the weight of the car that cracked the ice. The ice is a foot thick."

"Then what did it?"

"It's getting colder."

It is. And the snow's getting deeper. And the engine's still on.

It's getting late; they're getting tired. It's getting harder to believe Josh is really coming, but Aaron manages to keep their spirits up. Sandy's warmed to him and he doesn't think it's because she's had her orgasm. And yet he couldn't say what it was. In the dark, headlights shining nowhere in the snow, they talk of things that seem far away and unreal against the storm. At one point Sandy takes Aaron's hand and leans her head onto his shoulder. There's no sound coming from the back.

And?

Yes, she takes care of him; opens his pants and finds his prick in the dark. He wasn't going to ask.

Aaron thinks he sees Josh coming across the lake—on foot. But that doesn't make any sense, so he doesn't tell anyone what he thought for a second he saw. If it's him, he'll wake them up.

Jordan
Sudy

The Clown Joke

1

AL LOOKS GRIM. The mass of curls bouncing about through his sightline signals the actualization of his worst fears.

"How could this have happened?" he wonders. "Haven't I been a good father? Haven't I stressed enough the evil? Where did I go wrong?"

"I wanna be a clown! I wanna be a clown!" shrieks the child so to shatter windows in the mind.

"Now son, about this whole circus thing. . . ." Al begins, but before he can finish, the shrieking boy takes a deep breath and breaks into kid song parade, beating a metal bowl silly with a metal spoon, all the time singing out of time: "I wanna be a clown, clown, clown, me a clown, yeah a clown, I wanna be a clown. . . ."

Clowns.

Their impression pounds Al's temples. He massages them in aggravated little circles, and withdraws into hot reflection. He attempts to derive from where emanates his thorough disgust towards the red-nosed powdered rainbow-fro big shoe squirting flower wearing species.

Reflection complete, he repeats his conclusion aloud to his wife, who has, for several minutes, been chiseling through his wall of thought in an attempt to get this question answered: What is your problem with clowns, Al? It happens that the fruit of Al's reflection and the answer to his wife's question are one in the same. He says:

"I just hate those goddamn clowns."

Al's wife throws her hands north to the stars and spits, "well, you had better just hate those goddamn clowns some other day because today, today Al, you are taking little Billy to the circus," she flips to mommy, "yes sweetheart, I know you want to be a clown, that's wonderful," and back to Al's wife, "so you better fake it and play happy for Billy's sake. . . ."

"But you know about me and clowns. . . ."

". . . and yours," she caps the threat, and follows with a cold stare that burns Al's eyes to the floor.

He kicks an action figure across the kitchen and into a wall. Broken limbs scatter.

"Daddy!" screams Billy, "That's my favorite one! You killed Bob the Bionic Clown!"

Al cannot hide his smile.

"Really, Al," sighs his wife and exits into the living room, where daytime talk booms and booms. The Talk Show Host has invited a World Famous Speaker to the show so to impart tricks for sustaining a happy marriage. The Talk Show Host watches as a Member of the Studio Audience disagrees with the World Famous Speaker saying, "I simply don't see how 'checking the oil' helps in anyway to sustain a 'happy marriage'." The Member of the Studio Audience continues, "In fact, I don't see how anything you have said is relevant with respect to a discussion of marriage preservation at all." The World Famous Speaker pats roughly the pouring pores on his bald head. His retort is sharp: "Weeellll Maaaaam, ahem, may I ask how many marriages you have had?" "One," she answers. A smile creeps high onto the World Famous Speaker's cheeks and he says, "Well, I have had seven marriages, and that is what makes *me* the expert and *you* the tenderfoot." The Talk Show Host, looking quite satisfied with herself, leads the crowd into applause, and the screen fades to a feminine commercial.

Meanwhile, back in the kitchen, Al angrily thumbs two pink tickets.

"Oh, and Al?" his wife calls from inside the commercial.

"Yes dear?"

"You'd better believe we're going to check the oil when you get back."

"What?"

Al looks at the one-boy parade of annoyance: stamping his feet, smashing his bowl, belting his tune.

"Praising the clowns, my son, praising the clowns, my son, praising the clowns, my son, praising the clowns . . ." around and around the mind ran the thought until Al was himself physically round and round. He put his head on the table, closed his eyes, centered his thoughts, and wished all clowns dead.

2

Inside the circus tent, everything glows.

Al cringes, as children flow en masse with lightsticks as sabers toward the main arena; ready for battle. In his seat he looks on miserably as they wait like royalty to watch lions tamed, elephants kneeled, and death defying aerial assaults executed. He watches this war on sanity being waged, and curses again and again the court jester.

To the right Al sees his son, jumping up and down on his chair, waving his crayon sign:

Clown Rule!

A man nudges Al's left shoulder and says, "Quite a bold political statement for such a young child."

"Oh that," Al answers, wholly embarrassed, "He just forgot the 'S' in 'Clowns.'"

"Sure, Buddy. If that makes you feel better."

3

Honks the clown to the audience: "May I have a volunteer?"

The circus tent explodes in a burst of "Me, Me" as all goes dark, the drums roll, and the spotlight searches. Al slides low into his seat, and attempts to cloak himself by covering his face with his hands. He begins, "Please God, don't make me deal with this goddamn . . ." but his prayer is interrupted by the observation that his hands have turned red-orange, and the consequential realization that the spotlight has found him.

"You sir, step yourself to me!" demands the clown.

"Go Daddy!"

"Good luck, pal."

"Goddamn clown."

Al trips over legs and popcorn while off towards the clown below. Anonymity pinches his ass and he turns around to look, but lost somewhere between rage and darkness, Al can't see a thing.

In the circle of sand Al is sweating oceans. His eyes bulge out and away from the pressure of thought: "Get the clown, get the clown before he gets you!"

"Sir?"

"Yes, Clown" Al breathes through tensed teeth.

"Are you a donkey?"

"No, Clown."

A flower squirts wet in Al's face, and the clown screams, "Well then, you must be an Ass!"

4

"So what?" he wife yells, "So they all laughed at a stupid Clown Joke, who cares? There is absolutely no need for this," she waves an assortment of pastel brochures, "this shit is not happening. *You* are going nowhere buddy, or *I'm* going somewhere else!"

Al does not stop for her distant threat. He is lost in form. He is filling out applications for Clown College.

"Daddy's gonna be a clown, Daddy's gonna be a clown!" cheers Billy.

"That's right buddy, Daddy's gonna be a goddamned clown," says Al.

And scribbling nonsense all over the form, just like the directions ask, Al grins crazy, lost in thoughts of vengeance: "Get the clown, get the clown before it gets you."

"Never again clown, never again, I'll get you, I'll beat you down with your own stuff."

5

In Clown College, Al excels. He is a letter-winner in both Tricycling and Clown Car, of which he is named captain due to his small stature and uncanny ability to fit his entire head inside a glove box. He concentrates in Clown Philosophy, and writes his honors thesis on the Clown Joke. He studies it, and uncovers, through months upon months of intensive research and reflection: how it works, its form, its purpose. By Graduation he acquires the knowledge necessary to counter it. Al applauds himself at the ceremony for his achievement, as his family doesn't attend. His wife has left him to 'check the oil' with some other men, and has taken their son with her. Al does not care. He now has all he needs.

"All that's left now," he cackles, seated with the rest of his class and plush with the orange afro-wig of an honors graduate, "is to find that Clown and get him good."

"And so in closing," rants the King of Clowns, "my newly makeuped mates, my bumbling buddies, my squirting sissies, my honking homies, as you leave here today, and set out upon a world that adores your every flip and tumble, know this: I am your God."

And with that, the King of Clowns launches across the stage, going twice into backflip only to stick the landing effortlessly while juggling custard pies that he promptly throws into the face of the applauding Queen Mother amiss rabid applause.

Ascending his throne, he trips over a banana peel, and falls off the back of the stage. An ambulance pulls up, and seventeen red cross nurse clowns jump out. They raise the King of Clowns above their heads, throw him into the waiting ambulance, and file quickly in behind.

The crowd throws nuts as the King is sped off.

Al shakes his head, mutters "goddamn clowns," and goes skipping off into the sunset; his diploma in hand and revenge on his mind.

6

"May I have a volunteer?"

Al covers his face and waits for the spotlight. He can barely hold himself to his seat.

The spotlight hits him and he is before the clown who laughs and starts: "Sir?"

Al collects himself, thinks of the wife and the child he lost; embarrassment he has suffered; pain he has endured; the awful absurdity of Clown College— all in the name of retribution, all for this moment.

"Yeah, clown?"

"Are you a donkey?"

"Now Al, now!" screams his experience.

And calmly, very calmly, Al answers:

"Fuck you, clown. Fuck you."

Mark
Magill

The Duke of Penakeese Island

MY FRIEND HENRY wrote to me to say some magazine wanted "an unsettling & dark story that was not pleasant." The reason he wrote to me instead of calling like anybody else is that I'm on an island. And they don't have phones. They don't have electricity. They don't have anything but an old graveyard for lepers where I like to jerk off at night if the howling doesn't get too fierce. The reason why I jerk off in there is that they don't let women come on this island, at least women where hand-jobs would not be a preference. The reason I'm writing this at all is on the chance that it might get me off this goddamn island. The reason why I'm on this island is probably something you want to know, since everybody who comes poking around here wants to know pretty much the same thing.

The motto of this island is, "Shut up and keep chopping." The reason is that pretty much all we do besides jerking off and going to sessions is chopping wood. They actually give us axes. That's not really the motto, because they need to raise money to keep us out here away from the temptations of society at large. I'm not making that up. But if they put "Shut up" in the motto, people might wonder what we were doing with their money. There isn't any wood on this island except for a few scrawny looking trees that wouldn't keep a rat's ass warm. So they have to have some guy bring logs in a boat so we can chop them up, which is probably a good thing since even I can't polish my johnson twenty-four hours a day. And nobody could go to sessions twenty-four hours a day without getting hold of one of the axes and doing what comes naturally.

Henry said it's supposed to be a short story. If it gets in the magazine it will show that my remedial education is working and all that money is for a good cause. I forgot to say that besides the chopping and the hand-jobs, we have to go to school. It's in some half-assed building with one room and a picture of the Dalai Lama and the presidents in one corner. I have no idea what the Dalai Lama is doing here. The presidents make some kind of sense. So does the poster about sharks from the National Geographic.

But a short story is supposed to show some kind of transformation of the protagonist which is me, since Henry's not here and besides he's already transformed himself from being next in line to run his family's dry-cleaning business into a strung-out junkie with bad teeth. Which we're also supposed to be addressing in sessions. How to become a productive part of society and see the future in a positive light because young people act in accordance with the future they see for themselves and if the future includes robbery, arson and a certain amount of jail time, then those are the tools they'll use to get them to that future. They also say that they see progress if one of us who used to rob people and then shoot them or rape them now just robs them when he gets out of here. I'm not sure how long a short story is supposed to be, but I guess I can take some time out from my visits to the lepers' graveyard if it will get my ass out of here. Of course, if I really want to get out of here, I have to show some transformation of my own and not in the direction Henry finds so beguiling.

I'm sure you're wondering why somebody they sent out to this fucked up island is using a word like beguiling. You don't have to be stupid to end up here. You just have to get caught. You might say that amounts to the same thing, but I could argue with that. But before I go on with my transformation, I better tell you what this place looks like, in case you can't imagine it for yourself.

So this is an island. You got that part already. A few skinny trees a dog wouldn't piss on. A building where we live and eat and all. Two outhouses since there's no water here except what we get from the cisterns on the top of the hill. There's the school building. One room with the posters and stuff I mentioned plus desks for the seven of us. We're supposed to call ourselves students instead of horny, wood-chopping delinquents who'd like to get the fuck out of here. Each of us has his own desk. I mentioned there are no alternatives to jerking off here, which includes Margaret, who is the schoolteacher.

Before we got here, some guy kept sheep. There are a bunch of buildings where all the farm activity goes on, such as chickens, some pigs and all the other things we end up eating sooner or later. Then there's the leper cemetery up on the cliff. This place used to be a leper colony. You can read their names and when they were born and died. If you do the math, you can see some were just like eighteen or twenty. Some were old people in their fifties. There is one guy named Hammett Fulton who was seventy-two when he kicked. Men and women both, with names from all over the place. Hon Lee. Miriam Leibowitz. Milocsz Tadeiskiew. Anne Farnsworth. I like to think of the lepers getting together, falling in love, fighting over the women, dying of heartbreak, giving each other bunches of flowers. Not that any of that helps with my amusement up there. I've got some other sources for that. On the contrary, once I started looking into leprosy in the encyclopedia in the school, it kind of makes you want to puke.

The ocean waves smash against the rocks at the bottom of the leper cliff.

The whole place is covered with poison ivy, which finally dies in the winter. Then you get to freeze your ass instead of scratching it off. Which is why we spend so much time chopping wood, since the wind that blows over this place in the winter will knock you on your ass after it's done freezing it.

Before I forget, I want to say something about William Shakespeare. He wrote a play called "The Tempest" about a duke named Prospero who was stuck on an island like this. The only thing he had to keep him company was his daughter named Miranda. And an Igor type of guy called Caliban, plus a lot of other sprites and pixies and so forth. Well, the English guy who discovered this island, Penakeese, the one I'm stuck on, was named Mathew Gosnold. And he went back and told William Shakespeare about it. And he wrote the play about it, because there are all sorts of fucked up things that go on here at night. Ghosts, I mean. Mainly I don't give a shit. If some spook wants to fuck with me, fine. Whatever. But it shows you that this was one fucked up place all the way back then. Why else would they stick lepers out here instead of some kind of country club? Because the place is covered with ghosts, spooks, spirits, sprites and hobgoblins. Worse than the poison ivy, if you ask me. Not that they bother me, like I said. What do they do? I've seen them screwing, wading into the water, crawling on all fours. I've seen the ones without faces and the ones with too many faces. Did I think I was going nuts? Who wouldn't be nuts stuck out here for eighteen months? But I've seen worse right at home, no lie. It's what they call a dysfunctional environment. I'll take the spooks.

They have that play by William Shakespeare here, of course. Like it's their big claim to fame since it's about the only good thing they can say about this place. Margaret had us take turns trying to read it out loud in the class. I like that play, the way Prospero makes Caliban do his business for him and controls him with magic.

Which gets me to the visitors, which is what this story is supposed to be about. Two ladies and some old guy in shorts and what must have been their daughter. They came sailing up in their sailboat just before we were supposed to have our dinner. They rowed up to the dock in their little rowboat. Dean, the chief hard-ass instructor, saw them and sent Margaret down to meet them. I guess he was afraid they were going to deliver a couple of keys of crack or something. Why they would bring a teenage girl to a place like this beats the hell out of me. I guess just because they own a sailboat doesn't make them smart. Definitely not.

So Margaret goes down to the dock to meet these people and they ask her if it's okay to take a tour of the island and see how we're learning to become productive members of our community instead of hardcore cutthroats. Margaret, who doesn't basically know her ass from a hole in the ground and is new here besides, comes back to ask Dean if the people can take a tour. And Dean, who's been driving around on the tractor mowing some poison ivy says to get me, the senior student, to take some valuable time out from chopping wood and squeezing the squirrel to go down and show them around. Which I am happy to do, being naturally a friendly and outgoing type of person, unless you happen to piss me off, since I am from a dysfunctional environment.

So Margaret gets me in between my two principle activities and I go down to meet these people. I naturally check out the guy first, to see if he's going to be some kind of an issue, but one look at those shorts and the eyeglass strap and the dopey sailing hat and I figure no contest. The two ladies would be alright in a pinch, since they have considerably less weight on them than Margaret, who wouldn't do even in a pinch as I have indicated before. Now the girl is another story altogether and, being a happy, outgoing person, I could see right away that she was one, too. Which didn't get in the way of my trying to figure out how I could fuck her between the dock and the main building without getting mom and dad and whoever the other lady was in an uproar. All this is the result not so much of being raised in a dysfunctional environment as being a youthful offender who's been stuck on an island with nothing but poison ivy and a bunch of dead lepers' ghosts to look at.

So what did I do?

"Hi. I'm Mike, the senior student here. I've been asked to show you around and answer any questions you might have about the island."

So they introduce themselves, Mr. and Mrs. blah, blah, blah and their daughter, Miranda. That's right. I thought they were kidding. So I ask them if they know of the play by William Shakespeare called "The Tempest." And of course they do. So I tell them all about Mathew Gosnold, the explorer, and Prospero and Miranda. I tell them about how some people think the island still has sprites and fairies. I can see this gets right to Miranda. I don't mention the leprous ghosts fucking or drowning themselves and so on. I tell them about how a bunch of travelers gets shipwrecked on Prospero's island one day after Prospero and Miranda have been marooned there forever. They're all the people who plotted to send Prospero there in the first place. That's what the main story is about. I'm trying to get her to see me as some kind of modern day duke who's just waiting for the day when I can return to my dukedom instead of a hunchback type of character like Caliban, so I don't mention anything about him. The fact that Miranda is his daughter in the play is a little fucked up for my purposes but I'm hoping they don't notice.

These people also know about the graveyard somehow and they want to see it before it gets dark. That's fine by me. And, of course, the senior student has to show them the way so they don't get lost in the poison ivy. I don't tell them they *better* get there before dark or they might see something more than a few cute little fairies.

Off we go up the hill. I show them the barns and the pigs and the chickens and all that other farm crap we have to deal with. I show them the ten million sticks of firewood we've chopped since I've been here. I tell them how much we like chopping wood. The old guy, Mr. Blah, who's been hanging back, gets a funny look right about then, imagining us with axes, I guess. But Miranda's eating it all up. She must go to some kind of private school, because I don't think she's ever seen anybody like me before.

The cemetery is at the top of the hill. Right near the cliff. I don't figure I can get away with pushing the three of them off the cliff although I still haven't figured out a way to get to Miranda before they have to leave. But when we get to the top of the hill I can see right away these people aren't sailing anywhere tonight. I've never been on an island before I got shipped to this one, but I've been here long enough to know a storm when I see it. And I can see this one is no joke. I don't want to let on, of course, or Mr. Blah with the eyeglass strap might think they'd better get going. So I launch into every kind of history I can cook up about the island. How some people think it's a magical place. How people say they've seen fairies dancing at night and so forth. Miranda's getting into it, I can tell. She doesn't exactly say anything but I know the look. One of the ladies asks if I've ever seen any sprites myself. And I say it's a funny thing, but being out here all this time, surrounded by nature, by which I mean the birds and whatever the hell else they think nature is, not the poison ivy and the pigs, that I've seen a lot of unusual things. I even tell them how I like to look at the names on the graves of the lepers and imagine how couples must have fallen in love, as if the sprites and fairies put some kind of spell over the island, instead of the ghouls and ghosts that really run the place. I mention the bit about the bouquets and any other bullshit I can come up with, all the time I'm looking over their shoulders at the storm, trying to keep their attention until it's too late.

And pretty soon it is. The sky behind them gets real dark and the breeze, which usually blows pretty good around here, drops down to nothing. That's a good sign. Because generally when that happens it means all hell is about to break loose. So I start telling them about how there was a lighthouse here until it was washed away by a storm and how ships used to sink all over the place and people who tried to swim off the island for one reason or another were eaten by sharks or swept out to sea and never seen again. Anything I can make up to give them the idea that when they turn around and see what's coming, they're not going anyplace.

Which is what happens, because by the time we get back down the hill, the wind is howling and there's no way they're going to row that little boat back out to their sailboat. I lead them back down to the main house. Mr. Blah has a word with Dean who's not all that happy to have put these jerks up for the night but he doesn't have much choice because the rain is starting up now and it's promising to be quite an evening. Miranda's looking all shivery in her little shorts and I tell her I'll get her a coat to keep her warm. At the same time I'm giving a look to my fellow students, whose jaws are all hanging down to the floor, that they better not get any ideas. Since we all come from dysfunctional environments, they know what that look means.

It's already dark because of the storm and the main room is lit with candles and lanterns. Dean tells Roy and Jason to go check on the animals to make sure they don't blow away or whatever. And he tells me as the senior student to take our guests to the loft above the woodshop which is where they'll have to sleep. I get my coat for Miranda and some ponchos for the other people and I lead them over to the woodshop. It's not far, but it's blowing like hell and you can't see as far as you can spit. But I know the way since there's not much room to get lost on this fucked up little island. At least if you've been here for eighteen months.

The loft isn't a bad place. I like to hang out there myself sometimes when I'm in one of my friendly, outgoing moods. We use it as a rec-room. It has a warped old ping-pong table and some ratty old couches and one of those knock-hockey games. A real fun place. There's also a bunch of old National Geographic magazines and some other worthless stuff to read. With the storm blowing outside, it feels kind of cozy after I light the lanterns. Now I'm trying to figure out how I'm going to get Miranda away from the old folks. In the play by William Shakespeare, Prospero could put spells on whoever he wanted. Make them feel like they're being chased by dogs or bit by mosquitoes or just fall asleep. I'd like to put a spell on them, it's true, but I don't have the faintest idea how you do it. I'm wondering if I should tell them one of my ghost stories. Like the time I was on my way you know where when I saw two leper ghosts dragging something up the trail to the cisterns. I couldn't tell if it was a sheep or a person or a sack of potatoes. They were hobbling and shuffling along like mummies. I told you they don't bother me. They want to drag something, it's a free country. Then I could see what they were dragging was another person. But not one of them. I was hoping it was Dean the hard-ass instructor. Anyway, they got up to the cisterns and I heard a splash. The cisterns are where we get our drinking water, from catching the rain. Did I go up there and see what they'd dropped in? Hell, no. They're always up to shit like that. Did I give up drinking water for a while? What do you think?

Just then, while I'm thinking whether to tell them about the ghosts, a huge crack of thunder hits the place. I mean, I saw sparks flying around the room. And Miranda, who's standing near me, grabs my arm. So I naturally pat her on the head and tell her it's ok, just some lightening, which we get all the time. No big deal. Her hair feels so nice. Kind of curly and soft. Then the howling starts. And I don't mean the wind.

"What's that," she asks, all nervous and scared.

I know what it is but I say, "Coyotes. They swim over here to get the rabbits." I forgot to tell you that besides poison ivy, the place is covered with rabbits. I figure coyotes is better than what I know is really out there. "That's why we have to have fences around the chickens."

"What about the pigs?" she asks.

"The pigs can look after themselves," I say, like some kind of Joe Farmer. I never gave a damn about the pigs one way or another. I'm thinking maybe I should cook up something about the fairies and pixies and whatnot, since that's probably more her speed than coyotes or ghosts. The three adults are busying themselves trying to arrange the couches to make some kind of comfortable place to sleep, which I know is impossible since I've tried to sleep on those lumpy-ass things a million times. But Miranda must be one of those people who knows what you're thinking because she asks me in a low voice if I've ever seen any fairies. I'm hoping she can't really know what I'm thinking while I tell her sure, all the time, right after sunset, you know, when it starts to get hard to see. The fairies come out and you can see them kind of skittering across the top of the grass in the fields. I say grass instead of poison ivy for obvious reasons. They're like sparkly little lights dancing around with each other. And they sing a whistling little song because I guess they're happy to be dancing and able to fly around like that. She asks me what the song sounds like and I make up some cheery little tune and kind of wave my arms a little like I'm floating. This takes her mind off the howling, but it gets the attention of Mr. and Mrs. Blah and their friend, who want to know what we're talking about.

"Michael was just telling me about the fairies on the island," Miranda says. Michael, she calls me.

"Oh, really?" says Mrs. Blah, who seems ready to believe anything. "Have you seen them for yourself?"

I'm wishing I knew one of those spells, since Miranda was really getting interested, and now they're butting in.

"Oh, I've seen more than that," I say. "I didn't want to startle you before, but there's a reason why this island is kind of isolated the way it is. Ever since Mathew Gosnold the explorer discovered it."

"Why's that?" asks Mr. Blah, who now feels he's supposed to take charge. Maybe *he* can read minds.

"Ghosts," I say in a spooky low voice, as if I'm afraid the ghosts will hear me.

"Oh, really?" he says, same as Mrs. Blah but definitely not ready to believe everything, which I could care less. The three women seem a little more ready to go for it.

"Yeah," I answer. "At least that's what they say. They put all kinds of spells on people. Make them do all sorts of things. They say the Indians were afraid to stay out here at night. And they usually weren't afraid of anything. I told you it was coyotes and fairies, because I didn't want to scare you. Didn't you notice how Dean wasn't all that happy that you had to stay here? He's worried if the word gets out, people won't send money to run this place anymore and he'll have to get a regular job."

"Uh, huh," says Mr. Blah. He doesn't want to call me a liar and it's a good thing because that might make me forget my happy, outgoing side, which does happen once in a while when someone gets in my face. That also explains why I'm the senior student, since acting out gets you demerits against your release date and also why it's important to get this story in that magazine or whatever it is, although the way it's going, I'm not sure it's going to get me off this island anytime soon. If I wrote a play like William Shakespeare, maybe. That's the problem with remedial education. The stories that got you in the remedial situation to begin with aren't going to win you any points with the adjudication process, unless you have a happy ending, which I don't think mine does. At least I don't think I'm winning any points here, unless it's some kind of horniness contest. Because as it turned out, the quiet one, Mrs. Blah's sister or friend or whatever, had her eye on me the whole time. No, I'm not kidding. You can see this stuff happening on Open House Day. You know what I'm talking about. They think us cutthroat hoodlums are some kind of romantic outlaws, so they act all nice and friendly instead of locking their car doors like they would if they saw us coming down the street. So right in the middle of my telling them about the ghosts, Cynthia, which is what her name turned out to be, says she needs to use the facilities but she's afraid to go out there alone and could I show her the way? I know she means the outhouse, which kind of talk doesn't usually interest me, but after eighteen months, I'll take it. So I say sure. It's not too far, up between the house and the barn. I guess she's still thinking it's coyotes, but that doesn't make any difference to me.

She puts her poncho back on and we step outside. The wind is roaring and the rain is blowing sideways. You can hear the waves crashing all over the place. I kind of like it. She grabs my arm so I can lead her. Second one tonight, I'm thinking. It's so noisy it's hard to talk. She says something I can't make out. So she leans closer and yells in my ear.

"Why did they send you here?"

There it is. We're halfway between the woodshop and the outhouse in some kind of hurricane and she wants to know how I got caught.

"Politics," I shout. "They were trying to usurp my kingdom." I figure what the hell. It sounds a lot better than grand theft auto and felony arson or all the other little shit they like to tack onto the rap sheet.

"Some kind of drug war, you mean?"

Of course, she figures me for a gangbanger. Although I've always tried to be independent. A lone wolf, you might say. I just shrug and let her draw her own conclusions.

"I'd like to help you." she says.

I nod and try to look duke-like instead of some juvenile offender looking for instant gratification. We get to the outhouse.

"Can you wait here for me?" she says.

I nod again and she goes into the outhouse. It's raining and blowing like crazy. For a clever fellow, I'm not sure what to do next. I was wishing it was Miranda, first of all, but what the hell. Then, like right on schedule, what do I see but one of those ghosts, standing in the rain, on the other side of the outhouse. One of those sad leper ladies who probably never had a boyfriend, in spite of what I generally imagine.

"Great," I say.

She's got a big dog with her. Kind of nasty looking, like a police dog. Cynthia's still in the outhouse.

"What's up?" I ask the ghost. "Want to join the party?"

The ghost doesn't say anything. They never do. She just stands there looking sad. I don't blame her, really, since I know what it's like to be stuck out here with nobody on your side. I wonder why the world has to be such a fucked up place. I'm sure she didn't want to get shipped out here any more than I did. You might say in my case it's my own fault. But believe me, it's not what I wanted any more than she did. I'm kind of feeling sorry for her, so I reach out my hand. I mean, I know she's a ghost and all, so it's not like I could *do* anything with her. I just want to let her know I know how she feels.

Cynthia pops out of the outhouse while I'm standing there with my hand out like I'm trying to see if it's raining or not, which it is in buckets. Lightning is flashing all over the place. I must have this dopey look on my face, because Cynthia takes hold of my hand and kisses it. No kidding. The sad ghost is still standing there, and I'm actually kind of embarrassed, because I know she wanted someone to kiss her hand while she was still alive, but who would kiss the hand of a leper once you had a good look at it? The Dalai Lama or Abraham Lincoln, maybe. Or maybe even Prospero, the duke of Penakeese Island.

| H.E. | *At the Corner of Fort and Light* |
| Wright | |

1

WHAT I WANTED was to tell everyone that I thought the woman in the super-market was smooth, and that she made my guts go buzzed. But Mom would have slapped my face hard with love. So I quit jabbering. Just shut up fast and pulled my cap-gun out of my holster. And I shot the smooth woman as she pushed her shopping cart down the aisle—as she moved away from me.

2

Eve came first. Not the chicken. Not the egg. Certainly not a man. Not just crushes. At fifteen: a kiss, but no surrender. She touched me stronger with her eyes than the soccer player ever could with his hands. She asked to be held. The fight began. Intent is nine-tenths of the law.

True ladies don't whistle, they said in Sunday School.

This woman tried to feed me pancakes when I was fifteen. Alpha centauri flipped out of my pocket, and rolled—like a spurry jack—across the parquet floor, when she unbuttoned my Levi's. I just stood there against the wall.

"I tried to make you feel it. Fight me. Love me. Do something. Feel some-thing." That was what she said.

With erudition, I would do it now. So hungry, I was, that I could not feel my hunger then. But now, when it is too late, the anesthetic worn, I am ready—syrup on my bare, awake hands.

3

God's Adam. God's first man, and mine. Elements of subsets. Rakes his lawn, and waters and mows. He buys reams of standard bond. We speak in the metaphors of Nerfs on Sundays in his back yard. Adam, archangel in an oxford, defends the infield fly rule. We make militant love in a stomach-to-stomach safety sleep.

It was another old lie: It meant nothing. The italics are not mine. There is, I thought, more.

I say to Adam, "I trust you to not hurt me." Which is, I found out later, like saying, "I dare you to not hurt me." Which is saying, simply, "I dare you to hurt me." Which is just, "Bet you can't hurt me." Which means, if translated correctly—"Go ahead. Hurt me." Which is license, and not suspension. There were ledges. I jumped off.

4

When I woke today, I thought for a second that I was somewhere in Montana. For twelve nights in a row, I have slept in twelve different beds, for twelve different reasons which were all the same. I always wanted to be warm. I am closing in on home. I celebrate this season only because my godchild, who is four, was born on the twenty-fifth day of December: *I didn't know anybody would let people have birthdays on Christmas,* she said to me when she was old enough to understand birthdays.

And a Christ I once assumed, I now know only in the hands of other humans. My homage is paid. My rent is paid. And yet I wake, hanging on by the skin of my Christ.

Here, lovers move like guests: "I'm sorry. I didn't mean to wake you. I was just trying to remember where I am, and why, and which one you are."

It knows it needs, unable to fill itself.

5

We take off each other's socks. I kiss her stomach through her t-shirt. On her neck I taste the beer from the rowdy Guinness she opened. I learn her haunches with my mouth.

I like it like this. But price tags. Things cost. This is violence. I want a knife. Putting the steeple ghosts to bed, little girl comes into her woman. If I can touch it, I can catch it.

The sex show barker shouts to us as we walk past him on the sidewalk: "Hey girls, talk to a live naked girl for a buck. You don't need no lollipop to enjoy this show."

6

In a library without books, I held a pen that had no ink over a notebook that had no paper. Something other than blood pulsed through my veins. What pushed through my lungs was different from air. No thoughts ransacked my brain. With my teeth which are not teeth, I bit down on an angel who came from no heaven.

7

At pre-dawn, the bed goodbyed—those god-yes winter mornings. After midnight picnics and backrubs. All sexed out and places to go. Thighs tight as shoelace knots, beneath splashes of tepid starlight through the window. I'm running, to follow the moon through the first snow, tracing—into a big place.

Now, wherever I go becoming, I feel her damp hair brushing down my stomach. She said, "I'm going to marry him. I want respectability."

I hear my own words fall out of my mouth, and tumble across her cheek: "We both know I can't give you that."

I guess I always felt like we were just a perpetual game of Go Fish; but wherever I go here now, I must admit: I grew accustomed to the sinkered line.

Buttoning up the Levi's of a true fever. In the name of Christ their Lord, in the name of Mom and Dad. In the name of what the neighbors think.

I check my pockets twice for coins and bus tokens before I throw my pants in the washer. I do this, I suppose, to hold on to what I can, or what will have me, or what will sleep a soft sum-song in the palms of my open hands, or live by my biased, sweating bones. Or so.

8

A sudden Return to the Planet of the Het Set. He and I, we fuck and live a legally bound life. I spend my marriage coming to pass. Coming in order to pass.

He tells his friends: "She fucks like a bunny." He tells me: "You fuck like a bunny." "Is that good, or is that bad?" I ask. The next pay day he brings two rabbits home in a big cage. He puts the cage on our bed and we lie together watching them hump. He says to me: "Bunnies' asses fuck the best."

I know the clues. I can keep him happy. I take my clothes off and get on my hands and knees. It's not me. It's only rhythm and balance and sweat. He watches the rabbits and does me. I fuck like a bunny. But I feel nothing. I am an echo to a muted silence here. I have never yet felt anything that could be described as something. Folding up my desire for her, I keep it safe.

What says who cries when's enough. Pity our language; it's not enough to keep us honest. It's not really possible to spell *consummation* correctly. I'm homesick for a woman and a conversation.

There are nights with him when I cannot sleep, with this wheezing in my lungs. And so I hoard and hold her in my mind's own arms, before I know her face. I want to defect from his tundra, wake her, and lie under her carnival. Someday I will know her name, as a pleasure and a terror across my tongue.

I was breast-fed on the brimstone-boiled milk of a certain drastic theology, spooned strained faith and seminary blessings. But a running taste for passion is a loiny greed, like any other. And in all the world of Buster Brown boys, somebody touched tongues with a knowledge-wild woman. I can't go back again. Not really.

9

She brought me, jokingly, a yellow saucer of warm milk *because I can't find any cups* for which I was glad, because not only was I hungry but my arms ached from pulling in the life-saver all evening. I mean—there had been a rash of near-drownings at the pool. I really couldn't have lifted a full glass of anything. So I bent my head to the bowl on the table and went slurpingly down on my supper. And I suppose that was a good move because it turned her on, she said. Especially my milk mustache, she also said. And then she licked it off my face. And, well. This and that. Until my arms suddenly weren't tired, and the old familiar want began tugging at my thighs. She sat on my lap. And so. *I like this. I like her. I like her biting through my t-shirt for my collar bone.*

"Fran, stop." I heard the words come in my mouth. Out of the corner of my eye, I saw the wet spot on my gray t-shirt where her mouth had just been. "I know you've been with her, Fran. I don't care. You do what you want." She said, "That's all anyone can do." She went for my neck. Okay.

Next morning, I tried to get out of bed; but she told me to sleep. She made me Malt-O-Meal (which I hate) and ham and Tang. She packed a lunch for me. "I'll be home late," she said. I didn't ask. Thus. And so. "See you when I see you," I said. She gave me a pink hair ribbon, but my hair's too short. I guess I'll have to grow it out.

10

So we fought. I stung out of town on the red Yamaha, into the desert where I took off my shirt—thinking about coyotes my father and I had, years ago in this same flat land, shot with a 30.06. But today I found a trilobite and an arrowhead as wide at its base as a matchbook. Toward evening, against the sunset, I put on my t-shirt, over my sunburned breasts. When I got home, when it was dark, she pulled my shirt off over my head. And the blisters on my nipples opened wide to her touch, bleeding warm water across her sharp forgiven lips.

11

Meanwhile, the three words I wrote to her with broken crayons, in a fit of unforgiven honesty, weighed less than a clover. But, in a fact, they became poured concrete in the Converse high-tops I was wearing. They sunk me into the Pacific, beneath the spray and the foam, somewhere off the northern Oregon coast. If I could cry, I would cry. But I'm too big to be any woman's drowning daughter.

Nothing is cheap, that I know. Pure commodity rears up and hush: It's Independence Day—coming me into the apogee of skilled awakening; into the hungry palms of immaculate perception.

12

I chase a woman with a hunger across her face; for me, her hunger speaks, and I want to believe. Dream of a woman, I do, in a terrible white embrace: bleed me wet and home. Her gutsome blue eyes quench me my rage. Saturdays we heft up shingles, re-roof the house—a project almost completed. We avoid our wedding ring-less fingers, where we wear our invisible, indivisible hankering for each other.

What I am trying to mean is what is here. Picture Sangria: an elegant camper, treading forty. With dried mud caked onto the knees of her jeans. A breakfast fire. A tent. History textbooks stacked on the green and white lawn chair we bought at Sears.

"John Foster Dulles," she whispers into my ear, and her whispers scald me like spilt coffee. She knows what that does to me. Sangria says, "John Foster Dulles. John Foster Dulles." My ear is hot and wet, and I am long gone. My spine shivers, and she knows everything. I am licked. Nipples rise to receive kisses. A nipple for the biting. Suck, but don't bite; bite, but don't draw blood. A little blood, but just a little.

When I hold her, everything washes over me, resonates, and is gone:
We imitate the desires of others.
New and improved. Libidinal economics.
Why? Because we like you.
Your rationalism, your parking tickets.
Don't make me feel guilty about it;
now that it's over, let's just forget about it.
Hounded by predictability.
Your electoral college, your individualism,
your rechargeable batteries, your betrayals.
City.
White china tea cups.
Fort Ticonderoga.

Children, as function.
If I were twenty-three again, I'd play the stock market differently.
Our struggle to ambiguity.
Honey, just pay the man the fifty bucks, and
you and me will go up to the room and do the bird.
You display the wonderful traits of charm and courtesy.
I am your whipping boy.
There is no man in me.

A bird's wings, taut, in your green and green eyes. And I remember now: I am holding you. Here and now, in your green eyes I see that I am holding an obsolescing woman.

13

Out of the shower. The room is fogged. From behind, out of the humidity, a mouth opens wide and locks itself there. We fall asleep in the bathtub, in each other's arms. When we wake, the water has grown cold. We get out to return to bed. I lock the bathroom door behind you when you leave. I am sitting on the cold tile floor because if I stay close to you, I will say what I will regret. So hurry to sleep. Think me distant as initials. I am fine. I will be out in the smallest minute, to sneak into bed beside you and happily mumble mush into your graceful flesh—when I am certain you cannot hear me through the layers of your sleep.

But for now: The city stubs its toe in the night, tries to suppress its ouch, but can't. Me—I want neon; I want real, maybe a field of crickets and a hot train to hoo-hoo-soothe me to sleep. Me—I want hands, penny candy, Sangria's breath, light as a baggie, on my neck. I'm wishing for gravel.

14

The medium is flesh; now touch the same other for the body's sake. For life's sake, feel the metaphysic. Honor the body. Who feels philosophy?

Tonight the wind dies down; the wind hums back. We gust, and then it's gone again. We lie intimate, tangled as cursive. We stare out the window at the woman in the moon and at all the gold good conduct stars that have somehow, and by something, been pasted onto the forehead of the sky. I can see that there's nothing out there but time, but fire. Though bucking, it seems ride-able and, maybe, worthy. But I can't sleep. Your mouth slobbers copious dreams across my pillow. This is something almost close—almost very close, in fact—to what (once) I imagined I wanted to find.

| Kate Noonan | *Paper, Scissors, Stone* |

"WE MARRIED EACH OTHER for money neither one of us had,"

Jade was picking through a pile of rocks on the lawn looking for the right one. An unusual shape, a particular color, texture. Her mother's voice came from inside the house. Then her laugh. Jade had seen a play once where they had made a campfire of papier mâché logs, a red light bulb and a small fan blowing cellophane. From a distance it really looked like fire, it even felt warm, but when you got close you could see it was fake. Her mother's laugh was like that. She eyed a smooth stone and loosened the dirt around it with her toe. Sedimentary. Metamorphic. One of them hardened over time, and one of them crumbled. Which was which?

Jade kicked dirt into the blue hole on the lawn, a little at a time making a tiny avalanche that rolled to the bottom. The blue hole was a neighborhood anomaly. Jade wondered what it would look like if you were seeing it from an airplane. *A scar. The mouth on a giant clown.*

"You better not." Her little brother Rider was sitting on the porch steps eating the stiff remains of a peanut butter sandwich, in pajamas he'd been wearing all week. A line of ants was making its way up his pant leg. "You could fall in," he said. He licked the edge of the stale bread and squinted at the sun. Jade tossed in a stone and glanced toward the sidewalk where the two half-Vietnamese children they were now related to by marriage were playing. They were wearing clothes that were clean and fastidiously pressed.

New and Used. Words popped up in Jade's mind like flash cards.

Jade was wearing Marty's sweater. It hung well below her knees and she had to roll the sleeves up five times to see her hands, but that was okay.

It smelled like him: Dirty hair and menthol cigarettes. A person's scent can remain on things they touch for a long time.

Last year Jade lived with Tony and Dolores. In their dead son's room. His pillow smelled of medicine. The rest of the house smelled like death; a combination of mothballs, fast food and old flowers. You could leave the windows open all night and the smell would still be there in the morning.

When Tony and Dolores gave her back, her mother hired a teenager from the neighborhood named Marty to baby-sit. Once, he took Jade to the Rialto Theater and snuck her in the exit to see "Love Story." They sat in the balcony and toward the end when it was real sad and quiet, Marty made puking sounds and dumped a thermos of alphabet soup over the railing. When the manager came upstairs Jade started to cry and held her stomach. He shushed her with his finger and went to get her a free 7-up. Jade raised her eyebrows at Marty and grinned.

"On and off like a fucking faucet," he'd tell his friends in admiration.

Marty called himself the King of the Free Buzz. He said there was no reason ever to be starving or sober living in L.A., not with Happy Hour, Hare Krishna Temples and supermarkets everywhere you look. He told her he wrote the handbook on urban survival. He taught her how to get high on the gas from whipped cream cans and PAM non-stick vegetable spray, various methods of the dine and dash, and how to drive a waitress crazy. "Order a side of whipped cream. If they ask what else, say "Nothing thank you, the whipped cream will be all for now."

"I'll come back King of The Free World."

"Doubt it."

The white father of the two half-Vietnamese children, the man who had married Jade's mother sixteen days before, stumbled out of the house holding a bag containing two small square cartons of milk, and two donuts. He had carpet lint in his beard and he wasn't wearing a shirt. He had a scar on his arm where a tattoo used to be. You could still see a shape like a scorpions tail, and part of a letter that had either been an L or an E. Jade thought it must have hurt more removing the name than putting it there. She had written a word on her own hand with a safety pin once. After the first letter it wasn't so bad.

Kam-pu-chee-a. Kampuchea.

Marty had shown her a dumpster in the lot behind the grocery store where they kept magazines and newspapers tied up in bundles for recycling. She could sit inside it and read for hours, unseen. Some days the bundles were piled so high she felt like the princess in "The Princess and the Pea". Some days when the papers were low she would sit in a corner and drum on the sides to hear the echo. Most days she collected pictures of Vietnam from *Life* magazine, *Time* and *Newsweek*. A woman holding a dead baby to her breast. A monk on fire, cross-legged and faceless in the middle of a street. A blindfolded man at the business end of a gun. Three naked children, napalmed and running. Jade pasted these pictures in the scrapbook her grandmother had given her that had the word *Keepsakes* embossed in gold letters on the front. She carefully cut out each picture with the small scissors attached to the red Swiss army knife she'd stolen out of Tony's car.

Tony and Dolores were Italian. Their son and Jade were the same age, or they would have been, if he had lived. He was born three months before Jade, and died a day before her eighth birthday. He would be nine and three quarters. Jade was still nine and a half. They called him Little Tony. Little Tony had a blood disease. Jade's father and Little Tony died around the same time, and as best as she could figure it, her mother gave Jade to them as a kind of replacement. To cheer them up maybe. Jade's father had a tumor. A tumor is a physical anomaly. A person begins with a healthy brain that tells him who he is, and then for a reason no one could explain, something grows out of it, a separate organism that changes that person, makes him forget things, makes him sick, makes him shrink, and then kills him. This tiny thing no bigger than a pebble.

When Jade's father's got sick her mother started to drink full time. Sometimes at night she would come into the room that Jade and her sister shared and hover above the beds staring at them for signs of life. They would play dead, trying not to breath or move a muscle, each hoping their mother would pick the other. Sometimes she would hit them. Other times she would sit on the bed and cry. In the morning she would never remember, and if they tried to prove it by showing her the bruises, it would only make her mad. Jade thought her mother was like the edge of a cliff.

In a hospital somewhere her father was losing weight and strength and memory. In the house where they lived paint peeled and cracked, windows broke and stayed that way, and the weeds grew wild and ragged. Jade went to school less and less, bathed only sometimes, and instead of banding together, Jade and her sister and brothers developed an every-man-for-himself approach to their lives. They were four all together.

When their father died, they each went to different houses, where they waited until their mother would come sift through the ruins to determine what was worth keeping. A year later, they came together again, to this place, with its many rooms, its manicured lawn and avocado tree.

Sometimes, after a long separation, you simply pick up where you left off.

Jade's sister left a month ago. She threw a duffel bag into the back seat of some guy's car and they drove off without saying a word. She left pictures of Charles Manson on the walls of her room. "For effect," her mother said.

Her older brother Ben left forty-seven days ago, if she didn't count the one time she saw him. Marty, thirty-six. There was a calendar in the kitchen that helped Jade keep track of things.

Her mother's new but soon to be former husband tried to open the small cartons of milk for his children while they waited, staring at his clumsy hands as though hypnotized. Jade scraped dirt away from something black she hoped might be an arrowhead. The two half-Vietnamese children had been drawn away from their game of hopscotch. The boy kept chalk in his pocket and as soon as they arrived he would go to the sidewalk and draw the boxes, his talisman of order. Whenever a line started to fade he would stop the game and fill it in again. Jade watched the chalk get smaller, wondering when, if ever, he would run out, and what would happen then? He and his sister held one sticky donut each. Rider wrapped his arms around their father's leg and said "I want one too!" Jade's cheeks burned and she looked away. "Get off me," the man said. He took back the donut he had given to his son, tore it, and gave Rider the smaller half.

Dolores used to pet Jade like she was an animal. She would comb the tangles out of her hair and tie it back with ribbon. She would scrub her body with a brush like she was a cabbage, until her skin turned bright red. When she spoke to Jade she would always be looking somewhere else, as if Jade wasn't really there.

Little Tony had left shoes in his closet that had never been worn. Unopened jigsaw puzzles and a new baseball glove. A model fighter plane hung above his bed and Jade found the glue in a box on his dresser. Sometimes she would lie on the bed and look at the plane or the map of Africa on the wall. She would listen to the dead boy's parents speak to each other in Italian and cry in the next room.

She would open the tube of glue and put it in a small paper bag, put her nose and mouth into the bag, close her eyes and breathe in. She would begin to imagine the front door of her old house swinging open, her father standing in the threshold, suitcase at his side, saying "Here I am, I was only kidding!" Jade would list all the terrible things that had happened, and dispatch her father—avenging angel—to punish the wicked.

Tony knew a lot about World War II. He had a special shelf with maps and books. Jade liked the words Nagasaki and Mussolini. She heard him talk about the bombing of Dresden. Dolores had a cabinet of dishes and delicate figurines "All from Dresden." Jade imagined the bombing as the sound of a million cups and saucers crashing to the floor. Soldiers marching through the streets, crunching crockery into chalk under gigantic boots, the townspeople behind them desperately trying to fit the pieces back together, like Dolores' teacups that had been broken and glued, and broken and glued again.

Jade has a recurring dream. She is in the sea floating on her back, riding the surface on a raft of salt. The water is calm and metallic. She glimpses her father walking away up the beach, and her mouth begins to harden. She tries to call to him but she can't. A strange woman who takes his hand joins her father. Children appear and skip alongside as if they belong. Jade tries to call, her father looks towards her over his shoulder. This is the moment Jade always wakes up, with a lump in her throat that tastes like rust.

Jade once asked her father how to tell time. "You know how the earth rotates on its axis?" he said. Jade shook her head. "Well, the earth is actually spinning under your feet. It's spinning so fast you can't feel it. Time is like that." He pointed to the clock he kept on his night stand. "The hands of that clock are moving so fast you can't see them." Jade stared at the clock for a long time. She lay on the floor and tried to feel the rotation of the earth. Time passed, but she didn't see it. Her father came back after a while surprised to find she hadn't moved. He put the clock in the nightstand drawer, laughed, bent down to Jade and said, "And time stands still."

He was always playing tricks, and Jade was always falling for them.

The first photograph in Jade's book of keepsakes is of a woman standing in the middle of a dirt road. She is surrounded by tanks and people running in confusion. The woman is still and looks directly into Jade's eyes. Above the photograph is a word in bold type Jade thinks is the woman's name. She stares into the woman's eyes until she hears a sound like a snowy avalanche.

She falls into the woman's eyes, and stays there until her thoughts dissolve into space, and space to light. She repeats the woman's name over and over like an incantation: Kampuchea. Kampuchea. In the woman's eyes is a quiet place in which everything is recognized, everything acknowledged.

Jade holds the black shape in her hand and thinks the word *obsidian*, but it's only broken glass. Igneous. Of the fire. She remembers because she remembers the word ignite. Did Indians make arrowheads or did they grow that way? There are things Jade wants to know. Does moonstone come from the moon? Would she recognize it right away if she found one? Bone china really came from bones, skeletons crushed to a fine powder and fashioned into soup tureens and finger bowls translucent as skin.

The two half-Vietnamese children were called Lisa and Jeff. They were born in California, but by the way people stared at them—especially when they were with their Dad—eyes glazed with tenderness, guilty smiles—Jade could tell people thought they were real orphans.

Jade watched her mother's husband as he gently wiped milk from his daughter's upper lip. Her small face was upturned and her black eyes were trusting as a puppy's. He dusted crumbs from her skirt and Jade held her breath, but his hand didn't wander, and made no demands.

Rider lay with his back on the sidewalk, his face now powdered with sugar, arms splayed, outlined in chalk, in the cruciform shape of the hopscotch boxes, like a snow angel out of season. A small sticky Christ, saying "Look at me, I fit, I perfectly fit!"

The night of the blue hole Jade woke to a patchwork of sound. Shovel hitting earth, dirt being tossed and ice clinking in a highball glass. From her sister's room Bob Dylan's voice:

"All the tired horses in the sun/ How'm I s'posed to get any riding done?"

Outside the window her mother was digging a hole on the lawn, four feet deep and just as wide, methodically separating rock from dirt, dirt from grass, creating piles of each on the lawn. By the time the sun came up it looked as though a small meteor had struck, and her mother's eyes were black holes.

She was wearing a negligee and man-sized gray work gloves. Her blond hair was tied back with a silk scarf, and the black roots were so pronounced it reminded Jade of an opposite highway; a white road with a black dividing line down the center.

Someone had told her mother about a decorative pond that used to be there and in the middle of the night, fueled by scotch and Benzedrine, she'd attempted to unearth it. She hosed down the concrete, which still held flecks of paint. She spent the following day digging, buying more paint and brushes, laughing and explaining her project to curious neighbors, even enlisting kids to help scrub the concrete basin until not a speck of dirt remained. Jade helped her mother paint the hole sky blue and while it was drying, they went to the fish store together where Jade's mother let her choose several varieties of tropical fish, as many as she liked, and bought her a book that told about them.

When they got home, her mother, finally exhausted, retreated to her room. Jade lined up the bags of fish on the wooden floor of the living room. She lay on her belly and pressed her nose to each, imagining the homelands of these equatorial travelers. They had come far, she was certain.

She opened the book that would identify them. She recognized the Angel Fish and Goldfish. She read that some fish grew to the size of their environment. She wondered if that would be true of these, if they were suspended in this small space, only waiting to be released into a place where they could grow to the size of sea lions. She imagined how the pond would look when it was finished; with the blue walls it might look like a piece of the sky was captured in reverse. The water would be crystal clear so the fish would be like a reflection of birds, exotic jungle birds. There would be a wall of stones that warm water would continually cascade down, pooling into sea grass and water lilies. Seed pods would fall from the tree and land in the water like sad canoes without a destination. The fish would gaze toward the surface shadows. At night in the dark water their tiny filaments of light would shine like candle flames. They would glide and shimmer, and orbit each other in watery silence.

In the middle of that night Jade's mother filled the pond from the garden hose, and poured in all the fish. The next morning Jade found them dead, suspended under a thin layer of unseasonable frost that had gathered on the surface. Some had taken on the gray color of concrete. Some were transparent.

Jade's older brother Ben came out of the house that morning and walked toward Jade lying on the grass. Her nose was level with the edge of the pond. It smelled like the sidewalk after it rains. Jade felt nervous when Ben was around, because he wasn't afraid of anything. Ben would do anything on a dare, no matter how crazy, and he never cared what people thought.

When he saw the tiny corpses he shot Jade a look of accusation.

"She did it." Jade said.

Ben began to scream. He picked up rocks from the pile and began hurling them at the front door. He was screaming "Goddamn you! Goddamn you!" Pelting the door, and then their mother's car, screaming so loudly Jade thought his throat would rip apart.

Their mother ran outside yelling "What the hell is the matter with you?"

Ben was crying hard and whimpering. He covered his face with his arm and collapsed on the lawn. Jade pointed to the blue hole. Her mother clutched her bathrobe to her chest and said "What the hell is the matter with you? They're *fish* for Christsake!"

Ghosts were real. Tony and Dolores kept a photograph of little Tony on their mantle piece. The image seemed fixed until you saw it in natural light. Every morning Dolores would pull open the drapes, and the sun would shine on it, fading the image a little. Jade thought one day all that would be left would be the red stripe on the T-shirt he wore, like the grin on the Cheshire cat.

Jade remembered a commercial that she and Ben used to laugh at.

It was an anti-drug ad with a man in black hat and cape, moving Snidely Whiplash-like through a playground, offering drugs to children on swings. There was a boy who followed him around, attempting to thwart his efforts. Ben and Jade both reveled in hating that boy, he was a snotty, know it all kid, with a sing-song voice, asking

"Isn't it true that sniffing glue can damage your kidneys and liver?"

The man flicked his cape, looked into the camera and said

"Sure kid, why do you think they call it *dope?*"

Now Jade hates that boy alone, with a true and deeper burning kind of hate.

Only when she imagines his face, she sees Little Tony's face from the photograph, or Ben's face. She can't remember all the time, whose features are whose.

When, after a time, she could no longer conjure the image of her father in the doorway, she would lay curled in a ball under the covers on Little Tony's bed inhaling the last fumes from the hardening tube of glue. If she rocked a certain way the box springs would make a red sound that could have been his voice or hers—A rusty squeaking of something lost that begins to find itself again, has to account for itself after a long time.

Jade dreamt about salt. White crystals that sifted hourglass like into ant hills, and accumulated into piles and mounds. Salt that originated in her veins and erupted from parts of her body, from fingertips and belly button. White hills that grew mountainous and held her dune-like, in recline.

Once Jade lay in the dumpster on bundles of paper and opened a safety pin she found on the street. She scratched without conscious intent the letter K into the flesh on the back of her hand. Unsatisfied with the pink line that rose up, she pricked and pierced holes like a pointillist to see the tiny circles of blood emerge and congeal into a ceremony of letters.

She licked her hand. Red tasted cunning and brave.

Jade dreamt about white ridges of acrid, glistening salt.

There was a sound that would rise up in the back of her head, a white-noise kind of sound, like the low static from a radio between stations. Jade would lie and wait for that sound. She would poke holes in the bottom of the tube with a pin and gently squeeze. Cupping her hands around the opening, she would put her face to her hands, inhale the fumes and hold her breath until she felt she was drowning in air. The sound would rise up like a bubble and fill the back of her head, leaving no room for thoughts. This was the simplest kind of sorcery, so easy to make things appear or disappear.

There were things Jade could not recall. Like why when she thought of oranges, did she automatically think of blood? What happened to the blue sweater that she always used to wear?

Jade would bite down on the flesh between her index finger and thumb. She bit the tender webbing until it throbbed, and again until it lost feeling. It was the letting go, when she would release her grip, and her hand ached and pounded like her heart lived in it, it was the letting go she was after.

Jade hadn't meant to eat the glossy picture of St. Francis they gave to her at Tony and Dolores' church. It was the single tear drawn onto his cheek, his eyes that were like liquid, his long brown robes, the way his palms outstretched and beckoned, and all the surrounding green. She licked that tear that would never fall and felt butterflies in her stomach like eyelash against cheek. She felt shiny inside her chest when she licked the sad part of his eye. She licked his other eye, its cool and futile blue. She licked until his hands and face disappeared into pulp, she licked the cinnamon-stick color of his gown. She licked and chewed and swallowed what dissolved on her tongue, and what was left of the glossy picture of St. Francis, she stuck to the headboard of the dead boy's bed, leaving what looked like a bas-relief map of a lunar landscape in miniature.

Jade dreamt that she was floating, buoyant, held up as if hands were beneath the surface, and suddenly she was pulled down, into currents that were hot and then cold, and there was nothing she could grab onto to help her reach air. Jade dreamt until she woke to the ammonia smell of shame, her eyes crusted shut, her thin cotton pajama bottoms soaked through and clinging to her skin.

Jade used to dream bodies of water and feel rested when she woke. Now she woke with a thirst she stubbornly refused to quench. Jade would swallow hard and repeatedly, swallow tears, and swallow words, She would practice hate and silence so hard she would boil the water left under her skin. Swallow. Watch it evaporate. Swallow.

Jade peeled off her pajamas and put them in her suitcase in the closet. She removed the sheets from the bed and left them in a heap by the door. She sat cross-legged on the floor staring at them wishing they would simply combust. Ignite. Be consumed by flame. Sheets. Bed. House.

Jade wondered, would she, if ever lost in a wood, be able to identify flint? And if she could, would she be able to strike stone against stone to make fire? If she could she would make a bonfire. A hungry, beautiful bonfire that would send smoke signals to St. Francis as unmistakable as skywriting.

Her mother had a party that lasted three days. Lots of people came and went, and her mother stayed drunk but she seemed happy. She met her new husband on the second day. He wore a white rumpled suit and brought roses that looked stolen, somehow. On the third day he took everybody that was still there to Las Vegas. The man and her mother laughed throughout the ceremony. Jade wore the dress Dolores had given her, but it no longer fit.

The man got them all separate suites at the Landmark Hotel. He pulled Jade onto his lap and said "You don't have to call me Dad" and insisted she drink a glass of champagne. No one had money to pay the bill, so a truck driver the man knew in Bakersfield had to pick them up.

Jade screamed for him to pull over in the desert because she was sick from the stifling heat. She threw up on the shoulder of the road while they all stood and watched. The road was hot with the smell of tar. Her hair was too long to hold back, and her dress too short to pull down. She wanted to lay down on the asphalt and melt into it like a chocolate bar.

That morning of the dead fish, Ben took the telephone book and put it on the drivers seat of their mother's car so he could see out the windshield. He was thirteen but small for his age. Jade figured smoking had stunted his growth. He started up the engine and gunned it for a minute like he wanted someone to try and stop him, but nobody did. He took off down the street with the radio blaring, giving the finger to anyone who happened to be looking his way. Her mother got the car back a few days later, but Jade has only seen Ben once since then.

Tony owned a Carwash. He gave Jade a pair of Little Tony's overalls and she would go with him some days. She would sit in the back seats of Buicks and Oldsmobiles, Lincolns, Cadillacs and Camaros, as they were slowly pulled along on a track, the outsides being scrubbed clean, the insides reeking of stale cigarettes and new leather, after-shave and perfume, alcohol, vomit and sex. All day sweat would bead up on the windows and the back of her knees. Her chest would tighten under the spiraling pressure of the brushes, until the closeness made her rapturous and dizzy.

Sometimes she took things: sticks of gum, fallen coins, Saint Christopher medals, and kept them hidden in the pockets of the dead boy's pants as offerings, in case he somehow knew she didn't love his mother and father.

In case the dead boy knew and it made him mad. She kept some things for herself.

Jade snapped the Jesus from the crucifix that hung from the rear view mirror in Tony's car. The cross was metal and it left a green outline where Jesus had been. The body was a waxy cream colored plastic. It tasted like air freshener and fit neatly in one side of her mouth like the lollipops they gave her at the doctor's office. Independent of the cross Jesus looked like he was diving.

Last week Jade had seen her brother Ben leaning against a tree across the street from the house, attempting to be conspicuously invisible. He motioned her over. "I hear she got married." Jade nodded. "You think he'll buy me a motorcycle?" "Doubt it." "What's his name?" "Dick." Ben crushed his cigarette into the tree trunk and flicked the butt into the street. "Perfect." He raised his eyebrows, grinned at Jade and walked away.

Dick took his suitcase and his two children and piled them into a yellow cab. Lisa and Jeff pressed their noses to the window and giggled nervously as Rider licked the glass, meowing like a kitten. Dick picked him up by one arm and unceremoniously dropped him on the lawn. Rider hissed and tried to scratch him. "See you round" the man said to no one in particular. "Like a donut," Rider whispered and caught Jades eye conspiratorially. He smiled at Jade and she smiled back. 'See you round like a donut.' Marty used to say that.

Marty always knew what to say. They would go to the Wednesday night vegetarian feast at Hare Krishna Temples, and free pot-luck nights at churches sometimes, posing as potential converts. They would eat fast, Jade and Rider would fill their pockets with whatever food was solid while Marty listened to the Hell stories, and the God stories, and the Why-he-should-be-Saved. He would listen attentively with a serious look on his face, and when they thought they had him he would nod, and say "Yes! I *see*! But the thing of it is, I could give a rat's ass."

Tony and Dolores ate meat. They sat at a round table with a cloth made of tea colored lace. Jade sat in Little Tony's chair. It had a blue vinyl cushion on the seat that stuck to her thighs. Dolores served Jade's dinner on a plastic plate like she was a baby. She dished her out string beans from the platter that held the meat; an unidentifiable hunk of flesh, charred around the edges, bleeding in the middle. Jade stared at it. "Eat." Tony said.

The string beans were sitting in a pink stream of blood. "She cooks for you, you eat." Jade just sat there. Dolores said "This is Little Tony's favorite," "So," Jade said under her breath. "So? So eat." Tony said. He put down his knife and fork and stared at Jade who sat there, unmoving. The string beans looked like blades of grass in a killing field. "You will eat." said Tony. "It's poison." said Jade. Dolores started to cry and ran into the kitchen. Jade could feel Tony looking at her for a long time. Finally, he pushed his chair away from the table and quietly left the room.

At the Carwash the sunlight felt like switchblades when Jade came out the other side. She would keep her eyes open for as long as she could stand it. At the end of the day Tony would take a handkerchief from the pocket of his stained mechanic's coveralls. Snow white linen, folded and pressed into a square, its corners geometric and precise. He would tilt Jade's face toward his and gently wipe away the perspiration that collected on her forehead and in the hollow above her lips. With his large callused fingers he would trace the furrows on her brow until all was smooth again. "Like new." He would drape the handkerchief over her face like a veil, or across her eyes like a blindfold.

Jade would hold the linen to her face, breathing in its fatherly fragrance of rosewater and steam. Sometimes Tony would reach up and pull a quarter out of thin air. He'd buy her an Orange Crush and open the bottle with his pocketknife. Jade would drink it slowly, imagining the liquid as cold light moving through her. Jade would climb into the back seat of Tony's used gray Plymouth. She would sit on the smooth side, never in the indentation that still remembered the weight of a body. The engine would groan, pulling the weight of itself into a glide, like an old whale breaching the surface. Jade would push herself back and burrow in, her sneakers leaving a temporary imprint on the front seat. Tony would adjust the rear-view where the vacant crucifix dangled and swayed back and forth like a metronome, and sometimes their eyes would meet by accident.

When Tony delivered Jade back to her mothers house she refused to get out of the car. He talked with her mother on the porch for a long time. Jade opened the window a crack and heard him say "Forgive my broken English." Her mother said "Not at all," in a voice that tried to sound superior. Jade knew what Tony meant, but her mother didn't. English can be broken if it isn't strong. Grief breaks it. Jade got out of the car and walked past Tony like he wasn't really there.

Thirty-six days ago, Jade and Marty performed a soap ceremony. They dumped a box of laundry detergent in the William Mulholland Memorial Fountain, and watched from a bus stop in the distance, the suds blanket the street.

They shared a bottle of Peppermint Schnapps and Jade had her first hit off a cigarette. She liked the heat of it. Seeing the exhaled smoke was like proof she was alive.

"Why don't you burn your draft card?"
"Why don't you burn your training-bra?"

Jade gave herself tests of endurance. How long could she walk in the heat without water? How long could she go without food? Marty seemed to think survival meant having everything at your finger tips; a safe place to sleep, food to eat, stuff to get high on and people who like you. Jade knew it was really about how long you could endure without them.

There were things that looked exactly like what they were called: Amethyst. Emerald. And anomalies occurred that were beautiful; crystal could grow from a matrix of slate, ruby on granite. There were people in the world that could recreate entire civilizations from the fragments of things.

Jade wondered what they would glean from things like hearing your name called when no one is there. The empty space inside shoes.

Things you glimpse out of the corner of your eye that disappear when you point to them. Or the buzz that removes the silence from the air after someone leaves the room for good.

| Wanda Coleman | *Black Leather* |

THE ALARM HADN'T SOUNDED, nevertheless she woke with what she thought was the sound of a madness droning inside her head. She never touched alcohol, yet red and white lights flashed like internal fireworks or a bank of bulbs going off. A nightmare? She seldom had them. She seldom dreamed. In seconds, the phenomenon cleared, and she was peering into the familiar and comforting darkness that defined her apartment bedroom.

She was reluctant to turn on the light, because she needed more sleep. The glowing face of the clock read three in the morning. By that glow, she groped for the night table, squinting to make out the small plastic bottle with child-safe cap, the thought streaking through her cortices that she had no child.

She felt for the glass of water in its familiar place, anchored in the palm of her left hand, and felt to see if the bottle had fallen into the unit's half-opened drawer. Relieved, she squeezed its cylindrical body and flicked the cap-always-kept-loosened to the floor, pinched out one of the caplets, laid it to her tongue and washed it down with gulps from the water glass. Despite the liquid, her mouth seemed dry.

Now she was awake and sleepless. The alarm was set to go off in three hours. Without full rest how would she make the day ahead? It was cold, yet the room seemed airless. She got up and looked out her bedroom window. It faced the alley two stories below—a half-street paved in asphalt that divided the long blocks in this section of the urban ghetto; call it Ghost town, call it South Central, call it Hades.

She was startled as a young man sporting a fancy studded black leather jacket ran into her line of vision. He was headed west along the alley, glancing over his shoulders. He gleamed with sweat, was of medium build, brown-skinned with teeth that flashed whitely in the muted light from street lamps a half block away.

Something, some sense of something, caused her to hold her breath.

There was a swash of extreme brightness. A customized cruiser turned into the alley. Blackened by the shadows, it crouched low and crawled catlike for quarry. She felt a rush of terror as if she were the object of its hunt. Her hands went to the window, framing her face. She watched, frozen to the glass, palms to the pane, as the sedan's doors opened and four bulky young men, all variations on the theme of brown, leapt out and surrounded the young man on foot. There was music, the repeated boom-boom-boom of the latest sound. The sedan's taillights gleamed hot red. The men moved against the rhythm into the headlights. All but one wore a leather jacket. There was one in shirtsleeves. He reached out at the runner, cupped his hand and made a beckoning gesture that said, "Give it up."

She witnessed the movement of lips. Hard words and curses were exchanged. Did she imagine spittle flying? Or was it the effect of moonbeams dancing on blades? There was the distinct nod of heads, the brandishing of switchblades as the dangerous dance continued.

She tried not to hear the music. She tried not to think of movie scenes. This was a nightmare. What could hold her to reality? What could convince her that she was not dreaming? She pinched herself. Nothing happened.

They must be gangsters, she thought. They're all gangsters or posturing like gangsters.

The one in shirtsleeves skipped forward, knife stabbing the air with threats. Backed against a mesh wire fence, the runner held up palms in surrender, hand shaking side-to-side as if promising not to tell. Then he slipped out of the jacket, grasped the collar, raised one arm and held it out. He shivered in a turquoise T-shirt, upper arms fresh with newly developed biceps. The monster in the shirtsleeves snatched it away, donned it for a perfect fit then did a pirouette to the amusement of his cohorts. She imagined their laughter.

Just then, the runner attempted to escape by darting through them. They closed ranks, grabbed him and pushed him back. The fence shook as he bounced into the mesh. There was the distinct jerk of arms clad in black leather as they rushed him. When the quartet stood back, he runner dropped to his knees, clasping his side. The four assailants leapt back into the sedan. The runner rose to his feet again, staggered and weaved, holding his side.

The engine's roar was followed by the squeal of tires, then silence.

She was frozen to the pane, eyes on the runner. He seemed like some Japanese-made wind-up gismo winding down, or puppet with broken strings. What should she do? Surely she wasn't the only one who'd witnessed the commotion?

A lifetime ebbed.

The lights on back porches came on. She heard muted distant voices as awakened residents stirred. They came out in robes, or half-dressed, one man armed with a baseball bat, another carrying a shotgun. They made their ways across backyards, from backdoors opening onto the alley, the night air carrying the scent of anger at having greatly needed sleep disturbed.

Someone must have made calls she couldn't make because two police prowl cars and an ambulance inched through the onlookers blocking the alley.

She fought the impulse to throw on her robe and mules and run out to them. What would she say? That she saw it all. No, no license plate number, no description of the perpetrators. They were close, but not close enough. Good-looking young men who acted like animals.

How could she explain her terror as she watched, frozen to her bedroom window, without a cry of help to neighbors? What would she say to them? What would she see in their unsympathetic eyes? I took my medication. It does something to me. It removes me. That's why I didn't cry for help or go downstairs. That's why my hands are cold and tremble. That's why my eyes are still staring at that wounded soul as he collapsed in the alley. I can't see him now, because you're all standing in the way. But I know that he's there, and that if he isn't dead, he's dying.

It is a dry winter's morning typical of the southwest, dark and chilly. School started last week, she knew. The young man probably received that jacket for Christmas, a gift from someone close. His mother or father. In this part of town, only a parent could afford to sacrifice money for such an expensive jacket. What tragic irony in that kind of giving—unwittingly supplying some unknown fiend with the motive for killing one's child. It could have been anything, as it often is in neighborhoods like this. It could have been a bike or motorcycle, a wristwatch, a name bracelet. Anything that smacked of having more than others, however slightly more. To show any sign of prosperity when among the viciously poor was to invite trouble.

She had never given an expensive gift to anyone, nor bought one for herself. That kind of money had eluded her. Yet, she could imagine a mother or a father's pride. They had worked for their money, why not spend it on a daughter or son. She could see herself enjoying the thrill of shopping for and spotting the jacket; checking labels for designer, fit and price, taking it to checkout. She could see herself carrying it home, gift-wrapping the box with that giddiness that comes from anticipating the response the gift will bring-the delight in a youngster's eyes on the eve of manhood.

Not knowing then that it would lead to his manhood's being taken.

It was full moon at twilight, not long before sunup.

The crowd parted unexpectedly and she could see the body.

He lay facing the sky, soaked in blood. The turquoise T-shirt was virtually violet. The stiff fingers of his left hand were frozen upward, as if reaching out for help. He had not died at once, she realized. He had bled.

Black Leather

The crowd had quickly thinned to one patrol car, two officers talking to witnesses. Two blonde men in white uniforms and long white coats talk as they pull a gurney from the back of the white coroner's van. She cannot hear them, but imagines their clipped conversation—hears each word cloaked in a professional indifference. They've seen every form of cruelty and violence imaginable. This is of the more common, tamer variety. Another dream ended prematurely, another victim of the greedy night.

"They killed that po' boy back the alley, jes last night," someone will inform her the minute she steps out of doors for work. Their words will be flat, underscored by a weary tension. No one 'round here is ever stunned by anything that happens. The thought makes her tremble. What if I took an accidental overdose? They'd find me in here, cold. I'd be hauled off with an equal indifference. Without a single soul to discover my absence, even for the sake of mourning. They would probably call it a suicide, not knowing that some souls devoid of love and companionship nevertheless cling tenaciously to life, will give it up only by chance or act of God.

But that boy's death this morning was murder.

She imagines his face, magnifies it in her mind and erases the shadows. She gives him a full, sensual face, not quite handsome, but warm and open with thick, long lashes and full pugnacious lips. She gives him smooth skin. She places the silken stubble of an emerging beard across his upper lip and along his jaw. His uncombed hair is fine and curly with nappy patches hinting of mixed blood. He is not a smiler. His eyes are round and broody and when he looks at someone, they are immediately struck by their serious clarity. He has, she sees, a sensitive nature. Too sensitive to survive this impoverished neighborhood.

She cannot know him, yet she knows him. In another time and place she might have been an aunt, the high school English teacher, a lover. She might have said the important thing in the right way—the thing that might have kept him from going out that night, dressed for trouble in that black leather jacket; the thing that would have made him stay home with his parents, or spend the night with a friend. She might have given him a gift of money, enough to begin his education at a reputable university. She might have tempted him to not go out, to stay home, in bed, in her arms.

She had never been any of those things to a man. At least, not in a way that mattered enough to last any length of time. Inexplicably, the death of the teenager made her miss those lost opportunities. Was it too late? The mirror said so. The ringless hands that trembled said so. The mindless job of long hours among disinterested coworkers said so. When did she step into the spinster's clamshell? When did it snap shut?

Her withdrawal had been gradual. Somewhere, in the course of things, she had started going to doctors, asking for pills—to sleep, to get rid of anxiety, of weight, to steady her hands, to kill an illusive pain. The medicine cabinet had become a pharmacy.

What could she take to make her forget the slaying?

It began replaying itself.

She imagined what might have happened if she had run out into the streets screaming, "Let him alone, you beasts and bastards, let him alone!"

If she had grabbed up something to take with her, a frying pan like her grandmother used to wield at her grandfather; the broom, a butcher's knife. They would have probably laughed at her, waved their arms, gotten back into the sedan and driven off. The young man in the black leather jacket would still be alive. He would stare at her and not even offer thanks. No more than he would thank his mother for having been born. He would shrug and turn away and walk into the night. His parents would be grateful to hear the door slam announcing his safe return. The streets had spared their child. They'd have him one more day. His girlfriend would call, relieved when he answered the phone. He'd take her admonishment with amused silence, then tell her he'd be by after school. If his luck held, he'd graduate, go on to college, and then make something of himself—that black leather jacket retired to the rear of the closet, a reminder of the days when. . . .

But suppose they did not laugh. Suppose they were armed with heavy metal-guns. Suppose they called her nasty names and repaid her samaritan effort with bullets? She imagined herself laying out there, yards from that youthful stranger in the bloody T-shirt. She did not know him, she reminded herself. She was assuming these things about him, his innocence. Perhaps he had stolen the jacket. If so, death was still too strong a punishment for the crime. She dismissed the notion. She had lived long enough to know how guilt and cupidity were expressed in people's bones. That young man hadn't a whiff of either about himself. It was in how he held out the jacket, how that instant of surrender contained defiance and dignity—an acknowledgment of Fate?

She pulled one palm from the pane as if it were held there by suction. She looked at it. A purplish-brown line snaked in a diagonal across the pinkness, from just below the first finger to the tip end of the lower quadrant. A fortuneteller had once told her she had an exceptionally long lifeline.

She took a deep breath, left the window and went to her closet. She knew that they were busy below. They were placing the young man in a body bag and lifting him onto the gurney. She knew that they had removed his wallet and found his identification card. She knew that someone was in the process of contacting his parents. She knew that his girlfriend was sitting alone in front of the television set, unable to sleep, half-listening to the early news broadcast, angry and hurt that he hadn't kept his promise to spend the night.

He couldn't have been more than seventeen—old enough to call his own ill-thought-out shots, yet too young for full independence.

With each movement of her arm she saw the corresponding movement of his arm as he held out that jacket. One hand went to her throat. She was suffocating on the cold. Hastily she clutched each hanger, taking a blouse, suit jacket, skirt. She laid them carefully across the sagging single bed. The old dresser clock revealed time enough to shower, dress and read the morning paper over a bowl of hot cereal and toast. She'd eat slowly. She'd calm herself for the workday ahead.

The window drew her toward it. She looked out once more. It was sunrise. The sky was a crisp clear cerulean. Pigeons cooed in the eaves. The vehicles, the people—all gone. There was the telltale pool of blood and the broken yellow hexahedron marking the crime scene.

She felt a strange dizziness and leaned against the pane. It began to frost over with her breath. She envisioned all the young men found laying in all the dark alleys the nation round—a spectrum of skin tones and body types. She envisioned the funerals and the memorials, the condolences, the dead flowers—enough flora and cards to reforest a continent. She pushed herself away, spun around with a half-cry.

She steadied herself against the bedpost then rushed for the bathroom. Everything in it was yellow. She was caught in a blitz of cool yellow—the walls, the towels, the basin, the tub, the curtains, the light.

Impatiently, she rifled through the thin metallic medicine cabinet with its four wafer-thin glass shelves. Her eyes scanned label after label as she lifted first one bottle, then another. The tablets and caplets rattled as her hands flew. The vibrations made by her frantic flittings caused the upper of the thin glass shelves to dislodge. It cracked in half and the bottles it had held clattered to the cold tiled floor, peppering her feet with the multicoated contents as loosened lids gave way.

Gasping, she backed from the sink and collapsed on top of the lowered toilet seat. It was suddenly too hot. She perspired.

There was no pill she could find designed to stop the onslaught. This peculiar emotion was beyond any one thing she could name—grief, fear, regret? Whatever it was, it cloaked her with an unsettling snugness—not unlike tight black leather.

Her heart pounded oddly against her ribs. It was, she thought, as though something had entered her, and she was irrevocably changed—as though his life had somehow bled into hers.

And then she wept.

Melissa R. Lion	*The Second*

I AM THE SECOND WIFE, but he has others. The original wife, the first, is a woman I worked with. The third and fourth were wives of Joe's clients. They are sisters. And now there is the fifth. She is fourteen and her family belongs to our church. She and my husband were married this evening, at sunset, in a ceremony under God. We weren't allowed to attend. He said it would make her uncomfortable, that we should pray for them while we were home. We did not. The third and fourth curled each other's hair. The first sat in her room and talked in a low voice on the phone. I rearranged my room to better fit the new wife's things in with mine. And now the new smell, flat and sweet like baby powder, hurts my head.

The fifth and our husband are spending their honeymoon night together in the room next to mine. I hear his low, familiar rumble. She has been silent through the whole thing. She is here to make her parents proud. In the morning I will bundle up the sheet she is on and send it to her parents as proof.

He whispers now. When he speaks out loud he mostly makes up bible verse. He uses the old language and pronounces morals found at the end of fairy tales or embroidered on old ladies' pillows. But in bed, after sex, he speaks in a smooth whisper. He is breathy like a woman. He recites poetry. He has a perfect memory for it. He pauses like a scholar, not at line breaks but at punctuation. Perfect rhythm. He recites it, word by word. In the nights he spends alone, he memorizes poems from the Emily Dickinson and Walt Whitman books under his bed. I wonder if the girl recognizes them from lessons at school, but he picks the obscure poems and I doubt she's ever heard of them.

When he is quiet I tell myself that I need sleep. Tomorrow is important. The lighting people from the national news show will be setting up, and then the next day the perfect blond woman will be in our house interviewing us. Joe has a crush on her. He watches nightly, excited for her personal interest stories. That's what we are now, personal interest.

I wake early and find Joe at the computer. He is studying our stock portfolio. This is part of our income. The wives don't work. When we married Joe we gave him our savings for future investments. He is an accountant. When I met him he worked with a firm, but now he is independent. He manages the family's budget and the church's. He has a handful of wealthy clients who he's been working with for years. We live well, in house that Joe adds onto with each wife. We live east of San Diego. From our kitchen we have a view of a canyon and the avocado trees on top of the foothills and late at night I can hear the coyotes panting in our yard. Four miles down the road is man who runs a national white power group. I grew up in town and I am used to this isolation and the people that need it.

Joe provides for us from our stocks and his accounting. He explains the constant construction and cash always on hand by saying that God blessed him with the power of prediction, an eye for a hot stock. And I believe him, although he won't let us see the books. He continues to generate money and we continue to spend and I live better than I could have ever hoped for fresh out of college and working as a teller at a bank.

"Good morning," I say.

"Good morning," he says and motions for me to come near. He offers me his mouth and I kiss him. In his beard I smell the girl. She is sweet with a hint of musk. I breathe deep, trying to memorize her so I'll be able to tell later if it is her he is with on the nights he is supposed to be alone.

"Big day," I say and he nods, looking at the computer.

"The house looks great, thank you," he says and pats my hand. I want to thank him for noticing. Joe always notices. He can tell which of us did the dishes by the stacks and which of us scoured the tub by the spots missed. He prefers it when I clean the house, but each of us likes to think we do things better or more special than the others.

"You'll take care of her today?" he asks and I have to pause. Joe is asking me to mentor the girl. This is my first time taking care of a new wife. The first wife took care of the others and me. The extent of her training was showing us the trash and recycling schedule inside the broom closet and pointing to her bedroom door saying that she cleaned it herself and that we weren't allowed in.

"I'll take care of her," I say and I have visions of showing her to always clean her hair from the drain, and to place the groceries in the refrigerator with all the labels facing out. I get excited because I see the house coming together, and my work diminishing. I will have someone else help me take care of the others and Joe.

I make breakfast, taking care to make extra for the girl. I haven't met her yet. At church she stayed with the children at the Sunday school and never attended the service. I try to imagine her. I picture her mousy and hunched over. Maybe her breasts are too large and she's embarrassed. I see her biting her nails and pushing up her glasses. She is homely and I promise that I'll show her how to use make-up to accentuate her benefits and hide her flaws. She'll be eternally grateful.

I bring eggs and sausage and toast into the dining room and I want to drop the plates when I see her. Her skin is so white it's blue like skim milk and she glows. She makes the others look dim and unscrubbed. I see her pink scalp through a part in her white blond hair. Her eyes are a murky blue rimmed in red. She is smooth like the inside of a shell. I am shocked by how young fourteen is. She doesn't look at me, or down at her plate, but across my shoulder at the wall. She gnaws on her lip and squints, mean, then moves her lips like she's making plans.

I sit and try to act normal. She is thin, near the breaking point and I want to shovel more and more scrambled eggs onto her plate but Joe asks us to bow our heads for the prayer but I don't want to take my eyes off of her. I want belief to register. The prayer begins and everyone's heads are bowed but she continues to mouth at the wall.

Joe says a prayer about plentitude and the embarrassment of riches, "but I'd rather be rich and embarrassed than poor and proud," he says and I smile at my food so no one can see. I used to laugh at Joe's wisdoms because I thought they were jokes.

In our courtship he often asked me to pray with him and always wrapped up with a moral. After entering a drawing to win a washer and dryer at the supermarket, Joe bowed his head, "thou shalt not leave the house in dirty underwear," he said, "Amen." I howled and Joe gave me a smile. He laughed timid at first then laughing so hard he didn't make a sound. But I am the only one that laughs at Joe's prayers. The others don't even crack a smile, but when Joe and I are alone, when we're falling asleep I recount every comment that made me smile. He laughs with me, in bed, quiet, so the others don't hear. For him I remember them all.

The sisters act as if no one new is at the table. They continue to whine about life, shoes, magazine subscriptions and the first wife keeps her head down. She sits next to the girl and they contrast each other. The girl is white, white and the first wife is dark. She is not naturally so, she is dirty. Her black hair hangs limp around her shoulders and her skin is a mottled gray from not washing.

The girl chews slowly. I'd like to think she's savoring every bite, but when I look at her plate it is still as full as it was when I served her.

"Joe, I think we need to make more food for the meals," the fourth wife, says, "I mean the new one eats like a pig." And then she laughs in loud guffaws and I see the silver filling in her molars. There is mushy bread stuck to them. The girl looks up at the fourth wife with her eyebrow arched. The girl looks to Joe. He smiles at her and shrugs. He doesn't get involved in our fights, but insists we work it out ourselves. She looks back to the fourth who has stopped laughing and the girl narrows her red eyelids, squints. She moves her lips quickly, uttering something no one can hear.

"Kidding," the fourth says with a hidden genuflection under the table.

"I'm all done," I say and take away my plate. I take Joe's too and he thanks me, then leaves. The girl gets up and the sisters stay and pick at their plates. From the kitchen I hear them whispering. I get close to the kitchen door. I can't hear their words, but I hear their tone, sharp and hissing. I come out and act like I'm clearing more plates. They stop talking and I accidentally drop eggs onto the fourth's lap.

"She's just a girl," I say and leave them to clean up the mess.

Joe's room is hot and stuffy when I walk in. Sun is glaring through the sliding glass door and bouncing off the mirrored closets. I squint my eyes. I open the window and wave my hands in front of it hoping that some of her too sweet baby powder smell will disappear. The room is a mess, sheets off the bed and tubes and jars with their caps off. I pull up the fitted sheet and her blood in the middle reminds me of a Rorschach test. I feel generous and say butterfly, but I look closer. Two jugglers on a high wire tossing flaming bowling pins between them? I laugh then feel badly for the girl. Losing her virginity on a bed slept in by other women. There is nothing romantic about it. She is not Cinderella. We were grown women when Joe married us. We had choices. When we gave our approval for this marriage, he'd left out her age. He said someone new to the church. And we went along.

It was her parents who gave it away. After everything was agreed to her parents approached us at church. They were new to our chapter, from out of town. The father and his two wives introduced themselves and explained how proud they were that their daughter would marry into such a robust family. They explained that they had to pick her up at the day camp.

"How old is she?" the fourth asked.

"She is fourteen," her father said.

She gasped. Number three shook her head and the first walked to the car.

"She's mature," Joe said.

"Aren't they all," I said because I watched television—I saw how girls were getting taller, having periods sooner and because for the first time I saw Joe look ashamed.

I fold the sheet into squares and press it on the floor to make it smaller. I push it into an old tennis shoe box that still smells like rubber. Her parents have sent along instructions with her doctor's phone number and her allergies and a mailing label for the sheet. For a moment I think I should leave a note, but what to say?

Here is your daughter's blood. Life is lovely, wish you were here.

Instead, I write nothing. I wrap up the package in brown paper and stick on the mailing label. It has bunnies and tulips on it and a man's block letters. I leave the package next to our mailbox, COD.

The lighting people rearrange our living room. They remove shadow boxes from the walls and use extra care when moving the ceramic bunnies and wide-eyed porcelain children that the first wife used to collect. It has been years since she's added to her collection and after the lighting people move the figurines, they brush their hands on their legs leaving long, gray streaks of dust and cobwebs on their dungarees. These men are creating something.

They check our lighting in order of marriage.

"First wife's first," one lighting guy says and the others laugh, but she doesn't seem to notice. She sits with her face unmoving. Under the light the dirt on her shines. The oil in her hair creates a halo. They take notes and twist the lights up and down, but each time they are unsatisfied. She continues to have shadows.

"Lift your head up," they say, "swivel around," but she follows their instructions only halfway. Another lighting guy approaches her. He puts his finger under her chin and her eyes turn flat and cold. He pulls his hand away as if he'd been burned. It is the first time I've seen her touched.

We always tiptoe around her and Joe has stopped acknowledging her in front of us. They still sleep together on the appointed night and always near two in the morning I hear panting, her small scream, then silence.

I worked with her for a year before I married Joe. She was the senior-most employee at the bank. She was clean then and the district leader for new accounts. She had her very own desk. On it she had framed photos of faraway places. When she had a potential client in front of her she sat with one leg tucked underneath her and spoke with an accent. Her shiny black hair was piled on top of her head. She was very exotic to me when I was twenty-two.

I'd been only working with her for a few months when the Christmas party came around. My date was a boy from my high school who like me had gone to college, but never left home. His tongue was soft and he would sweat constantly. We talked about high school like it was our glory days. Both of us had been unpopular. Joe stood next to his wife, proud and sure. Late in the night he leaned in to give her a kiss and she turned her head away like someone had called her name. Joe looked down at his feet, cleared his throat and went back to looking proud. She left for the restroom and I introduced myself to Joe. We talked for a long time, and he often glanced around for her. He told me about accounting and the Ivy League school he'd gone to. He was blond and sharp and I touched his hand and flipped my hair. She had taken a taxi home and a few days later he called.

We went on dates and he told me about his church. And at first I was scared, but then he told me about the sisterhood between the women and communal lifestyle.

"Everyone takes care of each other," he said.

The next weekend he took me to a restaurant with leather bound menus and soft opera piped in through invisible speakers. He put his hand on my leg and touched the pockets below my knee.

"I want you to be my second wife," he said. And I laughed because I thought he was joking, but he continued, "I will take care of you, and she will take care of you and I promise to keep you happy. If you become unhappy you can leave."

He dropped me off at home and I thought about his offer. I would be taken care of by not one person, but two. The odds of my future happiness had increased. I would get a husband and a best friend. I pictured her dying my hair and taking me on safari. I called him in the morning before he was awake and said yes. When we married and I moved into their home, I found her collection of *National Geographic* with pages missing. Within weeks she stopped speaking to me.

They light me second and I try to be accommodating. I turn to the right, and to the left. I nod and look up. I smile and make jokes, but they seem unimpressed and they move on quickly without thanks.

I need to get the fifth ready. When I open our door she is up and moving, but then she drops flat on the bed. She pretends to sleep. Her skin is bright pink and her white hair sticks to her face. The radio is on and it is pop music. A boy band singing about love. She tries snoring and shifting.

"You need to get ready," I say and she still pretends to sleep. She is breathing hard to catch her breath, but she keeps her eyes closed.

"Were you dancing?" I ask and she shuts her eyes tighter. "You need to get ready," but she doesn't move. I throw a skirt and blouse on her bed and hunt around in her dresser for undergarments. All I find are white cotton panties with ruffles on the bottom. Little kids' underwear. I look for bras but there are none.

She squirms around on the bed and kicks off the clothes. I don't pick them up.

"Are you having a tantrum?" I ask and she snores loudly.

"In five minutes you will be in the living room," and I leave. I listen at the door and I hear the bedsprings creak and clothes rustle.

In the living room she sits still and I watch her from the entry where she can't see. They do not tilt her or twist her. Under the lights she glows. They keep turning the lights down. They complain about the iris, and the lighting meter. She is too bright; she has no shadows.

She smiles at the youngest lighting guy. He is red in the face and tall with a round middle. She makes a comment that I don't hear and he nods without looking up. She talks again and when he does look she tilts her head and flips her hair. She laughs at nothing and uncrosses her legs and hitches up her skirt to scratch her knee.

She is flirting and I am embarrassed for her. I feel pinpricks on my face, but she has to learn. She continues to talk and he says she's all set. "You're ready for your close up now," he says and turns off the lights. She doesn't get the joke. She lingers and sighs and fingers the cords. I should pull her away, explain to her that married women don't flirt. But she looks so awkward that I want to laugh, to call Joe over. He wouldn't get the joke.

"Movie star time is over," I say and pat her head to embarrass her more. She is sweaty and her hair sticks to my palm. Standing next to her I feel the moisture and heat radiating from her body. She grinds her teeth.

I point her in the direction of our room. "Off with you," I say and pat her bottom like she was a toddler. She walks away and I hear her call me a fucking bitch.

I show the men out and thank them again for their hard work then I find her in our room. Her feet are kicked up and she doesn't pretend to sleep. She is reading a paperback with a picture of a man and woman embracing in the breaking waves on the cover.

"Will you always call me a fucking bitch?" I ask and she kicks her feet.

"I know it's hard to believe, but you're married now. You have a new family and calling me a fucking bitch won't help you get by." She pulls a chunk of white hair through her mouth and flicks at the wet end with her little pink tongue.

"You'll get worms from eating your hair," I say. She twists around on the bed and I glimpse her white ruffled underwear.

"I am married now," she says, "and as a married woman, I'll call you a fucking bitch when I want." I am surprised by the huskiness of her voice. She is just fourteen and the swear words that came out of her mouth sounded natural. But she is small. The bottoms of her bare feet are pink and without calluses. She arches her eyebrow at me and there are no lines on her forehead. She is smooth all over. I am older and wiser.

"Apologize to me," I say and hear my voice, thin and unthreatening. I am no one's mother. I don't even take care of myself. I have no job and pay no bills. I have less responsibility than she does. She is supposed to be my peer.

"Fucking bitch," she says and flips back on her stomach. She picks up her book. My stomach feels light and cold and my fists are clenched. Her bottom wiggles as she kicks her feet. A drop of sweat falls down the side of her face and I want to punch her in the back. I want to call her a fucking bitch and see how she likes it, but how would I explain that to Joe? How can I make him see why I'd hurt a little girl? I back out of the room, and close the door quietly as if my courtesy would impress her, as if all of a sudden she'd realize how good little girls act. But she stays still behind the door.

The house is crowded and I have nowhere to go. The living room is full of equipment and wires. I hear the sisters in the TV room doing aerobics. They call out "yeah," and "feel the burn." Joe is in his bedroom and we are not allowed to knock when the door is closed.

In the backyard I catch the first wife smoking in a corner of the yard where it drops off into the canyon. She acts surprised and pleased to see me as she smashes the cigarette under her shoe. She thinks that by being nice I'll keep her secret, but we've all caught her. It is impossible to keep secrets in this house.

"So, what do you think?" I say and she swats at the air.

"Mosquitoes," she says and hits at her arms, then scratches. She smells like too much perfume and the scent of onions lingers under the flowery smell.

"Have you met her before?" I ask.

"I used to sit for her when her parents went on retreats. She used to spend the weekend."

"Joe said they were new," I say

"They were new to the church, he was a college buddy of Joe's," she says and wraps her arms around herself as if she's cold but it is spring in California.

"He doesn't lie to us," I say sure that she is the one lying.

"He didn't lie," she says and begins to walk away.

"She's young," I call out and she stops and turns. She smiles at me. Her teeth are perfect squares; they are still white despite her lack of care.

"You're jealous," she says and I hope she'll laugh, but she doesn't. She stands still, smiling.

"She's just very young."

"You'll get over it," she says, "trust me." And she walks inside. She is behind the sliding glass door and I see her as she once was, tall and foreign. That was before me. Now she is swollen and limp. For a moment I enjoy the view of the canyon and mountains on the other side, but I forget that it is an expensive view, one that we somehow afford.

It is my turn with Joe tonight. I curl up next to him and pull at his arm hairs. His chest is broad and muscular. He doesn't have the paunch other men his age develop. He makes an effort to work out daily. He says that he has to be four times as attractive as the average man. Five times now.

"Very exciting time, isn't it?" he says and I agree with him.

We've been married for more than six years. He is nearing fifty and I look at his face, checking for signs of age. But he looks the same to me. I know he's changed, he must have. But I guess it came slowly, over time, and I got used to it along the way.

"I love you," I say, because I do. When I was younger, unmarried and looking, I'd lie next to men and ask myself if I would mind them changing. If I'd still be satisfied with my decision when they were gray and their skin had begun to sag. But the truth was I didn't have to look into the future for that. I always felt there was someone better. There was always a man at the supermarket who was thinner and in better shape. Or a man in a class whose lips were fuller and softer.

When we'd gotten beyond phone calls and lunch dates, Joe lay with me in my own bed and asked about my history. Why I couldn't find a man my age or a single man I'd want to settle down with. I explained to him about the men I knew. He promised me then that he'd always keep me satisfied. He said that as my tastes changed, he would change with them. He left for his house and I slept well that night. It seemed to me then that a man who would make such a confident promise would be brave enough to follow through.

"You should wear your blue suit tomorrow. The newswoman will notice your pretty eyes," I say.

"You think I have a chance?" he asks and I pull at his hairs harder. I laugh and he laughs and my head bounces on his chest.

"Pick out everyone's clothes for tomorrow. I don't want to see jeans or collarless shirts," he says. "Please show her how to press her clothes."

"You don't think she knows?" I ask and he pulls away. My head falls off his chest.

"You're not jealous," he says.

"I'm concerned about her age," I say, "I didn't know she was so young."

"You gave your consent."

What I don't say is that it wasn't an informed decision.

"Jealousy is one of the eight deadly sins. Thou shalt not be jealous of your neighbor's house."

I don't laugh because it is sad now. He rolls over, puts his back to me and turns out the light. We don't have sex. He thinks that's punishment.

I wake early and Joe is gone. I put out dresses for everyone. They are our Sunday outfits—floral rompers and white collared shirts. We know the rules for formal events, hair simple, in a barrette and curled at the bottom, no hairspray.

The Second

There is music in the TV room and I peek in. She is watching MTV and dancing. She is panting and wriggling around with her hands on her hips. She flails as the song quickens. Her nightgown sticks to her and her white skin is red from the effort. There are women on the television in sequins and hot pants. They have glossy lips and blow kisses at the screen. She writhes with her eyes shut. She is off tempo and she is ridiculous. I leave her because I can tell myself she is just a teenager.

I dress in our room, grateful for the privacy. I pull on my clothes and brush my hair. I fix my barrette and pull again at my romper. It is blue with pansies. It is too tight in the front and my breasts are pressed against my chest. I pull again and it is still too small.

The newswoman shakes my hand. It is a tough, stunted shake and her rings hurt my fingers. She is compact in her suit, pressed in by a perfect tailor. She smiles and there is no lipstick on her teeth. She sits and her nylons scratch together as she crosses her legs.

"Have a seat," she says and motions to my own chair.

"You are the second wife?" she asks and flips her blue cards. I see "Number two" written across the cards she keeps.

"We're all set," she says to the lighting people. They flip on lights and turn on the cameras. For a second I lose her in the light, and then she comes into focus. I pull at my romper. I have to breathe shallow because it is too tight. I pull again and a stitch pops along my side.

"You don't have to be nervous," she says. "Take a deep breath." She inhales and clicks her acrylic nails together. I can't inhale deeply. I can barely breathe. She opens her eyes wide and smiles.

"Better now, right?" she says.

They tell her the camera is rolling and she thanks them with a smile. She touches my knee; her palm is warm but her fingertips are cold. "You'll be great."

She straightens up and clears her throat. She pulls a coral fingernail through her hair and the style doesn't move. When she speaks her voice is deeper.

"You are the second wife," she says and I tell her yes.

"Don't look into the camera when you speak," she says and I apologize and pull again at my romper.

"You are the second wife, but in a way you are the first."

"No, I'm just the second," I say with my best smile, but I feel my lip sticking to my teeth and I'm sure I look cross-eyed.

"You are the first woman to infringe on the original marriage," she says and I laugh. I tell her I'm not sure what she means and I try to figure out what to say. She repeats herself and this time she speaks slowly. She annunciates—I hear each consonant clearly.

"We are all consenting adults," I say which is my standard line to people who challenge me—my parents, and old friends from before Joe. I pull at my romper and press at the pansies trying to make them straight.

"That's not true either," she says and she leans forward like a real reporter. "There is a new wife who is not an adult. Isn't that right?"

"Her parents have given their consent," I say. The pansies just won't be straight or still, I am shaking and light-headed from not breathing right.

"She's fourteen," she says. "Would you like to have been married at fourteen to a man with other wives?"

My shoulders slouch and I give up on my romper. It is wrinkled and too small. I look at the woman and feel tired. She is very perfect. The lights make her hair glisten and I can smell the cinnamon on her breath from where I sit. When I was fourteen I had Barbies and would have never sworn at an adult. I would not have put my hands on my hips and danced until I sweat.

"She is mature," I say and the newswoman flips through her blue cards. She looks up at me and I try to smile again.

"You're done," she says and nods to the cameraman who shuts off the camera and flips off the lights, but large purple globes linger in my eyes.

"There are other things I can tell you," I say, but the woman is reshuffling her cards. "I'd like to explain how the house works, or why I've chosen this lifestyle. There are many more things you can ask," I say. People I've known might see this and all they'll see is me encouraging a fourteen-year old girl to get married. I want to explain myself. This is not the whole story. "Please," I say, "there is more."

"I'll ask the others," she says and stands she holds her hand out. "You were fine."

I don't take her hand. I leave the room without saying thank you. She interviews the rest behind a shut door and no one comes out seeming upset. They call us all back into the room together and Joe is joking with the newswoman. He bows his head and pulls at the tough skin around his fingernails. He is acting humble and women like this. She laughs and bats at him with her hand. They tell us to line up and sit on folding chairs, the most recent wife next to Joe and so on. I squeeze next to the first. Her smell is gone. Her hair is pulled up into a twist and I am at once surprised and glad that she will get into trouble for not wearing her hair down.

The newswoman asks Joe the questions and he smiles as he answers. He is proud. Often he motions to us with his hand. He sweeps over us from his seat, but one hand stays planted on the girl's knee. The newswoman asks him if he is five times a man and they both laugh. Joe leans forward and his hand moves up the girl's thigh.

"I am proud of my family. And indeed I am enough man for all of them, and more if you know of anyone interested," he says to the newswoman and winks just for her sake, but we all see.

"I can imagine that you are," the newswoman says with a bright smile. And I look at the rest of us, his wives. We are all dressed the same. Our floral rompers and white lacy blouses press all of our breasts down. We all have bangs and hair down and curled at the bottom. In the light our faces cast shadows, some in the eyes and others around the jowls. We are in various stages of decay. We are the same. We are all Joe's wives, our individuality is gone.

Joe kneads the girl's thigh. She uncrosses her legs and adjusts herself so his hand slips farther up. Joe shifts in his seat and his hand rests in the pocket her romper makes where her legs meet. The newswoman won't notice and she laughs harder at a joke I don't catch. The first wife stands, clean and dark, and crosses in front of the camera and out the front door and no one stops her. Not the others, not I, and not my husband.

| Cecile Rossant | *Horizontal Drainage* |

JANNIS INVENTS HER MOTHER and her mother's mother. The two older women stem from her younger body and feed off her urgent inquiry. Jannis cannot believe that her mother and the ghost of her mother's mother had never asked the important questions. Jannis' mother has never corrected her daughter's oversight.

Jannis' mother also invents. Her inventions appear simultaneously with the cartographic contours she draws around herself and which she has re-traced for over fifty years.

Succeeding map by model, model by map in turn: this is the first complicity between mother and daughter.

Jannis and her mother can both agree that Jannis' grandmother has never existed as a fully realized invention. She appears as gesture, dried-up, with no blood and no bones. Jannis' grandmother functions like a metronome ticking out a suggestive time.

Jannis' grandmother was in the kitchen preparing a *Kassler Braten* for the Thursday evening meal. The Kassler lay like part of a hollowed-out log on the kitchen table. Kneeling, with chest pressed against the back of the sofa, Jannis' mother perched her head on the cushioned rim in order to get a comfortable view out the living room window. From her station by the window, she waited for each hard knock as one after another cutlet shaped piece of meat was sheared off the log by the sure swing of her mother's cleaver.

The living room walls were painted in deep dark red panels framed in shiny white moldings; floral rings barely emerged from the high ceiling. The Oriental carpets, etched glass, polished wood frames of precious and decorative woods were of exemplary craftsmanship and quality.

The couch had its soft parts and its hard parts. A smooth wood sphere completed the well-padded man-sized armrest. The leather upholstered armchairs, the oval tea table, the yellow ochre lampshade with fringe border . . .

Jannis demands that her mother remember more. *What is happening beyond the window? How much can you see—are they shouting? Do the Jews enter the trains without protest? Can't you hear screams? I can't imagine the people not putting up protest. Some of them must be your neighbors. Don't you recognize anyone? Mama! How do you feel, watching all this?*

The living room was warm. The windows had not been opened since the Sunday before. Jannis' mother felt sleepy. She was on holiday. School would not begin until Monday and she had no special meetings planned. She had been sitting in the living room since the end of breakfast. Gazing all morning out the window had left Jannis' mother tired and a bit dull-witted. She couldn't be sure if she had heard shouting outside, if she had, it was certainly muffled. Jannis' grandmother was cooking the *Kassler Braten* for the midday meal. The smell had begun to reach the living room. In a few hours the guests would arrive. Jannis' grandmother was known for her *Kassler Braten*.

Jannis' family lives in her mother's childhood house. In fact, Jannis' mother has never lived anywhere else.

Outside were coats, so many coats. Coats clustered shoulder to shoulder. The dark ones outnumbered the colored. A few red coats and even white ones could be picked out—children usually wore those.

The police pushed them along. Many eyes were looking for something to fix on. Jannis' mother watched this from her window. They were being deported . . . but at the time she didn't see it in that way.

I don't remember recognizing anyone.

The train had been parked all morning. It stood at least 100 meters away from the station proper. Jannis' mother had noticed it standing there when she opened the front door to bring in the three bottles of fresh milk before breakfast.

From the living room window she could keep two entire cars and a half of a third in view without getting up from her position on the couch. A row of soot-blackened windows ran along the top of each wagon. Or perhaps they were simply painted over with dark paint. From such a distance it was difficult to distinguish.

No, let me remember—they were not windows at all. A narrow row of vents with slats turned to the horizontal position ran along the top of each wagon. She could not make out this detail clearly enough to say how it was. She counted one, two, three . . . five openings. Besides a slightly open door she could just make out a hand disappearing into the shadows. Jannis' mother traced along the hand's profile. The concentration strained her eye muscles but there was something satisfying in her ability to feel closer, to fight the corrosive power of the shadows and the distance between herself and the hand. *She clings to this detail.*

The sudden gunshot threw her back on her bottom. Then there was the galloping rhythm of the slats slapping shut. When she returned to her station the openings were closed and the thick shadows gone.

Jannis' grandmother called out through the open kitchen door. She asks Jannis' mother to buy a bottle of *Weizenkorn Schnapps* for the guests to enjoy after the midday meal. Of course Jannis' grandmother is too busy with the preparations to go herself. Be a dear, child, and run down to Stolz's liquor shop. Buy a bottle of *Schnapps*. Mr. Stolz knows which one we like. There is money in my purse, by the door. Go ahead, take it yourself, my hands are not clean.

Jannis' mother slipped into her father's great coat that always hung in the closet by the front door. She stuffed a ten mark bill she had found in her mother's purse into the miniature handkerchief pocket. She reconsidered and removed the bill to one of two breast pockets hidden in the inner lining.

To reach the shopping street Jannis' mother was accustomed to walk along side the tracks for about 500 meters. As it was a day in early March the air was still fresh and cool. She walked with her eyes partially closed and leisurely reviewed the image of the train car returning to mind. Being outside made it easier for her to understand the relative size of things.

From her house, the land sloped down towards the tracks. The train's adjoining cars must have been hidden by the patch of linden trees that in recent years had grown so thick and tall. Satisfied with her own reasoning, she opened her eyes more fully. She had already reached the first block of stores and offices belonging to her neighborhood.

The sun at her back was low enough to give her a long and thin shadow to follow. She laughed at how her father's coat distinguished her slightly unfamiliar silhouette. In the middle of the first block she was nearing Stein's Liquor Store. As she had been walking very close to the wall of buildings to catch a good look at herself in the display windows, the bold strokes of white paint making up the word *'JUDE'* jumped right out at her. She pressed her cheek up to the glass and looked in.

The place was a complete wreck. The wood shelves once integrated into the walls had been pulled down to the floor. Disorderly stacks and piles of paper were strewn randomly across the floor along with sharp fragments of wood broken off from the shelves. A row of naked bulbs described an obscene axis down the middle the ceiling. The carefully etched glass spheres that once covered them were all simply gone. There was only one bottle of alcohol visible in the entire store. Embraced by the soft cast shadow of the letter 'U', it stood open on the dusty step of the display window at the front of the store. A rod of light passed through the glass animating the small amount of clear amber spirits still remaining in the bottle.

Searching the large shadows in the store tired her. Jannis' mother returned to her feet and remembering her charge continued on to Mr. Stolz' shop which was at the first corner of the next block.

Mr. Stolz climbed up a few steps on the ladder attached to a track on the upper edge of the shelves at Jannis' mother's request for the bottle of *Weizenkorn Schnapps.* Here, my dear, he said and handed the bottle to her wrapped in white paper twisted into place at the bottle's neck. Jannis' mother thanked him, nodded to his assistant and left the store with her purchase. Once outside she slipped the bottle into the spacious front pocket of her father's great coat and started walking back in the same way she came. Although Mr. Stolz and his employee had not made any signs to acknowledge that Jannis' mother was wearing a man's coat, once outside, she began a count of the number of people who stole a second glance at her figure as she passed by. The majority of those to examine her most closely were women of all ages, both young and old.

Jannis' mother cut diagonally across a small park to a narrow dirt path that ran closer alongside the tracks than the paved road.

The train was now less than thirty meters to her left. Jannis' mother recognized one of the cars as that she had been so closely examining from the living room window. There was its identification number and the swatch of black paint almost in the middle of the car. Her fascination in comparing the two viewpoints drew her closer to the train.

She was studying the rust pattern below the window when she felt someone grip her arm hard. She whipped around and was relieved to see the face of a policeman. His face also looked familiar. She smiled pleasantly and explained that she was on her way home from the liquor shop where she had made a purchase for her mother. The policeman did not return her smile. He pushed Jannis' mother towards the train. She fell against a family of four huddled in a group in front of the steps to the car door. The man in uniform yelled at these people to enter the train and motioned with a nod of the head that Jannis' mother should do the same. Pointing to the rather large house behind the poplars she told him again that it was her house. She said she must go home, but the policeman ignored her pleas. He pushed her roughly up the stairs and through the door. On the second step, she slipped on the long skirts of her father's great coat.

The sight within the car made her gasp. All of the seats had been ripped out of the car. Everybody was standing. The car was so packed with bodies that no one had even enough room to remove his coat. The heavy air stank of sweat and wool coats worn all winter without wash. She gulped the air as if she were choking.

She protested. You have made a mistake. I am not Jewish. I live here, in that house, there. (It was no longer visible from within the train.) She spoke surrounded only by the Jews. She yelled out her protest even more loudly but to no avail. She was a rock sinking in the big sea.

The policeman was the only figure who could cut a path across the car. He had a stick in his hand. No one tried to smother him or to deny him a free way. He enjoyed a steady stream of oxygen rich air. He seemed certain to survive. He was employed, and he performed his job effectively. And he would do so too, tomorrow and the day after.

She realized now it was the coat she wore. What rightfully minded person would wear an absurdly oversized coat in public? Unless it was already clear that, permanently dwarfed and thwarted, one was already an outsider.

She could envision her pirouette to freedom that let it be known who she was. When freed her arms and legs would succeed to pull the rest of herself above it all. She was absolutely certain that she was not and could never be Jewish.

Jannis' mother began to twist in place. *She shows her daughter how she was able to distinguish herself from the wool fold that wove so many into one suffering body.*

With eyes closed she pressed her body against the others, turning in place to release the loosely held buttons. With one flap free, she twisted further trying to catch the open flap of her coat between her body and theirs. She believed in this possibility that the coat could fall away. Let them tug it off her pretty shoulders. She was a German girl in the midst of a pubescent bloom. She often counted the six new firm buds on her body.

The coat fell to her feet.

If she was mistaken for a Jew, it was clearly because she was wearing a wool coat several sizes too big. Jannis' mother made the vague assumption that a Jew might do such a thing. For example, the family is too poor to buy every member of the family a winter coat, so the eldest girl must wear the coat of her recently deceased grandfather. Perhaps a Jewish girl had been stupid enough to convince herself that she could conceal her identity by wearing a grossly oversized coat and thereby sneak away unattended.

But Jannis' mother had a vision of herself. Her bare arms and shoulders emerged from a well-tailored tunic dress. The dress was sewn from an eye-catching light red cloth. Her legs were also bare. (She wore leather tong sandals.) Her hair was carefully brushed away from a freshly washed face.

She climbed onto the shoulders of one of them. He was a middle-aged father of two. His wife in her plain kerchief helped her up. The wife was in fact very kind and had no objections when Janni's mother sat up on the shoulders of her husband of fifteen years. Janni's mother sat there, supple and confident and remembered the many times she had sat, with back straight on the back of her cousin's pony.

But the ceiling of the train was too low for her to sit up. She shifted into a different position, stretching out between two sets of shoulders as if the move were part of a gymnastic routine. She knew she had a fine voice. She would break into song. The melody would be simple, a song everybody should know.

Jannis' mother's eyes were shut tight. They opened of themselves with the policeman's staccato orders that each passenger must produce personal identification for inspection.

Jannis' mother was allowed to return home—*Does someone recognize you? Does someone recognize your name? What is it that makes the guard believe your story?*

She would never know. He looked at her. He took her chin in his hand. He examined her shoes and the buttons of her blouse and its sleeves. At the end he nodded to another man standing nearby who escorted Jannis' mother off the train. They all followed her with their eyes until she breathed the fresh air again.

She blew through the door to her parents' house as the food was being brought to the table. She did not attempt to report what had happened to her. She had not yet understood herself. In response to her mother's inquiry, she ran back to the foyer and pulled out the white wrapped bottle from the pocket of the borrowed coat.

Candice Rowe | *Bearded Irises*

I AM WEEDING my bearded irises. They're beautiful things, the pale purple of a thick vein under white skin, ruffled as a frail handful of bunched curtain. A lot of times when I'm outside, people stop their cars and compliment me on them. I live in a small town, so that's not so unusual, even in these days of general mistrust.

It is warm. I'm wearing one of my husband's old squash T-shirts. I've knelt forward, letting the still-chilled petals brush my cheek. The earth sends off its stored up nighttime coolness onto my skin. How long I stay like that, I'm not sure. Then, "Hello there," a voice says.

Using my shoulder, I tip back the grand straw hat I'm wearing. My daughter wore the hat at some garden wedding of a friend some summers ago. It's a wonderful hat, a yellow grosgrain ribbon securing it under my chin. Perfect protection from the sun. The man behind me is smiling, standing in one spot as though rooted, yet torquing around so that he doesn't lose sight of the street back over his shoulder. It's hard to tell how old he is. Not as young as my son, who is in his second year of college, not old enough to worry about.

"Those are some great flowers there," he says. He has hair cut close to the head, each strand separate with a mind of its own. His head reminds me of one of those oranges stuck all over with cloves intended as natural deodorizers the kids used to make as gifts for me at summer camp. His eyes though. They're a beautiful blue. Morning glory blue, delphinium blue, but there's something strange about them. When he smiles, which he seems to do when he thinks about how he should be smiling, one of his teeth is missing. A missing tooth says a lot about a person's upbringing.

He says a few more things, about the weather, my rock garden up on the side yard, and so on. But he's rushing his words to get somewhere else, you can tell. Then he's out with it. "I've been by your house before. I like to walk, you know? Do you think I could shampoo your hair for you?"

He's crazy, I think. Nuts. Out to Kansas, as my husband Daniel would say. So how can I get rid of him, I think.

"Your hair," he says. It's the color of burning leaves." He must sense I am trying to ignore him because he says, "I used to be a hair stylist. I've had New York training. I know good hair when I see it. It would be important for me. You'd really get a lot out of it too. I can massage your follicles for you. That could change your whole outlook on the day." He smiles vaguely, staring into the back yard at my smoke tree, the branches now a gentle haze of a blush.

A scam artist, I think. He wants to size up the house, the security system and come back later and rip off our Matisses and Picassos, if only we had them. The family silver, if we had that. The jewels in a vault, so to speak. I watch him as his eyes move conscientiously over the neighborhood's line of trees and neat house peaks. That's what's so odd about his eyes; they don't blink.

"What kind of shampoo do you use? Dark green shampoo strips the hair, leaving it vulnerable to attack," he says, looking right at me, but his vision falling off somewhere short of my face.

Or, I think, he could be a serial rapist. One of those charming men that wins the confidence of lonely or bored middle aged women, wooing them with poetry and a single wild flower, winning them over by making them feel singular in this world of mass everything. You know the type. You see shows about them all the time on television. Once inside the house, they play out the scenarios they've imagined since their boyhoods, which are invariably spent in orphanages, where their mothers, invariably heartless young prostitutes, have deposited them as though they are as valuable as empty milk bottles on the stoop. Theses are boys who crush the skulls of pet cats to idle away the hours.

He reaches out to touch a thick strand of hair sagging near my ear. My sun hat is knocked back a bit by his hand and my sudden move to avoid him. It seems at that very moment the sun shifts suddenly and full light falls on his face. He has a pale saddle of freckles over his nose, making him look boyish enough. There is an anchor-shaped scar by his left eye. I find myself compelled to touch the scar, ask him how he acquired it, even put the tip of my tongue to it to feel its deepness.

"I imagine," he says, "the warm water-not too hot or cold-running over your hair. With my fingers, I would smooth it back from your forehead. It would drift into the sink, darker now, it's always like that, and in thick waving ribbons. I would feel the outline of your head-there used to be a science like that," he adds informatively.

"Phrenology," I say, strangely unable to move away from him. "I saw it on television."

He looks at me as though he doesn't understand why I have interrupted him.

Then he takes my hand, still in my soiled garden gloves and we walk to the kitchen door. I am so concerned with break-ins that the door is locked, so I need to take off my gloves and fish the key from beneath the tub of nasturtiums by the back steps.

Then he is shampooing my hair. At first I am tense, my neck a little stiff with bending back into the sharpness of the counter and the kitchen sink. British doctors, I remember reading in the newspaper, recently announced a condition known as "Beauty Parlor Syndrome." When the neck stretches backward over the sink, the carotid artery is overextended, leading to a stroke. The woman the doctors were talking about first noticed a stiffness in her leg when she stood up from the chair, and by the next morning her speech was slurred and her face was numb.

I plan to mention this rare syndrome, but he seems irritated that he can't adjust the temperature of the water just so. "Forget the shampoo," he says, holding a squeeze bottle of dish liquid. At first I can't think beyond the white, curved expanse of my throat arching toward him. The carving knives are, what, five feet away on the counter? What does it take to hit a major artery? What does it take to plunge a single sharp blade into a single chamber of the heart? But there's worse. What if he doesn't kill first? There's biting, tearing of flesh, binding, trussing, insertion of foreign objects, unnatural acts.

"You're not relaxing," he says. He sounds angry. "The whole point is that you relax." For a single moment his hands stop moving over my head. I wait to feel the first jab of the knife as it slices through the skin, the first touch of his hands around my neck, tightening like rawhide in the sun. "Relax," he orders. I open my eyes, but all I can see are the bristles of his hair against the white expanse of the ceiling. As he bends over me I see that he has a widow's peak, as my mother used to call it, that deep v of hair some people have at the center of their foreheads. What did she says about the widow's peak? A good life, bad life, never trust those that have them? The only solid rule I can light on is that if a tiger cat has the fur line of a dark M etched over its eyes, it's protected by the Virgin Mary. My mind is a bit jumbled. He stamps his foot impatiently, like a naughty child. I can feel his tension through my scalp. I will myself to relax.

I give myself over to it. Maybe that sounds easy, but what other choices do I have? I think of my bearded irises. I think of the smell of mushrooms under a bed of ruff. I think of my grandmother pinning a tiny sprig of lavender to my dress when I was a child so that the earth could be a part of me as I passed through my day. Then I think of all the people I know who are dead now, family members, friends, a boy in high school who got killed in a car accident the week before graduation.

Timothy White his name was. I think of him still in a tweed sports jacket flapping at his sides, smiling at me across the expanse of heads in home room. Once in history class, during Mr. Lapsky's lecture on the Peloponnesian Wars,

Timothy White slid a mayonnaise jar of garter snakes from his desk and tipped it toward me. I thought myself very sophisticated, not the sort of girl who would be rattled by a jar of snakes. I straightened my back in my starched white shirt, straightened my plaid skirt, waggled my shoulders in complete disapproval of Timothy White's stunt and focused all the more intently on Mr. Lapsky.

Then Timothy White was dead, driving North, as he'd said in his goodbye note to his mother, in order to find the father he had never known. Whenever I think of him, I think of him on his Suicide Shift Indian motorcycle with the twin leather packs flopped over the rear wheels, riding into a roiling snowstorm until he's nothing but a tiny bead of black lost in a wash of white.

"You're done, Ma'am," the young man says. He's wrapped two kitchen towels around my head. "The comb out," he says, befuddled, looking around the kitchen. "I don't have the proper equipment." His eyes slide past the rack of knives easily.

"That's OK," I say. "I can take it from here."

He looks around as though he can't spot the door where we came in. "Can I get you a cold drink, some iced tea?" I say, hoping he won't accept, already planning to serve the drink to him in a plastic cup. It's over and I want him out. "A sandwich to take with you for the road?" That's something my mother always said.

"No, no," he says. "I have to get back. Be on my way."

"Your tip," I say, looking around for my handbag.

"No, no," he says. And like a man satisfied with the sex, satisfied for the minute anyway, he hurries out the door without so much as a good bye or a see you later or a take care.

My hair is tangled and wet but not unpleasant with its faintly lemon scent. Back outside, my irises have been warmed by the late morning sun. They are no longer cool to the touch, no longer giving off that damp, earthy smell of mystery and the unknown past. It's too hot to weed now, so I might as well brew some tea and relax in the shade of the ornamental cherry tree.

But before I rouse myself from the ground, I spot the shimmer of metal among the green iris fronds. It's a straight-edged razor, the kind you see in old-fashioned barber shops. How silvery, I think, not unlike the swooping petals of a silver gray iris washed in early morning rain. And when I put the blade to my cheek, I swear, the fist-sized shaft of the thing is still human-warm to the touch.

Joe
Taylor

Mademoiselle Preg. Nanté

MY PARENTS HAILED from a small European country best left vague. Off the boat, cattle car, steamship, or airliner they crawled, and into a dank apartment they entered, almost as if reversing the natural birthing process to find a womb and therein suckle. Within sight of the Statue of Liberty's arm, their problems began in earnest. As did mine.

A sub-sub clerk, perhaps in Kinko's where passports and green cards are made, or perhaps in the utmost bowels of the White House (I must tell you that as a native-soil American I have become negligent of my country's operations and can barely ascertain whether the Fifth War of Freedom was fought in the last century or was composed by Ludwig von Beethoven in the previous to last)—a sub-sub clerk somewhere, I say, having been deluged with prefixed *von's, uber's, ben's, de's* and consonantal horrors such as *Czsilov*, appended *Preg. Nanté* to my mother's patronymic. This dark joke surely was intended as a type of generic revenge on the sub-sub clerk's part, for that clerk must have noticed just enough rosiness in my mother's cheek to ferret the truth, perhaps even before Ma-ma herself had. Whatever the cause, the name officially appeared on Ma-ma's green card and visa. And when my father brought home his first paycheck, my mother blithely volunteered to take it to the bank whilst he reclined on a distinctly worn, mint green couch cursed with two ever-wandering springs. There he remained, hearing his bones pop back in place even as he popped open a can of the American beer he claimed to so dislike. Ma-ma jauntily tucked her green card and visa in a large purple handbag, the both slipping alongside Daddum's paycheck with her every growingly pregnant step.

"O-pen account," she told yet another clerk, as if intoning an incantation.

And how like an incantation it would turn out, for my mother convinced this second clerk to list Preg. Nanté as parcel of the account's official name. Well enough. Three weeks later, however, my father took it into his head to cash his own check. He may well have been unhappy with the beer ration he was receiving from Ma-ma, or he may have been influenced by some macho old-country male where he worked. The bank refused to deposit and cash his check without proper identification, which of course, would include *Preg. Nanté.*

Father was not in the least amused. And he was even less amused when Ma-ma had to trot to the bank, co-sign and deposit the check, delivering him his usual beer ration, minus the subway fare she'd expended. And he was even lesser amused when he learned the alternate spelling and meaning of this strange *Preg. Nanté.*

"Is it mine?" he growled one evening, staring over his American beer, which he'd popped most rudely.

I think, dear hearts, that I truly felt that question squirt through the umbilical cord to sour my digestion for the entirety of my last two trimesters. Moreover, I have a permanent twitch in my left eye whose origin I've often attributed to that question, for reading up on matters I learned that Daddums proffered his insult at the precise time the embryonic eyes are formed. Love—isn't it supposed to enter through the eyes, by way of an arrow? Just as easily, I warn, spite, resentment, world-sorrow, and other obnoxious anti-virtues might also enter.

Ma-ma let fly a cup of tea, breaking the thin blue china against Daddum's forehead.

"Oh Daddums," I would have warned upon seeing him walk in the door with his brows arched so evilly, seeing him reach into our fridge to pull out a beer so callously, before delivering even a welcome-me-home-nod, much less kiss. Yes, I would have slipped into my silky red slippers and run giggling to him before he could utter that damning question. But as we've discussed, my eyes were just forming, so I had no such opportunity.

Daddum's cruel question led to a week of raging silence and burnt meals. Consequently, poor Daddums ran through his allotment of beer three evenings before payday. And on payday, he once more attempted a solo journey to the bank, and he once more came tail-tucked home, having been forced to call my mother to come deposit the check.

Why didn't he simply open an account at another bank? You must understand that a certain class of men from my parents' fatherland foster eternal distrust of the other class of men who wear ties and suits. I've learned this attitude has a correspondent one in certain American men. So Daddums resorted to another solution: he located syrupy words in an English dictionary and he stole flowers from a neighboring complex's side yard until matters not only reversed but actually improved. His beer allowance was raised.

So it came to be that I was born. Ma-ma thought that *Preg. Nanté* had rendered her such a good turn that she should somehow pass the fortune along. Fully aware of the codified and hidden meaning by then, she shied from bestowing the whole name upon me. Instead, my middle name became *Nanté*. And soon enough, the odd name caught to become my given name, hardly a Christian one, but in these days who would ever notice that triviality?

Here floats the crux of this matter: at twenty-nine, I am single and I am named *Nanté*, yet I am not thus. It's not as if boys avoid me—no, I've been told that I'm quite attractive. Even girls have occasionally hit on me with their Sapphite smirks and slim shoulder swivels. See my above remark about these days being as they are. But no lasting relation—whatsoever its sexual attenuation—has formed. I look in the proverbial mirror:

"Nanté, Nanté," I whisper. "Soon you will be as old as Jesus when he died, as old as Buddha when he sat under the plane tree. And look at your thin self." I of course oblige and do. What I see is pretty enough, if one ignores the left twitching eye. But fact is that this eye is something I cannot ignore, considering its origin. Still, I hope it will someday dissipate like poor potty training, and I simultaneously console myself that women mature sexually in their early thirties while men mature sexually as boys. And there they remain.

If truth be known though, I fret that my snide remark about the blossoming time of women versus men could very well shift into a moot observation. So I pucker my lips, dab on Cherryblossom glow and incant before the mirror, "Nanté, Nanté, you must do something. Take the bull, as they say, by the horns." Isn't it wonderful how I've acquired an entire operant area of phrases that would befuddle either of my parents? And the finer implications of taking a bull by the horns have not escaped me either. Both Freud and Puritanism have become part and parcel of my make-up as a native-born American.

Let's slow down a bit. I'm in graduate school, microbiology, after a false undergraduate start in experimental psychology. The coupling and dispersing of cells has never ceased to amaze me. I have obtained a grant, I am an integral part of a grant, which no one understands, which boasts some vague intent of adding to the statistical knowledge of . . . hmm, cell division and reproduction. In defense of spending tax money, I must tell you that we don't hurt animals, though I do occasionally suffer personal qualms about drying living cells for slides or even zapping them with electron microscopes. At times, I discern a tiny, tiny wail. Nanté, you see, has become an integral piece of my personality. By that I mean that I am constantly aware of the profusions of life tumbling about. A type of Gaiea Theory is what I eventually want to work on in post-doctoral bliss. For instance, did you know that we now are pondering the possibility that life began—and still begins!—in the deepest seas, in sulphurous geysers miles down? I can just hear my daddums, reincarnated as a killer whale, finning above such a geyser and bellowing in whale song, "Is . . . it . . . mine?"

And that brings me to this conundrum: something's been going on in the lab lately, an oozing of micro-electric cellular energy that would do Genesis proud. "Nanté, Nanté," it burbles to me as I stare at the reflective glass of tanks and tanks of teeming algae or stacks upon stacks of happily procreating Petri dishes. So, to take the bull by the horns, I plan to entrap a student in medical engineering who's been hanging around the labs. He's trying to finalize some weird auto-immune device that measures cellular activity among white cells, even to the point of tagging them to discover their starting point and subsequently infuse micro-measures of antibiotics with a specificity never before imagined. His name is Will Carrollton. His hair is sandy and dandy. See how foolish I've become? Ma-ma would be so disheartened. Oh wait, I hear his footstep.

"Wi-ill," I sing, as lovingly as any whale on the sexual blorp.

"Uh, hi Nan," he responds, cocking his head. I've disturbed his vision of procreating white cells.

"Wi-ill," I sing again. People may say what they care about the usefulness of language, and after her experience with Daddums, my mother would certainly stand in the fore of its proponents, but that second singsong repetition of "Wi-ill" is all that's needed. Is it a verb? Is it a noun? Is it proper, is it common? Oh common, common. Oh proper, proper. So in front of chlorella, fruit flies, white cells, and a goodly part of the reproducing microbial kingdom, Will is kissing me. And I, I am kissing Will.

"Nanté," he gasps as I unzip him. Behind, cells are dividing profusely, happily. "Nanté," he cries again, his voice breaking as if he's fourteen.

My left eye twitches at his using my name. *Yes*, I think, *I soon enough will be*. And you, my bright young male biomedical wonder—if you ever even notice—you had better ask, "Is it mine?" gracefully. For dearest Ma-ma, she passed not only her biologic urges, not only her temper, but the intact half of her blue teacup setting directly to me.

| Robert Reid | *Asusinia Flower of the Dead* |

NACE THREADED HIS WAY through the jungle, pushing back the fronds of the thick growth. He smelled the sweet smothering odor of the asusinia (flower of the dead) and a vision of loveliness passed through his mind. He stopped in the darkness, just before light; and saw his mother's face on a pillow of white satin. He shook the image out of his head, and buried his nose in the bouquet of plumeria that he held.

Nace knew that darkness, death and the spirits of his ancestors lurked in the jungle. His mother warned him to be careful and avoid the trees with their ancient flowing and twisted roots. The Taotamona lived there, and they had been known to carry children with them to the spirit world, sometimes trapping them in the tree for as many as three days.

"Is that where you're going?" Nace asked his mother. Her bag was packed. She stood in the doorway of their small house that she called "the box." Her long black hair flowed across her shoulder as she turned to him.

"No," she said, her black eyes focused on his small face. She looked sad, as if someone had died. "I only told you that about the spirits to keep you out of the jungle." Her face softened as she leaned to plant a full lipped kiss on Nace's cheek. "I'm not going to the jungle, I'm going to America," she said.

The soldier waited beside the blue 1941 Chevrolet. He watched Nace, his eyes shadowed by the visor on his hat. The eagle on his hat brass burned in the sun and in Nace's memory.

"Let's go Olivia," the soldier said. He grimaced impatiently.

"He's my baby," Nace's mother said. She looked past Nace at the sparsely furnished living room one more time. The picture of her mother and father with her and Nace at Talofofo Falls hung on the wall behind the dark polished ironwood table. Nace followed her look. He saw the tears and realized that she wasn't coming back. He was too horror stricken to move.

"Me too Mama," he said.

She hurried, wiping her eyes, out the door, past the asusenia bush to the burning eagle. That night Nace noticed for the first time that the asusenia flower only opened, releasing its odor and sweet pollen, at night; and he was afraid.

Grandma Julia held him, rocking him back and forth as evening came. Wisps of smoke rose from the green valley below, and the smell of burning wood that meant barbecue for supper permeated the air.

She sang, "Mama's little baby loves shortnin', shortnin', Mama's little baby loves shortnin' bread."

Grandma was old and she and Nace were alone in the little house now. The coal oil lamp flickered and both Nace and Grandma Julia cried. Grandma put his mother's picture on the ironwood table and Nace continued to think of her as having gone into the jungle, snatched by an eagle.

She never returned. A few cards came from places like San Francisco and Las Vegas, advertising bridges and casinos. Two letters came from Denver. One of them contained a picture of his mother with a big white cat, sitting on the hearth in front of a fireplace. It was the first fireplace Nace had ever seen. His mother described the cold and snow outside; and she said the smell of wood burning reminded her of home. She missed Nace and Grandma Julia. Grandma Julia cried; but Nace didn't. He remembered the burning eagle and he knew that this was an imposter.

That eagle and his schoolmate, Madeliene Albright, came into his mind as he approached the house where he and his grandmother lived. Madeliene was three years older than Nace and her soft white skin, blue eyes and blonde hair fascinated him. Nace watched her from his third grade seat and felt all the love that Zane Grey's characters felt in novels like "The Thundering Herd" and "Light of the Western Stars." His taste for western romances had come with his loneliness as he learned to read almost anything to escape the slow time of his life with Grandma Maria. Everything that made life magic like Madeliene was out of reach. He read all the books he could find piled on a table in the used merchandise store that Buck Cruz opened in a quansit hut in Hâgåtna.

When he first saw Madeliene Albright the dull black and white of his life faded into background and an aura surrounded the star that made his heart throb. Once, playing ring around the rosy, as the children turned, laughing in a circle, he had come out of the broken circle to touch her hand. She came directly from the pages of Zane Grey. Nace was transported to a time and place where he imagined his dead mother lived when she wrote the letter.

Now, he looked at his brogans that he wore in the jungle to protect his feet from the sword grass and stickle burrs and wished for boots; and he wanted a real rifle to hunt deer and wild boar. His uncle wore engineer boots and khaki clothes. Nace often saw him cleaning the lever action Winchester .30-30, like the one the cowboys carried in their saddle boot, but Nace was never around when Tun (Uncle) Carlos went into the jungle to hunt. Nace missed a lot of things that the other boys had, but he had books; and he printed on them, Ignacio Natividad, and kept them all.

When he asked about his father, his grandmother said, looking down at her dark callous hands, that his father was a sailor named Bob. Bob had been transferred before Nace was born and Nace's Christian name was Ignacio Natividad Natividad.

"Does that mean I'm a bastard like Tony San Nicholas said?" Nace asked. He looked up into his grandmother's face.

She raised her face and her brown eyes met his. She put her hands over Nace's hands on her knees. "No," Your father was forced to leave and your mother stayed with me. Ask him why the Spanish named his family Santa Claus."

"Santa Claus has no children." Nace laughed.

"Not that he will claim," Grandma laughed; "but that Spanish gentleman has been down lots of chimneys, and he brought more than toys in his sack. If anyone calls you a bastard they are insulting your mother and me. You must fight." She put up her fists and showed Nace how to punch straight. Later his Uncle Carlos hung a punching bag from the ironwood tree in their front yard and his grandmother gave him a small pair of boxing gloves. After that Nace only had one fight. Nace was always good with his hands. He identified with the cowboys in the Western novels.

When Nace entered the house it was still dark on the western side. His grandmother knelt before a makeshift altar, her black hair flowing over her white gown, praying. The light from the lamp made her shadow loom over her small body as she fingered the prayer beads around her neck. A picture of Christ with a bleeding heart hung above her in the shadow. When he was smaller Nace thought the shadow was God's spirit listening to his grandmother's prayer for a new day free of transgression.

He went past his grandmother into the kitchen. Daylight from the window revealed the icebox and small white wooden table. Later Nace would go to the store with his wagon to get a fresh block of ice. Now, he sat down in one of the white wooden chairs made with slats on the back and seat. He put some of the kelaguen on his plate and began to eat. His grandmother told him stories about that being their meat during the war because the mixture cooked without fire. The cooking without smoke wouldn't attract the Japanese soldiers who would take the food when they discovered it. She told him how her older brothers had died in Hâgåtna defending the Island when the Japanese came. Only herself and Carlos were left of her entire family.

Nace was watching the Sunrise between two clouds when he felt his grandmother behind him. He turned and she was holding a letter.

"It's from your mother," she said. There was a sad look on her face and her voice was low.

"It's been a long time," Nace said. He saw again the image of his mother's face on the silk pillow, asleep and powdered as all the faces of the dead he had seen.

"She's in Detroit, Michigan," Grandma Maria said. "There's snow on the ground. It's Christmas and she wants you to come there."

"No," Nace said.

"She says she has a husband and can afford to have you come now." She wiped her eyes with the back of her hand.

Nace felt homesick at the thought of leaving when he saw his grandmother crying. He remembered the other letters. This was the only one that made him choke to stop the surge of grief.

"She says the man works for the car plant. They have electricity, a refrigerator and a little house. You'll be happy there."

Nace remembered the first time he'd seen an electric light. It was fluorescent and gave off a cold white light. Two tubes in a rectangular fixture lit the whole room at the funeral parlor. Nace was relieved when he and his grandmother got home to the warm light of the coal oil lamp. He associated the cold light with his mother whose image in his mind always threatened to leave and she finally deserted him. She was cold.

"Did this husband come down the chimney?" Nace asked.

| Italo Calvino | *Distance of the Moon* |

AT ONE TIME, according to Sir George H. Darwin, the Moon was very close to the Earth. Then the tides gradually pushed her far away: the tides that the Moon herself causes in the Earth's waters, where the Earth slowly loses energy.

How well I know! —*old Qfwfq cried*—the rest of you can't remember, but I can. We had her on top of us all the time, that enormous Moon: when she was full-nights as bright as day, but with a butter-colored light—it looked as if she were going to crush us; when she was new, she rolled around the sky like a black umbrella blown by the wind; and when she was waxing, she came forward with her horns so low she seemed about to stick into the peak of a promontory and get caught there. But the whole business of the Moon's phases worked in a different way then: because the distances from the Sun were different, and the orbits, and the angle of something or other, I forget what; as for eclipses, with Earth and Moon stuck together the way they were, why, we had eclipses every minute: naturally, those two big monsters managed to put each other in the shade constantly, first one, then the other.

Orbit? Oh, elliptical, of course: for a while it would huddle against us and them it would take flight for a while. The tides, when the Moon swung closer, rose so high nobody could hold them back. There were nights when the Moon was full and very, very low, and the tide was so high that the Moon missed a ducking in the sea by a hair's-breadth; well, let's say a few yards anyway. Climb up on the Moon? Of course we did. All you had to do was row out to it in a boat and, when you were underneath, prop a ladder against her and scramble up.

The spot where the Moon was lowest, as she went by, was off the Zinc Cliffs. We used to go out with those little rowboats they had in those days, round and flat, made of cork. They held quite a few of us: me, Captain Vhd Vhd, his wife, my deaf cousin, and sometimes little Xlthlx—she was twelve or so at that time. On those nights the water was very calm, so silvery it looked like mercury, and the fish in it, violet-colored, unable to resist the Moon's

140

attraction, rose to the surface, all of then, and so did the octopuses and the saffron medusas. There was always a flight of tiny creatures—little crabs, squid, and even some weeds, light and filmy, and coral plants—that broke from the sea and ended up on the Moon, hanging down from that lime-white ceiling, or else they stayed in midair, a phosphorescent swarm we had to drive off, waving banana leaves at them.

This is how we did the job: in the boat we had a ladder: one of us held it, another climbed to the top, and a third, at the oars, rowed until we were right under the Moon; that's why there had to be so many of us (I only mentioned the main ones). The man at the top of the ladder, as the boat approached the Moon, would become scared and start shouting: "Stop! Stop! I'm going to bang my head!" That was the impression you had, seeing her on top of you, immense, and all rough with sharp spikes and jagged, saw-tooth edges. It may be different now, but then the Moon, or rather the bottom, the underbelly of the Moon, the part that passed closest to the Earth and almost scraped it, was covered with a crust of sharp scales. It had come to resemble the belly of a fish, and the smell too, as I recall, if not downright fishy, was faintly similar, like smoked salmon.

In reality, from the top of the ladder, standing erect on the last rung, you could just touch the Moon if you held your arms up. We had taken the measurements carefully (we didn't yet suspect that she was moving away from us); the only thing you had to be very careful about was where you put your hands. I always chose a scale that seemed fast (we climbed up in groups of five or six at a time), then I would cling first with one hand, then with both, and immediately I would feel ladder and boat drifting away from below me, and the motion of the Moon would tear me from the Earth's attraction. Yes, the Moon was so strong that she pulled you up; you realized this the moment you passed from one to the other: you had to swing up abruptly, with a kind of somersault, grabbing the scales, throwing your legs over you head, until your feet were on the Moon's surface. Seen from the Earth, you looked as if you were hanging there with your head down, but for you, it was the normal position, and the only odd thing was that when you raised your eyes you saw the sea above you, glistening, with the boat and the others upside down, hanging like a bunch of grapes from the vine.

My cousin, the Deaf One, showed a special talent for making those leaps. His clumsy hands, as soon as they touched the lunar surface (he was always the first to jump up from the ladder), suddenly became deft and sensitive. They found immediately the spot where he could hoist himself up; in fact just the pressure of his palms seemed enough to make him stick to the satellite's crust. Once I even thought I saw the Moon come toward him, as he held out his hands.

He was just as dextrous in coming back down to Earth, an operation still more difficult. For us, it consisted in jumping, as high as we could, our arms upraised (seen from the Moon, that is, because seen from the Earth it looked more like a dive, or like swimming downwards, arms at our sides), like jumping up from the Earth in other words, only now we were without the ladder, because there was nothing to prop it against on the Moon. But instead of jumping with his arms out, my cousin bent toward the Moon's surface, his head down as if for a somersault, then made a leap, pushing with his hands. From the boat we watched him, erect in the air as if he were supporting the Moon's enormous ball and were tossing it, striking it with his palms; then, when his legs came within reach, we managed to grab his ankles and pull him down on board.

Now, you will ask me what in the world we went up on the Moon for; I'll explain it to you. We went to collect the milk, with a big spoon and a bucket. Moon-milk was very thick, like a kind of cream cheese. It formed in the crevices between one scale and the next, through the fermentation of various bodies and substances of terrestrial origin which had flown up from the prairies and forests and lakes, as the Moon sailed over them. It was composed chiefly of vegetal juices, tadpoles, bitumen, lentils, honey, starch crystals, sturgeon eggs, molds, pollens, gelatinous matter, worms, resins, pepper, mineral salts, combustion residue. You had only to dip the spoon under the scales that covered the Moon's scabby terrain, and you brought it out filled with the precious muck. Not in the pure state, obviously; there was a lot of refuse. In the fermentation (which took place as the Moon passed over the expanses of hot air above the deserts) not all the bodies melted; some remained stuck in it: fingernails and cartilage, bolts, sea horses, nuts and peduncles, shards of crockery, fishhooks, at times even a comb. So this paste, after it was collected, had to be refined, filtered. But that wasn't the difficulty: the hard part was transporting it down to the Earth. This is how we did it: we hurled each spoonful into the air with both hands, using the spoon as a catapult. The cheese flew, and if we had thrown it hard enough, it stuck to the ceiling, I mean the surface of the sea. Once there, it floated, and it was easy enough to pull it into the boat. In this operation, too, my deaf cousin displayed a special gift; he had strength and a good aim; with a single, sharp throw, he could send the cheese straight into a bucket we held up to him from the boat. As for me, I occasionally misfired; the contents of the spoon would fail to overcome the Moon's attraction and they would fall back into my eye.

I still haven't told you everything, about the things my cousin was good at. That job of extracting lunar milk from the Moon's scale was child's play to him: instead of the spoon, at times he had only to thrust his bare hand under the scales, or even one finger. He didn't proceed in any orderly way, but went to isolated places, jumping from one to the other, as if he were playing tricks on the Moon, surprising her, or perhaps tickling her. And wherever he put his hand, the milk spurted out as if from a nanny goat's teats. So the rest of us had only to follow him and collect with our spoons the substance that he was pressing out, first here, then there, but always as if by chance, since the Deaf One's movements seemed to have no clear, practical sense. There were places, for example, that he touched merely for the fun of touching them: gaps between two scales, naked and tender folds of lunar flesh. At times my cousin pressed not only his fingers but-in a carefully gauged leap-his big toe (he climbed onto the Moon barefoot) and this seemed to be the height of amusement for him, if we could judge by the chirping sounds that came from his throat as he went on leaping.

The soil of the Moon was not uniformly scaly, but revealed irregular bare patches of pale, slippery clay. These soft areas inspired the Deaf One to turn somersaults or to fly almost like a bird, as if he wanted to impress his whole body into the Moon's pulp. As he ventured farther in this way, we lost sight of him at one point. On the Moon there were vast areas we had never had any reason or curiosity to explore, and that was where my cousin vanished; I had suspected that all those somersaults and nudges he indulged in before our eyes were only preparation, a prelude to something secret meant to take place in the hidden zones.

We fell into a special mood on those night off the Zinc Cliffs: gay, but with a touch of suspense, as if inside our skulls, instead of the brain, we felt a fish, floating, attracted by the Moon. And so we navigated, playing and singing. The Captain's wife played the harp; she had very long arms, silvery as eels on those nights, and armpits as dark and mysterious as sea urchins; and the sound of the harp was sweet and piercing, so sweet and piercing it was almost unbearable, and we were forced to let out long cries, not so much to accompany the music as to protect our hearing from it.

Transparent medusas rose to the sea's surface, throbbed there a moment, then flew off, swaying toward the Moon. Little Xlthlx amused herself by catching them in midair, though it wasn't easy. Once, as she stretched her little arms out to catch one, she jumped up slightly and was also set free. Thin as she was, she was an ounce or two short of the weight necessary for the Earth's gravity to overcome the Moon's attraction and bring her back: so she flew up among the medusas, suspended over the sea. She took fright, cried, then laughed and started playing, catching shellfish and minnows as they flew, sticking some into her mouth and chewing them. We rowed hard, to keep up with the child: the Moon ran off in her ellipse, dragging that swarm of marine fauna through the sky, and a train of long, entwined seaweeds, and Xlthlx hanging there in the midst. Her two wispy braids seemed to be flying on their own, outstretched toward the Moon; but all the while she kept wriggling and kicking at the air,

143

as if she wanted to fight that influence, and her socks—she had lost her shoes in the flight—slipped off her feet and swayed, attracted by the Earth's force. On the ladder, we tried to grab them.

The idea of eating the little animals in the air had been a good one; the more weight Xlthlx gained, the more she sank toward the Earth; in fact, since among those hovering bodies hers was the largest, mollusks and seaweeds and plankton began to gravitate about her, and soon the child was covered with siliceous little shells, chitinous carapaces, and fibers of sea plants. And the farther she vanished into that tangle, the more she was freed of the Moon's influence, until she grazed the surface of the water and sank into the sea.

We rowed quickly, to pull her out and save her: her body had remained magnetized, and we had to work hard to scrape off all the things encrusted on her. Tender corals were wound about her head, and every time we ran the comb through her hair there was a shower of crayfish and sardines; her eyes were sealed shut by limpets clinging to the lids with their suckers; squids' tentacles were coiled around her arms and her neck, and her little dress now seemed woven only of weeds and sponges. We got the worst of it off her, but for weeks afterwards she went on pulling out fins and shells, and her skin, dotted with little diatoms, remained affected forever, looking—to someone who didn't observe here carefully—as if it were faintly dusted with freckles.

This should give you an idea of how the influences of Earth and Moon, practically equal, fought over the space between them. I'll tell you something else: a body that descended to the Earth from the satellite was still charged for a while with lunar force and rejected the attraction of our world. Even I, big and heavy as I was: every time had been up there, I took a while to get used to the Earth's up and its down, and the others would have to grab my arms and hold me, clinging in a bunch in the swaying boat while I still had my head hanging and my legs stretching up toward the sky.

"Hold on! Hold on to us!" they shouted at me, and in all that groping, sometimes I ended up by seizing one of Mrs. Vhd Vhd's breasts, which were round and firm, and the contact was good and secure and had an attraction as strong as the Moon's or even stronger, especially if I managed, as I plunged down, to put my other arm around her hips, and with this I passed back into our world and fell with a thud into the bottom of the boat, where Captain Vhd brought me around, throwing a bucket of water in my face.

This is how the story of my love for the Captain's wife began, and my suffering. Because it didn't take me long to realize whom the lady kept looking at insistently: when my cousin's hands clasped the satellite, I watched Mrs. Vhd Vhd, and in her eyes I could read the thoughts that the deaf man's familiarity with the Moon were arousing in her; and when he disappeared in his mysterious lunar explorations, I saw her become restless, as if on pins and needles, and then it was all clear to me, how Mrs. Vhd Vhd was becoming jealous of the Moon and I was jealous of my cousin. Her eyes were made of diamonds, Mrs. Vhd Vhd's; they flared when she looked at the Moon, almost challengingly, as if she were saying: "You shan't have him!" And I felt like an outsider.

The one who least understood all of this was my deaf cousin. When we helped him down, pulling him—as I explained to you—by his legs, Mrs. Vhd Vhd lost all her self-control, doing everything she could to take his weight against her own body, folding her long silvery arms around him; I felt a pang in my heart (the times I clung to her, her body was soft and kind, but not thrust forward, the way it was with my cousin), while he was indifferent, still lost in his lunar bliss.

I looked at the Captain, wondering if he also noticed his wife's behavior; but there was never a trace of any expression on that face of his, eaten by brine, marked with tarry wrinkles. Since the Deaf One was always the last to break away from the Moon, his return was the signal for the boats to move off. Then, with an unusually polite gesture, Vhd Vhd picked up the harp from the bottom of the boat and handed it to his wife. She was obliged to take it and play a few notes. Nothing could separate her more from the Deaf One than the sound of the harp. I took to singing in a low voice that sad song that goes: "Every shiny fish is floating, floating; and every dark fish is at the bottom, at the bottom of the sea . . ." and all the others, except my cousin, echoed my words.

Every month, once the satellite had moved on, the Deaf One returned to his solitary detachment from the things of the world; only the approach of the full Moon aroused him again. That time I had arranged things so it wasn't my turn to go up, I could stay in the boat with the Captain's wife. But then, as soon as my cousin had climbed the ladder, Mrs. Vhd Vhd said: "This time I want to go up there, too!"

This had never happened before; the Captain's wife had never gone up on the Moon. But Vhd Vhd made no objection, in fact he almost pushed her up the ladder bodily, exclaiming: "Go ahead then!," and we all started helping her, and I held her from behind, felt her round and soft on my arms, and to hold her up I began to press my face and the palms of my hands against her, and when I felt her rising into the Moon's sphere I was heartsick at the lost contact, so I started to rush after her, saying: "I'm going to go up for a while, too, to help out!"

I was held back as if in a vise. "You stay here; you have work to do later," the Captain commanded, without raising his voice.

At that moment each one's intentions were already clear. And yet I couldn't figure things out; even now I'm not sure I've interpreted it all correctly. Certainly the Captain's wife had for a long time been cherishing the desire to go off privately with my cousin up there (or at least to prevent him from going off alone with the Moon), but probably she has a still more ambitious plan, one that would have to be carried out in agreement with the Deaf One: she wanted the two of them to hide up there together and stay on the Moon for a month. But perhaps my cousin, deaf as he was, hadn't understood anything of what she had tried to explain to him, or perhaps he hadn't even realized that he was the object of the lady's desires. And the Captain? He wanted nothing better than to be rid of his wife; in fact, as soon as she was confined up there, we saw him give free rein to his inclinations and plunge into vice, and the we understood why he had done nothing to hold her back. But had he known from the beginning that the Moon's orbit was widening?

None of us could have suspected it. The Deaf One perhaps, but only he: in the shadowy way he knew things, he may have had a presentiment that he would be forced to bid the Moon farewell that night. This is why he hid in his secret places and reappeared only when it was time to come back down on board. It was no use for the Captain's wife to try to follow him: we saw her cross the scaly zone various times, length and breadth, then suddenly she stopped, looking at us in the boat, as if about to ask us whether we had seen him.

Surely there was something strange about that night. The sea's surface, instead of being taut as it was during the full Moon, or even arched a bit toward the sky, now seemed limp, sagging, as if the lunar magnet no longer exercised its full power. And the light, too, wasn't the same as the light of other full Moons; the night's shadows seemed somehow to have thickened. Our friends up there must have realized what was happening; in fact, they looked up at us with frightened eyes. And from their mouths and ours, at the same moment, came a cry: "The Moon's going away!"

The cry hadn't died out when my cousin appeared on the Moon, running. He didn't seem frightened, or even amazed: he placed his hands on the terrain, flinging himself into his usual somersault, but this time after he had hurled himself into the air he remained suspended, as little Xlthlx had. He hovered a moment between Moon and Earth, upside down, then laboriously moving his arms, like someone swimming against a current, he headed with unusual slowness toward our planet.

From the Moon the other sailors hastened to follow his example. Nobody gave a thought to getting the Moon-milk that had been collected into the boats, nor did the Captain scold them for this. They had already waited too long, the distance was difficult to cross by now; when they tried to imitate my cousin's leap or his swimming, remained there groping, suspended in midair. "Cling together! Idiots! Cling together!" the Captain yelled. At this command, the sailors tried to form a group, a mass, to push all together until they reached the zone of the Earth's attraction: all of a sudden a cascade of bodies plunged into the sea with a loud splash.

The boats were now rowing to pick them up. "Wait! The Captain's wife is missing!" I shouted. The Captain's wife had also tried to jump, but she was still floating only a few yards from the Moon, slowly moving her long, silvery arms in the air. I climbed up the ladder, and in a vain attempt to give her something to grasp I held the harp out toward her. "I can't reach her! We have to go after her!" and I started to jump up, brandishing the harp. Above me the enormous lunar disk no longer seemed the same as before: it had become much smaller, it kept contracting, as if my gaze were driving it away, and the emptied sky gaped like an abyss where, at the bottom, the stars had begun multiplying, and the night poured a river of emptiness over me, drowned me in dizziness and alarm.

"I'm afraid," I thought. "I'm too afraid to jump. I'm a coward!" and at that moment I jumped. I swam furiously through the sky, and held the harp out to her, and instead of coming toward me she rolled over and over, showing me first her impassive face and then her backside.

"Hold tight to me!" I shouted, and I was already overtaking her, entwining my limbs with hers. "If we cling together we can go down!" and I was concentrating all my strength on uniting myself more closely with her, and I concentrated my sensations as I enjoyed the fullness of the embrace. I was so absorbed I didn't realize at first that I was, indeed, tearing her from her weightless condition, but was making her fall back on the Moon. Didn't I realize it? Or had that been my intention from the very beginning? Before I could think properly, a cry was already bursting from my throat. "I'll be the one to stay with you for a month!" Or rather, "On you!" I shouted, in my excitement: "On you for a month!" and at that moment our embrace was broken by our fall to the Moon's surface, where we rolled away from each other among those cold scales.

I raised my eyes as I did every time I touched the Moon's crust, sure that I would see above me the native sea like an endless ceiling, and I saw it, yes, I saw it this time, too, but much higher, and much more narrow, bound by its borders of coasts and cliffs and promontories, and how small the boats seemed and how unfamiliar my friends' faces and how weak their cries! A sound reached me from nearby: Mrs. Vhd Vhd had discovered her harp and was caressing it, sketching out a chord as sad as weeping.

A long month began. The Moon turned slowly around the Earth. On the suspended globe we no longer saw our familiar shore, but the passage of oceans as deep as abysses and deserts of glowing lapilli, and continents of ice, and forests writhing with reptiles, and the rocky walls of mountain chains gashed by swift rivers, and swampy cities, and stone graveyards, and empires of clay and mud. The distance spread a uniform color over everything: the alien perspectives made every image alien; herds of elephants and swarms of locusts ran over the plains, so evenly vast and dense and thickly grown that there was no difference among them.

I should have been happy: as I had dreamed, I was alone with her, that intimacy with the Moon I had so often envied my cousin and with Mrs. Vhd Vhd was now my exclusive prerogative, a month of days and lunar nights stretched uninterrupted before us, the crust of the satellite nourished us with its milk, whose tart flavor was familiar to us, we raised our eyes up, up to the world where we had been born, finally traversed in all its various expanse, explored landscapes no Earth-being had ever seen, or else we contemplated the stars beyond the Moon, big as pieces of fruit, made of light, ripened on the curved branches of the sky, and everything exceeded my most luminous hopes, and yet, and yet, it was, instead, exile.

I thought only of the Earth. It was the Earth that caused each of us to be that someone he was rather than someone else; up there, wrested from the Earth, it was as if I were no longer that I, nor she that She, for me. I was eager to return to the Earth, and I trembled at the fear of having lost it. The fulfillment of my dream of love had lasted only that instant when we had been united, spinning between Earth and Moon; torn from its earthly soil, my love now knew only the heart-rending nostalgia for what it lacked: a where, a surrounding, a before, an after.

This is what I was feeling. But she? As I asked myself, I was torn by my fears. Because if she also thought only of the Earth, this could be a good sign, a sign that she had finally come to understand me, but it could also mean that everything had been useless, that her longings were directed still and only toward my deaf cousin. Instead, she felt nothing. She never raised her eyes to the old planet, she went off, pale, among those wastelands, mumbling dirges and stroking her harp, as if completely identified with her temporary (as I thought) lunar state. Did this mean I had won out over my rival? No; I had lost: a hopeless defeat. Because she had finally realized that my cousin loved only the Moon, and the only thing she wanted now was to become the Moon, to be assimilated into the object of the extrahuman love.

When the Moon had completed its circling of the planet, there we were again over the Zinc Cliffs. I recognized them with dismay: not even in my darkest previsions had I thought the distance would have made them so tiny. In that mud puddle of the sea, my friends had set forth again, without the now useless ladders; but from the boats rose a kind of forest of long poles; everybody was brandishing one, with a harpoon or a grappling hook at the end, perhaps in the hope of scraping off a last bit of Moon-milk or of lending some kind of help to us wretches up there. But it was soon clear that no pole was long enough to reach the Moon; and they dropped back, ridiculously short, humbled, floating on the sea; and in that confusion some of the boats were thrown off balance and overturned. But just then, from another vessel a longer pole, which till then they had dragged along on the water's surface, began to rise: it must have been made of bamboo, of many, many bamboo poles stuck one into the other, and to raise it they had to go slowly because-thin as it was-if they let it sway too much it might break. Therefore, they had to use it with great strength and skill, so that the wholly vertical weight wouldn't rock the boat.

Suddenly it was clear that the tip of that pole would touch the Moon, and we saw it graze, then press against the scaly terrain, rest there a moment, give a kind of little push, or rather a strong push that made it bounce off again, then come back and strike that same spot as if on the rebound, then move away once more. And I recognized, we both—the Captain's wife and I—recognized my cousin: it couldn't have been anyone else, he was playing his last game with the Moon, one of his tricks, with the Moon on the tip of his pole as if he were juggling with her. And we realized that his virtuosity had no purpose, aimed at no practical result, indeed you would have said he was driving the Moon away, that he was helping her departure, that he wanted to show her to her more distant orbit. And this, too, was just like him: he was unable to conceive desires that went against the Moon's nature, the Moon's course and destiny, and if the Moon now tended to go away from him, then he would take delight in this separation just as, till now, he had delighted in the Moon's nearness.

What could Mrs. Vhd Vhd do, in the face of this? It was only at this moment that she proved her passion for the deaf man hadn't been a frivolous whim but an irrevocable vow. If what my cousin now loved was the distant Moon, then she too would remain distant, on the Moon. I sensed this, seeing that she didn't take a step toward the bamboo pole, but simply turned her harp toward the Earth, high in the sky, and plucked the strings. I say I saw her, but to tell the truth I only caught a glimpse of her out of the corner of my eye, because the minute the pole had touched the lunar crust, I had sprung and grasped it, and now, fast as a snake, I was climbing up the bamboo knots, pushing myself along with jerks of my arms and knees, light in the rarefied space, driven by a natural power that ordered me to return to the Earth, oblivious of the motive that had brought me here, or perhaps more aware of it than ever and of its unfortunate outcome; and already my climb up the swaying pole had reached the point where I no longer had to make any effort but could just allow myself to slide, head-first, attracted by the Earth, until in my haste the pole broke into a thousand pieces and I fell into the sea, among the boats.

My return was sweet, my home refound, but my thoughts were filled only with grief at having lost her, and my eyes gazed at the Moon, forever beyond my reach, as I sought her. And I saw her. She was there where I had left her, lying on a beach directly over our heads, and she said nothing. She was the color of the Moon; she held the harp at her side and moved one hand now and then in slow arpeggios. I could distinguish the shape of her bosom, her arms, her thighs, just as I remember them now, just as now, when the Moon has become that flat remote circle, I still look for her as soon as the first sliver appears in the sky, and the more it waxes, the more clearly I imagine I can see her, her or something of her, but only her, in a hundred, a thousand different vistas, she who makes the Moon the Moon and, whenever she is full, sets the dogs to howling all night long, and me with them.

<table>
<tr><td>

Mark E . Cull
& Kate Gale

</td><td>

In Our Yard

</td></tr>
</table>

1
The Veil

I BEGGED HER, for what it was worth, she never listens to me, to wear at least a veil. But why, she asked, with that summer laugh of hers, her breath smelling like apples, her cheeks shining, why, when you already know what I look like underneath?

She had already insisted that my forcing her was out of the question. Sneaking out from behind trees, throwing her to the ground, pulling her by her hair, none of this was allowed, I must ask on one knee every time I wanted to touch her or she would run away. The veil, the veil! It was all I asked. She refused to wear any other scrap of clothing. She walked through woods and fields, just her long hair floating behind her.

I began to fantasize about her in veils. Every time I was with her, I closed my eyes, saw myself tearing a veil away from that face, kissing the lips, rushing down on her. She broke up my fantasies by laughing and humming to herself. I would have preferred a moan, a sigh, a whimper, an occasional scream.

After all, nothing we were doing could possibly be wrong. The big guy had set this all up; her, me, the garden, we were supposed to be doing these things together, and at the time, you understand, there was nothing else to do.

But she refused to wear a veil.

2
A New Roof

Our father was sullen, he obviously didn't get enough. But then Mother was always aloof, walking about alone, combing that long hair. When father would wake, stand outside, staring, not quite alive yet, he would call her right away, two short calls, like a dog barking. We kids slept all over the place, and we'd listen. I picked up my head anxiously, wondering what she would do. In my first twelve summers, there was nothing I could do but listen for his labored breathing. Most days she would already be off, bathing by herself at the stream. Sometimes we could hear her singing. She sang in a low voice, almost like a man's, and by the time she walked back to our fire, everyone was awake, and my father was sullen the rest of the day. Of the twelve children, seven were boys. That gave me an advantage right away.

Because what I wanted wasn't a man, not particularly, my sisters did, but I wanted the moon, or at least a moonlit garden. As soon as their cycles began, they were done shooting rabbits and chasing each other. They began singing lilting songs at daybreak, preening, wearing ostrich feathers around their necks. They wore veils to please their brothers, and four of the brothers paired off with sisters whose moves they admired, but right away, I could see there was a place for me. The three remaining brothers were without mates, and the brothers who had mates were still anxious, rumbling. My sisters now walked by the stream with my mother in the mornings singing a song that meant no, maybe later.

That's when I decided I wanted my own roof. I didn't like living under the big roof with all of us spread out, I wanted my own leafy patch. I wore veils, I wore sandals, I covered and uncovered. I became the place where my brothers wanted to be, and they built me my own roof. My father came by one evening to admire the pot I stewed in, and soon he was on hand to help my brothers build me the best of tents. My sisters and mother were distant, anxious, trembling. I did the family a lot of good. My mother and sisters had to give a little or the whole clan would have just camped out at my door while I perfected the skill of making the men want to build me the first real house. On my knees I could get my brothers and father to sing like parrots, to promise me enormous chimneys, fireplaces, log beds, and so the first real house was built, and the men sang like birds knowing that at night I would feed them, and they would feed me. We all kept our promises, and we all knew we were living according to plan. Our father said the big guy had planned all this, written a book on it, we were just following instructions.

3
After the Boat

The eight of us divided up almost immediately; my brother Shem and I were constantly fighting. He had told my wife stories of the first house and how it was built and sold her on the idea. The whole time we spent on the boat, my wife practiced techniques which she insisted would get her a house as soon as we landed. I really didn't mind, in fact, we were all willing to instruct her. What I didn't like was that Shem wouldn't let me teach his woman anything. Kept her squirreled away in his cabin, wouldn't let her out at mealtimes. Share and share alike is what I always say. She cared for the animals on the lower decks, but we saw her only two or three times the whole trip. So, it was no surprise that we all parted ways. Besides we'd seen enough of each other to last a lifetime.

In our clan, we started with the rules that we believed the big guy would make if he were talking to anybody which he doesn't do much these days. All mating was to be done with your mother's sister's children or with your own parents, no sibling stuff, we felt the big guy would want that to be off limits. It was a fair rule and kept us from the sort of anarchy the first family had experienced. Mating was done for life, supposedly, but if one got really tired of a mate, one could trade, if you found someone who was willing to trade. This helped cut down on the fighting some of the other clans experienced. We all travelled around enough that every few months we would meet with one of the other clans at an oasis or when the fruit along the delta was in season. One of the clans ruled you could only mate with siblings, in my father's clan, you could only mate outside the clan. This proved so difficult and there were so many who broke the rules that they had to give it up.

I traded with one of my sons after my wife started to do the singing by the river routine. My son had always missed his mother, so it worked out well for both of us. Unfortunately, when I ran into her, she would stick out her tongue and tell me, If I had known how marvelous my boy was, I would left you earlier, it was so much work to get you going. I don't know why I bothered.

But my niece was a pleasure, undemanding, uncomplicated without all the scheming, and vicious ideas about how I should kneel and beg at her slightest whim. She would shine into my face with her large moonbeam eyes, and it made me want to shout, Jennifer, Jennifer, thank God who created you. With her, I felt loud and large and boisterous, the leader of the clan, and she was shorter than me which was a blessing. I even taught my little niece Jennifer to moan, and moaning makes it all worth it.

4

Oklahoma

In our family, we grew up reading the Bible, praying, knowing God's word. My mother weaned me the day I started first grade, and she told me to pray, and

I knew then that I'd be a preacher some day. I could tell you about the work we did and about our crops and that sort of thing, but I'd rather just tell you about our family.

I was born in an old brick house, but when I was small, my mother moved us to a new white frame house. My sisters Meghan and Cleopatra took care of me when I grew up, and I loved them, although at the time, I couldn't figure out where my mother was. It wasn't until I began to get old enough to walk around the house by myself that I understood that my mother had a full time life just dealing with my father Michelle.

Michelle met my mother at a barn dance and knew immediately that he had to have her. She had long silky hair and very bad table manners, stable manners he used to call them, and he decided right away, she was a girl who wouldn't criticize him or follow him around checking up on him, besides she reminded him of himself. When he brought her home, his father just laughed. She's your half sister, he said. Michelle's green eyes gleamed in the candlelight, and he took her to the barn and had her on his father's sawdust pile. Michelle always said she never looked lovelier than when she had sawdust in her hair.

My mother was a saint, believe me. The first year, she gave birth to Meghan and Cleo and by the time I came along, she looked old before her time. She tried to let the girls know what was up. Some have said that she just left them to the hands of fate, but I know that wasn't true. She used to insist that we all sleep together. At night, Michelle would be out, visiting bars, going to whorehouses, who knows?

By the time I was ten, children started coming by, grey eyed children who looked just like me. By the time we had all reached puberty, and the boys were growing whiskers, it was clear that the whole neighborhood, in fact, our whole part of the city, was populated with Michelle's children. It became clear to me that my future girlfriends would all be my half sisters if I were to have a girlfriend, which I didn't intend to do. I had devoted my life to taking care of my mother and sisters. My sisters were both pregnant with Michelle's children by the time I was in high school, and the very sight of him was enough to make the hair on the back of my neck stand up. I didn't greet him with a Hey Dad, like I used to. Even when I'd begun to realize what a cad he was, I'd still been polite when he showed up at family gatherings and wandered off into the bushes with my aunts. Now I greeted him with a snarl, and since I was getting to be a man, he was staying away more and more. I prided myself that he was afraid of me.

My sisters never talked about him much. I had always understood that he had assaulted them on their fairy princess sheets, but they never really said so. They would sit with me in the evening rocking on the porch, singing to their unborn babies, and they'd put their arms around me. Mother would sit knitting; she was getting a bit lame, so sometimes she'd be so stiff at the end of the day that I had to carry her to bed. I'd lay her on the bed she used to sleep in with Michelle, and I would wonder how she could even bear being his wife, and I'd gently stroke her hair.

When my sisters' children were born, he rarely came by to visit, and I felt a rage for him growing in me. When he did come by, it was to send us all outside while one of my sisters would be alone with him for a while. He used to pretend this was because he wanted to talk with them, but none of us were fooled anymore. Cleo would emerge, eyes downcast, and then sit on the porch staring out into space, and he'd smile madly and call my sister Meghan. Meghan walked with a limp and slurred her syllables. She frothed at the mouth, and the bubbling around her lips combined with her glassy eyed stare used to give me the creeps, but I put it all down as being the fault of Michelle who had been harassing them since they were old enough to write. Meghan was still a beauty, green eyed, white skin, black hair, the loveliest hands, and she was constantly bathing. She bathed several times a day, a sort of insane ritual. Most of the time she walked around the house with just a towel wrapped around her.

My sister Cleo's daughter had an accident and was killed by a bus while she was still in kindergarten, but Cleo hardly had time to mourn before she was giving birth to another of Michelle's children. It wasn't until late at night that she would have time to cry, and I would hold her. I never had time for a girl-friend. I never left the house, it was all I could do to keep my mother and sisters going. I hated Michelle more every day. He would come by, take what he wanted from them, and I was left, my hands outstretched to catch their tears, all I got was their tears, but I was growing claws. I was definitely growing claws, and I was determined to use them.

One evening late, a troop of neighborhood children bicycled by our house pointing and laughing while we sat on the front porch eating stew. Every one of them looked just like us, and I shivered and held my sisters tightly. And then it came, the front doorbell ringing, and that familiar whistle, and there was my father Michelle. I stood up to greet him. We were just the same height, he and I, his hair was still light brown, and I realized that we looked nearly identical and that in the near darkness someone could mistake me for him, and I shuddered at the thought. My mother began moaning behind me, a sort of practiced moan, as if she were doing it on purpose, and my sisters both slipped down on their knees and begged him to leave them alone. Meghan had given birth to another child three days before, and Cleo only the night before. I saw my sisters kneeling in the lamplight, I heard my mother moaning, and my father stood there, lighting his pipe, whistling.

He was always rather fearless in his wickedness, that smile sitting jaunty as a girl on a swing on his features, his black hat with a feather cocked to one side. I did what I had done so many times I couldn't count them, I asked my father if he wouldn't like to go for a walk. My father took my arm, and my sister Cleo caught my eye, she knew she had both double crossed me and hoodwinked him, and my father and I were off together. My father would usually talk a little about his business and about the price of guns; he was a collector, and the fear would rise and rise in my chest, I'd feel it there in huge gulping swallows, and then he'd round some bend, press me against a tree, or have me get down, and he'd say, well, I guess it's your turn, boy, since the ladies decline my services this evening. So on this night, he was talking on, and feeling up a scar on his cheek with his fingers, and I wondered whether I wasn't surrounded by phonies, and whether I wasn't a phony too. I was younger than him, and stronger, and as we rounded the bend by the pond, he motioned to me to get on all fours, and I twisted around, threw him to the ground, and in less time than it takes me to tell you this, I had strangled him and thrown him into the pond. His body sank and then turned over and floated to the surface, his eyes facing up toward the moon, and I wondered if God was watching him. He'd gone so far from God's laws, I expected God didn't have any use for him anymore, but then what do I know of God.

I walked back toward the house where the women sat, singing a sad sort of river song. "Where's your father?" my mother asked, a slight gleam in her eye. I saw her now with a certain repugnance, she withered before my eyes, and without thinking, I reached out and cuffed her. Gone, I said.

I turned to my sister Meghan. Come on upstairs, I said. Her eyes widened, and she stumbled getting up. I herded her into the house and felt some satisfaction as she bustled to please me. All of my days of struggle seemed distant, I felt that I was finally inside the right story, an old story, living out a plan some big guy had set up for me.

| Greg Sanders | *The Gallery* |

MY FATE WAS DETERMINED by a visit, years ago, to the spiral Gallery, a structure no longer standing.

Some weeks before that visit, a sculpture of prurient content had reportedly become part of the Gallery's collection. An apocryphal tale had circulated about a band of ragged art historians who had bought the sculpture, of unknown age and provenance, attributable to some great *anonymous*, and installed it in the middle of the night. All but the least respectable papers ignored the story. But according to those few twenty-five cent dailies that picked it up, the "X-rated" sculpture was simply part of an effort by the Gallery's steering committee to stave off bankruptcy by whatever means possible. It was perceived as an ill-conceived act of desperation by an institution that was for the most part, dead. There was suspicion that promoters had hoped that by veiling the piece's installation in mystery they would in fact draw crowds. But no such occurrence took place and the Gallery's fate seemed sealed.

The popularity of the Gallery's architectural spiral and the myth that it effected hallucinations on its visitors had long since worn off. The strange and secretive design was now said to simply amplify thoughts and moods, rather than cause visions. According to the *New York Times*, that spiral hallway "texturized meaning" but did nothing more. Some theorized that because its great hall was shaped like the cochlea, the Gallery's amplification of sound was no surprise. Holdovers from previous decades spoke more generally, often with mist in their eyes, of holy convergences and the like, space that broke the rules of a Cartesian universe. But no matter what one believed, it was an undeniably decrepit building, fading quickly, and a poorly managed, insolvent institution. Many of its greatest works of art had been pulled and were now displayed at those monolithic institutions whose endowments seem never to be in doubt.

For decades the Gallery was an eyesore on lower Madison Avenue. It was built in the early 1920s by a trio of brothers; the mysterious Nahmans. Mysterious because they left no records of their lives, nor is it known where they went once their Gallery was completed. They were obsessed, so the Gallery's official history went, with creating a space unlike any other on the planet, and by most measures they succeeded. It's known only that the Nahmans' roots ran deep into Spain, to the medieval Catalonian city of Gerona. That city, its ancient section walled, its streets furrowed with narrow passages, is widely regarded as a birthplace of Kabbalah.

On that day of my first visit I was merely looking for some excitement. A bachelor of limited means, I sought out stimulation when things got dull, which was often. I had been working for some time in the state filing department of a large property casualty insurance company. My job involved analysis and facilitation with respect to the Company's compliance with statutes and regulations that govern insurance rates, rules, and forms. As an example, if I was told that the Company wished to begin writing general liability coverage for chicken feed manufacturers in Minnesota, then I would consult the *State Filing Handbook* ("The Bible"), see what one had to do in order to request adoption of rates, rules and forms in that state for said line of business, then follow the procedures exactingly. I would correspond with the Minnesota Insurance Department for perhaps three months, and if things went swimmingly, we would soon be insuring myriad chicken feed manufacturers in Minnesota. Simply put, it was a job—not thrilling or glorious in the least, yet above what I had expected out of life.

I picked a midweek afternoon to visit the Gallery. I guessed that attendance would be lower than on weekends and that my search for this mysterious sculpture would therefore be less inhibited. My plan was to take a long lunch. As I got off the bus at East 23rd Street and looked north up Madison Avenue at my destination, I was reminded, quite clearly, that the Gallery, its resolute dome stained with rust, its concrete patches of the previous decades discolored, was nothing more than a decrepit landmark, ironically "loved" by New Yorkers in the know and ignored by all but the most post-modern of tourists. Scaffolding had been erected over the sidewalk to protect pedestrians from debris that occasionally sloughed off the façade.

I entered through the heavy brass doors, paid the fifteen dollars admission, and handed my circular ticket to the usher, who had the unfortunate duty of dressing like a medieval steward of some unknown variety. Into the great, singular hall I stepped. Those who have visited the Gallery will recall that its main architectural feature is the one continuous turn that leads always to the right at a slight declination. On the left wall—the outside turn—sculptures were displayed, some on low pedestals, others, massive, glowered from great heights. On that day, the first of numerous visits, such works were an inconsequential blur, for I was interested in only the one piece of work I'd read about. It's sad, really, to admit that I felt a stirring, an expectant and bodily palpitation. Paintings, which hung along the inside wall, were of almost no interest to me: some lesser landscapes of the Hudson River schools; a few small reproductions of sketches by Goya; an abstract portrait of our famed mayor Fiorello La Guardia—these are some of the works I had my back to that day. I gave each sculpture a quick glance, not being sure whether the rumored piece was a literal rendering or a figurative sort of interpretation. As I walked further into that space that continuous curve, at first intriguing me with its subtle clockwise charm, was now becoming sharper, turning with an ever increasing period. On I walked, further into, and toward the center of, that strange and breathtaking space.

Finally, I came upon the piece. Unlike the other works, there was no etched plastic plaque, no indication of its origin or date of composition. Mounted on a thin stand that was nearly invisible, it seemed to hover in the air in front of my face. It was strange, to say the least, to see this piece of natural ingenuity removed from the haven of thighs, perineum, navel. This shimmering sculpture made of a solid yet mysterious material, wrought with delicate precision, glimmered luridly under the display lights. Fawning, engorged, two-feet in width—all in all, daunting. A gynecological still life, both titillating and repulsive. I breathed heavily with the exertion and strangeness of my search, and I was immersed in a sea of murmuring whose source I could not locate.

Things soon began to change. I felt as if a low-frequency vibration was passing through my body, as if I were part of a conduit. I could feel sweat gathering around my upper lip and along the lines of my forehead—the sweat of nervousness and dementia. Not since I had been an adolescent, during a mid-night fit in which, bolt upright in bed, I realized that death was inevitable and my life's memories would be extinguished forever and ever once I died, had I felt this kind of sweating. I was motionless, looking at the welcoming and giant sex. I had the feeling that heavy foreplay was about to begin, felt the expectant flush of fornication. My lunch hour had already officially come and gone and I was worried, slightly, about spending much more time here. Still, I wanted badly to reach out and caress the sculpture.

I turned and looked back down the hall to see if any spectators were about. Nobody to be found close by, the great hall unwinding, curving out of sight to the left. Empty. I went back and pressed my hand against the cold rim. I set off some type of modest proximity alarm. It beeped politely, and a red light the size of a button blinked solemnly from high above. I moved closer, rubbing the engorged lips, trying to warm them. They seemed to embrace me back, to warm to the touch, although I am uncertain if their pliancy was an illusion. A few people, defeated and perturbed by their long spiraling trek, did eventually come around that tight bend, but they retreated, walking backward, their eyes wide. I had that part of the great hall to myself.

From the topmost reaches of the sculpture a smooth little knob was peeking out from beneath its hood—a cautious turtle, a Cambrian arthropod. I anointed it with the last bit of moisture on my fingertips. I closed my eyes and pressed on it, rubbed that region and imagined a forty-foot tall woman bucking with pleasure. And just then a sound occupying all octaves rose from some small distance further along the Gallery hall, welling up from an abyss. It was a mechanical activation of sorts but without comparison to anything I'd ever heard. A deep rumble of bearings followed by the sound of air rushing through a narrow fissure at great pressure.

Things seemed different now in the gallery. The alarm had stopped and all murmuring had ceased. Stranger still, security still hadn't shown up. A bright light, emanating from around the tight curve and reflecting off the white wall, now illuminated the sculpture. I walked towards the light source and realized with amazement that the sculpture I'd been so intimate with was the last piece of art in the Gallery. That spiral hallway was near its end, turning in upon itself in tighter and tighter proportions until a man could no longer walk it. At that narrow end I squeezed my body in as far as it could go and saw, at the edge of my vision, a bright vertical slit. The very end of the Gallery! This narrow opening—a passageway for a circus thinman—was the source of the light. I reached my hand towards it, pushing my shoulders into the fold, emptying my lungs of air. With my arm and fingers outstretched as much as possible I could feel warmth at the tip of my fingers and a gentle breath tickling the hair on my arms. But the entranceway was slowly closing, the walls gently ejecting me back into the greater width of the hallway. I quickly returned to the sculpture and slowly caressed that button until I heard the opening of the passageway once again. Not hesitating this time, I walked quickly towards it.

Losing sense of time, dimensionality, and then consciousness itself, I don't know how to measure the amount of time that passed before I was cognizant of my own body. I was now a newborn being delivered into a smoke-filled New Orleans room on September 16, 1965, my birthday. Still covered in the lubrication of terrestrial arrival, my umbilical cord was adeptly snipped and tied off by a hand still unknown to me. Perhaps a doctor had volunteered to supervise my natural birth.

"Oh Christ, Dora," I heard a woman's voice say (this would be my Aunt

Julie), "he's a little trouble maker, I can see it in those eyes. And a horny one, ain't he?"

"Like his father," said another voice (this was indeed my father, who never stuck around after this day).

A small crowd was gathered in the room. I was now fully conscious, my mind that of the thirty-seven-year old who had entered the Gallery moments earlier, yet I was unable to communicate with any but the most infantile and shattering of squeals, one of which I let out. This sequence was to be repeated many times, and each time the invariability brought the utmost comfort to me. A time traveler now, how could I *not* get aroused thinking about the world that was to be mine, the women to conquer, stocks to buy, the civilizations to save.

My life—or each life in turn—would be spent accruing knowledge, memorizing the most spectacular stock performers and the events leading to the most disastrous failings of humanity. Passing through the next time, I would hope to change the path of our world, but inevitably would fail in all but the most mundane of tasks, that of making money. For the world, its course firmly set in motion, can be affected only fractionally by a single person, despite his wisdom above years. And life, especially with near perfect foresight, is invariably a rather dull endeavor.

Fresh from the uterus, I was hungry, cold, and irritable. As my mother, the Dora of above, tenderly fed me the first drops of breast milk, my mind would race ahead, planning my first leverage of foreknowledge, tallying my potential wealth, plotting my foreshortened life's stratagem for this go around. And then, also invariably, baby's meconium came forth from his virginal bowels and there the small gathering of young hippies gave a unified cheer and my mother held me high into a cloud of tobacco smoke, saying, weakly, "My little king! You're going to be my little fucking king."

Always, that spring day of renewal commenced with my dreamy march down the worn Gallery hallway towards that secreted button around which, I am now certain, the universe spun. The first year or more of my renewed life was invariable. I was happy to be swaddled, changed, fed, bathed, coddled, consciously savoring these times. In order to keep suspicion at bay, I could not feasibly do anything to affect my life or the world until I had reached at least two years of age. Needless to say, it would be physically impossible, nearly, to do otherwise.

After a few more passes through the Gallery's portal I was maximizing my knowledge of stocks, wars, women, minerals, and oil. Women, though thrown into the midst of the list, should perhaps be entirely excluded, for no matter how many times I had lived my thirty-seven years, I had not been able to improve upon a certain highly competent mediocrity when it comes to the act itself. I was, and am, still the same physical specimen, able only to perfect the mechanics of lovemaking, but unable to change who I *am*; although I gain knowledge, I am still Jonathan S., moderately handsome, shy sometimes to a fault, and rarely the sort of lover women swoon over.

It was not long in terms of my course of lives before I began encountering, on a recurring basis, a female who, I surmised, must also have discovered the secret of episodic repetitions, for I saw her grow closer to me with each new life I lived. Perhaps we were mutually circling each other, neither certain of the other's provenance, both hesitant to ascertain the truth girding the fellow traveler. While I always knew at what point I would encounter all my other acquaintances for the first time, she shifted about in the otherwise predictable timeline. At first she was a matter of curiosity, appearing momentarily in my life and then disappearing. Once, at my insistence, she even joined me for a cup of coffee in my later years as if we were acquaintances by some other means. This was early on, and neither of us was willing to ask the one important question that was so absurd as to be a reasonable cause for institutionalization, a chance not worth taking given the unknown lifespan of the decrepit Gallery that housed the all important portal. To be removed from the possibility of cycling through one's life again was unthinkable and I suppose akin death. In one life we might greet each other with toothy smiles at a polo game and retire to a willow's shade to sip Chablis. I recall a visit to one of my bankers in which she and I greeted each other in an antechamber as if we were the closest of friends, even though we had never met in that life. As time, or *our* time, went on we would make our presence known to each other at earlier and earlier stages of development. Of age roughly equal to mine, I had met her this last time at the country's top private grammar school where we had both managed to win full scholarships. We became companions, the best of friends until, in our teen years, the dam finally burst and we decided to marry as soon as was legally permissible.

It turned out that she, Alice, had been a cleaning woman at the Gallery and one night, piqued by the verisimilitude of the new sculpture, stimulated by its quiet proximity, and, as always, diligent in her work habits, she thoughtfully varnished the intimate region with a moistened cloth.

We waited for some time before having our first child. We now have three, the eldest being seven and the youngest not yet one. They are mortal, delicate things, and in need of Ivy League educations. We could not bear to leave them nor to leave each other for another pass through that spiral Gallery, even with knowledge of certain reunion, and so we allowed time to pass until, inevitably, the decrepit Gallery was emptied, demolished, and a glass tower, a residential high rise, erected in its place. Only yesterday we stood before the just-completed behemoth, acknowledging together the certainty of our mortality.

We will live out the rest of our years without hope of renewal, our vast knowledge being carried only forward until it is taken into the grave with us. Our doctors inform us that we appear to be rather oversensitive with regard to the effects of aging. With fear and awe I have counted several dozen grey hairs within my beard. Aging is an alien and frightening experience, for although we have lived for several millennia, we have no experience with the inexorability of physical decline. And if we are encyclopedic beyond our apparent years, we are like frightened children when it comes to reading the newspapers each morning, for we never know what new darkness the headlines will report. To alleviate this tension, Alice has decided to take up tennis. Given my years, I am surprised I never even considered the game.

David Pollock | *The Children's Hour*

THE GAME PRECIPITATION begins with a girl between ages fourteen and twenty-one. It's important that she is young-looking, only because a focus of the game is vulnerability. Now this girl may be called Diana, Susan or Mayor. When I play with my man-slave, Prince Alex of Westchester Heights, he hops around his aluminum cage and tries to lift the pet boulder to which his shackles are nailed. My man-slave makes me sick sometimes, he and that boulder. You should see what he does with it. He urinates in the tomatoes. He is ungrateful and he is stubborn. But I owe the success of our popular television show to the man-slave, so I put up with his tantrums and I indulge him in ways I'm not proud of.

"Me no want Mayor," cries Prince Alex. "Me want Diana or Susan. No Mayor!"

"Now, prince." I lift my folding chair from the lineup of folding chairs with missing legs and damaged seats and set it across from his cage so we may have a civilized conversation. "This *is* a game, which would suggest there must be rules. To completely disregard the game because of a detail, a trivial detail is ridiculous."

"Prince Alex say if detail so trivial, why not leave out detail?" Then he punches his chest with his left hand, a gesture he uses as punctuation for any thought he considers especially profound.

"It's not really the detail, is it, man-slave? What bothers you is the game itself. You hate the game, man-slave. You hate it."

I should say a few words about the decline of Prince Alex of Westchester Heights. I don't find the story particularly interesting because it's history, a stain. I get so frustrated when I stain my clothing, when I'm tipsy and dribble beer on a clean shirt, or shake off too close to home and sprinkle a pant leg, or step on a tomato a disgruntled man-slave has thrown from between his bars. Someone is bound to ask, "What kind of stain is that?" because I will stare at a stain convinced it's becoming darker, more visible. If it's an acceptable and

164

humorous story, I'll make it a light conversation piece, and if it's urine I will say it's sink water.

Timeline

Sept. 12, 1983

Prince Alex is conceived during Royal Exhilaration Days. Each day of this week a desirable lady of darker skin leaves her peasant village containing four public horses, two automobiles, a tomato garden and a well, and travels to the palace to lay on the Royal Mattress. The subject composes a four-hundred word essay addressing why she believes her child should be buried in the Royal Cemetery. A sensitive woman with a lisp, Juanita Dispenser argues that a kind nod from history is the only heaven a mortal can hope for.

The king places his hand over his heart. "Immortality," he declares, "is found in the history books alone."

Meanwhile, leftist forces grow. They fill blackboards with Royal statements they contradict with their own observations: "If the common people are free and benevolent, why do they not live in palaces, how is it that a village with population twenty has the same number of cars and horses as a village with population one hundred twenty, and why does Royalty enjoy sweet grape tomatoes imported from California while the rest of Westchester Heights must settle for what grows in their Royally-funded yards?" These leftists, third-hand royalty, the sons of sons of sons are commonly known as Libertines. Their earliest meetings occur in the damp basements of their parents' houses and in the backs of tea shops.

May 3, 1984

Prince Alex is born. Juanita Dispenser, holding a fresh life from her own womb, begs for custody. An agent of Human Affairs asks her to calm down. He punctures her neck with a dart containing the herbal tranquilizer Ricotene. Juanita discovers she is allergic to Ricotene when she dies twenty minutes later.

Libertine-led riots ensue throughout Westchester Heights. Most participants lack the proper ideology and are simply bitter that they too are not Royal. Nevertheless, the riots are hailed as the first victory of the Revolution.

May 24, 1984

Failed poet turned playwright, Gerald Sanders begins work on *Precipitation,* a show in which young girls are collected into oversized pickle jars, only to be removed via lottery on the second day of precipitation each month. Three female leads, Diana, Susan and Mayor are named after three of the king's wives. Sanders, a dedicated revolutionary, means for the work to satirize what he describes as "the games the king plays with his people, his chess set of beating hearts."

Precipitation becomes a popular post-revolution game; the original politics are lost to the pure pleasure of chasing young beauties through the rain.

Spring, 2000

Alex acquires the title "The People's Prince" after he works the assembly line at Jewman Roth's Pastoral Glove Factory, one of four remaining private industries in Westchester Heights. (The factory will become Royal property within a year; "inhumane" labor conditions are made "humane.") Alex's experience among the workers is mistaken by moderate liberals, Libertine-led apathetics as a benevolent class-crossing. In reality the job is punishment prescribed by the king for the prince's loose sexuality. Historians estimate that Prince Alex had been responsible for nearly twenty births, and had penetrated, in one way or another, over one hundred male anuses.

Historical anecdote: Prince Alex's fascination with the male anus nearly had him exiled to New Jersey when an agent from Domestic Affairs, performing his Royal rounds, a consequence of checks-and-balances, discovered Negro dishwasher, Abraham Meteslicierre in the Royal Game Room, naked and belly-down on the ping pong table, flattening the net. A knight from the king's ivory chess set protruded from between the dishwasher's meaty buttocks.

Prince Alex did himself no favors by entering the room with a jewel encrusted crate containing, among other items, an ivory pawn, an uncapped bottle of ketchup and a fine pair of oven mitts with a few blackened fingers. For the first time in three generations a member of the first family was tranquilized. A leak in the court, later revealed to be the secretary of Domestic Affairs, fed the story to *The Royal Times.* More riots ensued. The far left called for the prince's exile.

Alex was the People's Prince. Fearing a national disaster, The King spoke publicly: "Do not worry, good people. Your prince shall stay right here where you need him. Right now we are investigating. The suspect, Abraham Meteslicierre is in Royal Custody. He has denied any accusations of magic, of casting spells on Prince Alex or of holding a knife to his throat, thereby forcing him into— into shoving one of my prized game pieces into his rectum. Thank you, dear subjects, brave and benevolent peoples of my kingdom. I have no further comment."

2001

Gerald Sanders's *Precipitation* is performed at The Department for Public Transportation Royal Theater. The play takes four highway adoptions at the National Theatrics Awards, including the palace drawbridge for best original play. The king, although offended by what he describes as "misled political satire," is warned by top advisors to "shake no more fruit from their tree." The king does not understand but leaves well-enough alone.

April, 2002

Abraham Meteslicierre is relieved of all charges as the king fears his subjects will riot over just about anything. The Great Riot at Syluinischanyovichberg ensues after the prince publicly penetrates the dishwasher's anus on a water mattress in Syluinischanyovichberg Square. Alex's motive for the display had been to mock, in the fashion of fictional homosexual, Oscar Wilde, his own sodomy charges by allowing the people of Westchester Heights to witness him in action. The plan backfires when future chair of The Department Guaranteeing the Fairer Treatment of Children, Gertrude McGraw pushes to the front of the crowd and shouts in her banshee voice: "He is the people's playboy, and we are his toys!"

Three casualties due to trampling, The Royal Library of Eugenics and Other Pseudo-sciences is plastered with the people's food. Hundreds of vine-ripened tomatoes are the artillery of revolt.

By 2004 the king understands that his family's reign is finished. He curses himself for never having built a military, having believed that people did not like serving in militaries. People, he now understands, don't appreciate much. On the wet night of April 22, he packs his most treasured belongings into four trailers, and fills another three with the Royal Fortune. He takes with him his two favorite wives, Diana and Susan, and makes room for a few kids to ensure his legacy. Friends and top advisors are given airline tickets to the paradises of their choice. Those left in the palace, those with loose Royal ties, the poorly behaved, past threats to the crown (i.e., Prince Alex) are removed by leftist wrecking crews on May 1. *Precipitation* is performed on the drawbridge to a loud and excited audience; not a line of dialogue is audible.

In an act of spite, guised as a nod to the meek, the royal leftovers are forced into man-slave camps or Decharming Schools where they are beaten with concrete spoons and shocked into adopting primitive language and degrading style of dress. Once graduated the man-slaves are each given a pet boulder and a caveman suit. The less dangerous are provided with clubs. They are handed over to the lowest of the low in an attempt at reparation.

Before the reparation I picked tomatoes from the vines in my Royally-funded yard and sold them to children for quarters. One will pay seventy-five cents for a bruised tomato and glow right in front of you as the chunky juice rolls down her chin to her collar. When the leftists came to my shack and pounded on the aluminum door frame that has no door and offered me a man-slave, I thought he would be just like a child. I was wrong. They assured me, gloating Libertines with their bohemian white unisex gowns and their "How can Reconstruction Turn My Life Around?" pamphlets, that Prince Alex had been pacified at Decharming School. "Just look," they said, "at his caveman suit. And see the boulder? Listen to how he grunts. He makes *you* look like a prince."

I catch him sometimes, eyeing up my buttocks, licking his filthy lips. I've seen him with that boulder. He's still Royal all right. But the Libertines said that the lottery run by The Department for the Fairer Division of Wealth placed me as an entertainer and they offered me a television show.

"Wonderful," I said. "My mind is very complex and pregnant with entertaining ideas, not the least of which involves storing girls in oversized pickle jars only to let them escape. And tomatoes," I continued, "are often overlooked as being a fruit fit for drama."

My man-slave, hunched on all fours, howled into the damp afternoon. A pack of stray neighborhood children scattered into the alleyways like pigeons from a loud noise.

The Children's Hour Starring Master David and his Man-slave, Prince Alex of Westchester Heights

(Bubble-bubble, double-trouble, Master David and Prince Alex)

Hi, kids. Thanks for coming. You know, we almost didn't get here today. It's true, it's true. Prince Alex almost *escaped*.

"Shame on you, Prince Alex," shout the children. "Shame on you."

I was taking our man-slave for a walk through town. I waved hello to the mailman. He was happy to see me.

"We're happy to see you too!"

I waved hello to Gerald Apron, the friendly butcher. I was a little scared, friends, I'll have to admit. There was some *blood* on his *apron*. Nevertheless, he was happy to see me.

"We're also happy to see you!"

Then I passed town hall, where the mayor was watering the lawn. Oops, he said because he accidentally sprayed his pants, and it looked like he peed himself. But I could tell he was happy to see me.

"Hah, hah," laughed the children, "we're happy to see you as well."

Then I came to a brothel. Does anyone here know what a brothel is? The loveliest boys and girls are there, sprawled across the great marble steps. Each one held a plump tomato as if it were an apple. They waved hello. They were happy to see me.

"We're so happy to see you!"

But they weren't happy to see Prince Alex.

"Shame on you, Prince Alex."

Me lonely, said Prince Alex. Me want hugs. Me want *love*.

But that's not really what our man-slave wants, is it children? What does he want?

"He wants anuses!"

Oh, Prince Alex chased the lovely boys and girls all throughout the building. He chased a lovely Chinese boy up a wooden staircase. Prince Alex growled and sniffed just like a dog.

"Prince Alex," said the children, none of whom could believe what they heard. "That's disgusting!"

And he tackled the Chinese boy. He licked his neck and inserted three fingers into the boy's anus.

"Yuck," exclaimed the children. "Aw, yuck."

The owner of the brothel was very angry at me. She said I should learn to keep my man-slave tamed. She beat Prince Alex over the head with a tomato, then laughed so that her fat body quivered. "I'll call the police," she said. "They'll lock your horny little man-slave up."

"Not prison! Oh, Prince Alex, you're the worst!"

Don't worry children. We're here, aren't we? And isn't Prince Alex right here? Look at him pouting. Don't worry, man-slave. When we come back from this brief commercial break, we'll have a surprise for you. Plus, a game for all of the children in the studio audience.

And we're back! As promised, I have a big surprise for Prince Alex. Why do you look so glum, man-slave? Don't you want to be happy?

"Don't look glum," shout the children. "We're so happy to see you!"

Hear that, prince? You're welcome here. And just to show you that we're not mad about your misadventure at the brothel, here's your big surprise. Mystery guest, come on out!

Now, our mystery guest is cloaked, man-slave. Let's see if you can figure out who it is. The clues: He kept the dishes clean, but to you he was a penetration machine. A short time in jail he spent so that Prince Alex was not far away sent. A source of joy he was for you, in his rectum you fit a bottle, a chess piece and a cork screw.

Abraham Meteslicierre, uncloak yourself! Now, prince, here we have a box of ten items. Without looking reach inside. Whatever you grab Abraham will entertain us with it. How's that sound? Wonderful, I knew you'd cheer up, man-slave. And how about you, Abraham? Oh, Abraham, there's no reason to cry. There are children here. They don't want to be sad.

"Don't make us cry, Abraham. We're so happy to see you!"

Do you hear that, Abraham? You're welcomed here.

Anything, says Abraham, anything at all. Just keep me away from that animal. He's downright horrible. All he waaaants to do is stick things up my *poop* shoot!

Don't say those horrible things, Abraham. Look at Prince Alex now. Don't pout, man-slave. Abraham didn't mean it.

"Abraham loves you," shout the children.

I did too mean it! I swear on my mammy's grave! Keep that man away. Ain't nobody's ass but mine!

Now that's not true either, Abraham. Maybe Alex prefers your anus to others, but it's not just you. Today, for instance, the man-slave was wicked hungry for a Chinese anus. And don't think I haven't seen him eyeing up my own.

I don't care none, I don't care. Just let me out of these here cuffs and let me go on home. I got dishes to wash, and the sweet lord knows I want nothing to do with this here prince and what he wants to do with my butt hole.

"Hah, hah," laugh the children. "Abraham said 'butt hole'."

All right, Abraham. All right. It'll all be over soon. Now, prince, pick something from the box. Close your eyes. That's it. And let's see what you have.

I hope it ain't one of them ketchup bottles. I really hope it's nothing he wants to ram up my rear. Sweet Jesus, mother Mary, don't let him get me in the ass.

Me no want, says Prince Alex. Me no want book. Me want corkscrew. Me want toothpaste dispenser.

Oh, look. It *is* a book. *A People's History of the Revolution: Notes from the Underground!* You know what that means, Abraham. It means you get to *read* from it!

Me no want hear read, says Prince Alex. Me want pick again.

Now, man-slave, that's simply not possible.

Awwww, I don't know how to read none. I can't read pineapple from Big Apple.

"What?" complain the children. "What? That doesn't make any sense."

Just take the book, Abraham. Start at the beginning and work your way straight through to the end. That's it. No, Abraham, that's the end of the book. Turn it around.

I don't know. Like I said, let me go on *home*. I have a whole tub full of plates and forks and all kinds of my master's kitchenwares. If I'm late, he's gonna string me across the bathtub and get me with the red hot poker. I'll scream 'n' I'll yell 'n' I'll promise I'll never be late again, but he like to do me that way, and I don't know what's worse, having that animal experiment with my crack or work'n a free man for the devil himself! And when the wife come home she's gonna curse 'n' yell everyone from the Lord to her Aunt Susanna The Great from Southern California, The Rainbow State.

"Wow," exclaim the children. "You really said a mouthful, Abraham."

Enough, enough. Abraham, read the book please.

I don't know how to read a goddarned word of the king's English.

Abraham, we're running out of time here. Our friends in the studio audience would like to have their game of Precipitation for awesome prizes.

Me no want hear, complains Prince Alex. Me no like history. Me want *love*.

"Precipitation," chant the children, "Precipitation, Precipitation."

All right, I'm reading, I'm reading. Let's see what it says here. Once upon a time in the little ol' town a Weschedder Height was a little gal who had to get in the pickle jar. But I don't wanna get in the pickle jar, ma, I don't wanna have to run through the rain! Ohh, you must little gal, else big king gonna come on down the mountain and have ye all for supper in a big ol' pot for cooking stew! What kind of stew you want? I want stew with lamb, with carrots 'n' plenty of tomato. Mmmm-mmm. I love the toms. I wanna make me a stew 'n' have me a supper . . .

Afterword

When playing Precipitation, I am partial to a girl between eighteen and twenty. While it's true that Diana, Susan or Mayor should be as youthful as possible, there are problems with using children. An anecdote:

Bumbling Ogelman Fry was a purist when it came to Precipitation. He only played the game when there was actual precipitation in the air, he used three girls, Diana, Susan *and* Mayor, and they were always young, young, young. Sometimes—and I am not the one telling you this, they were too young to have been legally rented. Most of us were either passive to the Libertine revolution, or we were so jealous that we were not Royal we thought the revolution was a keen idea. Ogelman Fry however kept a secret chalkboard in his closet, just like a true super genius, and he deconstructed every sentence publicly uttered by the king or his press secretary. True, bumbling Ogleman Fry was dedicated to the revolution, but without the ideology. Revolution and deconstruction were games for him; he was both bumbling and compulsive.

One afternoon Ogleman left his abode, lit a bowl of cherry tobacco and thought, Yes, I believe it will rain today. I don't know where the man got his girls, but sure enough he returned home that afternoon with three twelve-year olds strung together with a velvet rope, in case one suffered pre-game anxiety. Listening to the thunder, waiting for the rain, he fed them wheat toast with marmalade and tea with some rum and left a bowl of sweet grape tomatoes on a small round table. By early evening drizzle fell. Ogleman set out three pickle jars in the basement, a stepping stool at each, and asked his girls to climb inside.

Now, if playing Precipitation in the puritanical sense one should have a brunette (Diana), a blond (Susan) and a miscellaneous girl of darker complexion (Mayor). Ogleman's problem was with his Diana, tiny creature with ravenous hair. The girls had not been in their pickle jars for more than five minutes when Diana started behaving not unlike my man-slave, hopping up and down and crying.

"Now, now," Ogleman spoke to her through the glass, "you will be released soon. There is nothing to fear, honey. Just wait until the rain falls a bit harder, then I shall chase you beauties through it."

She pounded on the jar. Her face was swollen and wet with tears. Susan and Mayor were humiliated by Diana's behavior. They each looked down at their bare feet.

The girls were never chased through the rain. As the all-important precipitation began to pick up, Diana hyperventilated, fell over and gave herself a nasty concussion. Ogleman felt horrible. He released the girls, laid the brunette on a sofa, pressed ice to her head and fed Susan and Mayor some more tea and rum and the sweet tomatoes. They explained to bumbling Ogleman Fry that Diana's mother was very poor and had sold the girl against her will. They on the other hand were proud to partake in such a game and looked forward to careers as famous actresses.

"Never again," he declared, "will I use girls so young, mere children. They fit the part, indeed, but I wonder if there *is* something potentially unethical about it."

I have heard Ogleman Fry say these exact words but we all lie to ourselves, and much more often than we'd like to admit.

Elizabeth
Ruiz

Cold Feet

IT STARTED HAPPENING about two days after my boyfriend and I broke up. He told me he was depressed and wanted to be alone. He wanted to be alone and depressed. Depressed and alone. To deal with everything alone was his deepest desire. And that was his entire explanation. That was all I got. After he told me, we cried for one day and one night and when I woke up the next day, I got dressed and told him he had thirty-minutes to get out. I went out into the streets of New York, walked around the block and sat on a nearby stoop to chain smoke cigarettes, finally caving in to a full-fledged habit after an admirable two-year hiatus. I saw him leave the building from across the street. He looked both sad and sheepish, stealing away like a thief in the glaring morning sun.

The best man I'd ever known in the biblical sense. A sensitive man. A perceptive man. A still-too-young man in terms of dog years. A man who at least tried to communicate. A man with interesting, if sometimes irritating, incongruities. An Ivy-League educated, blue-collar smarty pants, who could cry openly, but became a grunting, shouting, arm swinging, automaton before a television broadcast of just about any sports event, especially college basketball and the Mets. I too have always had a soft spot for the Mets and all losers who try and try. A romantic man, really. But a man nonetheless, and therefore unreliable in matters of love.

I know. That's a generalization, but generalizations can be useful if kept from the hands of idiots. And just as most hormonal women are volatile, most rich people are cheapskates, or most poor folk spank their children, for example, this generalization was also born out of plentiful, observable evidence.

Alone and depressed. Depressed and alone. The ex was a writer and had a particular fondness for romanticizing his misery, which always led him to make more of it. We were gonna move in together, when he got cold feet.

He told me he still loved me. That he loved me more than anyone in the world. That's why he walked out on me, of course. After three years of loving each other and all that crap you have to go through to keep a relationship on track. They all say some such similar shit. I love you, but. But, but, but. I've learned that words are almost always lies. I was sure he would eventually call me. When his dick became a perpetual piece of wood, he would call me and say romantic things that he would regret. But I wasn't about to listen. In fact, I wouldn't even answer the phone. All I wanted was my socks back.

So it was that two days after Valentines' day, the day my lover left me, a day which hadn't meant much to me since grade school, but that I'd now never be able to forget for the rest of my fuckin' life, that *I* began to get cold feet. 'Cause two days after V. D. day, in the coldest, darkest, most suffocating part of February, when bug-eyed, urban cave dwellers of every type consider drastic measures, did my feet start feeling unusually cold, freezin' crazy cold, as if I'd just come in from walking on ice. I had to wear thick wool socks to bed every night, but when I'd wake up the next day, the socks were nowhere to be found. Gone. Vanished. Disappeared. More than once, I turned the place upside down looking for the disappeared socks, but it was no use.

I admit I can be superstitious at times. Finding significance in meaningless coincidence, believing certain trinkets or articles of clothing to be lucky, for example. That's why twelve years ago I began a spiritual quest, so I could connect my physical existence to my other worldliness without falling into the traps of popular metaphysics, such as the New York Post Horoscope, palm readers and Chinese fortune cookies. All of which, I admit, I find attractive now and again the way I sometimes yearn for those rubbery, orange candies called Circus Peanuts even though they always give me a stomachache. So I began meditating and reading up on eastern religion, as well as the ways of Native Americans and Yoruba Santeros. I also read up on the Three Biggies: Christianity, Judaism and Islam, if only to see how their approach towards the same ultimate goal, the pursuit of love and truth, paled by comparison to eastern and indigenous religions. The Three Biggies place the believers so far from God that they have to go completely insane in order to believe God exists. Maybe that's why so many wars have been waged and continue to be waged in the name of the Three Biggies—because their most faithful followers are stark raving mad from the strain of trying to love and honor a distant impersonal God. An abstraction. A God that doesn't give a fuck. I've always been drawn to religions where God can be felt everywhere, especially in our own molecules. But being that close to God is a great responsibility—a responsibility that gives most people cold feet. Despite all the reading I did, though, it wasn't until last year, after my own deep dark depression, which took the form of a ranting rage, that I began to meditate on a regular basis.

I confess, I too am an artist. The specifics of what I do don't matter. But let's just say I feel I have a calling and believe there are ways to answer the calling while finding sustainable work that is not unduly punishing. Meaning, work where I don't have to eat the shit of the overpaid credentialed ones, the kind with family legends in the top Ivy League schools, who believe that it was solely their talent and efforts that got them where they are, and that the rest of us are either lazy or genetically deficient. For me, Corporate Society is anathema, but ironically working as a typist in a monster law firm pays just enough for me to eke out an existence in New York while paying (perhaps foolishly) my debts. And after sixteen years of "following my bliss" in the Joseph Campbell sense, of taking risks and even attending graduate school, I found myself where I was at age twenty-one, except with lots more debts, a slightly higher salary to pay them with and a bit more self-confidence. New Agers would say I must be doing something wrong, that I must not be visualizing my goals, that I must not really believe that I deserve the "golden opportunities" I so desire. To these types I would respond: Choke on a Latte! I very well do believe I can accomplish my goals, even against the odds and that I very well deserve to. But sometimes I get pissed off about how damn hard it is and how damn long it takes. How damn hard *everything* is for all of us who are not born into money, or the singular desire to chase it. Through the eighties I had read a lot of New Age psychobabble and had found some of it useful, but it wasn't long before I saw through the fast food, bourgie, wish-fulfilling philosophy. It was mostly a bunch of former, blow-dry hippies, trying most awkwardly to justify their privileged lives. The ex, by the way, would agree with every word of this.

Later on, I went into formal therapy, but right in the middle of the deep dark case of the uglies I mentioned earlier, I had to give my Jungian analyst her walking papers. For four years we had discussed my anger and depression, my childhood traumas, my dreams and even my Ancestral Rage, for she was convinced that my anger was more than just the sum of my childhood and adulthood, but perhaps the sum of the anger of my ancestors, a long line of Cuban peasants, rural townies and later on, assembly-line workers. For many months, our talks centered on the validity of my anger and the pain it sprung from, and especially how burned out I was, and how important it was for me to rest from my Gestapo job and make room for creativity. The shrink herself had said that the less time I spent at Crabass, Swine & More, the law factory where I cranked out legal documents for subhuman automatons, the sooner I'd recover. She had always been sympathetic about my tough, impoverished childhood and the subsequent hardships that kept me from fulfilling my goals. Our talks also included the ex, of course, who was not then an ex. We'd been together just over two years at that point. He was a sensitive, brooding type who required a lot of attention. I'd always been glad to give it—but now I couldn't. Now my own needs consumed me and I was afraid to lose him. But the shrink encouraged me to see the ex, who was not then an ex, for who he was, someone who loved me deeply and who had already shown more courage than the other Joes who hadn't cut the lemons in the past. She also suggested I might consider taking anti-depressants, such was the depth of my despair at the time, even though I'd once adamantly declared that I was only willing to take *illegal* drugs. Experimenting on myself, I said, was preferable to becoming a guinea pig to Western medicine, which I regard as completely inept with the exception of the inevitable surgery or antibiotics. But I was so down at the time, I even agreed to try an antidepressant.

While my analyst and I hunted for a pill-pushing psychiatrist that would accept my brand of health insurance, I came up with the brilliant idea of taking a short-term disability leave from my job. Lots of secretaries at the firm were doing it for diseases both real and imaginary, including depression. When I asked the analyst to sign the necessary form, it seems I struck her Achilles heel. She became evasive and put off the issue for several weeks until I finally confronted her.

"I'm sorry but I can't sign that form," she said, her words measured and her customary mask of compassion slowly washing over her nervous face. "I don't see how colluding with you to dupe the system is going to help you in the long run."

"Whaddya mean 'dupe the system?' My own supervisor told me to apply for disability! She's an absolute corporate stickler!"

My supervisor was a kind but cowardly black woman from the south. An old-school lady who didn't believe in rocking the boat or breaking the white man's rules. I'd nicknamed her "Aunt Jemima with Shoulder Pads," but not without affection and a tinge of admiration for her unwavering discipline, however misdirected I believed it to be. Needless to say, she wasn't the type who would ever attempt to "dupe the system."

"Well then I'm not going to help you *or* your supervisor dupe the system," said the shrink, starting to lose it. "I'll sign a note saying that I strongly recommend a leave of absence."

"I can't afford an unpaid leave of absence and you know it! Why don't you just read the form before jumping to conclusions," I said, sounding more desperate by the minute. I was hitting a wall and I knew it. She shook her head.

"I feel that what goes on in our sessions is between us, and I don't want to expose it or distort it to the outside world by permanently labeling you as depressed."

What the hell did I care about being labeled? I'd already been labeled and relabeled my entire life: Spic, Bitch, Artist, Non-Exempt, Debtor, Defendant. And if it would get me out of that hellhole, before I was driven to murder, they could call me whatever the fuck they wanted. I'd been going to therapy for four years to cure my depression, and now my spoon-fed, analyst, clad in crocodile boots, was afraid to give it a name.

"'It's not a *permanent* label,'" I barked. "It's only for three weeks. Aren't I entitled to feel better? Isn't that why I'm here?"

The shrink wouldn't budge.

"Why are you doing this to me? Why won't you help me?" I pleaded.

She maintained her pseudo-sympathetic expression; I wanted to rip the lips right off her perfect, Lancôme face.

"Are you saying I'm not really depressed?" I asked with all the sarcasm I could muster. "Is that it? That I've been coming to you for four years because I'm perfectly healthy! And you've been pushing me to take toxic medication, because I'm normal and happy! I'm not really depressed and *you're not really a psychotherapist!* Is that it?"

I suddenly realized I was shouting at the top of my tits, but it was too late. There was no turning back. I stood up, towering over her, and screamed in her face.

"What if I go out into the street and choke someone right now? Just strangle them until they turn purple and die? *Then* will you sign the fuckin' form? Huh? *Will I be crazy enough for you then?*" I picked up the swivel chair.

"What if I just smash this, sexy, little, designer, chair through the window? Huh? Will you sign the Goddamned form then?"

"Stop it!" squeaked the shrink. She tried to maintain her professional composure but I could see she was scared. I backed off, remembering how people like her, people who live by waspy ethics, regardless of their backgrounds, secretly hope little low-life, emotional Spic girls like me will resort to physical violence to resolve conflict. It justifies their buried prejudices and desire to maintain their foothold in the ruling class. But, besides this little victory, I was desperate. As it was now, if I told my boss the shrink wouldn't sign the form, she would think I had lied about being depressed.

"Fine. Seeing as I was never really depressed, and you're not really a therapist, I see no reason to ever come back here."

I walked out and never went back. That is, after one last mouthful—lots of clever things about her needing therapy more than I did and about her cowardliness and her sheltered, cushy upbringing, but mostly things like "You stupid, fuckin', stupid fuckin', stupid fuckin' bitch!" Here I had given her an opportunity to put her words into action, to give me some tangible support, but the shrink had gotten cold feet.

So you see, I am no picture of perfection, no goody two shoes. I'm a package complete with troubles, complications and bad habits of my own. The ex hung in there through all of this, listening patiently, but mostly staying out of the way.

"We'll get through this together," he said. He always knew what to say but seldom knew what to do. I, on the other hand, am a woman of action. I ditched the shrink and found an HMO psychiatrist. You know, the pill pushers. After two sessions, he admitted that psychiatry was still in its infancy, and that the garden-variety type of depression that I had was the trickiest of all to diagnose. Apparently, if I'd been a schizophrenic, a manic-depressive or a psychotic, there'd be lots of guaranteed treatment. But along with my traumatic, impoverished childhood, my Ancestral Rage, my A-negative blood, my un-canny love for all kinds of work that doesn't pay and my bad luck with men, I was also cursed with a seemingly incurable, garden variety depression. The HMO psychiatrist was sympathetic about my shrink's abandonment of me. He playfully opened up a book of psychiatric terms, put an odd Latin name to my condition and filled out my short-term disability form. He gave me a prescription for anti-depressants and, smiling, told me to enjoy my one-month vaca-tion. Here's a man to keep in touch with, I told myself on the way out.

I immediately filled the prescription, in case my employers investigated the claim. Once home, I flushed the pills down the toilet and went back out to the health food store where I purchased numerous nutritional supplements known to aid mysterious, garden-variety depressions. And it was then that I took up meditation again, but this time religiously.

So you see, for the eight months before my man left me, I was feeling pretty strong. I had conquered my depression, avoided pharmaceuticals, kept my job and even started a new project. And I was damned if I was going to let *his* shit lead me back into the downward spiral of fear and inertia.

During the low points, I imagined that he had never loved me at all. That it was only the sex that had tied him to me, or maybe the warmth with which my family embraced him. Warmth. Something completely alien to his own fam-ily. On occasion, we'd even felt free to smoke joints around my mom, a fairly nonjudgmental person so different from his own mother, who reminded me of Angela Lansbury, as the acutely controlling mother, in *The Manchurian Candidate,* only without the brains.

I speculated that maybe I'd driven the ex away with my noisy depression. The shrink had thought him more courageous than that, but what the hell did she know about courage? After all, she'd been the first to get cold feet. But, the worst of my depression had taken place almost a year before, I reasoned. And my rage had merely taken the form of screaming at reckless cab drivers, arguing with petty postal workers, conjuring revenge schemes against the corporate world, defending myself from all unethical people and crying to the heavens for help. And although I was sometimes difficult to be around, I didn't direct my rage at him. Not much anyway. I'd been heroic, I thought and—even though he wasn't much help—he had stayed and he had loved me. But I stayed too, and gave all the support and encouragement I could muster, which was quite above the average, if I do say so myself. As I said, the ex was prone to the blues too, only his depression turned him into a sniffling slug on the sofa; it was an inert depression and, as such, even harder to deal with, I thought. But as long as there was no manipulation or abuse, I stayed. Women stay. That's what women do. Because we know that as independent and attractive as our solitary lives can be, this kind of life always feels incomplete.

No sooner did I reason that real love should be able to withstand not only a few months of depression here and there, but death, disease and war, then I, once again, became filled with doubt. I was deep into the confusion stage. Maybe the truest reason he'd run away, was simply that he couldn't accept how I met life's challenges head on, while he withdrew into a basketball game on TV or buried his head in a magazine. Exhausted, after a few hours of my own conjecturing, I'd simply throw my arms in the air and say, "To hell with it." Maybe it was much simpler than all of that. Maybe he was just sick of my face.

Finally, I quit the self-blame/self-pity routine and started the sympathizing-with-the-ex phase. Reports from mutual friends revealed that he was a mess over the breakup and that made it easier. But maybe it was all the meditating or the stuff I kept reading in the Zen books, because more than ever before I felt compelled to be understanding. I had never once felt this way about any of my previous ex's. I kept telling myself that he was going through an excruciating time. After all, I was an older and more experienced person than he was. I'd lived through all manner of adversity, and knowing the risk of allowing myself to fall in love and to do everything and give everything in the name of this love, I had gone ahead and plunged in. I had to take responsibility for whatever came my way. It was, after all, his *right* not to want to be with me. And this man, who had been kind and generous to the best of his abilities, was now experiencing an all-time low, equaled only by the shock of menopause or maybe retirement, because the ex had recently been published, and while for a relatively secure writer this spells victory, for an extremely insecure writer it means that he got what he prayed for and now had to prove himself worthy. Feeling worthy was not his forte. What would be the use of my being vengeful or mean? Surely, if he'd been able to, he'd have stayed with me forever, such was the depth of his love for me, his soul mate. When I expressed this in conversation with friends or co-workers, everyone was impressed. They praised me for my wisdom, compassion, generosity and strength. They praised me for not falling into the trap of spiteful action, for keeping my dignity despite getting dumped. I meditated and prayed and went to Native American sweat lodges, fiercely trying to release all the fear and anger without having to lash out at anyone, including myself. After all, I was a veteran of this kind of pain, the ex was not. I'd been his first long-term girlfriend. I was a fully formed adult, and an attractive, intelligent woman. And if *he* did not want me in his life, it wouldn't be long before a new man, a better man, would come along.

I attributed all this compassion to the meditation. But meditation can be tricky. There's no doubt that it helps you focus on the present and avoid creating distress by clutching on to old thoughts that make you constantly relive old pain, but if you intellectualize it, it does nothing but camouflage your troubles.

The truth of the matter is, all that dignity was killing me. I missed him. I loved him. I wanted him back—mopey, obsessive, procrastinator or not. For what is love if not accepting imperfection? We each had a red mole in the same exact location, just above the right shoulder blade, we could read each other's thoughts, finish each other's sentences, and when we held each other at night, a feeling of peace and inexplicable bliss befell us both, no matter how hard the day had been. At night, we rested on a third body, a force which bound us inextricably, lulled us into a deep sleep with it's gentle vibrations and filled us with hope. We had dreamed of moving someplace where we could be closer to both nature *and* people. Now, the future was dead. Amazing how things projected into the future, things that do not yet exist, can cause such loss and longing.

My newfound compassion aside, every morning I'd wake up, either shaking and crying from a bad dream, or else awaken peacefully, but in a flash remember everything and burst into uncontrollable sobs. A piece of me had been ripped out and I cried. I cried until my tears and nose ran all the way down to my stomach, until my face was purple and swollen and unidentifiable, until I could no longer see, breathe or talk, until my heart was hurting, my head pounding and the absence of oxygen left me dizzy and weak. I cried until I felt I might actually die, and then my body would take over, forcing me to stop and breathe deeply until I was calm. Then I'd notice how cold my feet were and I'd lift the blankets and quilts required on February nights, only to find my feet naked and my socks disappeared, again and again, every morning.

I never questioned my sanity or any such nonsense. The fact is the socks were disappearing into thin air and that was that. I was down to my last pair of socks. I pulled them up as high as they'd go and tied shoelaces around my ankles. That seemed to do the trick. The next day the socks, tied with the shoelaces, had not disappeared. That night, I tried wearing them without the shoelaces, but the next morning they had vanished once again. I now had no socks left, and had to put my bare feet into my boots and run in the snow to the nearest discount store to buy some more. Interestingly, I remained unperturbed by the scientific improbability of it all. What bothered me was that every day that the socks disappeared, I felt weaker.

During this time, I'd had a number of interviews for teaching jobs, and noticed myself feeling shaky and uncertain while discussing matters in which I was normally confident. I was always cold, starting with my feet, and was starting to feel afraid as I had before my last big bout of the boohoohoos. I down played the fantastic fact of the sock disappearances and pondered its significance. It had been going on for a month or so, when I finally told my friend, Andre, what was happening. Andre, an astrologer, was not at all perturbed by the disappearing sock routine. Said that as a Taurus I had an uncanny way of manifesting my fears as well as my desires into physical reality. It was just a physical manifestation of my fear, which I should not try to negate. I asked why only my fears manifested themselves and *not* my desires, Goddamnit! He said that it was because of an afflicted Saturn, whatever the hell that means, and that in any case it wasn't a good month for interviews. Then, I told my friend Jill and her live-in boyfriend, Harry. Harry was skeptical. He said that I tended towards the irrational. Harry was a scholar and an old-school socialist, who buried his creativity under the icon of reason and was threatened by all matters metaphysical. He had seen me do this kind of thing before, he said, like the time I ceremoniously tossed an amulet, which I believed had been cursed by a Yoruba Santero, into the Hudson River, and Harry didn't think that sort of thing was helping me any.

"The truth is," I explained to him, "I didn't really know if the amulet was cursed, much less if curses are real. All I knew was that the trinket was behaving oddly. It didn't want to be with me, so I tossed it into the river. As for the sock thing, it happens every day. What can I say, Harry? The sock drawer is empty now. You can see for yourself!"

Harry suggested I go back to therapy immediately, with a Freudian analyst this time. Jill, on the other hand, didn't care whether the socks were actually disappearing or not (I don't think she really believed they were). She was concerned with my *feelings* about the disappearing socks. She said the fear and uncertainty might be a sign that I was holding something back.

One week later, down to my last pair of socks again, I sat home in my catatonic position. That's where in the dark, on my pale green, Louis XIV, velvet love seat, with gold chip painted wood frame which we bought from a Polish merchant in Green Point, I sit cross-legged, smoking a joint, my medication of choice, and stare at the television set in "mute" mode. I find television to be more interesting in "mute" mode and find comfort in the subdued, bluish light. I thought about what Jill had said about holding back. Maybe all I'd been doing was negating the negativity. Maybe I'd fallen into the familiar trap of judging my own dark feelings and forcing them into heroic ones. After all, the idea behind any spiritual path is to seek truth, to keep a positive overall focus, but not deny the existence of our darker impulses.

I'd been feeling abandoned, scared and lonely as hell, that was a given. But, after I stopped feeling sorry for both myself and the depressed ex, I had begun to feel angry. For the past week, every day had been a struggle not to call him up and rave about what a selfish little prick he was to walk out on a perfectly good relationship, with no warning and no obvious signs of deterioration. Sure, we'd had our ups and downs like every couple, but I remained supportive throughout the worst. There had been no betrayal, no deceit; we had never crossed any fatal lines. Just that I had noticed in the two weeks previous to the breakup, and for the first time since we'd been together, that our connection, that subtle body which thrives between two people who love each other, felt weak and malnourished. But that had only been for a couple of weeks. I had received no explanation for my sudden abandonment and was left holding the bag.

I thought about a time in the middle of my dark days when my self-esteem was at an all-time low. We were on the telephone. I was feeling needy and he distant. When I questioned him he became disproportionately defensive. We got into a heated nonsensical argument and he hung up on me. An argument so petty, I can't recall the details. I waited a while, feeling guilty for the neediness and then phoned back to try and patch things up. The line was busy. The line was busy all night. He had left the phone off the hook. All night, I was in a panic, given my emotional state at the time. In full-blown paranoia, I'd exaggerated the incident, thinking it signaled something fatal and that it had been all my fault. But now I saw it clearly. I had only wanted an attentive ear and a few simple words of comfort, and these had been viciously denied me. A low blow, I thought, considering my extreme vulnerability. But he had expected me to make my needs secondary, even when they needed to come first. What a fool I'd been, staying up all night, feeling guilty and wanting to apologize when he had clearly been a prick. Now I wondered how many other little abandonments I would recall in the months to come.

With that, I sped quickly into the full-blown anger phase. I was now, officially, *mad as hell*. Mad at the ex and his goddamned insecurities and his self-absorption. He made a commitment to me of body and soul. A sacred commitment which he broke. Sure he had a right not to be with me. And I had a right to express the pain it caused. He owed me. He had filled me with fear, and he had taken my socks, and anyone who disagreed, could eat a bag of shit.

I hastily put out the joint, a good buzz wasted by anger, and sprung up from the couch. I got dressed and put my ex-'s apartment keys in my pocket. We'd agreed to hold on to each other's keys, for a while, in case of emergency. You know, locking ourselves out of our apartments, his kidney stones, my night fevers things like that. I grabbed a coupla' bucks, lit a cigarette and bolted out of the building towards the E subway line on 8th Avenue.

Walking down the tree-lined streets of Green Point Brooklyn, I recalled all the times we'd grabbed each others privates in the night on those very same streets, in child-like defiance of the orderliness and stagnation of this working class, children-playing-ball-in-the-street, sweep-the-shit-under-the-couch, diaper changing, tulip planting, spouse cheating, teenage drug abusing, dog-shit-in-the-damp-air smelling, Englebert Humperdink, Spice Girls-listening type of neighborhood. I thought about the times we'd argued over where we'd live once we moved in together and how he kept insisting on Green Point. He romanticized the toxic riverfront, abandoned warehouses and dilapidated piers. He wasn't even perturbed by the fact that physicists had worked on the Manhattan Project in one of those warehouses in the late 40s, and that the entire waterfront was now owned by U.S. Waste. But it all makes sense now. Alone and depressed. Depressed and alone and ashamed in a toxic wasteland.

Once in the building, I was immediately assaulted by the smell of the garbage his eccentric Super insisted on keeping inside the first-floor foyer. I prayed that the ex's neighbor, Paul, a pretentious, but streetwise, painter queen who always glanced at me dismissively when the ex and I were together, would not see me. When the ex and I were together, Paul always gave me that look you get from jealous girlfriends. The one that says, "Your days together are numbered." Once inside the apartment, my heart pounded all the way to my central lobe and I thought everyone could hear it like in that Poe story about the murderer who kept hearing his dead victim's heartbeat, only in my case it was my own heart and it was screaming "Hey everybody, I'm about to commit a crime!"

I had no idea what I was gonna do, what shape my revenge would take. I noticed the place was much neater than it had ever been when we were together. This made me mad. When I'd been there before, there were always stacks of books and paper everywhere, in piles on the floor, leaning against the wall, on the windowsills. You had to tip-toe around them and it made you feel like you were in the way of his holy, knowledgeable existence, especially since he'd cringe and protest if you tried to move any of them. Now they were in brand new bookshelves or in the closets he had apparently cleaned out. He had been and still was a coddled boy. His parents, having risen from blue collar to middle class by working their butts to the bone 'til there was not a drop of love left in them, filled his apartment with furniture and his closets with stylish, casual wear. It looked like he'd been cleaning for weeks.

In the bedroom I noticed the light blinking on his answering machine. I pushed the play button. There was a message from a New York Mets sales representative trying to sell the best seats for the most exciting games of the season. The next one was a shrill, reprimanding message from his Mommy. My heart pounded louder and faster, afraid of what I might discover next. And here it was, after all, I'd asked for it—a message from a strange woman. It sounded like a young woman, early twenties maybe, with a small voice and a small soul whom he'd apparently met at some sports bar. She was enticing him to join her for the Duke versus someone or other basketball match, trying to be all sexy and sweet. Just the sort of shit I hate. So he wanted to be alone! So he wasn't interested in other women or any relationship whatsoever! Right. In a cloud of green, purple and black, I thought I'd take a scissors and cut everyone of his shirts in half, no better yet, I'd empty out all of his closets and bookshelves, dump the contents into a big pile and light it on fire! Better yet, I'd destroy his computer, every diskette and every piece of writing he'd ever done including all those shoe boxes filled with tiny little scraps of paper documenting every little precious idea he'd ever had! That'll show him. That rat pack, that procrastinating hoarder of books and clutcher of insignificant thoughts!

Fuck. These are such predictable revenge schemes. Wait. Don't act out of blind rage. I threw myself on the bed, screaming into the pillow, punching and kicking and failing my appendages about in a wild, one of a kind, seizure. After I exhausted myself, I thought how this meditation shit really does work. In the past, I would have acted from my first angry impulse, not having the presence of mind to just flail about like a moron first. I looked up from the pillow. There, on the bed in front of me, was a woman's bra and underwear. They had apparently been concealed under the pillow. I felt the pepper rise in my blood and was about to explode again, when on closer inspection, I realized they were *my* underwear and *my* bra. Disarmed, I remained unsentimental. I sniffed the underwear. *My* underwear. I wanted to make sure no foreign bodies had worn them. They were clean of alien scents.

I stared at the worn out satin panties, and slightly torn, black lace bra. Suddenly it hit me. I went to the kitchen, and after tossing the defunct undergarments into the trash, returned to the bedroom with an enormous garbage bag. I opened his sock drawer, or rather his sock drawers, as he had three of them filled to the brim. Not my colors to be sure, all Grey, White and Navy Blue, but socks just the same. This man had taken my socks and with it my confidence. The matter would be easily resolved.

On my way out I stopped at the "SpanAmerGroc." next door, that's short for Spanish American Grocery Store and bought an ice cold Diet Coke. Fulgencio, the Dominican grocer greeted me in his usual forthcoming way.

"Where you been? Iss been a long tine since I see you."

"My boyfriend and I broke up, "

"You left him?"

"Nope. He left me. Said he was depressed and wanted to be alone."

"That's a shame. Whass wrong with him! Such an esmart and beautifool lady!"

"I'll be okay." But despite my confident air, he must've seen the sadness in my eyes because he quickly replied,

"Don't worry. If it's meant to be he'll come back, if not you'll find another one—a stronger one. You will see."

I'd heard this kinda stuff from lots of people, but his sincerity touched me. Then he asked me if I had moved into the neighborhood.

"No. I just came to get my socks back." I opened the garbage bag and showed him the dozens of pairs of socks inside.

"Ah." he said, a glimmer of laughter in his left, middle aged, lonely eye.

Cold Feet

That night, I got a visit from my friend Edwin, a half-Jewish, half-Mexican theater artist with a great understanding for acts of passion. He too was unlucky in love and pushing forty. I'd nicknamed him the benevolent Don Juan in my therapy sessions, because he was unconscious of his hostility toward the female—always chasing the unattainable babes and betraying the real ones. He laughed when I told him of my revenge. He thought if I was gonna break the law, why just settle for a garbage bag full of socks? What the hell was that gonna prove? I wasn't sure what it was gonna prove, but I told him that in our WASP dominated, capitalist culture, the destruction or theft of property, even if only socks, was considered the worst offense you could commit, even worse than murder. He smiled at me, and passed me a beer.

I asked him how *his* love life was going. He told me he had been seeing a woman named Diana. She was an exceptional Diana, who traveled to third world countries on rescue missions for victims of terrorism. They'd been together going on five months. Now, I see Edwin about once a month, and this was the first time that he'd ever mentioned his exceptional Diana. I didn't ask him why two months earlier he had shown up at my New Year's Eve party, with an Asian cupie doll on his arm— a model, performance artist, tai chi instructor who, within sixty seconds of her arrival, handed everyone in the room a business card. I did, however, ask him if he loved his girlfriend, Diana. He paused, took a breath and non-chalantly replied, "Yeah. I love 'er. Sure. She's good to me." I nodded supportively, thinking how glad I was I'd never slept with Edwin, even though we'd both considered it once.

After Edwin left, I emptied out three drawers of old clothing, and filled them with my new treasure. I put on a pair of the ex's thick Grey socks. I needed to embrace the shades of Grey. In bed, I lay awake for a while, listening to my own heartbeat. Maybe it had all been for the best, I thought, for the first time since the ex walked out.

The next day when I woke up, the sun was shining and the birds were chirping. Spring had arrived at last. I couldn't remember my dreams and felt refreshed and peaceful. I pulled the quilt off and looked at my feet. The Grey socks were still on them. I sat up and moved towards the foot of my bed, and there, on the floor, at the foot of the futon, were all my disappeared socks. Grape, Cherry, Gold, Turquoise, Kiwi and Kumquat, all shining like the colors of the rainbow. By the way, did I mention that I have adorable feet? They're small, shapely and smell really good as far as feet go. At this moment, I understood why Herr Lugus, a German sound technician at the old Kitchen downtown, had once fallen in love with my feet. I looked at them with appreciation. I didn't know what the future held, but the day opened beautifully before us, my sock-clad feet and me, warm again and ready to walk into the world.

Steve
Lautermilch

Vellum

1

THE FINE GLINTS AND POINTS of the reflections coming off the water, warming his eyes and face. The flare of the planks bleached white, fire white in the sun. The figure bending over the last of the pilings, the hammer uplifted and steady, about to descend. The angled silhouette of an old man, working. Gnarled and bowed and warped as any plank or root, toughened by this northwoods soil, equal parts clay and gravel, stone as much as sand and loam. The handle high, the glare of the midday sun.

The boy and the man. Eyes meeting, the one facing the other. Out of time, the look passing between them, neither looking away. Not a face seeing itself in a mirror, more what the sun or a stone does, this looking not at but within. Through the other. Holding the gaze, not letting go, taking the look inside. Knowing the image will last, after the dark and the night have fallen. The boy, the old man. Unmoving. Unspeaking. The water. The rippled sand under the water and the watery sun cupping the side of the dock, lapping the beach.

The lake. A thing, not machine and not animal, something other, primal. A coupling, weird commingling of clay and dark water, midge-flitting air and pine-pitch scented shade risen to life and still in process, still gathering form. A canvas. Finding its shape and losing its shape. Shape of all shapes. Unfinished, raw.

2

John Corey. Two, close to three hours later. The boy coming out of the stone cottage with rod and tackle. Heading for the dock and rowboat, the oars over his right shoulder. Rod and tackle balancing in his left hand, the cane-sectioned length of the fly rod keeping time with each footstep. Mid-stride, slowing, breaking stride. In the shadows, at the edge of the lake, where the cedar trees crowded the bank. The man and the boy's father talking, the tones of their voices carrying. Not the words. The sounds almost metallic, echoing off the water. The boy's face falling, the slow turn of his face toward the cottage. Wanting to mask his disappointment. The two men, looking up from the weeds that ribboned the shore, the long drying streamers of brown green they were raking. Gathering into small piles. His father, motioning the boy to approach, nodding at the over-turned hull. The two adults, grasping the gunnels, swinging the craft upright and easing it into the water.

The length of nylon, loose coils in the bow. What had been a gallon paint can, filled with freshly set concrete. The end of the orange rope spliced, a loop around the basket sunk in the concrete. The boy eyeing the fine rope work, sliding the oar blades along the hull. Wading into the water, taking the line and drawing the boat to the end of the dock. In the sunlight the stems of reeds and cattails swaying, the lily pads moving, almost disappearing in the crest of the small waves. The old roadbed flanked by fence rails, a low depression swallowed up in the shallows.

3

Old John Corey. With his fingers Jamie followed the contour map of the wood grain of the study hall desk, the dark varnish of fingers and hands yellowing gold against the darker wood stain and ageing shellac. The wood moving under his fingers. His eyes closing. Tracing the letters blind, first names and last. The initials, words and images and numbers carved into the soft pine surface. His father. Saying the name, a hesitation touching his voice with a resonance. Something unspoken, unsaid. A tone almost of reverence.

The boy settling on the flagstone steps to the cottage, the father easing down alongside. Early afternoon, no use putting line in the water. Jamie would towel off from his swim, then follow the sand road back to the pond. When the sun fell behind the pines and the shallows began cooling there would be time for fishing. —Corey, his father repeating the name. A talisman.

—Saw to the cottages along the south shore, brought in the docks in the fall and put them out in the spring. Saw the boats were stored, the cabins winterized before the first snow. A tracker, when needed, a good one. Now and then called in when a hiker turned up missing.

Jamie saw the bowed back, the leathery skin, the wrinkles that creased, almost seemed to cut, slice into the neck. A turtle's neck. The boy looked down the path to the lake. A scratching among cedar roots, a chipmunk scampering to beg at their feet. Its pose. A beat. Impatient, well fed, moving on. The swollen knuckles, the long twisted bones of the right hand. The uneven set in the left forearm, as if the limb had been broken and paid only the simplest heed.

His father standing, pointing to where the sandy road curved behind a thicket of dark evergreens. Cedar and fir and spruce, the heavy limbs hanging over a small well. A walk, a grove of still darker, more thickly grown trees. Cedars again, and Norway pine interspersed with birch. The sloping shake roof blanketed with moss. Screens sagging and the front door hanging by a hinge. Off to the side of the screened porch, overturned and resting on sawhorses, the weathered hull of a boat, the open cracks and peeling wood orange and mustard gold with lichen.

—John's mother was French Canadian, Jamie's father had said, looking off. A shaft of sun slanted through the limbs, its spear point bright at his feet.— John's father was full-blooded Iroquois. The boy was raised above the border, drifted to the UP when his parents passed.

4

Jamie stopped his tracing. His fingers moving over the circles and loops and slashes, coming to rest at the edge of the grain leather cover of his Latin grammar, the textbook open beside the Latin dictionary. Two improbable, impossible birds. The black. The red. Each incapable of flight.

—*iam tum religio pavidos terrebat agrestis.*

The line, the long and short vowels, their rhythm on the tongue. Closing the dictionary, his fingers moving to the next line, his lips conjuring up the movement and tread of the meter. The flow of a weed bed in deep water, shadows moving at the edge of a woods. A single boat, the expanse of smooth water. A river mouth, the sea slick and glistening and without visible shore.

—*dira loci, iam tum silvam saxumque tremebant.*

Under his breath he sounded out his rough handwriting. —Even then, he had scribbled, *a presence woke fear in the natives. Even then the power of the place made the rocks and the forest shake.*

Two lines out of thirty, refusing to come into English. He set the dull pencil down. *Religio.* He knew or thought he knew what the word meant to his teachers, his classmates in the seminary. Here in the heartland. But what would the word mean in a land and time when a people, a folk, a region could respond instinctually, spontaneously, to the forces, the raw or subtle energies of a locale, an environment.

"Momentary gods." The jargon of the philosophers and anthropologists, their terms of classification. "Forces of nature." As if, with a code, a label, the places and their people could be explained and shelved and dismissed. All questions answered. Multiple choice. His fingers hovering. Shivering. All but touching, brushing the passage. And the images suddenly returning. The summer. The bent figure of that old man, the long nights alone on the lake.

The rippling call of the whippoorwill, the crazed laughter of the loon. The many-tongued chorus of the frogs, the triple call of the owl. The calling silence. Lying awake in his cot behind the drawn curtain until he knew he had waited long enough. Slipping out of bed and on bare feet moving down the hall and through the great room. Past the stone fireplace, the hearth still glowing. The braided rug. The brass lampstand, the hand-painted parchment lampshade where in a garden pond gold and orange and cream-colored koi swam in the dark. The screen door to the porch, the wood planks of the pier. The shore and firs, the stars and a moon. Petals and pollen, pistil and stamen of a night-blooming flower. A meteor shower over the lake.

That was the wonder and dread of the Latin, the chill moving through him now. The channel a dark glimmer beyond the pale rim of the sand. The far shore a ragged slash of black. The dip of the oars, his back leaning into the stroke, the pull long and quiet. His wrists and forearms feathering the oars, the blades making their funnels, leaving at the start and end of each pull the purling beads of black water. Floating on the black surface until they dissolved. Raindrops. Fat raindrops on dry sand. The night arched and moving over his shoulders, his shoulders arched and moving over the oars. The raindrops gone, absorbed in the sand.

The hours of those nights, the night-long rowing. The prow edging into a darkness not of air or fire but this water that opened and closed around him. Took him in. A pact, a wordless understanding that he had made with the night and sleep and what he knew waited and did not sleep under the flashing surface. In a year his mother would die of cancer and he would see face to face. But now he was crossing the lake and did not look back to the shore and the tree-shadowed house. There was only the hull of the boat, crossing to the opposite shore, the stem and stern leaving their wake in the night. And across the song of those ripples deep in the shadows where he would not look, the coals of the fire going out.

The floorboards and gunnels giving up the warmth of the long day and the day's slow going. The oar handles holding the warmth. The lid of the tackle box sliding open, the boat gliding on its own momentum. Shipping the oars, stripping out the line, beginning to work the cove.

The high trill of the tree frogs. The low, deep throbbing from the marsh and the lake edge. An outcrop of rocks over falling water, a solitary birch by the inlet. The floorboards cool under his feet, the breeze coming down from the banks even cooler.

No houses on this side of the lake.

5

Ohio. The seminary. No boat, no figure of John Corey, no dock or shore or cottage. The seventh row of the study hall, the third desk over from the wall. Where it was beginning and he felt it coming and knew there was nothing for it. It had come for him the last spring when the class was still translating Caesar, the Latin so simple there were evenings he never opened the dictionary, never touched the grammar. Only the subtle chill at his fingertips, the slow shift and change in the current along his arm. But it was not in his mind that the cold and pressure registered, it was his body that felt the change. As if in his blood moved another, a separate consciousness. The way the fish is unaware of the water until the sharp kill of the hook edges, penetrates its being, burns at the hinged edge of its mouth, the crease where the upper and lower jaws meet. A white coal, the soft skin. Then the perception comes, a flame that feeds at the back of the throat and along the serration of the gills. For what is swimming through its gills, feeding down its gullet and into its stomach is the taste of its own blood.

Castalia. The small village, and within the village the pool. *The Blue Hole.* An open cut, water running under ice. He had been standing there in the open, beside the open back door of the Chevrolet, staring up and into the night where the swelter of wings and tentacles and spinning bodies moiled and turned in a seething cauldron of gas. Eleven. He was eleven, it was eight years back. The day had been passed on the Lake, fishing off Catawba Island where their uncle had taken the brothers fishing, first from over the side for perch and then, in the early evening, along the rocky shore for the smallmouth bass that came into the shallows to feed.

On the way back from Port Clinton his uncle had left the main road to drive into a small village where they had stopped and Jamie had stumbled, tired and groggy and still half asleep, out of the car and into the glare of the streetlamp. Beyond the pool of the lamp where the mayflies and June bugs were swarming a second pool glimmered, made not of vapor but liquid. A watery eye, the circle of a glistening spring that stared, unblinking, into the whirling night.

—The door! Shut the door!

The slap of the command. Leaning the weight of his body into the car door, closing it with a quiet push. The child looking back at the adult. And the adult, darkened by the night into a silhouette, the black hair indistinguishable from shoulder and jacket. The momentary, impersonal shape of a beggar, some nameless cripple, faceless and unknown. Stunned, the child looking away.

Looking back. And the adult already changed. Erect, familiar. Face and frame lit by the streetlamp now. Recognizable.

By the time Jamie reached the small, illuminated pond the brother and uncle were gone. He could hear his brother's voice, the younger boy talking as he clomped across a footbridge to the waterwheel that drove the rapids and breeding ponds farther on. Alone. After a day of sweat and brushing shoulders, alone. Feeling the play of cool air in his hands, the rush along his legs. His body moving him now, his thin frame edging closer to the spring. Then the draft of a colder, darker, alien atmosphere, enveloping him, drawing him in. And the circle of soft light, glowing and swelling, glossy before his feet. A color his eyes had never before seen.

The Blue Hole of Castalia. Water flowing under ice. An open wound in the earth. It was as if he had stumbled and fallen, tumbling through a rip in the fabric of time, pitched from some mid-century escalator and by sheer misstep, some short in the cosmic circuitry, entered the mislaid spur of a wildcat tram or runaway subway, some wayward space capsule or time shuttle that set down on the moon decades before the *Eagle* and Armstrong.

It was blind and seeing at the same time. Bright and yet muted in it brightness. Distant and close. Its surface shone like glass, and like the molten glass his uncle blew at the glassworks in their hometown, the great tall-windowed factory that rose with its rounded chimneys and towered over the rooftops, this pool, this bubble, flowed and moved and swam under his eyes like a door, a furnace lid that opened into white heat.

The underworld. The other world. The blind side, the dark side of the mirror. The surface sizzling like ice that hovered between melting and freezing at once. The air circling the pool, wrapping his body, stealing his breath. Sucking it away like a funeral home or walk-in freezer at a meat-packing plant. He had heard the stories, but the words were no clue to the transparency and depth of the crystal world at his feet. Here wet-suited divers went down and returned without touching bottom. Tracer dyes released into these airless waters vanished without a trace. Weighted cords and lines lowered below the surface were snapped or became tangled or were drawn out of sight by an underground current so strong no sounding or measurement was possible.

Jamie. Someone was speaking. His uncle. The old man had returned, and his brother had punched the audio button near the kiosk. Now a metallic voice was talking into the night, talking to no one and anyone, breaking the reverie, reciting the prepared statement. How the physical depth of the spring was unknown although the apparent depth was fifty or sixty feet. How the spring found its source in an underground river, maintaining a temperature of forty-eight degrees winter and summer. How the flow of this water was unaffected by flood or drought, the volume maintaining a steady outpouring of 4,500 gallons per minute, enough to supply a city of twenty million. How the water was dead. Devoid of air, making it impossible for fish to live in the stream. How on the other side of the bridge, where the waterwheel turned and aerated the flow, a hatchery was maintained by the State Wildlife and Fishery Service, the fresh water supplying pond after pond of fingerling trout, rainbow and brook and brown.

6

That summer on the Upper Peninsula, the afternoon swim. The rocking, floating offshore platform, the raft anchored at the edge of the channel where the shallow water gave way to the deep. He would swim out from the beach, treading water and filling his lungs, his chest stretching to the limit, drawing in the last ounce of fresh air. Then the quick kick of the surface dive, the momentum of the jackknife and the first arm strokes taking his body down, his eyes following the chain links of the anchor to the muck and mire at the lake bottom.

The quiet of the deep, scissor kicks alternating with arm pulls, letting the momentum slow. The water temperature changing, the tepid waters of the surface falling away to the cooler layers near the bottom. The distant sounds of the oil drums under the floating deck of the raft, echoing, rumbling and muffled with the splashing sound of the waves. Distant now, removed.

This sweet drift. Close to perfect weightlessness now that the rope of the breath was released. The long glide in the dark. The body slowing down, the mind holding on. Then loosening. The lungs no longer struggling, no longer needing to breathe. Accepting the new element, enjoying the new world. The weed bed, its streamers swaying in the current. The occasional bass, the dark line running back from the gills, the darker line along the flare of fin and dorsal and tail. The strangely inviting heaviness penetrating his body, his mind. Light now, with a light that was dark and enclosing.

That cold all around him now. Coming to him, pressing from inside and outside at once. The dark wood of the desk, the carving of the crude letters. The pencil and the paper, and the books open beside the paper. The grammar, the dictionary. Not objects but windows and doors, rooms of power. The mind, its power of thought, its habits of concentration and awareness—only threads, the thinnest of veils. The mist that forms between evening and night, between night and morning, floating over the water and shore until the water and shore are gone.

7

His eyes. Blinking, focusing. The dark taking shape. Across the playing field the wind picking up, driving the crystals of the snow that had dusted the grass during the afternoon. His lips numb, his ears ringing. The surface of his eyes filling with the little sharp tears of the cold. The snow curling, forming wings, the lifting wings of a manta ray. The moon at the back of the wind swimming free, floating free of the clouds. The single, long breath of the moon, its light falling cold and pure across the frozen terrain.

A pocket of oak leaves, caught by the gusting wind. The brittle open hands of the leaves reaching first one way then another. Beyond the circle of pines, the trunk of the oak and its branches wild against the sky. The clouds closing against the moon.

At the corner of the building he stopped, turned, looked back. The wind stripping the landscape, emptying the limbs of their leaves. Unhurrying and unhurried. A hand that was closing, no different from the hand at the end of his arm that touched the coarse brick of the wall. Both apart from him now. The pleasure of surrender and release.

He was waiting. The heaviness had come and gone in the study hall, and he was waiting for the feeling to return. It could not be hurried. It was a shadow, a presence he could not name because it did not have either shape or form. Only a subtle pressure, like the weight of water that refused to be controlled. He was afraid of the feeling at the same time that he longed for its presence. And it was as if this faceless, amorphous pressure surrounding him, swelling and growing inside and outside his body, wiped something away.

The voice now, mocking him in his wait. —Where have you gone, Jamie Waters, long time passing? The words he used to sing on the lake. Only the words of the song had changed.

—Where have you gone, little one, long time ago?

8

He thought of the way the water was for the fish after the bass or the pike had taken the bait and turning, beginning its run, swam until the strength and the fight were gone. Drawn from its element, removed from the liquid it had taken for granted, the universe now a gift, a set of conditions that burned and sank in and drowned.

9

A winter, years later, Jamie would return to the village where his uncle had taken him as a boy. Interrupting his drive north, in the early night he would leave the state route to follow the winding road into town. At the edge of the village he would see the battered road sign, the black letters against the white enamel spelling out the fabled name. But when he would step from the car and follow the paved walk back to the place, the houses along the street asleep, he found the entrance chained and locked. Under the arch of grillwork, where wrought iron letters spelled in rusting, peeling paint the ancient name, he faced a tattered and warped placard, a public notice. *Closed.* The site was private now, purchased by a local firm that bottled water.

And there, seeing the shadows spill over the water, he read the notice and stayed. There was no reason for what he did; he was only aware that instead of returning back to the car and continuing north, he found himself crouching against the trunk of an ancient oak where he could wait and watch the pool through the chain-link fence. Not a meditation really, not even a vigil. And there was no slow or sudden revelation, no glimpse of some hidden and powerful truth. He simply waited, pulled, drawn by something in the place that kept him watching by the water until dawn.

A breeze came up at first light. Waves of morning sun came yellowing the steel posts and their diamonds of steel, the shadows casting a softness on the dark pool. Almost a canvas, the shimmer of sand and soft clay, foot trodden, wind swept. Then the wind began shifting directions, the light breezes crisscrossing, patterning the surface of the spring.

Under the rippling glow, caught in that hazy shimmering, rose the double trunks of a single tree. Rising, lifting side by side, a twin growth from a common root, stretching up from the rocky ledge, a cutback along the crest of a mountain pass. A clearing of dusty, needle-strewn basalt, the earth more stone than clay. The nubby, grain-leather, bone-hard scale of alligator juniper. The soft, shaggy, almost woven bark of ponderosa. Two trunks. Saplings. Shoots from a single stock. The pair of them planted, grafted together on the western curve of the Divide.

The sun coming up on his shoulders then, warming his back as it moved across his neck, the yellow catchlights brightening on the links of the steel fence at the edge of the spring. The diamonds of sloughed snake skin. And at the center of the well, the double trunk of the saplings, juniper and pine, the two of them unwavering until the sun fell from the rooftops, the glare erasing the vision.

A paper carrier, the wire saddlebags rattling as the bicycle left the sidewalk, the wheels coming down hard with their double thump. A car engine starting, the exhaust sending great plumes of white into the air. The wind in the oak leaves, brittle and harsh.

The ride out of town quiet, the wind humming a wordless, shapeless song in the curves. The car following the highway, the road turning north. Only the stop sign making him look down, surprised. His hands. Wet.

10

It was already late afternoon when he reached the cabin, the waters along the lake the slate of eroded desert at sundown. The sun had all but vanished, leaving only a glowing mirror over the woods and the waters; and following the sandy road away from the shore, Jamie found the old path leading back from the cabin, heading still deeper into the trees where the smaller, isolated pond was waiting. Not a lake really, not even a pool. A glacial basin scooped out of the earth and still twenty to thirty degrees colder than the spring-fed lake he had left less than half a mile to the south. But the clearing was still there, unmolested, and a little farther on the stream he would walk in the morning.

It was noon of the second day when he came across the kill. The brown eyes still open, the legs already stiff. The neat hole where the shot had entered, the splotch of dried blood caking the matted hair. A fawn, gutshot, left to clamber away and die. Corey had taught him the skills, and by midafternoon the fawn was dressed out and washed clean. Yet no one had taught him what he did next; and as he prepared the skin for the sequence of steps that would follow, what played through his mind were the stiff sheets of illuminated vellum he had touched only with gloves, the catch at the back of his throat telling him he had been holding his breath as the custodian brought the manuscript to the museum reading table and left the pages next to his chair.

He knew the formula, had written the sequence out. The woods and the lake were nearly deserted, and the small cabin his mother had left him waited back near the shore. He set the skin to soak, letting the stream darken the pattern of light and shadow, the running water softening and stretching the patches in its quiet flow. Soaked it a second time then, in still water, the loose length of the skin becoming a glistening mirror of the passing suns and the stars. Two weeks in lime, and the hair could be scraped clean. Two weeks more of continued soaking, the skin becoming workable now. A final rinse, a steady stretch, and the soft heat of the northwoods sun.

Apprentice work, this soft rubbing with pumice, the stone polishing the surface of the skin to a dull luster and sheen. Then the kneading of chalk, worked into the hide, rendering the skin an even white, the color of coarse meal. A final dressing with oil, then the cutting and sectioning into sheets. Vision, and vision's labor.

Vellum. The handiwork of a novice, performed for a scribe in a monastery scriptorium. And so his cabin along the lake became for those months a library, and the tools of his art became the learning he had acquired in the years overseas. As the skin was drying the ink was prepared. Soot from the fireplace, the flue. Liquid gum from a mail-order catalogue. Cuttlefish from a pet supply house. Lampblack. And again for a final time the water soaking, the ingredients of the ink blending with oak, apples, liquid flour, copper crystals till the time of preparation was finished and he stood at one end of the wood table, the ink and cut parchment laid out on the planks, waiting, ready for use.

11

Awake now. Breathless. Smothered. His limbs, arms and legs and hands and feet locked and unable to move, shackled in place. A light in the corner of the room, playing across the ceiling, the muffled sound of waves on a shore. His mind, forcing the lungs to keep breathing. And over every inch of his frame the presence growing, gathering force, sealing his will in a shell. The corporeality of the body—the physicality of the flesh, the bones and nerves, arteries and veins. Walling him off, skin and muscle and tendon one more room that closed him in, sealed him away.

He had waited, he had invited the presence, and it had come. A heaviness that seemed at first to enter from outside, but then gained strength and joined with the pressure that came from within. His skin and even his mind, his will and this inner sight that kept watching—all his consciousness little more than a sheet, a bed, that imprisoned him in their weight. He could turn his eyes, he could follow his thoughts. Yet their stream was one and the same with the walls that enclosed this room, this inescapable building where his every move was guarded and trapped.

The weight, the weight of awareness and concentration, always closing in, pressing down until his will, his mind, his identity were gone.

12

When he woke again he found himself standing in the corridor outside his room. How long had he been standing there? He could remember breaking curfew, leaving the building after night prayers and lights out, walking out to the pine grove and waiting under the wind of the winter storm. Could remember returning to the building, slipping down the tiles of the corridor and into his room.

The bells in the seminary tower tolling the quarter hour, the half, the three-quarters hour. The sequence beginning again. And another sound, the low flowing rhythm of a current over a streambed. Water slipping over pebbles, crossing over rocks and stones and gravel. The whisper of his feet, the whisper of his breath, moving down the corridor.

13

Again he lost track of time, or maybe he was moving out of time and time had lost track of him, the hours and the minutes no longer having meaning, moving no more in a line toward a predetermined outcome, rippling now like a stone in a lake in ever widening circles, rings thrown out from a center where something had gone under. Disappeared.

He was facing the prefect's door, his right hand suspended, the fingers and palm closed in a fist, a silent knock that would not sound, would not come down and complete its arc on the panel of oak inches away from its blind fall.

The ripple of the wood grain, grains of the polished bricks facing the alcove of the prefect's quarters. Only inches away, and the wood and the brick suspended, floating along with his hand in the air. Then the light entering from the hall, edging the pale yellow brick with a lighter yellow, feathering the alcove, caressing the floor and walls with the softness of dawn. His body softening then, the right hand and arm descending, the clenched fingers relaxing their fist. Neither completing the motion to knock nor withdrawing the hand. Simply surrendering, giving in to the needs of the flesh.

His feet. Moving away from the alcove, stepping into the hallway, the prefect's office behind them now. Again the lapping of water, the flow of a current over fine sand. Bending reeds, cattails, sawgrass. The slow, regular rhythms of their dance. His breath in time with his feet, crossing the polished squares. His body, the breathing of his lungs, the air escaping from his lips, all moving in sync, the rhythms of tree limbs and leaves and the calm, rooted stillness of the waters that flowed like the squares of tile at his feet.

His room, three doors to the left. His hands, depressing the lock, lifting the latch, moving the weight of the door on the hinges. The play of light, the shimmering of the ceiling. The whine and rustle and wash of the cars and trucks on the street, the surf of some inland, mechanical tide. The room opening around him, the walls bringing his body to a standstill beside his desk. The play of light on the floor.

14

He had been raised to obey. To listen, to understand, to respond. His parents, his teachers, his friends—they all had instructed him, and he had been their prize student. From each he had learned a different way of a thousand ways to anticipate another's needs until, through simple practice and the dint of repetition, he could read the speech of the eyes, hear the unspoken requests of the lips, meet the agenda of shoulders and arms without saying a word. Mindlessly, instinctively, unconsciously, he learned to survive.

Now a new kind of demand, a new manner of communication had made itself known. Physical, almost subterranean, the need had surfaced, making its urging felt not by words or thoughts or body language but by some strange working sympathy of pressure. A fault line that ran through his blood, a force field that would work its way through him.

This room, these walls and ceiling and floor. This desk and chair. Even the closet by the door, its shelves and hangers and hooks. The clothing that was there, the dark slacks and shoes, the pressed shirts and sweaters and parka. The clothing that was not there, the black folds of the cassock, the starched linen collar. They all had their place in the story.

The wind, driving a splatter of drops against the window, beginning to freeze again, the crystals of sleet and partially melting ice trickling down the fogging glass. All of it belonged, down to the single leaf that had caught in the left corner of the lower sash. Only his breathing, fogging the glass. Only these thoughts in his mind, setting him apart. He was the outsider here. He was the one out of place.

15

A rain had begun falling. In the middle of winter a spring shower, the aftermath of the storm that had passed earlier in the night. The snow clouds that had formed and gathered high over the city were coming to earth, falling and being transformed, each drop of water that had crystallized around its particle of dust thawing, returning as water now, washing roof and street and ground. The trickling rain streaking the glass. The leaf, the spreading fingers of an open hand, flattened now, pasted against the bottom sash.

16

His hands. He was looking down at his hands and seeing his fingers and palms, the creased skin and calluses smudged with ink and watercolor. The wad of paper towel, crushed, in shreds in the right hand. The fingers and thumb of the left hand, trembling, quivering a little from the effort. The soft lines, their cadence and flow on the surface of the paper. There had been no voice, whispering, asking him to listen. But his hands had whispered, and the paper had listened. Still was listening. And all the while, deep and insistent, the quiet force had been welling, calling him to do its bidding. For a time he had become other.

What he had drawn. What had drawn him. He looked at the sketch, stepped back from the tablet and let the image take form. The dark lines shone with light. Through a split rail fence, against the scud of waves, a landscape swept with the blur of storm clouds and heavy seas. The thick, rough bark of cypress trees. Flames, wrestling flames. As if water and fire had changed places, exchanged form.

There was a scale, a rhythm to the study, not unlike the bark of trees, their silvers and pewters and glints of gunmetal, the rough patterning finding its likeness in the waves and air where the watercolor and the texture of the paper became all but indistinguishable. Winter breath, steam rising from a lake, fog drifting along a reed bed. The fence rails of the foreground, the whitecaps and rollers in the middle and far distance. Turtle and snake, beetle and lizard, all just under the surface, hidden and playing and held in everything mottled and pied.

The cypress, anchored in the middle distance. The scrub juniper, shadowing the lower right corner. The foreground of rocks and boulders and sand, the leavings of a volcano when the deserts were seas. —*My ambition is limited to a few clouds of earth, sprouting wheat, an olive grove, a cypress.*

Was the scene closing? Or opening? Setting down the stem of the brush, leaving the drawing thumbtacked to the wall, he turned to the desk and opened the pages of a book. A journal, his day-book. And recorded the words.

What he did next he came to understand only at the end of his life, alone after the long years in the high desert, putting together the last grouping of his work. Picking up the dry stub of the brush, dipping it to drink in the puddle of dark water, then letting it drink again from the thumbprint of red color, he drew a line across the middle of the scene.

17

The brush at his fingertips drying now, the sheet of vellum still pressed between his hands. The colored pencils still in their containers, only the little jars of the ink he had prepared on the Upper Peninsula ready to hand. The gold, the black, the small vials of blue and white. And from his lips this trembling, almost a quivering that went out along the sides of his mouth, as if he were going to speak.

Standing by the window, the stiff parchment crackling as he held it to the night. The soft night over his shoulder, spilling across the portrait. Sloping, knotted, the curve of the rough forehead. The wild straggle of hair. Stubble, the sprinkled beard. The cut that scarred the edge of the mouth, a gash of white smoothness where the beard would never grow. A stippling, something torn away, freed only by ripping. The kind of mark not a single hook but a gang of hooks, treble hooks might leave in the lips of a fish if the fish survived.

The crevices of the face, the contours of eroded stone. The hollows of the shoulders, the left lower than the right. The skin, leathery under the tangle of hair, dark above the cording of the neck. The clarity of the eyes. Unmoving, as if able to see into the glare of sunlight, at home in the darkness of dark water.

The call for matins would be sounding, the bell ringing for morning prayers and chapel. Beyond the desk and bed, across the squares of linoleum, the wind was drying the wrinkled leaf the storm had pasted against the glass. His hands were quiet now, on the desktop lay the finished portrait. A face, the white pigment lightening the dark lines of the countenance. A face that had weathered, and in weathering done and become something more. Something other. As if within the image of this western face another, eastern presence had risen. Almost medieval, almost Byzantine.

A pond maybe, taking a reflection from the skies overhead. A lakebed, a watery mirror reflecting a moon-stubbled nightsky, itself a reflection of the earth it revolved around and looked on and always would hold and touch.

18

Staring into the night.

19

The wall of the high-school building, the handle freezing in his grip. He had broken curfew. Was risking expulsion. If a prefect or disciplinarian, if a teacher had seen him outlined among the pines, heard him returning, there would be few questions, only one outcome. Pulling open the metal security door, slipping inside. Holding down the handle to muffle the sound of the closing lock. The cold draft, flooding the corridor. The exit sign spilling its red glow across the polished tile.

Under the shell of his parka, under the shell of skin and bone, the small voice calling, singing to him from a great distance. —Where have you gone, Jamie Waters, long time passing? Less than a whisper, coming from somewhere inside of him, a place he had forgotten. —Where have you gone, long time ago?

Diza
Sauers | *Roan*

FOR TITO, THE WORST PART about burying horses is having to quarter them, to cut them up so they fit in the hole. That's what gets to him most, even more than finding them dead, which is, naturally, a shock and disappointment. More than the bloat or glazed eyes or how the lips part into a grisly yellow tooth smile when you drag them, what really undoes him is all that sawing and hacking you have to do unless you have a back hoe. Tito doesn't own a back hoe. He has a tractor, which helps to haul the carcass all the way up from the highway. He has a truck, a 1953 Desoto and an old parked bus, but he does not have a back hoe.

Tito is burying one of his horses. Not a good horse or a friend horse, but a horse who holds no memories for him, a bony, nameless roan that wandered out on the highway and got mowed down by a semi. No one was hurt, except the horse who probably didn't feel a thing. At least that's what the driver kept saying. "He just stood there," he said, sipping coffee, nervous, moving a toothpick from side to side in his mouth, "Just stood there looking at me. Wasn't nothing I could do." Tito didn't say anything because it wasn't worth it. The driver's pin point blue eyes told him enough, that and his tremor, jacked up on some sort of shit for sure. Tito didn't want any trouble. The horse was old, probably found a tear in one of the fences and wandered out in the road at the wrong time, in the wrong place. The semi wasn't damaged at all, except for some tangled hair and a large bend in the grill, so Tito shook the man's clammy hand and sent him on his way. Then he called his son, Len, to come help him clean up the mess.

They've already slung ropes around the horse and dragged him back down to the field. They've piled brush high on him so that he isn't so visible, only a brown heap down by the trees. It's late, the sun hanging low and watery, the color slipping out of the sky, making eerie slanted rays. In the streaked light, Tito finally gets a solid take on Len who looks worn out with his red rimmed eyes, his face gaunt. "Go home," he tells him, "You look like shit."

Len drops his hand over his face, rubs his eyes, "Thanks."

"We're not cutting today. Too late. So go on." For Tito, the horse is easier than any of this, Len looking so beat, the house growing dark up on the hill, none of the windows lit, Helen sitting in the dark, waiting for them to come and turn on lights, shower, get ready to go. Tito would rather be here, stacking brush, not talking, not thinking about the viewing or anything beyond that. "Go on," he told Len, "We can take care of this later. You should be there. Take your mother. She'll want you there."

"You should be there," Len says quietly, staring at him, then he looks down at his feet, swallows. He rocks the tip of the shovel back and forth, tosses the handle toward his father, shrugs, turns back toward the house.

"I'll be there, I'll be there." Tito calls after him, but Len doesn't turn around, he jams his hands down into his pockets and keeps walking toward the house looking smaller the closer he gets.

In places, Tito's field dips and swells down to where a row of apricot trees and a small wash hem it in. The slope rises gently up to the house, bare except for some loose rocks and scrub, chamisa skeletons, sworls of flattened and dry deer grass. Tito's other fields are more orderly, furrowed rows waiting for the next season, his pinon groves, his orchards, but this one sloping patch is left barren. Out here he has buried everything that's died on him, his horse, his first wife, some dogs. Under his feet, small silent graves radiate in every direction and that's something he can understand. He doesn't have time for church or candles or all that smoke and bells. Church is somebody else's idea of a good time.

Just a few hours ago, he and Helen fought, bitterly, on this spot, about where to bury their son, Bear. For now he's laid out in the chapel in a closed coffin covered with roses, lilies and larkspur. They can't agree on where to leave him. Tito wanted Bear to go to rest here, in the field with everybody else. Helen wouldn't hear of it. She cried. She spat words at him and at last she stumbled down onto her knees, clawing up handfuls of the rocky soil, spitting and choking on bitter words. Tito lifted her, rocked her, told her she could bury Bear where she wanted. But it saddens him to think of the narrow Church grounds, closed in, carved granite dates announcing everything to anyone who might happen by. Tito can't understand that when out here, on the hill, they could let him spread out, thicken and move around in the mud, let the apricots soak down into him.

Depending on what he's burying, Tito usually digs more than one hole. When he buried his best dog, Pooch, he dug seven. For Reyna, he filled the slope with small shallow ponds. It depends on how much he wants to forget. Usually, he digs until his brain is numb, until he can only feel the ache of muscles, and the shovel an automatic part of breathing. Then, when he's not really thinking, he puts the body into one of the holes. By then, flesh is one more step, part of the endless digging, tossing dirt, stepping down, stepping up, smoothing the dirt in circles. He doesn't have to think about the body, he just thinks about filling the holes back up, patting all those holes shut with the underside of his shovel so that they all look the same. By then no one, not even Tito, can remember what went where. Of course, then the slope is full of brown mounds and scars, but a season of hard weather takes care of that.

Tito marks a plot for the roan down near the edge of the field beneath a tree. He counts off an eight stride by six stride hole and digs in, breaking through the soil frozen for the first inch or so. It takes a while to break down further into the cold clay and rocks. Behind him, the lights in his house go on one by one, then back off. A motor starts, makes its way down the drive, then fades out into a whine on the main road. He digs until his arms begin to burn and ache, until the ridge of the blade bites into his foot, until he's standing one foot down in the ground, drenched with sweat. Only then does he leave his shovel standing up in the center of the shallow hole, starting back up to the house to shower, shave and go sit with his boy.

Under bright lights, Bear's casket wavers, bursting with flowers, waxy and unreal, blooming bright in the night. Wild roses spill down the side between bright patches of purple and yellow. Babies breath fans out in a cloud. The coffin is polished, glossy and smooth. Tito knows what kind of wood it is but he can't think of the name. Yesterday he stood there beside Helen and nodded his head yes in front of the right coffin but now he can't think of what it is called.

Faces unpeel and swim back toward him one by one, shining and floating in the candlelight, filing out. Helen walks out leaning on Len's arm and Tito lets them pass. He studies the small moons of dirt under his fingers, pulls a horsehair off his pants. Father Joe walks up slowly, his face flushed red, and he reaches out to hold onto Tito's shoulder, grips him to the bone with fleshy fingers, then walks on. Tito remembers the father from back when they were kids. The priest was a real pissant with fat red cheeks, always in trouble, frying ants and holes in spider webs, putting sugar into gas tanks during mass. They spent one summer hand-fishing together, laying on the banks of the river, reaching under to stroke the golden silken bellies of trout, sometimes grabbing a handful of screaming muskrat instead of Tito's tired and bony shoulder, aching here in the last pew, Tito's son up there in the basket.

Cedar. The casket is cedar, smooth to the touch, fragrant. That's what the scrawny woman with the black swooping hair told them. At the funeral home she told them all about the different types of wood available, listing prices and virtues spiraling all the way up to Mahogany which was way beyond them. That room was filled with caskets, like barges, shining, about to let loose from their moors and embark. Tito didn't really listen, except for the part about $950 and thirty days to pay the bill. They sat opposite her long desk sunk into over-sized chairs while she arranged everything in her date book. Tito watched her eyebrows lift and lower, swim around on her forehead while she talked on and on about the flowers, the visitation, the plot, the church, flipping back and forth through her file, her fingers loaded with large turquoise rings. It was cold, there, in her office, with only a high narrow window up behind her desk, a brilliant square of blue. An electrical space heater blew on her feet and Tito stared at that, the grill growing cherry red, fading back out, then swelling orange into red again.

More faces pass by him, more hands press him on his shoulder, his cheek, reach for his hand. There are some cousins and friends and people he doesn't know. Ed and Ophelia make their way down the aisle last. Ed looks bad, gasping shallow like he needs air while Ophelia holds him up by the elbow. Tito waits for them to go by before he studies the altar again, narrow and confined.

There is one head left near the front. Bear's wife, Wendy, suddenly stands up and turns to go, fists clenched. Dark smudges circle her eyes. Her hair stands up, frizzy on her top, floating behind her. Tito knows there are certain people that have broken something inside of their heads and they just wait for a chance to get rid of it, to lay it down and walk away. He has known this all along about Bear's wife. When she stops at his pew and sits down next to him he doesn't move. He doesn't say anything.

"You can have them," she says quietly.

Tito nods and stares up at the white wall with the heavy wooden cross hanging off it. When he closes his eyes he can see crazy crosses in wild bright colors, burnt deep on his lids.

"I hate this." She spits the words out. They both stare up at the front as if something moved, maybe changed. She adds quietly, "I can't come tomorrow. I'm not doing this again. I'll be here when they put him down but I'm not going to sit like this again," she says firmly, as if Tito might argue, but he doesn't move, not even his hands.

"You can have them all," she says.

Tito turns and stares at her, her eyes strained and muddy colored, looking just to one side of his face.

"His shoes," she says and stands back up. "Everything. Come tomorrow." She backs out the pew and walks on, never once turning back. Bear's shoes are in a muddy heap on the bottom of a closet. There aren't so many, not like Tito imagined all night and through the morning while he stood outside digging and digging. Every time the shovel bit into the sole of his foot he saw shoes walking, shoes clumping, shoes with holes and one wet foot. He shoveled a mountain of shoes. But there are so few, criss-crossed, a couple pair of scuffed boots, dress cowboy boots with chains, sneakers with tangled laces, one pair of black and white dancing shoes.

"Tell me a story," Lena sits on the edge of the bed hugging a stuffed sock monkey. She is fresh from her bath, pink, and in blue pajamas with feet, a robe belted around her middle. She fixes her monkey's hat so that it pulls down over his eyes. Tito hates that monkey. He hated it when Helen gave it to Lena for Christmas three years ago and he still hates it. It's sewed out of some kind of brown sock material and has a jaunty silly hat with a red tassel. Worse, are the red lips on its face and the same obscene red lips where the tail leaves its body. It has stringy arms and legs and bright black eyes. Lena calls it Munk-a-lunk.

"Tell us a story," she says in her Munk-a-lunk voice and wiggles the monkey in the air.

Tito carefully unfolds each sheet of newspaper, lays it out flat before he wraps the shoes, one at a time. He stretches and winces at his digging muscles, "About what?" he asks her.

"About you, silly," she says and falls back laughing. Munk-a-lunk peers over the edge of the bed. "What are you doing with dad's shoes?" Munk-a-lunk asks. "Going somewhere with dad?"

The shoes are very dirty, very, very dirty and it takes Tito a while to wipe all the mud, so carefully, from the place where it's caked between the heel and the sole. He knocks the heels slowly on the floor to knock the dirt out, then he sweeps the dirt into a little cone. Each shoe gets two sheets of paper, the ends tucked neatly down into the hole before they slide into brown shopping bags. One pair to a bag. Lena and Munk-a-lunk stare over the edge of the bed, a patch of shiny drool on Lena's cheek.

"Don't know no stories?" she asks finally.

He starts to tell her about the dead roan they just dragged in but he stops in time. He folds a shoe up in a piece of paper, "I was in a fire once," he says, grabbing onto the first words appearing in his mind. "A big one, but I didn't die."

"Here?"

"No, far away, once, in California."

"When you were little?"

"No, when I was big. I was out working. Building a house."

"House?"

Tito nods, "It was early, morning. I was mixing cement when I saw a fast fire coming, a brush fire with a wind. It was jumping up at me, chasing me. I knew I couldn't run fast enough. No one could run that fast, so I turned on the hose, stood under the water. That fire blew right by me, a big tall wall of fire, pulled the air right out of my lungs, singed my hair. And right when the fire came I felt a rush at my feet, a rustling and you know what that was?"

"The fire," Lena says, breathless.

"No, rabbits. Those rabbits were running as fast as they could and when they smelled that water they dove all around my feet. I had rabbits up to my knees squirming and squiggling to get next to me, under that water. Then the fire hit, a wall, almost knocked me down. Then it was gone. Just like that. All gone."

"Gone," Lena says faintly.

Tito wraps a boot slowly thinking of that burnt and smoking field, how clear and beautiful everything was, dreamlike, a world he didn't belong in. He took a step. "And those rabbits," he adds softly, "Were dead. Every one." He can see the shriveled up raisin eyes, how peaceful and heavy they were as he stepped out of them, piled high around his feet, the roar of the fire already dim behind him.

"All dead?" she asks, "All dead?" her eyes widening, hugging her Munk-a-lunk closer to her, shrinking into the bed.

Tito drops a boot into a bag, embarrassed. This wasn't what he wanted to tell her at all. It was the moment, incandescent and pure, his eyelashes singed, smoke all around him. Out there in that field no one knowing whether he was dead or alive, and in that instant he realized fully that his existence was his idea and his alone. Everything that he was or would be rested in that moment, in that idea of himself.

"All of them died?" Lena spells this out, leaning forward to make sure, her head and neck sticking out, some hair fallen into her eyes.

"Great," Wendy says grimly, stepping into the room, setting a box down in the middle of the floor, "Know any others?" She sits on the edge of the bed, and pulls Lena next to her. The box is a tumble of clothes, a bright red shirt, a tan hat, some jeans. "You can have those too," she says.

"That's dad's hat . . ." Lena says solemnly, pointing. Wendy pulls her to her feet and heads her out of the room, Lena and the monkey straining to see what's behind her.

"I didn't mean . . ." he starts

"Forget it," Wendy says and drags Lena out, "Forget it." She starts down the hall and calls behind her, "We're having dinner if you want something to eat."

Tito finishes packing the shoes and straightens out all the bags, lines them up in a row by the door. He can't imagine what they could be eating. He can't imagine what she's told the child. In the kitchen, Lena's shrill voice rises on the word "shoes," then tops out on "bunnies."

He couldn't eat even if he wanted to. Already there is too much inside of him, all these boxes of Bear's clothes and shoes, where to put them so that Helen isn't upset, Bear's coffin and the funeral, the horse stretched out at the end of the hill, waiting. He can't imagine what they could be eating.

Bright yolk pools on both their plates. Lena holds a piece of tortilla up to her mouth and looks at him blackly. She chews slowly, studying the food in her hand. Without looking at him, she folds and folds the rest of the entire tortilla into her mouth. She chews with her cheeks bulging, turning her hands in front of her, showing herself they're empty.

Tito accepts coffee, turning the mug so that the faint orange lip mark on the rim faces away from him. Wendy wipes the counters, the walls, the baby's face and takes her to bed leaving behind only two wet circles on the table where their plates were. Tito takes it all in, the bright alphabet letter magnets on the refrigerator, postcards of small sunny beaches tacked up neatly in a row above the sink, a sprouting avocado seed. When had all this happened?

Down at the end of the hall he can hear Wendy starting back, closing doors and switching off lights, making her way through the house, toward him. Tito tries to see her differently for a moment, not as the surly woman from Seattle who always stayed out in the car while Bear poked in his head to say hello. He tries to imagine her the way Bear saw her.

She swings around the corner and drops the box of clothes down on the table in between them. Then she brings the bags of shoes and boots, one by one, piling them up on the table too. Tito watches her disappear behind the mound of Bear's belongings. Although she tries to hide it, he can see the strain in her face, puffy and pink around the nose, a slight give in the way she walks, almost a limp and he knows that this is what Bear saw too: a thin woman with a limp, walking toward him. She sits down across from him breathing a little heavy, reaches for a cigarette.

"When he was small," he tells her, "He looked like that, like Lena. Once when we were planting he found a packet of carrot seeds. He dumped the whole packet down in one row and grew the most enormous carrots I'd ever seen." Tito holds up his hands to measure out an absurdly long carrot, "Burst right up out of the ground."

Wendy lights her cigarette, taps her foot, puts her thumbnail between her two front teeth, tries to smile.

"Enormous," he adds.

Tito knows that he should be asking the important questions, question about the immediate future and the welfare of the child but her face stops him. He tries again with a story about how one time Bear ate a bee, but Wendy's face is smooth and uncomprehending, staring at him like he is speaking in another language. This isn't the Bear that she knew at all, her Bear wore these clothes, stood at that stove, sat in this chair. Slowly it comes to him he didn't know her Bear either. They are not the same person. They are not even the same idea.

When Tito thinks on these two men, it feels as if Bear never existed at all. He sips his coffee once, then again quickly. In his palm, the beginning swell of a blister throbs, pink and angry. His nails are caked with dirt. He can see how easy it would be for Bear to spin off into nothing, that sharing his memories with her is like ripping Bear up into small then smaller pieces, letting them go by the handful in the wind. Tito's boots hang heavy, out of place on the bright orange throw rug. He would like to be in his car, on his way home to his horse waiting for him to come and finish the job. It is when he thinks of the horse, collapsed under the tree that he knows what he will give her, a little jagged splinter he's lodged down inside of him for years. It isn't a story about Bear but that's not what she wants. She wanted her own notion of Bear, something she could keep for her own.

"One year, the rio froze early. Like now, October, the ice thick and cold," his voice boomed, startling them both. He stops, clears his throat, begins again. "The boys, of course, all piled down there to play. This is the rio Hondo, not the Grande, the one out back," he says and nods over his way so she'll know. "Sometimes it used to freeze solid, all the way down to the bottom, but not so often. Other times it floods, you know." He feels like he's wasting words so he gets quiet. Wendy inhales, blows her smoke up in the air waves it slowly away with one hand. "So . . ." she prompts, her voice flat, a smudge of lipstick on her front tooth.

"So this one time, all the boys they go off down there to go running around, only the ice, it's not so thick, see, not so thick. They get this idea, like boys, to throw some big boulders down in there. They launched them good, too, real high so they came down, punched big holes right through that ice. Big round craters. Some of them didn't break all the way through those ones just rolled out there and got stuck. They ice was littered with rocks, big rocks, holes, what a mess." He stops, sips his coffee. Wendy is listening now, leaning a little forward. She wets her tooth, wipes the lipstick away with her tongue. Her smell is faint, like a vegetable, nothing like it should be. He taps the side of his cup slowly, "But then, they got bored so they decided to get wild, rough, you know. They start spinning each other around, and Bear, he decides to go a little crazy with his younger cousin, Celso. He takes him by the hands and starts spinning fast, then faster in a circle. Only thing, his hands slip and Celso, he goes flying crazy through the air, spinning around, sails right out onto the ice, slides a ways, slips right down one of them holes. Slick. Right down. Kerplunk."

He can see Bear in his mind, turning, then feeling those small hot hands, that weight spin off, whistle through the air, knocking Bear down into the snow. "Bear, he fell down. Sat right down, but those other boys, went running out across that ice to get Celso out. One big kid, Lalo, he comes skimming and running across that ice, feet flying and slipping, then tripping. He shot right into one of those rocks, split his head right open like a melon. Smack. Broke it right open."

Wendy winces, but Tito keeps right on going because he's just getting to the good part. "So Bear gets up. Them other boys are all gathered around the kid with the broken head so Bear runs out on the ice to the hole Celso sunk through. He reaches right down into that black water pulls that Celso right up soaking and gasping from the cold. Carries him home, too, warm inside of his jacket. Didn't even catch a cold."

Of course the real story is much simpler than this. When Tito was small he watched while two older boys chased each other out on the river. One tripped and fell, snapped his neck and died. Tito stood, rooted on the bank, hidden behind a tree. He knew the boy was dead from the way his neck was snapped back and the way the other boy ran, wide eyed and breathing hard, right past him, back for help. Tito did not run. He clenched his hands, turned away and walked quickly, without stopping, all the way home, into his house, then into a closet where he pretended to be asleep. He didn't even open his eyes after his mother threw open the door and found him there, screaming about all the mud and snow he tracked all through the house, melting on all her nice shoes and stockings.

But, for a moment, Tito can see this other story too. Now that's he told it, it seems like it might have happened, Bear and Celso out there spinning around on the bank, sailing through the air. He watches Celso slide backwards, the surprise on his face as he tips down into the hole, his red mittens sinking down into the water. He watches all of it happen just like he said. He knows both he and Wendy can see Bear now, standing straight and tall, scooping his cousin up out of that ice, striding back home with Celso wrapped up next to him. They sit quietly, neither stirring. Tito finishes his coffee, gets up to rinse out his cup and leave.

Wendy stabs her cigarette out in the tray, "Wait," her voice so faint he can hardly hear her over the water running. "I have more," she says, "I'll show you."

Wendy opens up one of her closets and hands him a box, full of sharp tools. Tito lifts it, sets it down by the door but when he goes back she hands him another, this one a tangle of electrical wire. She hands him a box full of Christmas ornaments and one of wrapping paper. She gives him a half-used bag of alfalfa pellets and a leash, a box of belts and rags. They move faster and faster. Wendy digs out boxes, empties drawers, scoops out shelves. She gives him blankets and pillows, wire hangers and garden hoses, half empty buckets of paint. She clears the closets of all that she can and when they are done she helps him carry everything out to the car.

By the DeSoto, boxes lean and totter, piled up on each other, sinking into the icy mud, which claims everything, the boxes, their boots, streaked on their clothes and hands. It will take at least two trips back and forth to get so many boxes back home. Wendy sets the last carton down, "Wait," she says, and runs into the house, comes back to the door. "Everything will fit in there," she calls, tossing the keys to Bear's yellow truck from the door. She rubs her arms, like she's numb, her pale face lashed with one mud streak. Her hair hangs limp around her shoulders, pushing against her face, fallen and confused. "I'll see you tomorrow then," she says finally, in a loud voice, then she closes and locks the door.

When the back door swings open, iced water rushes out, then the dank, clammy smell of fish. In the dim light, blocks of ice glint covered with the sleek bodies and tails of fish, bags of cubed ice and bright packages of frozen fish stacked, slanted, waiting. Tito hadn't thought about this, the deliveries. There's maybe half a load of fish in there on ice, but nothing to do about it now except shove it over and begin loading up the boxes of Bear's belongings. Tito stacks and packs the boxes, side by side with the ice, enough room so nothing will slide around, then he lurches the truck up onto the road, on their way home.

His lights catch on trees, phone poles and mailboxes, the curves jumping up at him driving a different way home. Although he knows the road well it feels unfamiliar from the inside of the cab, the seat too far back, the wheel loose. Loud head banging guitars thrash on the radio where Bear left them. Tito gropes for the knob, spins the music up too loud, then turns it down low, but he leaves it on the station. The cab smells musty, of goats and coffee, of fish. He cracks the window and lets the heater blast on his feet, smelling the night rushing by.

Tito doesn't touch anything that has been left behind, not the ashtray full of twisted cigarette ends, a woman's lipstick on the seat, an empty, split styrofoam cup. It is enough that he must find a place for all the fish and the boxes down in the extra shed without Helen seeing and growing upset. He can't think about that, already it is rushing closer to him. Here he is, roaring through the night in his son's place. He's not sorry that he told Wendy the story that he did, leaving Bear walking back across the ice. He can see it again, Bear picking up Celso and walking across the ice, when he lifts his foot off the gas because he's not seeing Bear grown, carrying his cousin, he is seeing Bear tiny, just a moon head, dark eyes and a blue snowsuit, cold and whining. Walking, they were walking down over the bank, a short cut, across the rio, over to the back road. The thaw was on, early spring, ice and mud, everywhere. The rio rushed by, swollen. They crossed the way they always had, on a long felled tree that spanned the width of the river. The huge gnarled roots provided a step up onto the thick trunk, worn from so many crossings. Foot holds were hacked into the trunk so they could cross.

Bear was heavy in Tito's arms but he held him tightly, Bear's jacket rubbing against his cheek. He could feel Bear's body tense, his arm squeezing Tito's neck while behind them, Helen waited. Tito kept telling her to wait until he crossed so that the log wouldn't bounce or jog. It was easy until about half way out when Tito could feel a light spray on his face and smell the water black and fast, small pieces of ice broken up, pooling, rushing under the log. Bear shifted, fussed, and Tito slowed down to edging one foot next to the other, the log a little slick in places. He was almost across when he felt the pressure of Helen stepping up onto the log behind them, her weight coming up through his leg. Bear twisted back to see her, calling her name. Tito tried to catch himself, leaning first one way, then the other, but Bear kept twisting and turning. Tito swerved to one side and felt his foot slip, reach out and sink into air.

Tito rolls the window down further and lets the wind dig into him. He leans forward into the wheel, high beams curving and leaning, following the white lines up and down, pulling him down the road, swing left, jog down a small dirt drive. Tito pulls into a lot where two dull eyes stare back at him until he gropes for the knob, shuts his lights off. He is out of the cab, standing out in the cold before he realizes where he is, in the church lot. Frozen, rutted tracks criss and cross all around him but the only other car out there is Father Joe's. The church's high thick walls face him blankly, and the heavy wooden door pulls back at him when he tries to open it, but he wrenches it open.

The room smells cold and sickly with perfumed flowers. Candles smoke in the corners, pale and exposed in the small blare of an electric light. Only the father is there, in a regular shirt and pants, pulling a jacket on. He looks up, startled, "They've gone home, Tito," he says. "They all left. Go on home. We'll see you in the morning." In his voice there is a whiff, a suspicion that he thinks Tito is all messed up or drunk. The father doesn't want any trouble. Tito has several things he could say right then but he's not sure if they would make sense, so he tries to explain why he is there, but before he can work it all the way through, he starts to feel wobbly. The cold, damp air on his face pushes on his eyes, and for the first time all day he feels cold, really cold. The walls should be warm but they are only frozen mud, not any kind of earth holding in the heat.

"I need to sit for a minute," he says, lowering himself gingerly, startled, like is catching up to himself from a long distance. The room is blindingly bright, every single pew defined, the flowers illuminated, even old Joe's face, pink, almost translucent, seems focused and vital. The father comes closer, leans down and looks at Tito, draws in a sharp little breath. His slack eyes wander from Tito's mouth to his face. He stands, then shrugs. "Can I do something?" he asks in a tired voice.

The father, Tito knows, is a drinker. He would like to go back to his house out back and build a nice little fire, pour some brandy and lemon into some hot water, fill it to the brim a couple of times, then begin to drink in earnest, two fingers deep, straight from his coffee mug. He is not lost on Tito.

Tito smiles at the father and shakes his head no. "I just want to sit for a bit. Not long. You go home. I'll tell you when I leave."

The father looks around, relieved, then, smiles, pats Tito on the shoulder, "Have it your way," he says, "Knock when you go."

The door booms shut, the priest fades away, a shuffle in the gravel, back to his house. In the corner a bald electric light throws ridiculous shadows. The lamp, an old iron rooster, beak open, foolishly crowing, has no lamp shade and makes no noise as Tito snaps it off. Moonlight jumps into the room, casting hard blue and white shadows. The altar, half in shadow half in light, swells. The casket is shiny, satin smooth, dense under his hands. Flowers brush up against his face, the petals fleshy and cool, the bouquets surprisingly light. He lays them gently, one at a time, on the railing and the ground around him. He just wants to see the coffin, bare, sleek, glowing pale in the muted light. The lid isn't so heavy. It glides up on oiled hinges, easy, in one lift.

Tito hears a long wail, which is Helen, then the shock of cold. The swift current tumbled them, but Tito grabbed hold of his boy, struggling for air, so they were pulled feet first downstream until a pocket pulled them under. Down in that green ringing cold, Tito saw Bear's mouth dark, his eyes blurred first then growing whiter. Tito pulled him closer but Bear grabbed a fistful of hair, next to the roots and pulled as hard as he could. Tito couldn't get his footing, and as his movements slowed, a stillness filled him, so that the ache in his head and ears softened, and Bear's thrashing so close, filled him with a clear surge.

It wasn't love or anger that rushed into him, fusing their two bodies together, it was something just beyond them, unrecognized, beyond the cold beating into them, an idea of themselves which was inseparable. If he squeezed hard enough, they would reach it, that single moment, transformed, he could squeeze it into them, reaching beyond who they were spinning around and around, floating, without weight.

So he did, pulling his son closer in an embrace, holding them down, lungs bursting. And even after he could feel the rock and gravel solid under his feet, Tito let the moment carry them a bit further, crouched on the river bottom, feeling the force strangling him in his chest, his arms locked around Bear.

One arm around his shoulders and the other under his knees, Tito rises, in one swift movement, up, and carries him out. He walks in an even line straight down the aisle, pushing open the door, carrying Bear back out to the ice, to the back of his truck.

Tito pulls fish out, one at a time, dropping them with heavy thuds around his feet. He grabs bags of cubed ice and larger blocks. He heaps fish and ice, scooping them out of the truck and piles them up around his feet. Then, he quietly trudges back and forth, again and again, wiping his feet carefully at the doorway of the church so as not to track any mud down the aisle.

Up there, at the altar he breathes heavily, but in the moonlight it is beautiful to see: the glimmering ice spread over the fish, the heavy sagging salmon, a whole school of slippery trout, a bloated heavy fish, speckled with pink scales the sizes of pennies, golden flat eyes and a puckered mouth. Tito buries them all so that they swim and twist back and forth by each other, swimming both north and south. He packs the ice so tight down and around them that the fish are suspended, dark beneath the ice, caught in their own frozen strip of water, distorted in blue light.

Slowly, he lowers the lid down over the packed and leveled ice, sealing the coffin back up. The roses and larkspur are replaced and rearranged, blooming light and lovely, as they were before. Then very quietly, Tito gets down on his hands and knees and mops up his tracks, in careful, deep circles, backing the whole way down the long tile aisle, right on out of the church, wiping up any traces that he was ever there at all.

The ride home floats by, slow and easy, the back weighing down the wheels, keeping them on the road. Tito's mind is tired, spinning again over the simplest thoughts: how he will cut the lights, then coast down his drive, all the way down to the shed beyond the house where they sometimes put up guests, unloading the delivery truck, quickly, quietly. He will stand in the shower long enough to rub off the day, then slide into bed next to Helen, warm, placing just his feet over hers, gently so as not to wake her. He can see her now as if she were beside him, standing there, tomorrow at the church in front of the yawning open hole, watching the casket slide down on greased ropes. He will let Helen lean into him, her perfumed shoulders and powder floating up gently at him, her hair pillowed and soft to the touch. Maybe he will hold her elbow while she stoops to pick up a small handful of holy dirt to toss down into the hole. He will take a much larger handful, a handful of pebbles and dirt. When he tosses them they'll roll down like loose teeth or clattering hail. He'll wait a minute, then do it again.

Ahead of him there is nothing but some startled trees, then the break out into the field beyond, the moon washing out the bowl like a giant crater, empty and wide. Tito slows down to clear the curve, the one where the roan died. He cuts the lights there and slows till he finds his drive. Starting up his hill he keeps the engine in low gear, crawling home. Moonlight seeps into the fields around him making them look pocked and pitted, the road full of gulches, but Tito knows it is just a trick of the light. He shifts his weight, presses his foot down harder on the gas. The heater blasts so hot on his boots he smells leather heating, shoe polish melting, but Tito keeps his toes there, his mind loose and wandering. He thinks about the ruts in the road, the packed boxes, the melting ice, the roan stretched out and waiting next to the grave, a small disturbance down by the trees.

Vincent Collazo	*Modeling for Maya*

EXHIBITIONISM PAID HIS BILLS. In front of large groups and small he'd drop his clothing to the floor, stretch and contort his body while they'd scratch and smush images of him onto paper and canvas. They called themselves artists and he was called model—but they ingested his life essence while he fed off their energy, that which they named talent. His extraordinary ability to hold a pose kept him in demand, overriding his cold affect. Ideally, a model was warm and pleasant, but he did not view the process as a cordial one.

I'll suck up your energy and you can suck mine, and if you're good you'll end up with more, but if I'm better you'll leave with less.

He felt Maya understood this. They'd never spoken of it but he could feel her psyche focused on him, in a conscious struggle with his. They'd had some majestic battles during her classes—while her students drew, blithely unaware. She'd pace around the room, behind the easels, staring at the students' work, offering criticism, comparing their lines to his body. Her gaze was powerful— she knew what he was doing, and she reciprocated. Maya requested his services frequently, and he felt a thrill each time he came to her class.

Twenty minutes posing, five minute break. Twenty on, five off. But he needed no rest between poses. He'd spend the five minutes examining the works created, while the artists cowered from his silent judgment. He had a piercing eye for talent; when he failed to linger at a drawing or painting he could sense a student correctly assessing that their work had been summarily dismissed.

Maya had made a special call to him, asking if he'd model for a second time after the class he had scheduled. It was odd that the teacher had called him instead of the modeling coordinator, but he assumed that the coordinator was out sick. He'd accepted gladly—it was always better to model a "double" class, as he wouldn't need to travel to another school for work that day. The first class had only one or two truly gifted students, but Maya's presence made the experience worthwhile. She looked into his depths, and he tried to fathom hers.

He took a half-hour break for lunch then returned for the second class-hoping that they would prove more deserving of his efforts.

They were late, which was not a good sign. Maya sat at the front of the room with a circle of empty chairs surrounding her, and he felt the insult for her. In the midst of his reading a chapter of Nietzsche he was roused by Maya saying, "Shall we start then?" He hadn't previously thought of Maya as having a keen sense of humor, but with the room still bereft of students he could only believe she was kidding. He finally decided to admit to confusion by saying, "But the students haven't arrived. . . ."

"Oh, didn't I tell you? This is to model for me personally."

No, she hadn't told him. It felt odd. He'd only modeled for classes, not individual artists. "Oh, okay," he managed.

"I've been commissioned to paint a mural for the lobby of a building downtown," Maya explained, "and I need to practice my drawing. I hope it's all right with you, modeling just for me."

Technically, he should have been getting more money for modeling for her individually. She was taking advantage of her position in the school to get a lower rate. He didn't feel he could turn her down or re-negotiate at this point. It made him uncomfortable.

He took his clothing off and she sat him in a chair directly in front of her and asked him to face her—a very easy pose. Yet she was dissatisfied and walked toward him to rearrange him. Maya was tall and powerfully built. She had long, shining, red hair, which, though obviously dyed, was quite stunning. She brusquely placed his arms on the chair rests saying, "Imagine you're an Egyptian statue."

Those words had the effect of changing the nature of the session. Suddenly he believed that she was in some way coming on to him. *Why else the mystery about modeling for her and not a class? It was a trick so that I would agree to do the job without knowing what it was. I probably would have done it anyway, and Maya is quite attractive, for a woman her age. She's probably fifteen years older than I am. Egyptian statue. Why does that sound like a sexual image to me? Uh-oh, better stop thinking about these things, I'm starting to get aroused. No place to hide sitting here naked. Let me think about what I was reading.* Anything done out of love is done beyond good and evil. *I don't know if I agree. The statement posits that where love is concerned we cannot use the faculty which most distinctively marks us as humans: the ability to come to a moral decision. Are love and morality truly mutually exclusive? How would Maya look if she were undressed as she was drawing me? Oops. Another little rise. Well it's probably still within normal parameters for penile elongation fluctuation due to temperature changes. It is rather warm in this room. Should I ask her to open the window? God, if I actu-*

ally speak to her somehow that would seem even more intimate. It's a situational feeling—modeling in a warm room alone with the teacher. I'm not actually attracted to Maya—how could I be, I was never aware of it before. Except right now I'm having a difficult time remembering that I'm not attracted to her. Oh my god, more arousal. Nietzsche's no good, better think of something else. Plato perhaps. The Waters of Forgetfulness would be a wonderful blessing at this point. Plato is so dry—among the least likeable philosophers. Also the most sexless. Made a career out of stuffing his own words into the mouth of Socrates. Now Socrates, on the other hand, wasn't averse to a little sex on the side. He was always eyeing some fair youth—he didn't even care about gender. A truly liberated philosopher—how do I keep getting on to sex? I'm really showing too much now, I'm sure Maya's begun to notice what's going on. But she generally works oblivious to outside forces, so maybe she hasn't. What a powerful way of drawing she has. She really rakes the charcoal over the paper with authority. I can hear each stroke that she puts on. There's a rhythm to it. Stroke, stroke, stroke-stroke. Stroke, stroke, stroke-stroke. It's really too much to expect me to maintain sexual decorum at this point. Jesus, I've got another ten minutes to go before a break. I'll never make it. This is torture. I'm sure she knows anyway. What if for once in my life I'm not a complete professional? What if I just let myself go? That would be nice. Oh god, there, I've done it. I'm at "half-mast." The pressure is off now. Oh, she is beautiful. I guess I've always known it. Imagine if we were to be together. . . .

So he allowed himself to become fully erect, and casually placed his robe on at the end of the twenty minutes. He cooled down during his five-minute break and told himself that he would never repeat that performance. When the modeling recommenced she again placed him in the "Egyptian statue" pose and began to stroke away. He couldn't bear it for very long. Again he allowed himself to "rise" to the occasion. Again she worked through as if this were perfectly normal. *She* was the consummate professional, he thought, then cringed as his mind turned the adjective "consummate" into a verb, and his body responded to his fantasy: glistening atop the head of his penis was a tiny jewel of pre-come.

It went on like this for the full three hours of modeling. He chastised himself at the end of each twenty-minute pose for allowing prurient thoughts to dominate his body and promised silently it wouldn't happen again. But as soon as he was facing Maya, and felt her penetrating eyes measuring his proportions, he could not help being sexually stimulated anew. By the end he was emotionally and physically spent, and thoroughly embarrassed. Yet Maya asked him if he would like to do another session over the weekend at her studio. He barely managed to say yes, and get the information about where and when, before practically running to the men's room, where he masturbated furiously. That was over pretty quickly, but now he had several days to anticipate what would happen at Maya's studio.

The next day he realized he was completely unnerved by his loss of control. He had an overwhelming desire to share the experience, but he hadn't any friends with whom he could be that intimate. A therapist would be a good sounding board, but he would never subject himself to that kind of scrutiny. One might think that with the abundance of twelve-step groups now extant, that one of them would address this particularly peculiar situation, but alas, it was too particular or too peculiar even for the twelve-step contagion. So he did what came most naturally to him: he went online.

It wasn't hard to find an e-pal in a chat room. He tried at first to explicate the inner workings of his system of thought regarding modeling. Although it seemed very clear in his mind, he now found that words didn't seem to be enough to convey the essence of the energy-sucking game he played with artists. The e-pal wasn't getting it. So he shifted gears and went straight for the "juicy" stuff.

". . . as I thought about her I popped a boner as hard as a frozen cucumber, right in front of her! And she acted as if nothing had happened!!!"

. . . and so on, in that vein, with lots of excitable punctuation and rapid-typing misspells. The e-pal's conclusion, after having extracted every detail of his experience, was, basically,

"what's the problem? You like her. She doesn't seem to care if you get hardons. She maybe enjoys it. She invited you to her place. Have a good time. As for the professionalism—gimme a brake. It's not like you're a lawyer or doctor violating a code of ethics. You're a model who takes off your clothes forgodsakes."

He took offense at the suggestion that he was *merely* a model, and abruptly ended the communication with the e-pal. He believed his standards to be loftier than those of bloodsucking lawyers and bloodletting doctors. But, although he did not receive full understanding, the e-catharsis felt good. Besides, he did want to go through with his next session with Maya, and he'd gotten affirmation in that regard.

That night he brought himself to sweet sleep by re-playing in his mind the session with Maya, embellishing until it was a new scenario, which contained personal touches which served as a sort of dry run for his upcoming meeting with the art teacher. The imaginative practice session proved, in the end, to be anything but "dry."

The subway ride to Maya's Upper East Side studio was one of great agitation. He alternated between pretending that this was just another straight modeling job and letting his fantasies go way beyond the bounds of what might reasonably occur. But what *was* reasonable about any of this? He squirmed on the hard plastic subway seat, stood up and paced, then bolted back down to a seat, unable to contain his extreme uneasiness.

When he finally got off the subway he felt as if he weren't dressed well enough to even be walking on Maya's block. The doorman announced him. He half-expected to be turned away—he'd probably built up the modeling incident in his mind out of nothing . . . he needed to get out more, associate with people in a normal fashion, he'd probably imagined her invitation—but no, the doorman listened to the phone for a moment, then opened the door, granting him a professionally courteous smile.

The elevator and hallway were overly gilded and there was far too much detailed carving on the ceiling, but the lack of taste was counterbalanced, in his mind, by the amount of money such ostentation required. He exited the elevator onto an extremely long corridor lined with "forged" paintings from Masters. It was a journey through time, with representations of da Vinci, Rembrandt, Whistler, Picasso, Pollack and some unfamiliar contemporary abstractionists. Was Maya the source of this counterfeit stroll through Western art history?

He raised his finger to ring the bell but the door opened preemptively, with Maya standing on the other side, beaming. She invited him inside. The apartment opened out into wide proportions, which he was unprepared for a Manhattan home to possess. How could she afford such a place? Was she really that successful an artist? Or did she have—not believing he hadn't thought of it before—a husband? He'd have to check her hand for a ring. They traversed the length of the apartment and she asked if he wanted anything to drink. Did she mean alcohol or a beverage? Through his confusion he said no.

"Then shall we get right to work?"

"Yes, please." The "please," he realized as soon as it flew from his lips, was extraneous. She smiled and led him to her studio.

She placed him in a new seated position, foregoing the "Egyptian statue." Was it a sign of a change in her attitude? What was her attitude? He'd decided that he would let himself get turned on immediately, without a struggle, and if something were going to happen between them, he'd know it. She *did* have a ring, he now noticed—a plain gold band, clearly a wedding ring. He resolved it didn't matter to him if she were married—he wasn't looking for a relationship he was looking for . . . what? A quickie? He could get that elsewhere, without the elaborate set-up of this modeling charade. No, he wanted an unusual experience.

Naturally it failed him. Now that he wanted to display his erection to indicate his continued interest, he could not attain one. The more he thought about it the less likely it seemed to be possible. He was modeling and she was drawing, and that was all. Except he was not able, in his "weakened" condition to receive any of her energy as she drew. Was she taking it from him? He couldn't tell, which probably meant that he was "losing" this battle so badly that he didn't even know it was happening—exactly what he did to unsuspecting students. He could not rally himself. Between his sudden exhibitionist "impotence," Maya's wedding ring and his doubt about why he was here to begin with, he was thoroughly distracted.

She drew in the same fashion she had before: stroke-stroke, stroke, stroke, stroke. Her passion was clearly for her craft. *She's an artist working, has no interest in me except professionally. Sometimes things are what they seem to be, and nothing is buried underneath; layers of deceit need not operate in every human interaction. She had been commissioned for a mural and needs practice.* His current chagrin superseded his previous humiliation, and he actually blushed for the remainder of the session.

Maya declared the session finished, but as he moved toward his things she said, "No, don't get dressed yet, I've something I'd like you to see. This way."

He followed her, and felt oddly vulnerable walking naked through her home, and wondered what she could show him that would be hindered by his clothing. They arrived in the bedroom and she stopped to face him in front of a large, round, canopied bed. She glanced down at his genitals, penis still limp.

"I thought you were interested in me," she said.

He was so flabbergasted, all he could manage to say was an echo. "Interested. Um. Interested."

"Yes," she said, "interested," and cupped his scrotum in her hand, which contracted in response. He felt blood rush to his penis as it filled and grew, and he sighed relief—as much because his "equipment" was in working order as because Maya was making his fantasy reality.

With her free hand Maya gently shoved him so that he fell through the laced canopy and on top of a blue satin sheet. As he lay on his back she quickly disrobed, but it was not at all like a striptease, but rather more similar to a businessman returned home at the end of a long day. She folded and laid her clothing on a late Victorian chair, then approached him.

She was beautiful—tall and strongly built. Her formidable breasts only sagged a little from age; her legs had a minimal amount of cellulite. Her pubic hair was bright orange. He now knew that the hair on her head was originally the color of her pubic hair. She dyed the hair on her head to compensate for graying and the almost inevitable darkening of red hair. *There's irony in Maya deceiving the world with a lie (a dye) which held a more essential truth than her mismatched roots.* As his mind played with these words and concepts his penis dove. She lunged at him, vaulting onto the bed with great agility, landing straddled upon his genitals with her full weight. She rocked herself back and forth and as he once again grew to his proper proportions he could feel her wetness.

He looked up at her breasts, nipples erect, sweat beading across her torso and upper lip. He moved his hands to touch her breasts but she grabbed hold of each of his wrists and pinned his arms down, outstretched over his head. Her face was close, and she was breathing harder as she continued to rub her vagina over his penis. Stroke, stroke, stroke-stroke-stroke.

It was agony, it was delight. He wanted to kiss her, but her mouth hovered a tantalizingly short distance from his lips. He wanted to touch her, but she kept his wrists firmly pinned. He squirmed underneath her, and she seemed to enjoy that. At length she lifted herself enough to position her vagina directly above his erect penis, then lowered herself onto him, and he watched his penis disappear from sight. She was so lubricated he glided in, with no friction whatsoever.

He had no breath; he could not believe this was happening. She raised and lowered herself over and over, as he lay motionless, more and more aroused. As she moved he noticed the optical illusion which made it seem as if the penis was attached to Maya, entering him. Stroke-stroke, stroke-stroke-stroke. Like her drawing rhythm, her sexual motion was hard, fast and determined. After she thrilled him with some long and slow strokes he exploded inside her. Only after he came did his think: *should I have been concerned about birth control or is Maya on the other side of menopause? What about disease? Why didn't either of us take precautions? I did bring some condoms.* He didn't voice his thoughts, choosing instead to lay in bliss. Maya's orgasm had consisted of violent jerking, and she'd released his wrists as she collapsed on top of him, and rolled him briefly over her only to return his compliant body underneath her considerable mass. Once her paroxysms ceased, which wasn't for several minutes, she lifted her vagina from around his penis, creating a popping sound and a bit of pain in his penile head. She immediately re-clothed. He remained on the bed, still trying to take in the experience, vibrating. Maya brought him water and began to busy herself with some paperwork she brought in from another room, and he felt he was being given a signal that it was time to leave.

"I'd love to draw you again," Maya said. "I'll call you to set up an appointment."

He agreed but left doubting that she'd call, after having been whisked out so quickly following their sex. *Perhaps her husband was expected shortly, and Maya didn't want to seem tacky by mentioning him.* And yet, there was something else in the way she'd treated him that made him believe she wouldn't see him again. *A coldness, a calculated coldness.* He laughed at himself for expecting warmth and affection from her, when all they were doing was basic, animal fucking. This was no relationship. They weren't dating. They weren't in love. He had made no attempt to speak to her throughout their sexual encounter, and she offered no verbal communication either.

Before Maya left she handed him cash for his three hours of modeling. When the exchange of bills from her hands to his took place, he was momentarily confused. He *had* modeled, but being given money so soon after having sex created uncomfortable undertones. He took the money. He *had* earned it, and *he* knew how.

On the subway ride home he began to play one of his favorite games—categorizing people. Usually it was a rapid and facile exercise, but today he was unsure whether the mustachioed man in a cheap suit was a giver or taker. Was the teenager with the stocking rolled on top of his head as tough as he made out or was he posing? The woman with the three rambunctious children—was she trapped in her life, with a bad marriage and unfaithful spouse, or was she a loving mom exhausted from the process? Nothing seemed simple. He gave up the game.

He entered his apartment and saw the words he himself had scrawled onto the large white erasable board: LAUGHING LIONS MUST COME. It was from Nietzsche, but its brilliance as a watchword had faded.

He got online to re-establish a connection with the e-pal he'd previously written to about his initial stirrings for Maya. His idea was to report on his success, but the triumph he boasted of was not heartfelt. He accepted the e-pal's congratulations anyway.

He spent the next few days waiting for the phone to ring. If someone had observed him during this time it would have appeared that he was actually reading books, writing notes, watching television, surfing the Internet and listening to music. But the truth was that when the phone rang all other activity immediately stopped, most tellingly his heartbeat. Upon coming home he rushed to check his answering machine, but it was invariably a call for him to model, and not with Maya. He longed to phone her at the school where she taught, but felt it somehow inappropriate. At night he fantasized calling her at home—she was listed with information, he'd checked—but this, he felt, was bordering on insanity. Did he secretly wish to speak to her husband? What would he say? *"Hi, you don't know me but I fucked your wife the other day and I'd really like to do it again. Is she home?"*

So when the phone rang and it truly *was* Maya, he had to perform some sort of reality check, to make sure he wasn't imagining it. He drove his thumbnail into his forearm and saw the indentation it created clearly—a detail which his dreaming mind would be hard pressed to conjure with such quick accuracy.

"How's this Friday night for you?" Maya asked, businesslike, studying her calendar.

"Fine. Friday's fine."

"Listen, we won't be able to use my studio. Would it be all right to do it at your place?"

He'd agreed, of course, and set about getting his apartment in order for a social visit. Not many people crossed the threshold of his home. He felt unworthy to have her under his roof, and wondered how she would feel in a space which would practically fit inside one of her enormous closets.

Maya did not care that he had a small home, didn't, in fact, seem to notice. She set up her easel and paper, ordered him into some standing and recumbent positions and drew, as usual. His penis rose in anticipation, thrilled to be under her penetrating eye once more. After three hours had elapsed she put down her charcoal, took his hand and led him to his bed. "Okay, lover. Let's see what you've got."

He had hoped—dreamt—that they'd be able to perform some very specific sex acts that they hadn't gotten to during their first round of pleasure seeking. But Maya, apparently, had a different idea—or rather, the same idea, one of repetition. She disrobed, more quickly and less fastidiously than before, and once again climbed atop him, straddling his genitals with hers. Again he was pinned down while she rocked back and forth and got his penis inside her, whereupon she rode him until they both shuddered from their simultaneous orgasm.

She placed money for his modeling on the table before she left, and then arranged another session for the following Friday. "Listen," Maya said. It was an unnecessary imperative. When she spoke he couldn't do anything but listen. "I think I should have a set of keys."

He looked at her blankly, unable to process what she had said.

"I don't like having to wait on the street while you come down to get me after I buzz. If your building had an electric door . . . anyway, it'd save you having to walk down then back up the stairs. So suppose you just bring a set to me at the school—you can drop it off with the receptionist."

"Okay." He couldn't find a reason not to fulfill her request. It made sense. Yet he felt uneasy because he associated giving away one's keys with a certain level of intimacy they had not attained, nor could he imagine them achieving. *But keys are merely objects, and objects only contain the emotional content that we imbue them with. The root of fetishism, then, is an emotional vacuum filled by the object.* He was proud of his little analysis and wrote it down in his journal as soon as Maya had gone.

Modeling for Maya

I have to kiss her. The thought played in and preyed upon his mind. *That's such a junior high school expectation,* he chided himself in his journal. *Mouths meet and pretend to exchange something, but it only amounts to saliva and groping tongues. When we kiss we mime some primordial urge to be fed by the mother, regurgitating digested food into her baby's eager mouth. Birds do the same thing, why is it so important for a human to do so? I'm vaguely disgusted by my own bent towards this instinct. Ashamed that I cannot easily rise above it.*

There were other sexual longings he possessed in relation to Maya that required explication. He wanted to be on top of her while they had intercourse *(the need to dominate and be in control is not a lofty one),* to go down on her, find her clitoris with his lips and tongue and stir her into a frenzy *(to bury oneself and merge into the Other's identity, to crawl back inside the womb, and to control another's behavior, under the guise of giving them pleasure—even perhaps the muted homosexual wish to suck on a penis—certainly the act of cunnilingus is rife with possibility for psychological exploration. In fact, cunnilingus is so charged an area that some men will not deign to perform it, complaining of a smell or the less definable "otherness" or the even less distinct "ickiness"),* to suck upon her nipples *(the mother and child again, in a more tender and infantile form).* There was more, but in truth he did not want to explain his desires away. *I want, like all of us, to give in to my desires, whether or not they are ideal or even good for me.*

Friday could not come soon enough.

In the ensuing days he read more Nietzsche, wrote more exposition on his "condition," defined variously as lust, perversion and human. He listened to Billie Holiday moon about *her* lovers. He rented pornographic videos and imagined Maya in every "starring role." He masturbated constantly and without thought. None of this assuaged his unrest, so he decided it was time for a field trip. He took himself out on a date to the zoo.

While the giraffes, elephants, red pandas, polar bears, zebras, gazelles, tigers, seals, rhinos and the rest of the impressive menagerie held their own particular fascinations, nothing so moved him as his visit to the baboons. They were unapologetically all over each other. They chased one another with great abandon, jumped and humped with no ostensible motivation. Their red rumps blazed with passion as they had actual and simulated intercourse to satisfy their needs for sex and dominance. He felt all too distant from their free and loose ways until one baboon came close to where he was seated, and sat flush against the glass wall which separated them. It did not look upon him directly, but glanced at him out of the corners of its eyes—eyes that, upon close inspection, looked remarkably human. They sat together quietly for some time in what he imagined to be a tandem meditation, and he gained a sense of peace from this encounter.

Thursday night. Just one night to go before Maya's next visit, and he was in the midst of another bout of fitful sleep. Perhaps he was engaged in a pleasant reverie involving Maya, for surely all his dreams included her. There was a strange yet familiar sound. The door to his apartment creaked open, a shaft of light removed the shadows from his home and a silhouette stood ever so briefly under the doorframe. The door closed behind it and Maya came directly to his bed.

"I couldn't wait," she declared, and threw her clothing off and her hands upon his body.

"Wait a minute," he said, sleep beginning to clear from his head. "Why didn't you call?"

"What's the difference," she said, "I'm here."

She clambered on top of him and although she was entirely lubricated he was nowhere near erect. "Don't you want me?" she asked.

"I want you to call before coming into my apartment."

As a response she placed her mouth over his penis and sucked on it, roughly.

"Maya, no," he said, but she continued.

"Stop, Maya!" he yelled, but she didn't stop and placed her large left hand around his throat, which had the dual function of preventing him from yelling and cutting off his air and blood circulation so that blood was sent to his penis—a coerced version of erotic asphyxiation. His penis engorged, seemingly of its own accord, having nothing to do with what was in his mind. Once it was fully erect Maya assumed the genitalia straddling position, pinned him down with real, not mock, force, and proceeded to writhe upon him.

"I've begun the mural," she informed him.

He was too stunned to yell or even mildly protest. The sensations of her vagina overwhelmed his ability to resist. He asked himself if resistance was indeed what he wanted. "My . . . mural . . . is . . . going . . . to . . . be . . . incred . . . ible!" she proclaimed as she contracted and wrenched uncontrollably from her orgasm. As she did so, he, too, came, but there was a feeling of intense sensitivity, which left his penis feeling chafed.

She rose out of him, dripping with his semen.

"I'll let you get some sleep now," she said.

As she dressed he managed to tell her, "Maya, I don't ever want you to come in again without calling first."

"Didn't you have a good time?" she asked.

"I don't want you to do that again. Do you understand?"

She shrugged her shoulders, which he took to mean that she would comply without comprehension. But in the morning he had the lock changed, in case she'd missed his point. He did not sleep further.

He rose to begin a full day of modeling appointments, but he felt so disconcerted while he stood naked in front of the morning class that he canceled the afternoon class, saying he was ill.

Once home he went online and wrote to his e-pal of his most recent experience with Maya.

". . . it's not as if I was, well, "violated". . . I mean, I got an erection and she makes me come, so that can't really be called rape, can it? It's more an issue of inconvenience. She doesn't respect that I might not be in the mood (or even awake), or even that she should bother to ask. It's like I'm some sort of abstract dildo she's using that happens to be attached to a human body. Maybe *she* views *that* as being the inconvenience—this human being thing getting in the way of her crass pleasure."
E-pal wrote:
"I think, by definition, a penis can't be raped by a vagina. if it's erect it's responding positively and there's no coercion, and if it's *not* erect it can't be "had" and there's no crime.

I know it sounds like a Catch-22, but it's a true one. Maybe you just got in over your head with this woman's game playing. I agree she shouldn't have come to your apartment. . . ."

This was fairly standard thinking, and indeed the dictionary clearly defines rape as something that happens to a woman. One could broaden the definition, without too much objection, to include a man suffering nonconsensual anal penetration, as long as one qualified it by naming it *homosexual* rape. Even so, the perpetrator must perforce be a man. He was not arguing that he had been raped, quite the contrary. But since the word hung about like a stray cat who'd been given a bit of milk, he became interested in exactly how to define what *had* happened to him.

Literature has given us "The Rape of the Lock," he thought but if my memory serves me correctly, the lock of hair in question was "raped" in the sense of being abducted. Perhaps the definition of rape needs to be extended to include the phallus—I could write a poem entitled "The Rape of the Cock," to make my case, although if I wish for it to make an imprint on our culture, I'd best turn it into a hip-hop song:

her pussy covered my jimmy sayin' gimme gimme gimme
so what could I do y'all? she had her hands over my balls

she squeezed out some juice from my thumpin' machine
sayin' to me "boy I'm gonna make you cum clean"

The exercise of creating this whimsical song lightened his spirits, and he found himself de-emphasizing the negative aspects of his last encounter with Maya. Perhaps the next time they met he would get to do some of the things *he* wanted to do—act out *his* fantasies for a change. He'd definitely have to speak to her about it.

He awoke that night to some pounding in his head, which turned out to be his door. Maya was on the other side, frustrated that her key didn't work. He looked at her distorted face through his peephole and said, through the door, "I thought you agreed to call me before you came here."

"Open the door," she demanded.

"Maya, if you'd just called I would have invited you over. I don't understand you."

"Open the door." Her face was livid.

"I think you'd better go home. We'll talk about it tomorrow."

Her response was to pound on the door with both hands, yelling out "Open up you fucking thief! You stole my money! Open the door and give it to me!"

He could hear movement from his previously sleeping neighbors and he considered his options while she added kicking the door to her assault. He could call the police, but how long would that take? What would he tell them? *Yeah, we've been fucking but I'm not in the mood tonight. And last time she broke in she forced me to have sex.* It wasn't liable to go over so well with the cops. He could try to keep it simple and say that they had broken up and he didn't want her in his home. What would Maya tell them? She had already created a lie about stolen money, how far was she willing to go with it? He didn't want to find out, so he opened the door.

"What the hell do you think you're doing?" Maya asked as she charged through the door. "Embarrassing me like that. You're going to get it now." By which she meant the usual treatment. She straddled and rode him, but this time she did it with her back to his face—apparently as punishment for the rudeness of his attempt to lock her out. He laughed at his previously imagining he could converse with Maya about the sex they were having, as if she would consider altering her behavior to better suit his needs. She wanted only one thing and would not be swayed from her path—it would be easier to stop a wrecking ball in motion with bare hands. She was a Juggernaut, and he'd thrown himself under the wheels of her carriage, and if he was crushed it was not a matter for an exalted god to be concerned about. Only devotion, blind

226

and complete, was expected of mortals in relation to their betters. *"Forgive us our betters . . ."* passed through his mind as Maya furiously pounded them both into the climactic completion of their sexual act.

"Give me your spare key," Maya said, almost immediately afterwards. He found he could not lie and say he hadn't gotten a spare; he retrieved the key and handed it to her.

"I've finished the mural," she said. "It's a brilliant piece. You should go downtown and see it."

He said he would.

She dressed and left. As loud as her entrance had been, so her exit was just that quiet.

There was nothing left to gain by consulting with his e-pal. He had only to await her return, to pay homage or make whatever sacrifice was necessary. It wasn't so bad. She didn't ask for his life or his firstborn son. She didn't even want a tithing from his meager income. She merely required a small sampling of his seminal fluid, extracted from him in an ecstatic ritual during which he was permitted to have personal contact with the deity. This duty was an honor.

A month later she had yet to reappear. He was convinced she would though, because she had taken his key, which he had given readily. Each night he lay in bed, staring at the door in unholy anticipation, counting his heartbeats. Every locked door was now an illusion—for rage and overpowering hunger lurked on the other side. For the rest of his life, he knew, through his shame and glory, that he would await those forces, powerless to stop them, unable to comprehend, but willing to worship at their altar.

| Henry | *Funeral March* |
| Alcalay | *for a Marionette* |

RAINING. A Friday night, late December, the week between Christmas and New Years; what I like to refer to as the perineum of the year. There must be plenty of people all over this long dirty city having better nights than me, I thought, as I walked down Lexington Avenue wearing an oversized trenchcoat and a grey chalk-striped suit with lapels so wide they should have come with turn signals. Yet I wanted to think I looked as if I had stepped out of a picture I'd seen recently on the cover of a James Cain novel, *Double Indemnity*, where the figure in the sepia-toned photograph wears an extravagant, double-breasted suit and, since I know the train he is boarding will carry him towards his destruction, the suit seems even more beautiful.

I was on my way to Ray's apartment to see what I could say to Harold. He had a problem; he was facing five to fifteen years in prison. And I am a lawyer.

One night the previous October, Harold climbed into a friend's car and was driven out to Little Neck, a quiet community of tree-lined streets and single-family homes in Queens, near the Nassau County border. There Harold sold an ounce of cocaine to a pair of undercover cops. Harold had been set up by a friend who had been set up by a friend who had been set up by another friend and back and we can go until we come to the day Jesus himself was indicted. Now Harold was torn between trying to set someone up himself or simply pleading guilty in return for a reduced sentence. Using the excuse that I am a jurist I wished to speak with him, to palpate and inhale his agony firsthand.

Those days Harold was staying with Raymond, who lived three flights above the Stolen Moments, a topless bar on Lexington, just south of Grand Central. Climbing the stairs to Ray's apartment, I could hear the jukebox. *Fly, Robin, Fly*, it insisted, beckoning me but I resisted and knocked on Ray's door. He opened the door and gaped at me with his usual expression of chagrin. Then he moved aside so I could enter.

"I can't shake hands with you, my hand's still fucked up from the shooting," he said. In October, Ray had shot his roommate in the leg and himself in the hand. Accidentally, of course, and no charges were filed. Afterwards his roommate chose to move.

"That's okay with me, Jim, I don't want to touch you either." I waved hello to Harold who leaned against the sink wearing only jockey shorts and loafers. He wiped his eyes and sniffled. Him I definitely didn't want to touch. Shoving Ray's clothes aside, carefully I hung my coat in the apartment's one closet. Walking back to the kitchen I resisted the impulse to shoot my cuffs.

"So," I said to Harold who leaned against the sink by the gap where the dishwasher used to be. Ray had put pillows and a blanket down there which was where Harold liked to sleep. The old roommate as well. Hell, I'd slept there myself.

I looked at Harold who looked back with out speaking. Now and then a sob or shudder convulsed him but between them he seemed fine.

"What's going on?" I asked.

Raymond answered for him. "He just got back from trying to set these two guys up to sell some coke to the narcs but then at the last minute they backed out."

"How come?"

"They didn't want to go to Queens."

"Oh."

Since Harold had been busted in Queens any set up he put together would have to take place there.

"Hey, whose are those?" I asked Ray, pointing to a set of dentures on a plate by the sink.

"Anthony's," he replied with a shrug. "I didn't care but he insisted, until he pays me." Anthony was the super. Now and then Ray sold heroin. Just enough to get your hopes up when the urge struck but not enough you could count on him. He was more reliable in high school. Sometimes he used to let me go with him to see his supplier whose apartment was in Jackson Heights. On summer nights I'd wait outside, leaning beneath the sycamores. A breeze would blow through the treetops, the blinds in someone's window would flutter and the first floor widow's wind chime would tinkle in the dark. Then Ray would appear in the doorway, the yellow light of the hallway lighting him from behind. He'd shuffle down the steps, opening his hand to show me a fistful of glassine bags.

"Hey, that reminds me," I said, meaning Anthony's teeth. I went over to my raincoat and removed a plastic bag of watercress which I rinsed in the sink. "Ray, got any salt?" Reaching into a cabinet above the sink —for some reason all the cabinet doors had been removed—Ray handed me the dirtiest shaker I'd ever seen. Even the sides were sticky. Whatever was inside was more yellow than white. "Oh, it's salty enough already," I said putting the shaker on the counter, eating my watercress right from the bag; God forbid I should have to see what kind of plate he'd come up with.

"Aren't you cold?" I asked Harold. "Why don't you put something on and we can talk?"

"He always takes his clothes off first thing when he gets back from trying to set someone up," Ray explained. "He hates the clothes he has to wear to look right and can't stand to wear them for one extra second."

"Has Harold forgotten how to talk?" I asked Ray in an annoyed tone. I'd known Harold as long as I'd know Ray, all of us since we were ten. There was something provocative about his refusal to dress which I struggled to deny. Sometimes it was like that when we went swimming as children.

"Come on Harold, lighten up," I said. "Want some watercress? How much more time you got to set someone up?"

"All the time I want, long as they see me trying, not just dragging things out." He hugged himself and shivered. "It's hard to set someone up."

"Someone you don't know, sure it is. Next to impossible. Someone you already know, that's another story. How in the world are you ever going to get a stranger to go to Queens?"

"Yeah but he won't do that," Raymond interrupted. "He says he won't set someone up he knows."

"Can we just let Harold speak?" I glared at Ray until he signaled his retreat by smiling and pushing his glasses up his nose. "Here is my advice to you," I intoned, giving in and shooting my cuffs. "Think about setting someone up you know or think about doing time. What if you set up a female? Does it matter to them what gender?"

Harold shrugged. "I don't know. I don't see why."

"Setting up someone you know, setting up perhaps a female; all of a sudden the pool you have to pick from has expanded exponentially." I gestured to Harold that I'd like a cigarette. He pulled a pack of Camels from the ragged waistband of his shorts and tossed it to me with some matches. The pack was warm which I found both stimulating and repulsive. Setting someone up, though I'd never done it, didn't seem to me to have to be as big a deal as some people made it. For years growing up in Queens I'd heard there was a tradition where if you set someone up and he found someone else to hang it on, the two of you went out for fried clams at the Howard Johnson's on Queens Boulevard to prove it was nothing personal. Which is why among Jewish users there was rarely any violence.

I lit the Camel, tossed the pack to Harold and asked what they were offering for a guilty plea.

"I can plead possession of an ounce and get three years."

"Serve three or be sentenced to three?"

"Serve three."

"Serve three, that's a little much, don't you think? If you had done your deal in Manhattan you'd just bargain it down to possession of a quarter and get, say, a year. Then in eight months you'd be out. Times I eat lunch during sentencing sessions down on Centre Street, that's just what I see." Finished with my watercress I looked around for Ray's garbage; every week he put it someplace else. Easy to see in this world who's never had a maid.

"What's Malcolm say?" I asked. Malcolm was Harold's lawyer. Malcolm Seifert from Douglaston. Avid collector of Marvel comics, grossly overweight, a wheezing whiz at ping-pong, Malcolm worked as a lawyer at Legal Aid.

"Malcolm says take the deal." Harold uncrossed his arms to light a Camel, then covered up again. He stared at the floor, his mind somewhere else. Harold at 17; he's standing in front of the pizza place on Union Turnpike dressed in jeans, a t shirt, a leather jacket, a sweater tied around his waist. But he's not standing still at all, he's in the middle of a deal; fencing something, or breaking and entering, or moving some smack or weed. He's handsome and doesn't know it, and if he did he wouldn't care and so the girls who hang out smoking and chewing and wearing too much makeup vie for his attention but to no avail. Harold at 17 has no time for them, already he lives in an adult world of hustling and petty crime.

"Maybe I'll make us some spaghetti," says Ray, standing in the middle of the kitchen, but I don't think he will.

"What do *you* think I should do?" Harold asks me. His hair's no longer shiny and it's thinning and instead of a wiry build and hard mocking eyes, now he's put on weight and his eyes are guarded and if he goes in for three years he'll be 32 when he comes out. But he's been to reform school and Rikers and if anyone can handle it, he can.

"Just don't wind up in Comstock if you can help it," I say, recognizing that whatever it takes to set someone up, he no longer has it.

"Why's Comstock worse than anyplace else?" he asks, turning to stuff his cigarette butt down the sink. Ray starts to protest but falls silent, figuring, I'm sure, since I'm the same way, he'll make a fuss the *next* time.

"Ah, it probably isn't, only I went up there this past Monday to drop some appeal papers off and I'd say the place looks pretty rough."

"Shit, they're all rough," Harold snorts, gripping himself. "Go in a man, come out a broad."

"Well I don't know about *that*," I say before it hits me my job isn't always to make every one feel better. "Anyway, I had fun. Want to hear what I did?" Harold nods and lights another Camel. "Well, it's such a fucking drive, five hours each way, and all I'm doing is dropping off some forms and then coming back. I had to pee so I stopped at this souvenir stand where they had these antlers with a strap attached so you could wear them. Real antlers, not plastic. I go up to the register wearing them and the guy taking my money makes a joke and says now that I've worn them I can't bring them back. I couldn't fit in the car with them on so I took them off but when I got to the prison I put them back on. I mean, I figure, the guards don't care, they're getting paid by the hour, what's a little joke on the client?"

"And the client, man, freaks. He's some older guy who tried to hire the wrong guy to murder his mistress and he's looking at a life sentence. 'Who are you?' he starts screaming, his voice all full of tears. 'Who are you, where's my lawyer?' I try to tell him to relax and sign the papers, we'll get him out of there but he freaks out so much the guard comes by to see what's happening. I got those papers signed and left, I was so relieved I didn't live there I didn't mind the drive back."

Harold doesn't think its funny. "You keep pulling stunts like that, they'll disbar you."

"No they can't disbar me," I tell him. "Since I'm not admitted in the first place."

"What does that mean, you're not admitted?"

I'm surprised Harold doesn't know the lingo since in his life he's spent as many hours huddled with lawyers as normal people with their therapists. "I mean I've never passed the bar exam so technically I'm not a lawyer."

"Well, what have you been doing all these years I thought you were working as a lawyer?"

"Well, that's not to say I've not been working. I work more or less as an assistant lawyer, I help out at my uncle's firm doing what needs to be done. Like galloping up to Comstock; you think the firm would send a real lawyer on an errand like that? Think what it would cost them in billable hours."

Harold snorts in this way that once used to mean trouble. "Your family sent you to college and law school and you come around in your big-ass suits and really all you are is a messenger? Man, where's that at?" he asks and cackles. "And you tell *me* to get dressed?" He cackles some more.

Turning I see Ray in the next room, sitting on the floor, fixing a radio, using pliers and a screwdriver. As he works he whistles the theme from *Alfred Hitchcock Presents*. Though I'm dying for a cigarette I know better than to ask.

"I don't know, Harold," I tell him, intent on the last word. "At least I'm not the guy who sold coke to two guys wearing acid-washed jeans."

"I've told you a million times I couldn't see what they were wearing before

I handed them the coke since they were in the front seat. By the time I saw it was too late."

"Acid-washed," I snort, though without conviction.

Drifting in from the next room came the sound of a sax and a piano. Ray had gotten the radio working. "You hear that?" he asked proudly. "Wayne Shorter; 'Drinking and Driving Blues.'"

"That's not 'Drinking and Driving,'" I said after a few seconds. "That's 'Teru.' 'Drinking and Driving Blues' is on the other side. Same album at least."

Ray cocked his head. "You sure?" he asked.

"Positive."

He shrugged. "Anyway," he said. "All beautiful music begins with a broken dream."

"You know what? You're terrific," I said sarcastically.

Ray smiled. He took off his glasses and rubbed his eyes. Outside an ambulance shrieked past. Ray can fix anything. He fixed Ronnie the night Ronnie died. That was Ray's big secret, which he told me one night years after it happened, both of us looped on the F train: Ray and Ronnie shooting up in the basement of Ronnie's mother's house by the park in Queens. "Help me out Ray?" he asked, extending his arm, offering Ray the syringe. So Ray did him. Then he pulled the point back out, wiped the blood on his jeans, handed it back to Ronnie. Ronnie smiled his thanks, started to get up from his seat but his nose began to bleed and he sat back down abruptly, splintering the stool, sprawling on the floor, out cold. Ray stared, not sure what to do. Tell Ronnie's mother, upstairs watching TV in her bedroom alone? Call 911? Grabbing his stuff he ran out the side door to the park, hoping there to find someone who'd know what to do. Running around the park, bouncing from one knot of people to the next, a dexedrined dragonfly in blue jeans, asking, "What do I do, Ronnie's out, who knows how to give a saline shot?" Nobody knew. Nothing was done. Next morning Ronnie's mother found his body in the basement. Now sometimes in the middle of the night Ray wakes up to find Ronnie sitting by his bed, extending his arm with a smile, offering his syringe.

My gaze took in the calendar Ray had on the wall. Three days left to go before the old year fell away like a dry scab. The new year yawned like a fresh wound, all that time to fill. I watched as Harold tore the cellophane off a fresh pack of Camels, lit one and stared out the window. Following his gaze, I saw it was still raining. I figured I'd wait till it stopped. Maybe if I hung around long enough someone would come by with stuff to sell. Heroin is good any time but somehow when it rains it's even better.

Ursula K.
Le Guin

The Ones Who Walk Away From Omelas

WITH A CLAMOR OF BELLS that set the swallows soaring, the Festival of Summer came to the city Omelas, bright-towered by the sea. The ringing of the boats in harbor sparkled with flags. In the streets between houses with red roofs and painted walls, between old moss-grown gardens and under avenues of trees, past great parks and public buildings, processions moved. Some were decorous: old people in long stiff robes of mauve and gray, grave master workmen, quiet, merry women carrying their babies and chatting as they walked. In other streets the music beat faster, a shimmering of gong and tambourine, and the people went dancing, the procession was a dance. Children dodged in and out, their high calls rising like the swallows' crossing flights over the music and the singing. All the processions wound towards the north side of the city, where on the great water-meadow called the Green Fields boys and girls, naked in the bright air, with mud-stained feet and ankles and long, lithe arms, exercised their restive horses before the race. The horses wore no gear at all but a halter without bit. Their manes were braided with streamers of silver, gold, and green. They flared their nostrils and pranced and boasted to one another; they were vastly excited, the horse being the only animal who has adopted our ceremonies as his own. Far off to the north and west the mountains stood up half encircling Omelas on her bay. The air of morning was so clear that the snow still crowning the Eighteen Peaks burned with white-gold fire across the miles of sunlit air, under the dark blue of the sky. There was just enough wind to make the banners that marked the racecourse snap and flutter now and then. In the silence of the broad green meadows one could hear the music winding throughout he city streets, farther and nearer and ever approaching, a cheerful faint sweetness of the air from time to time trembled and gathered together and broke out into the great joyous clanging of the bells.

Joyous! How is one to tell about joy? How describe the citizens of Omelas?

They were not simple folk, you see, though they were happy. But we do not say the words of cheer much any more. All smiles have become archaic. Given a description such as this one tends to make certain assumptions. Given a description such as this one tends to look next for the King, mounted on a splendid stallion and surrounded by his noble knights, or perhaps in a golden litter borne by great-muscled slaves. But there was no king. They did not use swords, or keep slaves. They were not barbarians, I do not know the rules and laws of their society, but I suspect that they were singularly few. As they did without monarchy and slavery, so they also got on without the stock exchange, the advertisement, the secret police, and the bomb. Yet I repeat that these were not simple folk, not dulcet shepherds, noble savages, bland utopians. They were not less complex than us. The trouble is that we have a bad habit, encouraged by pedants and sophisticates, of considering happiness as something rather stupid. Only pain is intellectual, only evil interesting. This is the treason of the artist: a refusal to admit the banality of evil and the terrible boredom of pain. If you can't lick 'em, join 'em. If it hurts, repeat it. But to praise despair is to condemn delight, to embrace violence is to lose hold of everything else. We have almost lost hold; we can no longer describe a happy man, nor make any celebration of joy. How can I tell you about the people of Omelas? They were not naive and happy children—though their children were, in fact, happy. They were mature, intelligent, passionate adults whose lives were not wretched. O miracle! But I wish I could describe it better. I wish I could convince you. Omelas sounds in my words like a city in a fairy tale, long ago and far away, once upon a time. Perhaps it would be best if you imagined it as your own fancy bids, assuming it will rise to the occasion, for certainly I cannot suit you all. For instance, how about technology? I think that there would be no cars or helicopters in and above the streets; this follows from the fact that the people of Omelas are happy people. Happiness is based on a just discrimination of what is necessary, what is neither necessary nor destructive, and what is destructive. In the middle category, however—that of the unnecessary but undestructive, that of comfort, luxury, exuberance, etc.—they could perfectly well have central heating, subway trains, washing machines, and all kinds of marvelous devices not yet invented here, floating light-sources, fuelless power, a cure for the common cold. Or they could have none of that: it doesn't matter. As you like it. I incline to think that people from towns up and down the coast have been coming to Omelas during the last days before the Festival on very fast little trains and double-decked trams, and that the train station of Omelas is actually the handsomest building in town, though plainer than the magnificent Farmers' Market. But even granted trains, I fear that Omelas so far strikes some of you as goody-goody. Smiles, bells, parades, horses, bleh. If so, please add an orgy. If an orgy would help, don't hesitate. Let us not, however, have temples from which issue beautiful nude priests and priestesses already half in ecstasy and ready to copulate with any man or woman, lover or stranger, who desires union with the deep godhead of the blood, although that was my first idea. But really it would be better not to have any temples in Omelas—at least, not manned temples. Religion yes, clergy no. Surely the beautiful nudes can just wander about, offering themselves like divine souffles to the hunger of the needy and the rapture of the flesh. Let them join the processions. Let tambourines be struck above the copulations, and the gory of desire be proclaimed upon the gongs, and (a not unimportant point) let the offspring of these delightful rituals be beloved and looked after by all. One thing I know there is none of in Omelas is guilt. But what else should there be? I thought at first there were no drugs, but that is puritanical. For those who like it, the faint insistent sweetness of *drooz* may perfume the ways of the city, *drooz* which first brings a great lightness and brilliance to the mind and limbs, and then after some hours a dreamy languor, and wonderful visions at last of the very arcane and inmost secrets of the Universe, as well as exciting the pleasure of sex beyond all belief; and it is not habit-forming. For more modest tastes I think there ought to be beer. What else, what else belongs in the joyous city? The sense of victory, surely, the celebration of courage. But as we did without clergy, let us do without soldiers. The joy built upon successful slaughter is not the right kind of joy; it will not do; it is fearful and it is trivial. A boundless and generous contentment, a magnanimous triumph felt not against some outer enemy but in communion with the finest and fairest in the souls of all men everywhere and the splendor of the world's summer: This is what swells the hearts of the people of Omelas, and the victory they celebrate is that of life. I don't think many of them need to take *drooz*.

Most of the processions have reached the Green Fields by now. A marvelous smell of cooking goes forth from the red and blue tents of the provisioners. The faces of small children are amiably sticky; in the benign gray beard of a man a couple of crumbs of rich pastry are entangled. The youths and girls have mounted their horses and are beginning to group around the starting line of the course. An old woman, small, fat, and laughing, is passing out flowers from a basket, and tall young men wear her flowers in their shining hair. A child of nine or ten sits at the edge of the crowd, alone, playing on a wooden flute. People pause to listen, and they smile, but they do not speak to him, for he never ceases playing and never sees them, his dark eyes wholly rapt in the sweet, thin magic of the tune.

He finishes, and slowly lowers his hands holding the wooden flute.

As if that little private silence were the signal, all at once a trumpet sounds from the pavilion near the starting line: imperious, melancholy, piercing. The horses rear on their slender legs, and some of them neigh in answer. Sober-faced, the young riders stroke the horses' necks and soothe them, whispering. "Quiet, quiet, there my beauty, my hope . . ." They begin to form in rank along the starting line. The crowds along the racecourse are like a field of grass and flowers in the wind. The Festival of Summer has begun.

Do you believe? Do you accept the festival, the city, the joy? No? Then let me describe one more thing.

In a basement under one of the beautiful public buildings of Omelas, or perhaps in the cellar of one of its spacious private homes, there is a room. It has one locked door, and no window. A little light seeps in dustily between cracks in the boards, secondhand from a cobwebbed window somewhere across the cellar. In one corner of the little room a couple of mops, with stiff, clotted, foul-smelling heads, stand near a rusty bucket. The floor is dirt, a little damp to the touch, as cellar dirt usually is. The room is about three paces long and two wide: a mere broom closet or disused tool room. In the room, a child is sitting. It could be a boy or a girl. It looks about six, but actually is nearly ten. It is feeble-minded. Perhaps it was born defective, or perhaps it has become imbecile through fear, malnutrition, and neglect. It picks its nose and occasionally fumbles vaguely with its toes or genitals, as it sits hunched in the corner farthest from the bucket and the two mops. It is afraid of the mops. It finds them horrible. It shuts its eyes, but it knows the mops are still standing there; and the door is locked; and nobody will come. The door is always locked; and nobody ever comes, except that sometimes—the child has no understanding of time or interval—sometimes the door rattles terribly and opens, and a person, or several people, are there. One of them may come in and kick the child to make it stand up. The others never come close, but peer in at it with frightened, disgusted eyes. The food bowl and the water jug are hastily filled, the door is locked; the eyes disappear. The people at the door never say anything, but the child, who has not always lived in the tool room, and can remember sunlight and its mother's voice, sometimes speaks. "I will be good, "it says. "Please let me out. I will be good!" They never answer. The child used to scream for help at night, and cry a good deal, but now it only makes a kind of whining, "eh-haa, eh-haa," and it speaks less and less often. It is so thin there are no calves to its legs; its belly protrudes; it lives on a half-bowl of corn meal and grease a day. It is naked. Its buttocks and thighs are a mass of festered sores, as it sits in its own excrement continually.

They all know it is there, all the people of Omelas. Some of them have come to see it, others are content merely to know it is there. They all know that it has to be there. Some of them understand why, and some do not, but they all understand that their happiness, the beauty of their city, the tenderness of their friendships, the health of their children, the wisdom of their scholars, the skill of their makers, even the abundance of their harvest and the kindly weathers of their skies, depend wholly on this child's abominable misery.

This is usually explained to children when they are between eight and twelve, whenever they seem capable of understanding; and most of those who come to see the child are young people, though often enough an adult comes, or comes back, to see the child. No matter how well the matter has been explained to them, these young spectators are always shocked and sickened at the sight. They feel disgust, which they had thought themselves superior to. They feel anger, outrage, impotence, despite all the explanations. They would like to do something for the child. But there is nothing they can do. If the child were brought up into the sunlight out of that vile place, if it were cleaned and fed and comforted, that would be a good thing, indeed; but if it were done, in that day and hour all the prosperity and beauty and delight of Omelas would wither and be destroyed. Those are the terms. To exchange all the goodness and grace of every life in Omelas for that single, small improvement: to throw away the happiness of thousands for the chance of happiness of one: that would be to let guilt within the walls indeed.

The terms are strict and absolute; there may not even be a kind word spoken to the child.

Often the young people go home in tears, or in a tearless rage, when they have seen the child and faced this terrible paradox. They may brood over it for weeks or years. But as time goes on they begin to realize that even if the child could be released, it would not get much good of its freedom: a little vague pleasure of warmth and food, no real doubt, but little more. It is too degraded and imbecile to know any real joy. It has been afraid too long ever to be free of fear. Its habits are too uncouth for it to respond to humane treatment. Indeed, after so long it would probably be wretched without walls about it to protect it, and darkness for its eyes, and its own excrement to sit in. Their tears at the bitter injustice dry when they begin to perceive the terrible justice of reality, and to accept it. Yet it is their tears and anger, the trying of their generosity and the acceptance of their helplessness, which are perhaps the true source of the splendor of their lives. Theirs is no vapid, irresponsible happiness. They know that they, like the child, are not free. They know compassion. It is the existence of the child, and their knowledge of its existence, that makes possible the nobility of their architecture, the poignancy of their music, the profundity of their science. It is because of the child that they are so gentle with children. They know that if the wretched one were not there sniveling in the dark, the other one, the flute-player, could make no joyful music as the young riders line up in their beauty for the race in the sunlight of the first morning of summer.

Now do you believe them? Are they not more credible? But there is one more thing to tell, and this is quite incredible.

At times one of the adolescent girls or boys who go see the child does not go home to weep or rage, does not, in fact, go home at all. Sometimes also a man or a woman much older falls silent for a day or two, then leaves home. These people go out into the street, and walk down the street alone. They keep walking, and walk straight out of the city of Omelas, through the beautiful gates. They keep walking across the farmlands of Omelas. Each one goes alone, youth or girl, man or woman. Night falls; the traveler must pass down village streets, between the houses with yellow-lit windows, and on out into the darkness of the fields. Each alone, they go west or north, towards the mountains. They go on. They leave Omelas, they walk ahead into the darkness, and they do not come back. The place they go towards is a place even less imaginable to most of us than the city of happiness. I cannot describe it at all. It is possible that it does not exist. But they seem to know where they are going, the ones who walk away from Omelas.

Contributors' Notes

HENRY ALCALAY lives in New York. One of his earlier stories, "Paid on Friday," appeared in Red Hen Press' *Blue Cathedral.*

MARGARET ATWOOD has received numerous awards and several honorary degrees. She is the author of more than twenty-five volumes of poetry, fiction, and nonfiction and is perhaps best known for her novels, which include *The Edible Woman* (1970), *The Handmaid's Tale* (1983), *The Robber Bride* (1994), *Alias Grace* (1996). Her novel, *The Blind Assassin*, which won the prestigious Booker Prize, was published in the fall of 2000. *Negotiating With the Dead: A Writer on Writing* (2002) was published by Cambridge University Press, and her novel, *Oryx and Crake*, was published in 2003. Margaret Atwood currently lives in Toronto with novelist Graeme Gibson.

ITALO CALVINO was an Italian journalist, short-story writer, and novelist, whose whimsical and imaginative fables made him one of the most important Italian fiction writers in the 20th century.

KAREN J. CANTRELL's short fiction and non-fiction have appeared in *The Palo Alto Review* and *Prision Life*. She is completing a novel as well as working on a collection of contemporary micro-fictions based on stories found in *Grimm's Fairy Tales*. She lives in New York City, blocks from Ground Zero, with her two children.

WANDA COLEMAN has worked as a journalist, scriptwriter, medical secretary and occasionally teaches at university level or conducts writing workshops. A former columnist for *Los Angeles Times Magazine*, her honors include fellowships from the National Endowment for the Arts, John P. Guggenheim Foundation and the California Arts Council. She received the 1999 Lenore Marshall Poetry Prize for the most outstanding book of poetry published the previous year (*Bathwater*

Wine, Black Sparrow Press)—the first African-American woman to receive the award. Her work has appeared in over 70 anthologies, including Terry McMillan's *Breaking Ice*, Paul Hoover's *The Norton Anthology of Postmodern American Poetry* and *The African American West: A Century of Short Stories*. She was the first African-American to receive an Emmy in daytime television writing. Coleman's fiction appears in *High Plains Literary Review*, *Obsidian III*, *Other Voices*, and *Zyzzyva*. Her *Mercurochrome: New Poems* (Black Sparrow Books) was a bronze-metal finalist in the National Book Awards 2001. Her new books include *Ostinato Vamps*, University of Pittsburgh Press, 2003 and *Wanda Coleman's Greatest Hits 1966-2003* (Pudding House Press, 2004). She resides in Los Angeles with her family and husband of over twenty years, visual artist and poet Austin Straus.

VINCENT COLLAZO was born in the South Bronx and raised on Long Island. He has written two plays—*The Dust Bunny Murder* (produced in New York City) and *The New Astorians,* a full-length musical. His short fiction and poetry have appeared in various magazines and he has recently completed his first novel, *Sanity's Bane*. He performed excerpts from his one-person show, *Queerer Than Thou,* at the 2002 Local Produce Festival and 2003 Brooklyn Artists Exposé. He resides in Brooklyn with his beloved, Heather Faraone, and their dog and cat, Eclipso and José.

MARK E. CULL is the author of one short fiction collection, *One Way Donkey Ride*, which was published in 2002 by Asylum Arts and has co-edited two anthologies of contemporary short fiction, *Anyone is Possible* and *Blue Cathedral*.

KEALA FRANCIS lives in Colorado with her husband and two young children. She grew up in Hawaii and has lived in Europe and Asia. Keala is working on several short stories and a novel. "The Clot" is her first published story.

KATE GALE received her Ph.D. in American Literature at Claremont Graduate University. She teaches English and Hyper-Opera at California Institute of the Arts. She is the author of seven books and co-editor of three anthologies, *Anyone is Possible*, *Blue Cathedral* and *Fake-City Syndrome*. Her five collections of poetry are: *Blue Air, Where Crows and Men Collide, Selling the Hammock, Fishers of Men* and *Mating Season*. She is the president of PEN USA, Managing Editor of Red Hen Press and Editor of *The Los Angeles Review*. Her current project is *Rio de Sangre*, the libretto for an opera by Don Davis.

RAY GONZALEZ, is the author of *Turtle Pictures* (Arizona, 2000), which received the 2001 Minnesota Book Award for Poetry, and a collection of essays, *The Underground Heart: A Return to a Hidden Landscape Arizona*, 2002), which received the 2003 Texas Institute of Letters Award for Best Book of Non-fiction. He is the author of nine books of poetry and two collections of short stories, *The Ghost of John Wayne* (Arizona, 2001, winner of a 2002 Western Heritage Award for Short Fiction) and *Circling the Tortilla Dragon* (Creative Arts, 2002). His poetry has appeared in the 1999, 2000, and 2003 editions of *The Best American Poetry* (Scribners) and *The Pushcart Prize: Best of the Small Presses 2000* (Pushcart Press). He is the editor of twelve anthologies, most recently *No Boundaries: Prose Poems by 24 American Poets* (Tupelo Press, 2002). He has served as Poetry Editor of *The Bloomsbury Review* for twenty-three years and founded *LUNA*, a poetry journal, in 1998. He is Full Professor in the MFA Creative Writing Program at The University of Minnesota in Minneapolis.

JAMES HARMON has been published in literary and critical journals including *LA Miscellaney*, *The Los Angeles Review* and the *Criterion*. He is currently pursuing a Master's degree in English at Claremont Graduate University.

STEVE LAUTERMILCH, a poet and photographer, lives on the Outer Banks of North Carolina and offers workshops in meditation, dream study, and writing. He is the author of nine chapbooks of poems, most recently *The Small Craft*, co-winner of the first Aldrich Museum competition. Poems from a new artist's book *Spirit Writer* have won the Luna Prize from CETOS and received a Pablo Neruda Poetry Prize in the *Nimrod/* Hardman Awards. His story "Vellum" is part of a larger collection, tracing the development of an American artist.

URSULA K. LE GUIN, writes both poetry and prose, and in various modes including realistic fiction, science fiction, fantasy, children's books, books for young adults, screenplays, essays, verbal texts for musicians, and voicetexts for performance or recording. She has published five books of poetry, nineteen novels, over a hundred short stories (collected in eight volumes), three collections of essays, eleven books for children, and three volumes of translation. Few American writers have done work of such high quality in so many forms. Three of Le Guin's books have been finalists for the American Book Award and the Pulitzer Prize, and among the many honors her writing has received are a National Book Award, five Hugo Awards, five Nebula Awards, the Kafka Award, a Pushcart Prize, the Howard Vursell Award of the American Academy of Arts and Letters, and the L.A. Times Robert Kirsch Award.

ALAN LINDSAY lives, writes, breaks rocks, and burns trees at his home in the woods. His poems and stories have appeared in *The Bend, New-Works Review, Wired Hearts* and various other publications. His novel *A.* was published by Red Hen Press in 2004. He attained an M.A. in fiction writing and a Ph.D. in English from the University of Notre Dame. He teaches literature and writing at New Hampshire Technical Institute.

MELISSA LION received her MFA in Creative Writing from Saint Mary's College of California. Her fiction appears in the spring 2002 issue of the Santa Monica Review. She lives in San Diego with her husband and is currently working on her first novel.

MARK MAGILL is a founder of *Bomb Magazine* and a contributing editor to *Tricycle: The Buddhist Review.* He wrote and co-produced *Waiting for the Moon*—winner of the 1987 Sundance Film Festival. The film was later chosen for the permanent collection of the Museum of Modern Art. He devides his time between New York City amd the Catskill Mountains, where he keeps bees and is an active member of the North Branch Volunteer Fire Department. His most recent book is *Why Is the Buddha Smiling?*

DENNIS MUST is the author of *BANJO GREASE, Selected Stories* and a forthcoming second edition from Red Hen Press. His plays have been performed Off Off Broadway and his fiction has appeared in numerous journals and anthologies including *Blue Cathedral: Short Fiction for the New Millennium* (Red Hen Press), *Rosebud, Portland Review, RiverSedge, Writer's Forum, Salt Hill Journal, Sun Dog—The Southeast Review, RE:AL, Red Cedar Review, Sou'wester, Blue Moon Review, CrossConnect, Exquisite Corpse, Big Bridge, Linnaean Street, elimae, The Baltimore Review, Green Hills Literary Lantern,* and *Pacific RE-VIEW.*

KATE NOONAN is a playwright and filmmaker from Los Angeles, CA. Works written for the Theatre include "Without Gravity" and "The Skin of Our Town." Ms. Noonan is currently in post-production on her feature length documentary film on the life and work of pioneer Performance Artist Rachel Rosenthal. "Paper, Scissors, Stone" is her first published short story.

DAVID POLLOCK received his MFA from New School. His work has appeared in *The Mississippi Review.* He currently lives in New York City.

ANNE RANDOLPH is delighted to be *past* General Director of Central City Opera, Opera Colorado, Opera Memphis, and the Colorado Symphony. She has worked as an Editorial Fellow with Fulcrum Publishing in Colorado and devotes her full time to writing fiction. As a Stage Director in theatre and opera, she has worked across the United States, as well as in London at the English National Opera and the Netherlands Opera in Amsterdam. She has been awarded grants from the National Endowment of the Arts and the National Institute of Music Theatre. Her screenplays have won awards with WorldFest Houston International Film Festival, Chesterfield Film Company, the New York Drama League, Empire Film Company, Writer's Network, and the Writer's Foundation.

ROBERT REID has published short stories, essays and plays in *Confrontation: The Literary Journal of Long Island University, Poems and Plays, International Third World Studies Journal and Revue, American Culture and Literature* (published by Hacettepe University in Ankara, Turkey), *The Prague Revue, The Annual Czech Language Anthology of the Jama Cultural Foundation* (Prague, Czech Republic), *Fiction and Drama: The Literary Journal of The National Cheng Kung University* (Taiwan), *Anyone is Possible* (Red Hen Press), *The Acorn, Breakfast All Day* (Dieppe, France), *Missing Spoke Press Anthology, The CLA Journal, The Southern Quarterly, Blue Cathedral, The Micronesian Educator, The Potomac Review* and *The Southern Quarterly*. He has worked at the King Saud University in Riyadh, Saudi Arabia, Bilkent University in Ankara, Turkey, The University of Kentucky in Cumberland, Kentucky, Tennessee, Wesleyan College in Athens, Tennessee and the University of Guam. He lives in Al-AIN, United Arab Emirates and teaches in the division of Culture and Heritage at UAE University.

JEWELL PARKER RHODES is a novelist, the Virginia G. Piper Chair in Creative Writing and Artistic Director of the Virginia G. Piper Center in Creative Writing at Arizona State University. She has also served as Director of the Master of Fine Arts in Creative Writing at Arizona State University (1996-1999). Rhodes's latest historical novel, *Douglass's Women*, was published by Atria Books, October 2002 and won numerous awards, including the 2003 American Book Award, 2003 Black Caucus of the American Library Association Award for Literary Excellence, and the 2003 PEN Oakland Josephine Miles Award. Her short fiction has been anthologized in *Gumbo, Children of the Night: Best Short Stories By Black Writers, Ancestral House: The Black Short Story in the Americas and Europe*, and *African Americans in the West: A Century of Short Stories*. She has received a Yaddo Creative Writing Fellowship, the National Endowment of the Arts Award in Fiction, and was selected as Writer-in-Residence for The National Writer's Voice Project.

CECILE ROSSANT, who was born in NYC, spent several years in Tokyo working as an architect before moving to Berlin. Her collection of short stories, *About Face*, is published by Red Hen Press. Her stories have also appeared in *Salt Hill*, and the *Ex-Berliner*.

CANDICE ROWE has published literary nonfiction, a chapbook of poems, and short stories that have appeared in journals such as *CutBank*, *Natural Bridge* and *Greensboro Review*. She has an MFA from the University of Arizona and was the recepient of a grant from the Massachusetts Cultural Council for her fiction. She is finishing up a novel about a teenager who disappears from Provincetown without a trace in the late sixties.

ELIZABETH RUIZ is a writer and actor. Her plays have been produced at Intar Theater and the Public Theater in New York and her work appears in various collections including *The Brooklyn Review*, *The Best Stage Scenes of 1999* and *Fake-City Syndrome*. Elizabeth has taught writing at Brooklyn College, Hunter College and John Jay College of Criminal Justice and is a professional interpreter of Spanish and English.

GREG SANDERS lives in New York City, where he earns his living as a technical writer. His fiction and nonfiction have appeared in a variety of venues.

DIZA SAUERS has published in various magazines and is a recipient of two Arizona Commission for the Arts Fellowships. She teaches at the University of Arizona.

E. C. STANLEY taught psychiatry for some years before becoming interested in abused children. Eight years' work in a clinical setting with a high incidence of adult survivors of childhood abuse provides the factual content for Stanley's short stories, although each individual story is carefully fictionalized. Literary fiction offers a mode that is less subject to sensationalism than most others and hopefully will provide an audience who can incorporate such atrocities into a thoughtful appreciation for abused childrens' plights. "It's About Justice" is part of a larger collection, still being readied for publication as *Someone Else's Children*, since so often such stories only come to light when the state, a therapist, or an adoptive family steps in. When not tied to a computer, E.C. enjoys Asian movies, ethnic food, and gardening organically on a New York City rooftop.

Contributors' Notes

JORDAN SUDY is learning. He lives in San Francisco, CA.

JOE TAYLOR is the author of the storynovel *Oldcat & Ms. Puss: A Book of Days for You and Me*. He has a second novel forthcoming from New South Press, entitled *The Once and Future Bunion*. Over fifty of his stories have been published in various literary magazines and anthologies. He teaches at The University of West Alabama and is also the co-director of Livingston Press there. The story "Mademoiselle Preg. Nanté" comes from a collection in progress entitled *Child's Play*.

JILLIAN UMPHENOUR, a Native Californian, recently moved to Tigard, Oregon where she writes short stories. She began her writing career as a film and music critic for The Orange County Review in 1984. She's also an experienced advertising copywriter and graphic designer. "Morton's Cow" is her first published piece.

TERRY WOLVERTON is the author of five books. Her most recent, *Embers*, a novel-in-poems, was a finalist for the PEN USA Book Award and the Lambda Award. *Insurgent Muse: life and art at the Woman's Building*, a memoir (City Lights Books) was the winner of the 2003 Publisher's Triangle Judy Grahn Award, finalist for the Lambda Book Award, and named one of the "Best Books of 2002" by the *Los Angeles Times*. Her novel, *Bailey's Beads*, was a finalist in the American Library Association's Gay and Lesbian Book Awards for 1997. She has also published two collections of poetry: *Black Slip*, a finalist for a Lambda Literary Award in 1993, and *Mystery Bruise*. Her fiction, poetry, essays and drama have been published in periodicals internationally, including *Crab Orchard Review, Prairie Schooner, Glimmer Train Stories*, and *Zyzzva*, and widely anthologized. She has also edited fourteen successful compilations, most recently *Mischief, Caprice, and Other Poetic Strategies*.

H. E. WRIGHT did graduate work at the University of Maryland and at the University of Utah, where she taught. She also taught at Salt Lake Community College. She then developed creative writing and computer literacy programs in a Baltimore middle school. She recently returned to her native Utah to write full-time.